Yearning for Yuri

Demetria "Mimi" Harrison

Published by:

Boss Status Publishing

304 S. Jones Blvd.

Suite 2222

Las Vegas, NV 89107

Books published by Boss Status Publishing are available at special discounts for bulk purchases in the United States by corporations, institutions, and other organizations.

Edited by Pitta-Gay Powell

Cover Design by M. Pirro

Harrison, Demetria

Yearning for Yuri by Demetria "Mimi" Harrison.

ISBN-13: 978-0-996-94070-2

A CIP catalog record for this book is available from the Library of Congress.

Printed in the United States of America.

Acknowledgements

First and foremost, I must give thanks to my Heavenly Father for giving me the strength to write this book. I am blessed and grateful, glory be to God. Thank you, God, for giving me a creative mind and the will to never give up. To my children: Benjamin, Shamika, and Sharoni'a, I love you. To my seven grandchildren: Ziah, Bryana, Khaaliq, Nevaeh, and Akeem Jr., Royal and Khloe, we made it through this.

My extraordinary mother Cathy, I love you and thank you so much for being here and never once judging me. And Pops ("John") you were right there with us.

To my Father Charles, I love you daddy. Thank you for being a great parent.

To Alicia, a special thanks for always popping up on me, and making me have a better day.

My COO, Best friend, Sherice Sr., Captain you always make it happen. I thank you for all you have done to get the revised version of this book out when I was unable to. You're my muscle. I owe you one. Lets take BSP all the way up.

My girls 4 life. My Top Dogg, My Sister Charleszette, theres no me without you. Mel, Vick, Devon, Adrial, Mary Kay, Carla, Nicky, Tracy, Nilla and Mardae. We down like 4 flat tires.

My fly Con AkA Prison pals! Tracy, Tess Peaches, Kim, Toya, TT aka Belinda, Duchess, we all get another chance! Change is good. See you on the other side. MeQuetta you make me laugh! Also Carrie Neighbors thank you for typing the revised version, you are heaven sent. On my journey through Federal Prison, at FCC Coleman Camp, I have met some of the most beautiful and courageous women. Thank you ALL (you know who you are) for treating me with nothing but love and respect. For throwing me some of your creations, "Yearning for Yuri" has a part of all of you included as well.

To my promotion team, Kreelona Willis, Alicia Boo Mills, and Anthony Hurd, this couldn't have happened without all your hard work and dedication to the project.

To Chad (J Bo) Brown, it's almost over Bro.

With God's will, this book should be released around the same time that I will be released from serving a Federal prison sentence that more than likely saved my life. It also made me see life for what it is. "Change your thoughts, change your world" (a quote from RDAP).

It wasn't easy and in the process I not only lost one sibling, but two. Rest in peace to my brother Greg Mitchell and my sister Megan Gamble. Also several cousins and friends, bless their souls. To all inmates doing time, state and federal, keep your head up. Know your time is coming, and when it does educate the young teens about the consequences of coming to prison, before they end up on the road to self destruction. We all know if we're in the game, there's only two options out: Prison or death!

P.S. Big Shoutout to Ms. Cuttino for making sure that I didn't miss my brothers' homegoing when I was incarcerated. I am eternally grateful to you for that.

Thank God for bringing me out!

Sincerely,

Demetria "Mimi" Harrison

Pro-Logue

Barbara could not believe her eyes! She always strived to be the best wife and mother that she could be. She loved her husband dearly. She was now standing at her bedroom door, staring through a crack; her heart dropped to her feet. All she could do was hold her breath, in total silence.

She watched in disbelief, as her husband, Eugene, long-stroked this woman from behind, with more sexual passion than he had ever had with her. Tears began to roll down her cheeks as she stood there, filled with horror.

He held onto the woman's waist, pounding his monsterous dick further and further inside of her. The woman's head was buried' between Barbra's two favorite pillows that she cuddled when Eugene wasn't around to hold her. She fell into a silent jealous rage feeling vengeful and hurt. As he reached his climax, he screamed out a name that would change everyone's life forever.

"Oooh Yuri, I'm cumming! I love you baby."

Then, drained of passionate energy, as he pulled his soft shaft out of Yuri, in his peripheral view, he caught a glimpse of Barbara removing the 9 millimeter out of her underwear drawer.

In a cowardly voice Eugene yelled "Oh my God!"

Both he and Yuri jumped up in shock, never knowing that Barbara had entered the house. As she stood there with fire in her eyes, enraged, she cocked the gun. Barbara screamed at the two lovers, in the top of her lungs,

"WHY?!"

Bang! Bang! Bang!

Chapter 1

Today was a very special day for Barbara. All of her hard work and sacrifices had paid off. Her only child was walking across the stage, in her cap and gown, looking beautiful. As Yuri's name was called, Barbara couldn't stop the tears of joy from falling.

Eugene held his wife and said, "You have done a great job."

Barbara divorced Yuri's biological father when she was a teenager leaving herself as a single parent, until Eugene came into their lives. Although Barbara was a busy attorney, she made sure her family came first.

Barbara worked at one of the top law firms in Washington, D.C., so she made sure her only child had the finest things life had to offer. Barbara came from very humble beginnings. She was part of a large family: six sisters, and four brothers. She was the youngest, and always received her older sisters' hand-me-downs. Her mom and dad were not wealthy, but they made sure all the children were never hungry and always clean. Whenever Barbara thought about getting married, she always dreamed of a fairytale ending, just like her parents.

Barbara's mother and father were married for sixty years. Her mother died after losing three children, and her father died one month later, from a broken heart. As much as Barbara loved her siblings, she vowed she would never have as many children as her mother had. She dreamed that she would only have two children. That would be the perfect family, a boy and a girl.

Barbara worked her way through Howard Law School. While at Howard, she met Yuri's father, Mike, who was also a student there. He was in Medical School. Mike was just starting his residency and she was in her last year of Law school, getting ready to take the bar exam.

Barbara was a beautiful young lady that all the men wanted to date. She was smart, and possessed a shy but strong-willed persona that was a magnet for men and women alike. Barbara was also a virgin at the time she met Mike. She was saving herself for her husband. She had it all planned, just like the story she was told about her parents.

Barbara and Mike fell in love; she knew this was the man she wanted to spend the rest of her life with. When he proposed, he was so romantic, it was indeed like a dream come true. It happened one night over dinner at their favorite restaurant. Mike made the night so special, one that Barbara would never forget. As she sipped on her glass of chardonnay and Mike stared at her in amazement of her beauty, she felt something in her mouth, as she was about to swallow. She gently used the tip of her tongue, to not allow what she felt to go down her throat. After fishing it out of her mouth, Barbara was in total shock! Mike was sitting across the table from her, with the biggest smile plastered across his face. Barbara said softly, "Mike, you didn't."

He reached over to take her hand in his and said, "Yes, I did, Barbara. I love you, and I want to spend the rest of my life with you. Will you spend the rest of your life with me?" Mike then reached over, took the ring, and placed it on her finger.

Looking at each other intently, in that moment, it felt like no one else was in the room but the two of them. Barbara answered, "Yes, Mike, I will be your wife, and I love you, too."

As she marveled at the half-carat diamond on her left hand, Barbara was not afraid. She had waited so long for this moment. She was also ready to make love to Mike. Tonight she would give him all of her: mind, body, and soul.

Making love to Mike was what Barbara wanted, even though she was a virgin that had vowed to remain pure until marriage. As they made their way to the hotel room, her heart was pounding, but she enjoyed the fact that Mike couldn't keep his hands off her. As they entered the suite he picked her up in his strong arms and carried her over the threshold. "Tonight," he said, "It will feel like our wedding night." He laid her on the bed and gently undressed her, taking his time, exploring every inch of her body. Kissing her soft lips, making his way down her neck and whispering softly, "Barbara you are so beautiful, I love you." Taking off her dress, and her bra, he stopped to take off his own shirt and in less than 10 seconds they both were naked.

Their eyes and hands and mouths devoured the new territory, savoring the sight, feel, and taste of each other. As Mike looked at her, he thought about how long he had desired Barbara. He wanted to take his time, since she was a delicate virgin. As he carefully entered her, she softly moaned, holding tightly to him. He whispered, "Relax, I won't hurt you, baby." She followed his instruction, and even though the pain was intense as he worked his way inside, it was a good pain. She wanted to feel all of him, so she let go and began to move her body with his. Soon there was no more pain, just the pleasure of Mike rocking her slowly. Her body was feeling things it had never felt. Mike cradled her body, held her and screamed, "Oh Barbara, baby I, I, I love you, I love you!" At that moment their hearts were connected and she felt all of his love. Now it was her turn to give him all of her, and she was not going to hold anything back. Barbara felt liberated and knew this would be the man that she would spend the rest of her life with.

Two months later, after learning the news that Barbara was expecting, he could not believe that during their first night of love making they conceived their child. They realized that they needed to move forward with their plans to marry.

Barbara and Mike were married, then Mike graduated from med school. After 3 years of working at Howard University Hospital as an emergency room resident, he was able to move Barbara and their young daughter, Yuri, into a five bedroom home in Silver Springs, Maryland. Once they were settled, Mike and two of his fellow residents decided to go into private practice and start their own group. They were fortunate enough to land several contracts for emergency services for DC and Maryland hospitals which made him and his partners extremely wealthy.

Barbara and Mike were the perfect couple with the perfect child. Mike was a successful doctor, and Barbara, a successful attorney. They kept Yuri in private schools, where she took dance and piano lessons. When Yuri turned five, she became acquainted with her neighbor, Chanel. Chanel had a brother named Chance. Chanel was six and Chance was eleven. They were great playmates for Yuri, and their parents had also graduated from Howard.

Chanel and Yuri hit it off immediately and they were inseparable. Chance never paid the girls any attention. If Chanel got involved in plays or anything at school, Yuri and her parents would be sure to attend. Chanel was a year older but she was in the same grade as Yuri. Her birthday came after the cut off, which caused her to have to wait a year to start school.

Their friendship grew stronger with every passing year. When Yuri was nine, she desperately wanted a brother. She would beg her mother to have another child. She wanted to have a sibling like her best friend Chanel had. Her mom explained that she was swamped at the law firm and that her dad could barely get away from the hospital. Barbara told Yuri to consider Chanel and Chance her brother and sister, "You guys do everything together anyway. When I take you shopping you ask me to buy Chanel the exact outfit and her mom does the same." Yuri thought about it, and her mom made a good point. Barbara added, "If we have another child, you won't be able to get all the wonderful gifts that we shower you with. One day you will grow up and we'll have to pay for your college education. Even if you get a scholarship, we will still have lots of expenses to cover. So, Yuri, it's your choice." Yuri thought about not having as much attention paid to her and not receiving all the gifts. She decided she did not need a brother, after all.

As time went by, Yuri started spending less and less time with her parents. Barbara would ask Chanel's family to pick Yuri up after school, and sometimes it would be 8pm when Barbara got home. Chanel's mother didn't mind and she would make sure Yuri had dinner and all her homework was done. Mike was swamped; running from hospital to hospital. It would sometimes be days before he would come home. When he did return, he always came bearing gifts for the ladies of his life.

Yuri missed eating dinner and watching T.V. with her parents. She missed her mom helping her with her studies. Chanel's mom did a good job of standing in but she just missed her parents. It sometimes seemed that they forgot she existed. Chanel's mom was home by 4:30pm everyday with dinner on the table by 6:30pm. Even though Chanel's dad was a big-wig at the government agency where he worked, he made sure he was home to eat dinner with his family. After the meal, he would spend time with Chance, playing his Madden football game. It seemed like they had the perfect family that Yuri once knew and enjoyed. She felt very alone. All Yuri kept thinking was that work had taken over her parents' life, which made her feel unloved. Even though she received anything material that she asked for, all she really wanted was quality time with her family.

The years were going by so fast and now it was Yuri's thirteenth birthday. Barbara would make sure that it was unforgettable. Yuri was doing very well in school, so Barbara told her that she could invite two of her friends to go with them to New York City. Barbara was going to take Yuri on a shopping spree. Her dad told her, "Even your friends can buy whatever they want." Yuri couldn't wait for the day to come, to go to New York. She had heard so many wonderful stories about the city and she knew that she would have a ball. Of course, her first choice to go along with her would be Chanel, and then she thought of Marie, her other friend from school, whom she had met recently. Marie's parents were not doing as well as her parents and Chanel's financially, but she and Yuri had a lot in common, despite their different backgrounds.

Mike told Barbara that he couldn't go on the trip, but she could take his credit card and spend as much as they wanted. Barbara smiled and kissed her husband. After all this time, she still felt his love and she still loved him, too. Yuri hugged her dad and said, "Thank you Daddy, you're the best." He sighed contentedly because nothing made him happier than to know that his little angel was on cloud nine. Off he went to save lives. Barbara packed everything into her Volvo and they were on their way to the Big Apple.

When they arrived, Barbara woke the girls so they could see the bright lights of Times Square. They were remarkable. Chanel had been there with her parents twice before, but it was the first time for Yuri and Marie. Their eyes lit up and they had the biggest grins on their faces. Chanel and Marie were happy for Yuri, plus, they got to spend a few hundred a piece on Mike's black credit card.

Barbara looked at Yuri and said, "Happy Birthday, my angel. I know I've been busy lately, but I want you to know that this weekend it's all about you, so please enjoy yourself, Angel. Let's check into the hotel and tomorrow we'll shop 'til we drop!"

Yuri leaped over the arm rest and gave her mom the biggest hug that she could give her. She smiled from ear to ear and said, "I love you, Mom! Thank you."

When Yuri, Barbara, and the girls went out to start their shopping, they left the car at the hotel. The traffic was so hectic that they decided to walk or catch a taxi. Yuri had been to Chevy Chase to shop in Maryland, but she was now looking at all the designer stores right here in New York City, and she wanted everything, just like a kid in a candy store. As she walked past the Gucci store, she saw a bag that caught her eye. She begged her mom for it. Her mom had four or five of them and she was ready for her first.

Barbara told Yuri, "Those bags are really expensive, and I work hard to buy them."

Yuri's response was, "But Daddy said I can get whatever I want."

When Yuri walked out of the store with the $550 bag, she was all smiles. Chanel and Marie were happy for Yuri, as well. Yuri had managed to spend over $2,500 before the day was over. She had bags from Gap, Victoria's Secret, Guess, and every other store she could think to shop in. Her pride and joy for the day was the Gucci purse.

After shopping, Barbara drove the girls to City Island. They had a delicious dinner of fried crab legs and steak. When they returned to the hotel, the girls had a slumber party, talking and painting each other's nails. While the girls were having their fun, Barbara exited to the connecting suite to call Mike. When she did not get an answer, she gave up for the night. She knew he worked really hard, so she went to bed, sure that either he was asleep or in the operating room.

Sunday morning came swiftly, and the girls were already awake. It was time to be on their way back to D.C. While they were driving, Yuri out of nowhere said, "I love New York City and when I grow up, I'll live right here, in Manhattan. " Her mom interrupted her thoughts and said, "I have no problem with that as long as you finish college, young lady. After that, you can live anywhere in the world you want." Yuri, listening to her mom, could not respond. College was the last thing on her mind because she had her own dreams. If her mom said she had to go, then she would go. Until then, she would dream of the day when she could return to the Big Apple.

When they arrived back in D.C., they dropped Marie off at home and then they went home. Chanel got her bags and ran across the grass toward her house. She yelled back, "Thank you, Mrs. Jones. I had a wonderful time!" Chanel then looked over at Yuri and said, "I'll see you at school tomorrow."

Yuri and her mom walked into the house. It was empty. Mike was not at home. It appeared he had not been there all weekend.

Barbara thought to herself, "They are going to work my husband to death."

The next morning came and Barbara still hadn't heard anything from Mike, so she decided to stop by the hospital to surprise him. She missed him so much and couldn't wait to see him. When she arrived, she asked the head nurse, "Could you please tell me which unit Dr. Jones is working?"

The nurse looked puzzled and said, "Actually, we thought you guys were on vacation until tomorrow."

Barbara felt this strange sensation come over her, and immediately dismissed all the negative thoughts and possibilities that were flooding her mind. With great disappointment, she politely thanked the nurse and drove to her office.

During the drive, Barbara replayed the conversation over and over in her mind. Her head was pounding. The last thing Mike said to her was that he was swamped in the ER. She started thinking it must be a misunderstanding, because it was not like Mike to go away and not inform her of his whereabouts.

She could not get this out of her mind; she had to pull the car over. She thought back on all the times that she had called during the night for him not to answer. She felt so stupid. All the signs were there, she just refused to recognize them. She thought about how they had not made love in over a month. She tried not to show any emotion when the nurse said that Mike was not at work, although she was burning up on the inside. She was now determined to get to the bottom of whatever Mike was doing. She was hoping for the best, but her gut told her that whatever he was doing, it wasn't good.

Three days passed; she watched his every move, and nothing happened.

On the fourth day of her patiently watching, Mike strolled out the double doors of the hospital laughing with a blonde that stood around 5'8. Mike likes tall women. Barb knew she was about the same height as the blonde. The blonde could not have weighed more than 110 lbs wet. She was so thin, it looked like a good wind could blow her away. Barbara was thinking "the blonde couldn't be more than 30 years old". Not pretty, but attractive in her own way.

The botox and fillers gave her an unatural look, "peculiar" Barbara thought.

As they got closer Barbara asked rhetorical questions to herself, " What's wrong with her lips? Is she even real?" She had an obvious lip implant. If that wasn't enough, her 36 double D silicone breats stuck out like two Italian Mt. Vesuvius's. These large breasts did not fit her small frame.

Barb said to herself "typical bimbo." She thought once again, "I am sure she can't be the one."

They jumped into her Mercedes Benz coupe. Mike then leaned over and kissed the blonde passionately..It was as if he couldn't get enough of her rubbery duck looking lips. Barb proceeded to follow them to an unfamiliar restaurant. Barbara scoped out the scene. She wanted to leave but she couldn't. She watched him pay the bill and both got back into her car. She followed them to their next location, which was the Marriott Hotel. Barbara put on her glasses and scarf, walked into the lobby, and watched Mike and the blonde check in. Mike never even looked around, as if he was single and free, without any obligations. She listened and learned the room number.

On the way up in the elevator, she decided to call Mike, and to her surprise he answered on the second ring. She said in the most normal voice she could, "Hello baby, how's work? I miss you."

He responded, "Hello, my love, it's crazy around here. We had a whole family come in from a car accident and we're swamped."

Barbara asked, "Well, I was hoping you could make it home for dinner tonight."

Mike answered, "I know it's impossible. Don't wait up for me. I love you dear, I gotta go." He hung up the phone without giving her time to say another word.

She held the phone in her hand in total disbelief that he just dismissed her with that a lie.

Twenty minutes had passed and it was time for Barbara to make her move to the door. She was having second thoughts, and considered just leaving and going home. But no she had come too far; she had to confirm what she already knew. She had sensed it all along; all the signs were there. She knocked.

"Room service," she yelled.

When the blonde cracked open the door, Barb forced her way into the room, knocking the blonde onto her flat pancake ass, but she bounced back up like a yo-yo. Barb rushed into the room feeling offended and bitter. Mike was lying naked in the bed with the sheets covering half his body. He looked as though he had seen a ghost! She ran by the bed in a rage, grabbed the ashtray from off the nightstand, clobbering Mike on the side of his head as hard as she could, almost knocking him unconscious, blood splattered everywhere. He let out a horrific scream. "No! Mikey, are you ok?" Blondie yelled.

Barbara could not believe what she was hearing; that was her name for him so many years ago! It reminded her of when their love was strong. Barbara screamed at the top of her lungs "Mikey my ass, bitch, who the fuck are you, and how long have you been fucking my husband?"

Barbara then ran in a rage straight for the blonde, punching her on top of her head as hard as she could. Mike was still dazed from the ashtray, trying to get it together. As he watched Barb pounding the blonde, it took him back to his college days when he played the Mario Brother's game. Barb was 'Donkey Konging' the hell out of Blondy! Barbara was working on mad adrenaline. Mike jumped up and grabbed Barbara and told her to stop it..

10

As the blonde continued to sob, Mike brought himself to say, "She's my mistress and I love her."

Barbara felt a pain go through her heart. She felt betrayed. She could not control her emotions. She ran out of the hotel crying.

She jumped into the rental car, speeding through the streets. She ran a stop sign, almost air lifting an old man that was struggling on a cane to cross the street. Barely missing him, he stuck up his middle finger cursing at her. She continued speeding through the streets, not knowing her destination, just wanting to be as far away from the man she had once planned to spend the rest of her life with. She thought to herself, "does 'till death do us part' mean anything to people any more?" She never saw the Eighteen-wheeler until it slammed into her driver side door. Just like that, Barbara was unconscious.

There was a sanitation truck driver sitting in his truck who watched the whole thing unfold. He could not believe his eyes. He knew there were no survivors. He dialed 911, and jumped out of his truck moving toward the wreckage, but he couldn't tell if they were dead or alive...

Chapter 2

Yuri graduated at the top of her class, receiving a scholarship to Spelman University in Atlanta, GA. Once the graduation ceremony was over, Barbara and Eugene presented Yuri with a Tiffany and Company necklace and bracelet set.

Mike and Anna, *the blonde*, now his wife, had also come into town to see his first-born graduate from high school. Mike gave her a new Apple computer and a pair of diamond earrings. Yuri's half-sister, who was 3 years old, gave her a big hug. She worshipped her big sister, already, even though Yuri did not feel the same. Yuri was still bitter about how her dad had cheated, and conceived a child with Anna, before the divorce was even final.

Chanel ran over and gave Yuri a big hug. She said, "We made it, girl, and we are going to take Howard University by storm!" What Chanel didn't know was that Yuri was planning to leave D.C. altogether.

Yuri just smiled and said, "We sure are, Sisters for Life." Yuri walked over to her mom and told her she was going to hang out with a couple of friends who were having a party, and not to wait up. Yuri was now a high school graduate and could stay out a little later.

When Yuri arrived at the apartment, to her surprise, there were candles lit, a bottle of champagne, and the table so nicely decorated, it looked like something out of a home and garden magazine. All he had on was his boxers; there he stood all 5'11", light skin, smooth, even skin tone, curly hair and his well-defined body which she always admired. She just could not get enough of Chance. She had been sleeping with him ever since she was fourteen years old.

One night, while her mom stayed overtime at the office and her dad was at the hospital, she stayed at Chanel's house. Chanel had fallen into a deep sleep, and Yuri had crept into Chance's room. By the time Chance woke up, Yuri already had his dick in her mouth. Chance was startled and tried to collect himself, to figure out what was going on.

Now fully erect, he said, "Whoa, Yuri, hold on! What are you doing? If my mom or dad catches us we're going to be in a shit load of trouble."

Yuri did not listen to him and she wasn't letting go of his dick. She continued to suck him with passion, slowly moving her head up and down, and stopping only to catch her breath. She looked up at him, as her head moved in slow motion.

He looked into her eyes with so much pleasure, "Yuri, you're too young for me. Stop it!"

She paused, held his dick in her hand and just for a moment released it from her mouth, and whispered, "Shush," then moved her warm mouth back to his dick and sucked him like she was every bit a woman. He couldn't resist anymore and gave in, taking all the lust he had and making passionate love to Yuri. Chance was her first, and now she would lay claims on him. She could have him anytime she wanted. She was his for the moment, and she loved every minute of it.

Yuri had matured so much, and Chance had fallen in love with her. Chance was six years older, but it didn't matter to him. No woman had made him feel the way Yuri did. He couldn't help but reminisce about how she sucked his dick, licked every inch of his balls, and nibbled all around the crack of his ass. When the love-making was over, she swallowed every drop of his cum. Chance had become her love slave.

Yuri prayed that Chanel would never find out that she had been seducing her big brother since she was a young teenager. It would definitely break Chanel and their parents' hearts. It was a secret between her and Chance, and as far as she was concerned, it would remain that way. Chance thought that he was the only one that had been inside Yuri, but she was sexing six other guys.

Chance pulled Yuri in the door of his apartment and started undressing her immediately. He pulled out the strawberries and whipped cream, and without hesitation, their bodies intertwined. While not letting go of each other, they licked every possible place and brought endless pleasure. Yuri was the dominant one who always took charge, and Chance was submissive to her; but this night Chance would take the lead as he began to spread the whipped cream over her clit. He could not resist the sweet taste of her. He licked and sucked and held her hips as she moved them in a circular motion, staying in the rhythm of his tongue. She could not control herself as he held her clit in his warm lips. Yuri moved her hips faster and faster, as she was familiar with this feeling she was having. She could not hold back any longer; she squirted in his mouth as he held onto her. She was shaking uncontrollably.

His tongue was still giving her great pleasure and she screamed, "Stop it, stop it Chance! I can't take it anymore! I am about to cum again, please let me go!"

Grabbing her ass harder, he wouldn't let her go. She continued to move her hips and fuck his mouth and was brought to ecstasy once again. Chance was erect and ready to fill her. He wanted her to taste her sweetness on his lips, and she did not resist, as she began to kiss him. She loved the way she tasted, oh so good. He put his dick inside her and began to stroke her, going in and out, whispering, "Yuri, I love being inside of you."

She was always wet; it was like being in a tight moist glove. When he could not take it anymore he did what he knew Yuri liked best. He put his dick in her mouth, and let her swallow all of his love. Yuri felt if she swallowed his cum, it would not be inside her to conceive a child, so instead she drank all of them.

Chapter 3

Yuri was planning her trip to Atlanta, to see what Spelman was really about. Chanel was wishing that Yuri would just stay and go to Howard with her. Yuri had bigger dreams. She didn't want to stay in the city that she'd been in all her life. Yuri thought D.C. had become nothing but boring and everyone said, Atlanta's the city of opportunity for African Americans. Black Hollywood, as they called it, and she was ready to find out. Before Yuri left, she stopped by Chance's to give him his treat, which was her! She told him that he better not cheat because she would only be gone for two weeks. He pinky swore that he wouldn't. She had him so sprung that she knew he wouldn't.

Eugene was going to take Yuri to the airport. Barbara was at the house getting ready for work. She was running late but she wanted to see her baby off. She said, "I hope you like Spelman and if you do you'll be living in Atlanta." She took Yuri and Eugene's hands and said a prayer. When she finished her prayer, she said, "A family that prays together, stays together." Once the prayer was over Eugene ran to the bathroom and grabbed a hot face towel.

Yuri had two and a half hours before her flight. Eugene complained, "It took your mother all day to get out of the house, like she suspected something."

Yuri said, "I don't think so, I think your conscience is just eating at you."

While Eugene was driving, Yuri started rubbing on his pants, and his enormous penis immediately bulged, like magic.

He said, "Yuri, you're gonna make me," and before he could say 'wreck' she was unzipping his pants and putting his big penis in her mouth.

Before he got lost in the passion and crashed, he pulled over at the park and fucked Yuri, just like he had been doing for the past 8 months. Once they got in the back seat of his GMC truck, Yuri climbed on top of him and rode his big dick for the next twenty minutes. Instead of letting Eugene cum in her mouth, he was the only one that could cum inside of her. Eugene sucked on her titties and called her name, as if she was the love of his life. Yuri knew that Eugene had fallen in love with her. She did not feel the same.

It just so happened that one day Yuri had been running late for school, and she ran into the bathroom, only to see Eugene standing there with the largest penis she had ever seen. The shit was damn near hanging to his knees! This was fascinating to her. He had not used the bathroom after waking up, leaving his dick hard as a brick. When Eugene saw her standing there, he was very embarrassed. He apologized, even though he was the first one in the bathroom. Yuri walked over to Eugene.

He was puzzled, "What's wrong?"

Yuri grabbed it and started kissing on it. Eugene was confused and aroused at the same time. He pulled it away from Yuri and asked her what had come over her. She had never made any attempt to come on to him in the past. Now she had him in her mouth stroking away. His penis was 9" or better. Yuri put it down her throat like she was a porn star. He couldn't resist. After that, they continued to sleep together, right under Barbara's nose.

When Yuri arrived at Hartsfield Jackson Airport she was amazed. She had never seen so many black people in her life. People were walking fast to get on the escalator, almost knocking her down. This would most definitely be an interesting two weeks. She caught the MARTA transit to the West End train station where the Spelman shuttle was waiting. She jumped on it and in five minutes she was at her destination. As she observed her surroundings, she could see college students of both genders everywhere. After finding her designated dorm room, she got settled and tried to become familiar with the people and the area. She then walked past Clark, Morehouse, and Morris Brown. She wanted to take in the scenery. Everyone was smiling and doing their thing. Guys were checking her out as she walked by, and the girls were making passes at her as well. Yuri was gorgeous at 5'9", 135lbs, and soft smooth skin the color of caramel. Her measurements were 36-26-40. She was built like a stallion with her jet black hair flowing down her back. Her dark brown eyes and sexy smile, not to mention her sparkling white teeth with the narrow gap, drew men to her.

She did not know what to expect if she chose to move out to Atlanta but she sure loved the attention. She had what appeared to be an unconscious sexual rhythm to her strides as she leisurely strolled about taking in and savouring the scenes and sounds of her surroundings. This was her chance to start fresh and she was estatic.

Chapter 4

Yuri ran across a young woamn that had seen her walking around like she didn't belong. The woman said, "Hello, what's your name?"

She responded, "Yuri, and you are?"

"I'm Candice." Candice asked her where she was from. Yuri said she was from D.C. and Candice said she was from Chicago. Candice said to Yuri, "You must be new to the area because you look lost."

Yuri said, smiling with perfect white teeth, "Actually, I just arrived here today." They began to walk and talk. Yuri asked Candice about her major, and was she on scholarship? She told Yuri that this was her last year at Spelman and her major was business and accounting. Yuri said, to her surprise, "I'm here for the same thing."

Candice responded, "I'm not on any kind of scholarship, but my family was not fortunate enough to put me through college. After high school, I packed and left the south side of Chicago behind. I did not know how I was going to make it, but I stepped out on faith."

"So when you got here how did you make it?"

"I got a job at the restaurant around the corner, Busy Bees. That's where all the ballers go and dine. One day this nigga named Q, who always sat in my section, told me that I was too sexy to be working there. He said his boy had a couple of bartending jobs at his strip club, and if I was interested, he'd turn me on to him. He said that I had a very nice body, and that the waitresses in the club could make just as much as the dancers. He also said he would give me his boy's card and number, but only if I went out on a date with him. I told him that would be fine. The first day that I was off, he picked me up. I was living around the corner in student housing. He asked me how many of us lived in my house. I told him six, but I wasn't trying to be there long. I told him I would have my own apartment soon. Q kept looking at my shoes and my clothes like they were not suitable. Before we had dinner at Houston's, he took me to Lennox Mall. He bought me an outfit and shoes from Bloomingdale's. After he purchased it, he said he'd wait for me to change in the dressing room. I was a little embarrassed that he would buy clothes for me and make me change. After I was dressed, we walked down to the MAC store where they did a complete transformation. I never would wear eyelashes, now I had them on. I couldn't help but admire myself and how my new look enhanced my beauty. When he walked back in, he could not believe his eyes. He handed me this very expensive bottle of Creed perfume and said, 'This will complete you!' When I turned around to look in the mirror, I thought to myself, 'Where's Candice?'

He said, 'You look like a piece of candy.' Candy would later become my name at the strip club."

Yuri was sitting, listening to Candice tell her fairytale story. Candice went on to say that Q did give her the card for his boy after dinner, and it read "Body Tap". She thanked him and told him that she was so glad that after all those months of sitting in her section, that he had finally acknowledged her presence.

16

Yuri asked, "So did you keep talking to Q?"

Candice continued, "Q was a very busy man and he was in and out of town to New York. He was into real estate. When he was in town he would stop by the club to check on me, and also to get a lap dance or two from the dancers. We went to dinner a few more times. By the beginning of my sophomore year, I made enough money to get my own apartment in the West End. The guys that came into the club paid me nice cash just to get drinks. They always tried to get with me but my mind was on graduating. I would watch the dancers make thousands of dollars in one night. The ballers would 'make it rain' as we call it here in the ATL. That means 'throw stacks of money in the air'. I wanted that kind of money. I was already playing around the poles, so I knew how to work it. I finally asked Jinx, the club owner could I dance. He told me that I could start out on Amateur Night and if I was good, I'd have a spot. After one month of Amateur Night, I was a front runner; I had all the men lusting for me. White men were leaving thousands of dollars, and telling me they would give me anything I wanted, to be with them. As I got better, I received more gifts. This one night, Q was in town and asked the bartender was I waitressing tonight. She told him actually... and that's when I popped up and said, "Hey good looking, my name is Candy, and would you like a lap dance?"

He looked at me and said 'Damn, girl, I sure do.'

That was the first time that I slept with anyone around the club. He smiled when he saw my new apartment. It wasn't the best, but far better than the frat house that I had been in. Q told me that the club had done me good and he was glad I was still in school trying to graduate. 'That's my Candy', he boasted. He made love to me and put me to bed. When I woke up, he was gone. He left me a letter that read, 'Get you some new furniture.' I counted the money, and I couldn't believe my eyes! It was $10,000! I bought new furniture and put a down-payment on a new car, too. He has helped me ever since."

Yuri said, "So you paid your way through school, dancing?"

Candice replied, "Yep, every step of the way. I dance but I don't sleep with the guys coming into the club. I'll be a senior this fall. I now live in Buckhead, in a beautiful condo. I drive a CL550. God has been good, and it's only getting better. Candice told Yuri to thank God that she was on scholarship and that her parents would help her with the rest, "As for me I had to do what I had to do to make it, and soon I won't be dancing anymore."

Yuri said, "I would love to go to the club and see you dance."

Candice said, "Now I do more private shows and not so much clubs. The private shows bring me triple the dollars of what the club brings."

Candice asked Yuri how old she was. Yuri responded, "Seventeen but I have a birthday coming in a few weeks, when I graduate high school, and I can't wait."

Candice told Yuri that she would take her to the club before she left town. She added, "If you plan on living here, you'll have to get a fake ID."

Candice told her that she had a class to get to, but she gave Yuri her cell phone number so she could call that weekend, and they could link up. Yuri told Candice it was nice meeting her, and then they parted ways. Yuri admired how everyone went on about their business, not worrying about if someone were straight or gay.

The first week at Spelman had gone great. Every night Yuri called Chanel and told her what was going on. She told her how there were so many handsome guys. Even though she liked older men, she still had her eyes on the younger ones too.

Chanel told her she was ready for graduation and to get out of her parents' house in the fall. She would be moving into an apartment with a roommate, right by the University.

Chanel asked, "Have you found anyone you like?"

Yuri answered, "Of course I haven't, and anyway we're both going to keep our virginity until the right men come along to marry us."

Chanel responded, "And you know this."

Chanel was still a virgin but Yuri was out of control. Chanel knew everything about Yuri except all the guys she had relations with, not to mention her brother, Chance, and Yuri's step dad, Eugene. Yuri kept all of that information to herself.

The weekend had come, and Yuri gave Candice a call. "Hey Candice, it's Yuri."

Candice answered, "What's going on sweetheart?"

"I just wanted to see if you were doing anything this evening. I was bored and I'm tired of this campus."

Candice said, "You haven't even begun to get used to it."

Yuri said, "I will try not to." They both burst into laughter.

Candice said, "Actually, one of the dancers is having a birthday party, so take out your best outfit, because every baller in town will be in the place. For the record, not to be offensive to urban labels like Baby Phat, but we don't wear those.

Yuri laughed and said, "I may be young, but I'm ready!"

When Candice showed up, she had washed the 550. It was shining like new money.

She looked at Yuri and said, "You clean up well, if I must say so myself."

Yuri had put on a mini from Arden B. and her 5 inch Jessica Simpson heels. Her long hair was flawless. Candice was looking like a movie star. She had Robin Jeans with a tight fitting top. Her Christian Louboutins had to be well over 6 inches tall. She had a Louis Vuitton bag that had to cost three thousand dollars or more. Her weave was hanging down to her ass.

18

Yuri thought, 'I want to be in the major leagues like Candice.'

They pulled up to the door, bumpin' Jeezy. The valet guy greeted them like they were celebs.

He said, "Hey Candy, I see you brought a friend."

Candy smiled and walked straight past the crowded long line. Yuri had never seen anything like this in her life. Candice was strutting like a top model through the club. All the dancers greeted her with a kiss on both cheeks, and all the men watched her big, firm ass pass them by. The women wore fly designer dresses.

Once they got by the VIP section, a guy motioned for them. They went in, and the cats all had on Chicago White Sox and Detroit baseball caps. They had watches on that Yuri had only seen in magazines, and the chains they wore lit up the club. There were so many bottles of Grey Goose, and Perrier-Jouet that Yuri thought she was dreaming.

One of the dudes asked Candy, "Who is your sexy friend?"

She answered, "Everyone, this is my girl, Yuri she's from D.C. Yuri, these are my Chi Town and Detroit playas."

Yuri smiled and whispered "Hello," shyly, and one of them said, "Loosen up, and welcome to the A."

They walked over to the stage, where the birthday girl was totally naked. Her body was beautiful. Yuri couldn't tell her true ethnic background, but she was tanned with soft skin. Once she made eye contact with Candy, she ran over and they hugged and did some kind of booty dance to greet each other. It was cute. Even though she felt a little out of place, Yuri got with the program fast. She threw back a couple of shots to calm her nerves. Candy introduced her to the birthday girl.

"Yuri, this is my girl, Passion."

She said, "Hey Yuri."

As the song "Independent" came on, by Lil Webbie, Passion jumped up and screamed, "It's on! I gotta go make this money."

The club got so hype and money was being thrown from all directions. All the girls ran to the stage. They climbed the poles and flipped around like acrobats. It was amazing!

Guys were grabbing Yuri's hand, trying to hold her in conversation.

Candy said to Yuri, "There will be plenty of days for this when you move here; trust me, you will see them all again."

When the night was over, Yuri was drunk. Candice walked her to her room, tucked her into bed and went out on her date.

19

Yuri woke up the next morning with a hangover. Candice had left aspirin and ginger ale on the table for her.

Yuri thought to herself, "I like Candice, she is the shit, and last night said it all."

Candice played hard to get with all the D boys because she said they didn't like to pay. She was pulling in checks from ball players and corporate white men.

The following week passed fast. Yuri was ready to go home, even though she'd had fun. She had never gone two weeks without sex during the last two years of her life. She fantasized about how Eugene would fuck her when she returned home. She could not wait to put her lips on his extra-large penis. She called and left a message on Candice's phone, when she didn't pick-up.

Yuri said, "Thank you Candice, I had the best time of my life, I don't know how I could ever top that, so I owe you one. I will keep in touch for sure, see ya."

Chapter 5

When Yuri arrived at the airport, back in D.C., to her surprise, her mother, Barbara, was in the car with Eugene. She ran and hugged her. Yuri was really disappointed, but could not show it. She spoke to Eugene. He spoke back to her. He asked her how the school was.

She said, "Wonderful." All she really could think about was the strip club.

Yuri said to Barbara, "Momma, I can't believe you're not working today."

Barb responded, "I wanted to take my baby to this new restaurant and spend some time with you. You'll be graduating in a few days, and I know how it goes after that, you'll be out doing your own thing, then you'll leave town for Spelman in August. I just wanted to get all the time I can with you."

Yuri smiled as they drove off.

After dinner, Yuri jumped in her Honda and drove straight to Chance. She didn't call. She wanted to surprise him. When she got to Chance's house, he opened the door, looking like he had been asleep. Yuri pushed him in, barely closing the door. They kissed and undressed as she pushed him to the ground. There they were right on the hardwood floors, fucking like they were in the bed. Chance was in love and she knew it. Right before he was about to cum, Yuri began to suck that dick like only she could.

Chance screamed, "Here it comes." Yuri took it all in. When they finished he said, "Please let me hold you for the rest of the night."

Yuri made excuses, "I just got home and I need to be with my family. I told them I was going to get something to drink and now that I got one, I have to go."

Chance said, "I am so tired of you fucking me when you want, and leaving me like some sad dog in heat. Are you fucking someone else?"

Yuri kissed his lips and said, "It's just you and me."

Once Yuri got home she called Chanel and told her about the strip club, and how Candy had everyone on her coat tail. Marie was also on the phone. They said they wished that they could have been there, but neither Chanel nor Marie were fond of strip clubs, and they were still too young.

Three days until graduation, and Yuri was excited. She went with Chanel to shop for dresses to wear. In just the short time that Yuri had been in Atlanta, her style had changed. She no longer wanted the dresses in Arden B. She went into Nordstrom and found a two thousand dollar dress that she had to have. She called her father, Mike, and made him send five hundred dollars for the Gucci shoes she wanted. Because he felt guilty for leaving the family, he still gave her whatever she wanted.

When Yuri got home from shopping, Eugene was sitting in his room reading the paper. She took her bags to her room. She went back by his bedroom door, and asked, "Did you miss me?"

21

He looked up at her sexy naked body and said, "I did, but Yuri, we can no longer do this."

She walked toward him, with lust in her eyes, saying, "We will stop, but right now don't you want me?"

She laid on the floor and started playing with herself. Eugene tried not to look but he had become aroused and was rock hard.

Yuri said, "I know you want me, and I want you, baby. I need you," she sucked on her titties.

Eugene could no longer resist. He ran over and dove straight in. He fucked her for hours right on Barbara's floor.

Eugene had fallen for Yuri once again. She had a spell on anyone she slept with. The following days leading up to graduation, they had sex every day, all day. Yuri was glad Eugene was on vacation. His extraordinary big dick was all hers.

Chapter 6

Yuri woke up with the second worst hangover she had ever had. Atlanta, and now her graduation. After she had left from making love to Chance, she went to the graduation party. They had been taking jello shots and she was drunker than she would ever be again.

Carlos was a boy from school that had always had a crush on Yuri, but thought she was a virgin. Carlos came over to her and said, "Hey Yuri, are you ok? You look pretty drunk."

Yuri responded "I'm ok." Carlos said that Chanel and Marie were gone, and he would take her home. He put her in his car and they drove off.

Yuri started fondling Carlos. He said, "You are drunk."

She agreed, "I am drunk, but I know what I want." She pulled at Carlos' pants. With an erect penis, Carlos swerved, almost hitting a car.

"Look Yuri, I have always admired you and would never take advantage of you. You're drunk and not in your right mind."

Yuri was still rubbing on his pants and said, "Just for your information, Carlos, I will let you in on a little secret, I'm not a virgin, and I'll suck your dick so good to where you will want to marry me." Carlos' penis got really hard at that point.

Carlos unzipped his pants, and once he pulled it out, Yuri looked at it and laughed hysterically, as if Carlos had made a joke. Carlos was looking puzzled as to why she was laughing. She had gotten him hard and ready, and now she fell on the floor of the car laughing.

"What's so damn funny? You told me you were not a virgin and how you wanted me."

"I did, until I saw what you were working with." She continued to laugh hysterically. She added "Wow, your dick is small!" She looked at it, as it went soft, laughing even harder. "I have seen babies' dicks larger than yours." Carlos was embarrassed and upset. She had totally done a three-sixty on him.

When he pulled up to her house he said, "You are a cruel bitch."

She laughed "And it still does not change the fact that your dick is little."

He growled, "Get the fuck out of my car."

When Yuri got into the house she was very loud. Eugene came down the stairs to see what all the noise was about. "Hey Eugene, baby, what are you doing, good looking?" She giggled uncontrollably.

"Yuri you are drunk and loud, and you're gonna wake your mother."

She agreed, "I'm drunk and I want to wake you up", as she reached for his 'love stick'.

23

"Are you crazy?" he whispered.

She stumbled and said, "About you," flirtatiously.

"I'll help you to your room. You need to lay down and sleep this off."

The next morning, Yuri lay there with the worst headache. She thought about Candice, and how she had left her the pills and ginger ale after her hangover in Atlanta. She didn't even remember how she made it home after the graduation party, let alone how she made it to her bed. She vowed to never get that drunk, ever again. She retraced her memory from yesterday. She had graduated, she remembered her Tiffany and Company set that Barb and Eugene had given her was on the dresser. The gifts from Mike, Anna and Janie, her little sister, were there. She tried to sit up, but her head was throbbing. She laid back down. Then she remembered going over to Chance after the graduation. After that, everything else was a blur.

Barbara had already left for work. She didn't have a clue that Yuri had come home drunk and delirious. Yuri finally made her way to the bathroom. She grabbed two alka-seltzers and drank them down. She ran a hot bath and relaxed until the throbbing stopped. Once she dried off, she put on her robe. As she was walking to her room she bumped into Eugene.

"Damn Yuri, you were drunk out of your mind last night. I had to help you to your room, I'm glad you made it home."

"So am I," she said, not knowing who brought her home.

"I have one more day of vacation, so I think I'm gonna go catch a movie."

Yuri dropped her robe. "We can make a movie, Eugene."

Eugene promised himself that it was over with Yuri. He loved Barb and would never want to disappoint her. He knew how much Barbara cared about him and how happy she had been.

"Yuri, we discussed this." Yuri walked up and planted a kiss on Eugene's lips, slowly caressing his penis through his pajamas. "Yuri, I will not do this anymore."

As the swelling started and she took his penis to her mouth, Eugene could no longer resist. As she took him in her mouth he fell back against the wall, and grabbed her head.

"Damn, Yuri, you make me feel so good." Eugene picked Yuri up and took her to the bed.

They did not fuck that day, they made love.

Barbara had not seen her beautiful graduate since yesterday. She decided that she would take Yuri out to lunch, just the two of them, and then do some shopping. She told her secretary to cancel all of her appointments until the next day.

"I'm going to spoil my daughter. We are going to have a wonderful day."

24

Her secretary said "Have a great time, Mrs. Jackson."

While on her way home, she grooved to Al Green singing "Love and Happiness." Barb was in a good mood, her child had walked across the graduation stage yesterday, work was going well, and she had her husband. Nothing could steal her joy.

Barbara arrived home. When she saw Eugene's truck, her face lit up with a beautiful smile.

She thought to herself, "Maybe I should give my husband a special surprise."

She had been so swamped at work, that she was neglecting her wifely duties. I'll make love to my husband before we head out. Barbara unlocked the door silently. She wanted to sneak up on Eugene and give him the ultimate surprise. She walked in the door and immediately took off her shoes and suit jacket. She knew that Yuri would be asleep, after her long evening. She crept up the steps, unbuttoning her shirt. Once she approached the double doors of her bedroom, she could not believe her eyes.

Her heart dropped to her feet. All she could do was hold her breath, as she watched Eugene's extra-large penis go in and out of the woman. Eugene smacked her ass while he stroked her from behind with more sexual passion than they had ever shared. As Barbara looked on, tears began to stream down her face. She had already been betrayed by Mike, when he left her for the white blonde.

Barbara stood there frozen, in utter disbelief. Now Eugene was pounding this woman. She was moaning and groaning as she climaxed.

As he reached his climax, he screamed, "Oh, oh Yuri, I'm cumming! I love you, baby!"

Passionately drained of energy, he pulled his now soft dick out of Yuri, with no condom on. In his peripheral view he caught a glimpse of Barbara pulling the 9 millimeter from the underwear drawer.

"OH MY GOD!" screamed Eugene.

Yuri and Eugene jumped up, in shock, never knowing that Barb had entered the house. She stood there, crying, with fire in her eyes. She cocked the gun in rage.

He said "Barbara put that down before you hurt someone."

She said, "I can't hurt anyone more than you've hurt me."

When the paramedics arrived, they hoisted Eugene onto the gurney. Barbara had shot him once in the leg. When he tried to run, she put one in his ass also. She had turned the gun on Yuri next, but as she gained her sanity, she dropped it.

She screamed, "You little bitch, get the hell out of my house! I never want to see you again! All your life I have gone out of my way for you, and this is the thanks I get." As the police handcuffed and took Barbara away, Yuri stood there, crying. She mumbled "Sorry Mommy, I'm so sorry.

<h2>Chapter 7</h2>

Yuri packed some clothes, not knowing where she would go. She did not want to go to Chanel's. If they found out that she had been sleepinwith Eugene, her mom would not have wanted her over anyway. She drove around crying, and finally prayed to God. "Dear Father God, I am coming to you the best way I know how, Father. I have committed the ultimate sin. Father, I don't know why I have these sexual urges to sleep with men, and especially my mother's husband; please forgive me! God, I have never been touched or molested, but yet I love sex. Take this sexual demon away from me, Father; I need you right now. Lord, please let Eugene be ok. It was not his fault, Father God. I was being Eve, and he gave in to me. Father, I know I am so wrong, but right now I'm begging your forgiveness, that if you can forgive me, so can she. In the name of Jesus, I pray. Amen."

Before Barb was released on bond, she sat in her cell, picturing Eugene stroking her only child. Her tears could not stop flowing down her face. She thought, "What did I do to make him run and sleep with my baby?" She totally blamed Eugene. She had thought Yuri was still a virgin. However, seeing how Eugene was long-stroking her, with his oversized penis, she could not have been a virgin. How long had they been sleeping together? All sorts of thoughts came to her mind.

She went back to the day that she had opened her eyes, after coming out of the three-month coma. The strange man was sitting there. Once he saw her open her eyes, he ran to get the nurses. Everyone was running around, as if they had seen a ghost. She did not know she had awakened. When Yuri arrived, Barb was sitting up.

With tears in her eyes, she ran and hugged her mom, saying, "I missed you! Thank you, Father, for bringing her back to me."

Once the doctors checked her vitals and CAT scan, they told her it was a miracle that she had no brain damage. She was not paralyzed, and she would be out of the hospital in about a week.

Barbara said, "So I have been here asleep for three months?"

The doctor responded, "Sound asleep, and thanks to this guy, you lived." The stranger was standing there smiling. "I'm sure you guys have some things to talk about."

The doctor gathered his things and exited the room.

"Hello Barbara, my name is Eugene Jackson, and I'm so happy to finally meet you."

Barbara responded, "Do I know you from somewhere? It's not clicking in my head, I apologize."

Eugene said, "No apology needed. No, you don't know me. Actually, the day you ran the red light, leaving the Marriott Hotel, I was sitting on the other side of the street in my sanitation truck. The guys were picking up the trash. That's when you came speeding through the red light and the 18-wheeler that had the right of way, plowed into you on your driver-side door. You were immediately knocked unconscious, and you were stuck in the car. I jumped out of my truck and dialed 911. I ran to try and free you but the doors were jammed. I pulled and pulled with the help of other concerned on-lookers. Once the fire department and the EMT's arrived, they had the proper tools to pry the car doors open and free you, and you were then rushed to the hospital."

He took a deep breath and continued, "I felt so sorry for you, and plus I had never experienced seeing anything like that in my life, only on television. I made it my business, every other day after work, to visit, and relieve your daughter. Your daughter was very distraught. She said all of your siblings were in different states. They were able to come for the first month, but had to return home for work. Your daughter, Yuri, and I took turns sitting with you and waiting for you to wake up."

Barbara said, "You don't know me and you've taken the time to sit with me, while I lay here unconscious, for three months? Wow!"

"No, I didn't know you, but God said for me to do it, so here I am."

Barbara sat in silence for a minute, and then she said, "Thank you very much. I guess I would have to say that you are Heaven-sent." Eugene gave her a pleasant smile.

Barbara pictured that day in her mind. She had just left the hotel after catching Mike with the blonde. His naked body was a constant replay in her head. Her blood pressure went up and the nurse came in to calm her down.

The nurse said, "Whatever you are thinking about right now, you shouldn't, because your blood pressure is up, and we don't want you slipping back into a coma."

Barbara took a deep breath and said, "Well everyone, I just want to say thank you. I don't know how I can ever repay any of you for your kindness, and I don't know what I would have done if you were not around."

Eugene said, "No need to thank me. I enjoyed sitting with you, it reminded me of the book *Sleeping Beauty.*" She smiled, and he continued, "When you get out of here, maybe you can have lunch with me."

"You have sat with me for ninety days, I would never have you take me to lunch, it will be on me," Barbara said. Eugene left his number on the table and he was gone.

After two more weeks, Barbara was out of the hospital. She was ready to get back to the law firm. She filed for divorce from Mike, and as soon as it was final, Eugene proposed to her. Eugene and Barbara really hit it off. Even though he drove a garbage truck, she still liked him. Besides, he had to be a special guy to sit with a complete stranger for three months in the hospital.

Eugene stood 5'11" with a dark chocolate complexion, a big bird nose, with a protruding crooked front tooth. Eugene wasn't ugly, but not exactly handsome either. His big heart and loving ways made up for his looks. Truth be told, Gene was a love making machine, he made Barb see stars when they made love on their wedding night.

27

Yuri was glad her mom was happy again. The only issue Yuri had was now she could no longer sneak the guys that she had running in and out of the house when Barbara was in the hospital. After six months, Barbara and Eugene were married. They told everyone how they had met, and they all loved their story. It was like a fairytale.

The guard at the county jail opened the cell, "Jackson, your bond has been paid, and you are free to go."

Chapter 8

Yuri ended up calling Chance. "Hey Chance, I'm on my way over I need to talk to you.

Chance replied, "Um, I'm a little bit busy right now, can it wait?

Yuri said, "Get rid of the bitch. I'm on my way!" When Yuri arrived there were no traces of a woman. Chance made her leave without even letting her finish the meal that he prepared for her.

"What's wrong Yuri?"

"Mommy just shot Gene! For what, I don't know. They were arguing and all I heard were gun shots!"

Chance felt so bad for Yuri, he grabbed her and held her tight. "It's okay, are you alright?"

"No, I don't know if Gene is dead or alive! There was blood all over the place. I'm scared, and I don't want to go back to that house! I want to stay here with you."

"Yuri I would love for you to stay here with me, but Chanel has been staying here. She's going to summer school at Howard, and since this is closer for her to get there, I'm stuck with her. I'll get you a hotel room for a couple of days, and I'm sure that everything will die down, and you'll be able to go back home."

Yuri thought, '*If he only knew*!'

"Thank you, Chance," Yuri murmured. When Yuri arrived at the hotel she showered, feeling nasty and pathetic. She felt sorry for Eugene. Eugene had tried to end it so many times, yet she still seduced him. She scrubbed her body as hard as she could, but Gene's scent seemed to remain on her, even after scrubbing for over thirty minutes. She dried off and lay in the bed. Usually she would call Chanel, but she couldn't. She knew her mother would never expose the real truth to her neighbors, and it would be swept under the table. She felt lonely and unwanted. Chance dropped her off and did not even try to stay. Barbara had told her to never come back home.

Yuri was bombarded with the reality of her situation -What would she do? Where would she go? Her birthday was a week away, and she couldn't go home. Yuri decided to call Candice. The phone rang and Candice answered.

"Hello, how are things coming along? This is Yuri."

"Hey Yuri, everything is going great down here. You graduated the other day right?"

"Yes, I did, and in a few months I'll be attending Spelman."

"Good for you, and I'll be graduating with my Masters' degree around the same time, Chi-ching," Candice giggled.

"Candice, I was calling you because my 18th birthday is next Friday, and I was going to fly down to Atlanta. I was trying to see what was a good area to get a hotel?"

Candice responded, "Well, you know I'm still alone in my condo, and you're welcome to stay with me if you would like."

Yuri exclaimed, "Really? That would be great! I'll check on a flight, or I might just get my lil' Honda serviced and drive. Either way, I'll let you know."

"Ok Yuri, good hearing from you. Talk to you later." Yuri took anything she had, valuable, including the diamonds her dad bought for her, and the rest of her gifts from graduation. Her best clothes from the closet were now in two bags.

She rode past her house one last time. "I'll be back one day," she said.

Chapter 9

Yuri drove through the night. She had cleared out the two thousand dollars that was in her savings account. Candice had thought she was coming to vacation for her birthday. Never would she have told her that she was coming to Atlanta to stay. She would hang with Candice, and hopefully find a roommate and job after a short time.

Yuri had gotten tired from driving, so she popped in the CD that she had brought from Atlanta, the last time she was there. Candice had been bumpin' Young Jeezy 'Trap or Die' on the way to the club, and Yuri liked it. The music and Red Bull that she drank revitalized her. Once she arrived in Gwinnett County, she called Candice.

"Hello Candice, this is Yuri. I arrived a couple of days early and I was wondering does your offer still stand?"

Candice responded, "Of course, girl, where are you?"

"I am passing Jimmy Carter Boulevard on 85 south." Candice told Yuri to keep driving until she got to 400 North, and exit on Lenox Road. Once she got off, she needed to make a left, and the condo was on the right, across from the interstate.

Yuri arrived, Candice gave her a hug. "Welcome back, Yuri, I see you could not get enough of the A."

"I couldn't! I loved it, and I didn't want to spend my 18th birthday in DC. Oh, and while I was home, I was able to get an ID that says I'm twenty-two."

"Good for you girl! I know you're tired after driving through the night. There are his and hers towels in the bathroom; you can put your things in there. I have finals, so I'm gonna go and study."

Before Yuri showered, she admired Candice's condo. It was immaculate, with granite counter tops and stainless steel throughout the kitchen. The furniture looked very expensive. Behind the couch was a big photo, on the wall, of Candice laying on a mink rug, wearing a seductive dress. She looked beautiful.

When Yuri stepped into the bathroom, it was like being in one of those bathrooms on MTV Cribs. There was a small flat screen television on the corner of the wall. The shower was bananas! It had fifteen different jet settings for the Jacuzzi. The tub sat separately in the middle of the floor. The décor was brown and peach with fresh flowers sitting in the corner. After the jets had taken over and her body was clean, she fell into the Pottery Barn duvet, luxury linen, and slept the whole day away.

That evening, when Candice came home, she yelled throughout the house, "Yuri are you awake? I have some dinner for you."

Yuri said, "Yes, I'm just relaxing. I thought my bed at home felt good, but this bed makes me want to lay here forever."

31

While eating the rice and California rolls they listened to Usher sing 'Confessions.' Candice asked Yuri, "Do you have any confessions?"

Yuri hesitated, "Well, my mom thinks I'm a virgin, and actually I'm not. I have slept with a few boys and a few men."

Candice responded, "Well, I sure hope you're not fucking for free."

Yuri burst into laughter. She said, "My mom and dad took care of me, so I never asked."

"You never asked," Candice replied with a strong look on her face.

"No, I always had my own."

"Don't you know your pussy is a lethal weapon, and you can get anything you want with it? Here, in the A, men and women pay for pussy all the time. Not often do I give my goodies away, but when I do, they come out of their pockets generously. "Like the director of a symphony, she waved her arm around the room and said "How do you think I got all this? So please don't run around here talking to any of these Goofy Nigga's unless you consult with me first. Got it boo?" Candice stated firmly, with her Chi-Town accent.

"I got you," said Yuri.

The next day, Candice drove Yuri around. They drove down Lenox into downtown Atlanta. They passed the underground. Yuri looked around, taking in the scenery. She had always heard people talk about it, and now here she was, seeing it all. They rode past Auburn Avenue, and then past Martin Luther King's grave. As she was admiring all the sites, her thoughts were interrupted by Candice's phone ringing.

Candice answered, and the voice on the other line said, "Hello, how are you, darling?" and Candice replied, "Oh just showing my little sister around town."

Yuri felt good to hear "little sister," and she blushed.

"Six o'clock? I'll try to change my plans; will it be worth my while"? She smiled and said, "Ok I'll see you then." Candice hung up the phone. Still smiling, she looked in Yuri's direction and said "That was this white guy that I've been dating, if you really want to call it that. He says he wants to spend a couple of hours with me. We may have sex for about twenty minutes, if that, then I sit and talk with him. Before I leave, he gives me no less than twenty-five hundred dollars."

Yuri's mouth hung open in disbelief. She was shocked at what Candice had just said.

"They give me anything I want. I have a nice body, but the body you see, this guy paid for it. He has given me twenty thousand dollars. I went and got my breasts done, now I'm a C-cup, and then I got lipo and a tummy tuck. The doctor took what was left of the fat on my stomach and put it in my ass. The power of the pussy!"

Yuri idolized Candice and soaked up all the game that Candice had told her, now Yuri thought about the strip club that they had gone to, and all of the females with the forty-five inch booties. Some looked like you could pop them with a pen. But the men loved it.

Chapter 10

The week had gone by so fast. Yuri was having a ball. She knew that she had been at Candice's for a week. She tried to give Candice four-hundred dollars of her savings, but she would not take it. That was peanuts compared to what she made. Men gave her that just for a conversation.

Candice said to Yuri, "Today is your birthday and I'm going to take you out tonight. Jeezy is having an album release party at 'Club Chaotic', so you can use that money to grab an outfit."

When they arrived at Phipps Plaza, Yuri spotted Ludacris.

She got really excited but Candice told her, "Girl, they are regular people just like you and me. Don't get star struck, you will look like a groupie. If you want to fit in keep your head up and act like we are celebrities too. This is Black Hollywood." Yuri smiled, listening to every single word Candice was saying.

Once they left out of Saks Fifth Avenue, Yuri had her outfit for the night. A pair of True Religion Jeans, a sexy tank top and a pair of Gucci shoes that were on sale, but still totaling up to five-hundred eighty dollars. Yuri didn't really care about the cost; she wanted to look as good as Candice. The Dominican Beauty Salon was next. Yuri's hair was beautiful as it swung down her back. Candice's 18 inch Remy weave was already done and flawless. Now it was time to relax, until the party started.

When they pulled up to the club, Yuri could not believe her eyes. There had to be well over three thousand people outside the club. Candice paid the valet one hundred dollars to park her car. Yuri was out-done.

'One hundred dollars to park!' she thought.

Once they got to the door the guy said, "What's up, Candy?"

She answered, "Nada, just ready to get in here." They cut the line and walked straight through to VIP. Candy told her, "That is what we call bossing up. Now let's get it."

The club was packed, but Candice went straight to a table. The guys that were there had on at least five hundred thousand dollars' worth of jewelry.

"Hey Candy, with yo' fine ass," one of the guys said.

Candy responded, "Hey Bone, what it do boo?"

He said, "Just kickin' it." Yuri was glad Candice knew people, because if you weren't in VIP, then you were holding up the wall.

Candice introduced her, "Guys this is my little sister from DC, and today is her birthday."

The other guys asked how old? Yuri said, "twenty-two."

34

"Cool, Happy Birthday. Grab y'all a drink and let's kick it."

Jeezy came out performing 'Trap or Die' and the club went crazy. This would be an eighteenth birthday that Yuri would never forget.

Before the night was over, at the club, Bone said to Candy, "My man's tryin' to get at yo' sista and I'm tryin' to take you down."

"Stop it Bone, I'm going home alone and so is Yuri. She can get his number and see what goes down from there."

When they got in the car Candice explained that Bone and his crew were D'boys, and if they thought a chick was thirsty, they would short-change them, so she treated them like they treat women.

"But if you want to give him a call in a few days, it will be better when he is by himself, than to get with him after the club. You won't get short-changed that way."

Yuri had so much fun, she knew that Atlanta was her home. The following week, Yuri told Candice that she wanted to stay in Atlanta. If she could crash out just a couple more weeks, she would then find a roommate to share an apartment with. Candice said, "That's fine, mi casa, su casa."

Two weeks had passed and Yuri was ready for the ATL. She now knew the do's and don'ts. She knew if she slept with a man, her body was no longer free.

Yuri decided to call Troy. He was the guy who was with Bone on her birthday, two weeks ago. She called him and he answered, "Paper Entertainment, this is Troy."

She said, "Troy, how are you?"

"I'm good, who am I speaking with?" Troy asked.

She said, "This is Yuri, Candice's sister. Were you busy?"

"A little, but I have a minute, what's up, Momma? I have been waiting on your call."

"I was getting settled in, but I'm calling now."

He chuckled and said, "Is that right?"

"Yes," she replied.

"So when are you going to let me take you to dinner?"

She responded, "Whenever you're free."

He countered, "I'm free tomorrow evening, how's your schedule?"

She shot back, "I am pretty much open until I find a job."

He replied, "I have a job for you," laughing.

She giggled back, "Well I'll take it."

Still laughing, Troy said, "Ok, I'll give you the application when I see you. I'll pick you up around sevenish."

She hesitated, "No, we'll meet, just call me and let me know where."

"Ok sexy, will do, I'll holla."

Yuri put together her outfit of what she wanted to wear. After she was happy with it, she relaxed and finally called her best friend.

After one ring, Chanel asked, "Girl, where the hell have you been? I've been calling you since your birthday, and you haven't answered. I even spoke with your mom and she acted like she didn't know and really didn't care. I know she had the ordeal with Eugene, but why is she acting like you fell off the face of the earth?"

Yuri replied, "Wow, you are going one hundred miles per hour, slow down girl."

"No Yuri, I've been worried."

"Well, after Momma shot Eugene, I just wanted to stay out of the way. She was angry, so I let her vent. I am grown and I needed a vacation."

Chanel asked, "Where are you?"

Yuri responded, "I'm in Atlanta and having a ball."

Chanel said, "You what?" Yuri explained, "I drove here, and I'm staying."

Chanel was puzzled. "But you have no money to live alone."

Yuri said, "Actually, I am staying with the girl, Candice, that I told you about; she has a two-bedroom condo that is to die for. She got mad niggas on her heels and she pays them no attention, unless they are bringing something to the table."

Chanel responded sarcasticly "She sounds like a high class ho to me!".

"Yes, Chanel, I hear you. How are your parents doing?"

"They are great. It seems like the older they get, the more they fall in love, "Chanel mused.

Yuri asked "How is Chance doing?"

Chanel responded, "He is being Chance. He moved Shannon into his apartment. They've been dating for the last six months, but now it's serious."

Yuri thought about the day she went to see him, after Barb had shot Gene. He made her leave right before Yuri arrived. Yuri replied, "Oh that's good for him, I'm glad he found someone to treat him right." Unlike herself, she thought.

"Yuri, have you spoken to Marie?"

"No, if I haven't called you, Chanel, you know I haven't called anyone else."

Chanel chuckled. "Well, it's good to hear from you, and don't ever take this long to call me back!"

"Yes Chanel, I love you, good night."

Yuri laid in bed thinking about Chance, and she got moist. She had not had sex since she had screwed Eugene. She now wanted Chance to give her his special treatment. She was definitely jealous of the thought of him sleeping with other women. She prayed and fell asleep.

Chapter 11

Troy met Yuri in the Lenox Mall parking lot. She jumped into the Range Rover he was driving and they sped off. Troy said, "Damn, you are sexier than I remember."

She replied, "That is because you were drunk and full of those back woods when we met, but thank you."

"Where you wanna eat?"

She said, "I'm not picky, you choose." He pulled up to Benihanas. While they ate, he talked, and told her about how he gave all of the parties. Yuri looked on, sipping her Saki. She thought 'Troy is sexy and he can get it.' They ate and took two shots of Patron.

Troy was about to drop Yuri off when she said, "So soon, I thought we were hanging out?"

He replied, "We can, I just thought you were ready to go home."

Within the next hour Yuri and Troy were at the Intercontinental and she was sitting on his dick. Troy had gone through a whole pack of rubbers. Troy's dick was a nice size. Yuri would have given in even if it was small, as bad as she hated small dicks, but tonight she got lucky.

After no sex for a month she was a wild animal.

"Suck this dick, Yuri," Troy moaned, because he had not had head like Yuri gave in a long time.

She sucked on the tip, and licked all over his balls. She put his whole dick in her mouth and played a tune with it on her tonsils.

Troy started shaking and asked, "Where do you want it, on your stomach or on your back?"

She took it down her throat. Deeper, barely getting her words out, "right here." Troy was totally aroused, and he came straight in her mouth.

After Yuri showered, she told Troy she couldn't stay because she had a few things she had to do. In actuality, she had nothing to do, but he had satisfied her strange appetite and she was ready to go.

When she got to her car she finally asked, "If possible, can you give me some gas money?"

Troy was so overwhelmed with her work, that he slipped her three crispy hundred dollar bills.

Yuri really didn't want any money she just remembered what Candice said to her and she smiled and said, "I will be in touch."

He grinned, "You better, because I will hunt you down, mamma. Damn, you the shit."

Once Yuri told Candice that she had slept with him, she said, "That was quick, but did you check that niggas pockets?"

"No, I didn't check his pockets."

Candice shook her head. "Girl, not like that. It's a figure of speech. Did you make him pay?"

"Well I did ask him for some gas money, and he gave me three-hundred dollars."

Candice smiled. "You must have whipped that young snapper on him, because those niggas hate giving up money for pussy. They feel they are ballers and women give it for free. I am not going to come down on you. You will learn."

Yuri was relieved both from Candice not coming down on her and from her sexual urges.

While Candice was at school, preparing for graduation, Yuri went off with men that she met at gas stations, restaurants, or any other of a dozen places. Some of the men who had small dicks paid out the ass, the guys with big dicks pleasured her and gave her a hundred or two.

Chapter 12

The fall had come and Candice graduated with her Masters in Business Accounting. She asked Yuri why she hadn't enrolled in school, and what was she going to do? Yuri had started selling her body, and when the money got good, she forgot about Spelman all together. She told Candice that she would wait for the next semester to begin. She knew she had no intention of ever going.

Yuri had finally met the infamous Q. He was finer than Candice had explained, and he looked tasty. When she introduced them, Yuri could barely look into his eyes. Q had bought Candice a diamond bezelled Rolex for graduation. He always showered her with expensive gifts. They might sleep together and then he was gone. He didn't have a ring on, but he must have had someone somewhere. Yuri was puzzled but let it be.

Q wasn't very tall. At about 5'8" he had an aura that demanded attention and respect. With an East Coast swag, island-bronzed skin, mesmerizing black eyes, thick eyebrows, a rather large nose and perfect curls on his head, he must have had Italian in his blood. His pearly white smile made Yuri think,"men around here are truly into their teeth."

Candice and Yuri went out every weekend. On one particular night, Yuri met Shane. Shane was six feet two inches, with a basketball player's body. He was dark milk chocolate with a baby face. His lips were juicy and ready to be licked. The waves on his head looked like the ocean. Yuri could not take her eyes off him all night.

She thought, 'I would fuck him right here in this club.'

Candice followed her stare. "Are you watching Shane, the tall one over there? That's his name, yep, and he is rich as hell. I used to check for his boy, he had a whole lot of money, too. We still talk but he got locked up for some Mortgage fraud and is in Jessup, Georgia on some Federal shit. He used to treat me right." Yuri never really heard one word that Candice said.

A waitress walked up with a bottle of Moet. "Compliments of the guy over in the VIP." Yuri took her glass and motioned him a toast. He smiled and gave a sexy nod. Yuri watched him out of the corner of her eye, until he finally walked up. "Hey Candy what up? And who do we have here?"

"Hey Shane! This is my sister, Yuri. Yuri, Shane."

"Hello Shane, it's a pleasure to meet you."

"I don't usually step to women, but you might be my future wife."

Yuri blushed. "Sounds good to me."

Shane smiled, showing a row of perfect white teeth. Yuri thought, 'you could be my husband any day.'

She felt her heart beating fast. No man had ever made her heart beat like Shane. The short sleeved sweater he wore showed every muscle in his arms. Yuri studied his body as if it was a biology test.

He said "Damn baby girl, you sizing me up?" Yuri was in a trance and never heard a word. She just watched his lips moving, wishing they were between her legs.

"Yuri!" Candice screamed.

"Oh, Yes," she finally replied.

"Shane said he would like your number, so you guys can get to know each other."

"That's fine, its 202-466-7834," Yuri said, "Now hand me your phone and I'll call myself so I can have yours, also."

Shane smiled and gave her the phone, when he touched her hand, electricity went through her body; it felt like she was struck by lightning.

He took the phone and winked, "I am looking forward to hearing from you, ma."

She replied, "Likewise."

Yuri woke up in a sweat, she had been dreaming, and it was all about Shane. They were married, living in a mansion. Shane Jr. was in her womb. Everything she wanted, he gave to her. He bought her cars and yachts. They went on extravagant vacations. When Shane Jr. was born, he was treated like a prince. Shane Jr. was a replica of his dad. They were the perfect family. Just like her parents. That is what woke her out of her dream. She thought about her father, Mike, and how he did her mother, Barbara, and now she was back in reality; the real world.

Yuri had a date at noon, with a guy she met weeks before. He told her he was from Miami and comes in from time to time. He told her that if she had sex with him he would pay her one thousand dollars. Yuri stepped her game up, since the three hundred dollars she got from Troy. Now they paid five hundred dollars or better. One guy even paid fifteen hundred dollars the second time around. Yuri had told the man from Miami that she was in town for one more week, and arranged the date. She met him on the other side of Atlanta. Not where she was currently living. They got a hotel room in Lagrange, Georgia. Yuri put her mean face on and was ready for Mr. Miami.

She told him she would shower, and then their fun could begin. Once out of the shower, she walked out with her towel wrapped around her body. She stood in front of the bed and dropped it. Mr. Miami's eyes got big and he became erect. She grabbed the bottle of champagne and poured it on her titties, and sucked on her nipples. He wanted to touch her but she was still standing, giving him a show, without even touching him. He jumped up and started getting undressed. Once he was naked, he pulled out his small dick. Yuri noticed it and every juice she had worked up evaporated.

She finally said, "I would feel better sucking your dick if you showered, you did just get off a flight." She bent over and said, "Then you will get to fuck all of this," with her lips opened.

Mr. Miami ran to the shower.

41

Yuri took him a glass of champagne. "Here you go, sexy, drink this so you won't come so fast."

He drank the champagne down. As he dried off and stepped out of the tub, he fell flat on his face. Moving quickly, Yuri got dressed. She grabbed the thousand dollars that he had given her, plus an additional two thousand that was in his pockets. She slipped the expensive watch off of his arm and cursed him, "You little dick motherfucker, don't ever insult me like that!" She had slipped Visine in his drink and left him helpless, right where he lay.

Yuri arrived at Candice's place and she was in the shower. Yuri stashed the money and the watch where all the rest of the stolen items that she had taken from men with small dicks. Yuri hated little dicks with a passion. She punished any man that stepped to her with one. Some got Visine in their drinks, some got Mickey's, and some would take a shower only to return and find all their belongings were gone, along with Yuri. Married men had it the worst. She always carried handcuffs. She would play her dominatrix game and get them aroused, and if it didn't stand over a few inches tall, then they were doomed. She tied them up and robbed them. Clothes gone, and wedding band taken. She would say, "Married men should not cheat on their wives," especially if he wasn't packing. Married men even got their balls shaved completely. She made sure their better halves would know. Yuri had no conscience.

Yuri knew that it was time to move to her own place. One month had passed and over the month she had racked in twenty-thousand dollars. Not including the jewelry that she had taken. She found a loft in Midtown that she liked. She thanked her big sister, Candice, for letting her crash for the past few months without paying her one dime. Candice gave her a few pictures that she would not use and helped her pick out furniture at 'Styles by Designs'. The 17th Street loft was perfect. There were all the shops and restaurants and anything else that she needed. Publix grocery store was even in walking distance.

Once Yuri settled in, she relaxed and started thinking about Shane. A month had passed and neither of them had attempted to call. She visualized about his well sculpted lips, the perfect white teeth that he displayed whenever he smiled, how his arms bulged out of his tight knitted sweater. The thought of all of this made her wet. She grabbed the large vibrator out of the night stand and pleasured herself.

Yuri walked around her new neighborhood looking at the area. Atlantic Station was adorable. As she passed the Twelve Hotel, she checked out all the expensive cars that were around. All black men owned these cars. Atlanta was most definitely 'Black Hollywood'. She walked into the Publix and purchased some fresh fruit and flowers for her bathroom. She thought to herself how the fresh flowers always made Candice's condo look and smell so good. She grabbed a couple of T.V. dinners and headed back. When she arrived home, she decided to call Shane.

"Hello, may I speak with Shane?"

"This is Shane."

"This is Yuri, Candice's sister."

"Oh, hey Lil' Momma, I'm in a meeting, can I get back with you?"

"Sure anytime."

Yuri found the guts to call her mother. The phone rang until the answering machine came on.

"Hello mother, I know I am the last person you want to hear from, but I had to tell you that I love you and miss you so much. I know that you put Gene out and filed for divorce, but the truth is I was the" (beep), time was up.

Yuri could not find it in herself to call back, to let her mother know that she had seduced Eugene. She fell asleep.

After days of wondering if Shane would ever call back, he finally did. Yuri was mad because it had taken him so long. When they had exchanged numbers, neither had called for a month, and she was the one to make the first call, only to be told that he would return her call later. Yuri was excited, even though she gave him a nonchalant tone. Shane's voice sounded as good as he looked.

"Hey, Lil' Momma, sorry it took so long to get back with you, but I've been so busy with work."

"That's fine, Shane, if you don't work, you don't eat."

Shane said "That's right. I have one more day here, in LA, and I'll be back in Georgia. If it's possible, I would love to take you to dinner. Will you be free?"

"If I wasn't, I am now."

Shane laughed. "What about Saturday, around seven?"

"I can't wait," slipped out of her mouth.

Shane said, "I will call you as soon as I land."

Yuri laid around all day, thinking about Shane. She wondered what she would wear, how she should comb her hair, and what about her make-up? She wanted to look her best to please him. She called Candice to ask what she should wear. Q picked up the phone.

Yuri smiled. "Hi Q, is Candice around?"

"Hey Yuri, she's in the shower and asked me to answer the phone. How's everything goin' at the loft?"

"It's great, I love it, and I know Candice is happy to have her space back."

"Actually, she misses you, you're the little sister she never had."

"Can you have her give me a call?"

"Sure, I'll tell her."

"Thanks, Q."

43

"See you 'round, Yuri."

Yuri had gotten her call from Shane after he landed. He told her that once he showered he would pick her up. She told him where she lived. He was familiar with the area. Once he arrived, he greeted her. He opened the door of the black Maserati. The black and beige leather seats were customized. The radio played Maxwell. Yuri felt like his queen already. When they got to the Capital Grill, Yuri smiled.

"This is my favorite; my parents always brought me here." Yuri ordered steak and shrimp, and an apple martini.

Shane did not eat meat, he had shrimp and grits, with a Coors Light.

He said, "So you're from DC? What brought you to Georgia?"

"I was supposed to start Spelman this semester, and now I'm going to start in January."

"Why are you waiting?"

"I don't know I just wasn't ready."

"Well, Lil' Momma, 'a mind is a terrible thing to waste.' The sooner you start the better. What are you going to major in?"

"Business Accounting."

"So you're good with numbers, huh?"

Yuri smiled and said, "Enough about me, what is it that you do, Shane?"

"Real Estate, I buy and sell foreclosed homes and apartment buildings. The market has crashed so much, that eighty percent of the property in Fulton County is up for grabs. It's a billion- dollar industry. It has made me wealthy; I also have a lot of property in Los Angeles."

Yuri asked, "Is that where you're from?"

"I was born in Phoenix, Arizona. As a teen we relocated to LA. Now I have homes here and out there. Maybe one day you can accompany me there."

Yuri blushed, trying not to look too pleased. Shane made Yuri feel like a child who was about to receive candy. While Shane talked, Yuri just stared. She never heard another word that he spoke. He thought she was listening but she was totally in a trance. Shane had put a spell on her, he had her hypnotized. Shane's last words were, "Are you even listening to me?"

Embarrassed, like the first time when she met him, she said, "Sorry, I was thinking about something."

He grinned "I hope it was me." If he only knew.

The date went really well. Yuri wanted so much to ask Shane upstairs and knock his lights out. Before she could ask him up, he said, "I have an early meeting, but I would like to see you again. Would that be fine?"

"Sure Shane, anytime. I had a lovely evening."

"I will call you soon, Lil' Momma, goodnight."

Shane had been on Yuri's mind so much, that she had forgotten her sexcapades. She thought, 'If Shane becomes my man, I will never sleep or cheat with another man, I will make him so happy.' Yuri had spent over five thousand of the dollars that she had stolen, and knew she needed cash. Rent was fifteen hundred dollars, dinner, groceries, toiletries were an additional thousand, and clothes two thousand. The twenty thousand dollars she had was getting short. She decided she would take a trip to DC. She would then pawn or sell the jewelry that she had stolen from all the men.

Chapter 13

Yuri arrived in DC and Chanel picked her up from the airport. She was so happy to see her best friend. They embarrassed each other with hugs and kisses.

"Wow, Chanel, I love your new car."

"Momma and Daddy bought it as a combination graduation-going to college present. The old jeep finally gave out on me, and when I came home from work last month, it was in the driveway. I wondered whose Impala was sitting there, who had stopped by. So when I went in the house and no one was there, I asked momma who had left their car. She said, 'You did Chanel.' I was so excited; my favorite part of it is the sunroof. Girl, I think I am the shit now."

In unison they burst into laughter.

Yuri replied, "Well, I'm still pushing the 2008 Honda, but soon I'll be jumping into something slick."

"Damn Yuri, you look good girl! I love the Louis bag, and you can leave those Chanel shades when you go," she giggled.

"So how is your brother doing, Chanel?"

"He is great! he's been talking about marriage."

"Is he in the same apartment?"

"Yes."

"Let's stop by so I can say hello."

When they pulled up, Chanel said "I need to take this call," with a smile on her face. "Go ahead up he will be glad to see you."

"I bet he will," Yuri thought. She knocked on the door.

"May I help you?" a woman's voice asked.

"Yes, I'm Yuri, Chanel's best friend, she's in the car, but I was looking for Chance.

As he approached the door, it was like he had seen a ghost.

"Hey Yuri, how are you?" They hugged.

"I'm ok, Chance, and I see you are, also."

"This is my fiancée, Shannon."

"Hello again, we just met."

"Yuri, I have heard so much about you. Chanel misses you a lot."

"I miss her even more, but I love Atlanta."

Shannon was beautiful. She was Indian and black with hair down to her butt. Her skin looked like she tanned every day. "Would you like something to drink?" Shannon asked.

"No thank you." Yuri said. Yuri was jealous. She thought of all the places she had left her piece of love, on the furniture that was there, even on the kitchen table. Now this pretty bitch was asking her, 'did she want anything?'

Chanel finally showed up. "So, Yuri, I see you've met my future sister-in-law."

"Not if it's up to me," thought Yuri before she replied, "Yes, I have, and you were on the phone a long time, who is he?"

Chanel blushed, and said, "We will talk later. We just stopped by because I knew you'd love to see Yuri. We'll go ahead and leave you love birds alone."

"It was nice seeing you, Yuri," Chance lied. Chance felt awkward as Yuri shot daggers with her eyes through his body, making him feel guilty.

"And it was a pleasure meeting you, Yuri," Shannon added.

"Likewise, Shannon." Yuri was burning on the inside. Even though she never wanted to marry Chance, she didn't want anyone else to have him, either. She thought, if it was up to her, there would never be a wedding.

Yuri checked into her hotel. Chanel asked, "Why not just go home and sleep in your own bed?"

"Because Momma doesn't know I'm even here, and I have business to attend to," Yuri said, "but you're going to stay here, with me tonight, and tell me about this man that's making you smile."

Once their pajamas were on, Chanel told Yuri about the new man in her life. His name was Terrance. He was from the west side of Philly.

"He had come down to Howard's homecoming because his cousin is a Q-dog there," Chanel said "You know I don't drink, but that night, I took regular shots, a couple of Jello shots and whatever else shots they had." She giggled. "After all the liquor, Marie tried to make me leave, but I wouldn't; I cursed her and fought with her. After all the fussing, I fell down, only for him to come and help me up. I cursed him, too."

Yuri said, "Get to the good part."

"Well, before the good part, it gets worse. He didn't mind the name calling; he pulled me up and asked Marie where the car was? On the way to the car, when I could no longer walk, he picked me up and carried me the rest of the way. I was dizzy and everything was spinning. My stomach had balled up into a knot and before I could say 'put me down,' I threw up all over his shirt."

"Yuck," said Yuri

"Instead of dropping me, he still carried me to the car. He told Marie to get me home and give me some Pepto-Bismol. Marie thanked him and apologized," Chanel grimaced.

"The next day, after I gained my composure, I called and asked his cousin was Terrance still in town." Luckily, he was. He put him on the telephone. I said. 'Hi, I'm Chanel, and I am really sorry about last night, I do not normally behave like that, and I know you probably want to kill me.'"

"He said, 'Apology accepted, only if you take in a movie with me. I'll be going back to Philly tomorrow night, though.'

I told him we could do a matinee the following day, because I couldn't get out of bed that evening.

He said, 'that's fine.'

I couldn't believe it."

"The next day we had dinner and a movie at the new cinema. We talked for the rest of the day. He's a junior at Princeton, and he's majoring in Architecture. He has no children and loves to cook. You know my weakness is food."

"Boo, you still have a nice slim body," Yuri responded.

"Now he comes into town every weekend, and when he's at school we talk through breaks, and all night long until one of us falls asleep, like school kids," Chanel giggled.

"Sounds like you're in love."

"No, not yet, but he might be the one who could take me down."

Yuri thought about how Chanel was in college and was still a virgin; Chanel thought Yuri was a virgin, also. Yuri was a 'ho,' but she was not ashamed of her profession.

The next morning, Yuri went to the Russian at the pawn shop. Her dad used to do business with him when she was a child.

When Yuri walked in, Zlotnick greeted her, "Hey Yuri, you have really grown up. Looks like life is treating you great."

"Well, I can't complain."

"So what brings you by?"

"I have a couple of pieces that I want to get rid of."

Zlotnick looked at the rose gold Rolex, inspecting it well. The three karat diamond earrings were as clear as the blue sky. He asked her where she got all the nice pieces.

"My boyfriend was murdered, and left it all in my apartment. I gave a few of the most expensive pieces to his mother and kept these." He inspected the last piece. It was a canary pinky ring.

He thought, 'Whoever her boyfriend was he had great taste.' "Well, I know it's well over forty thousand dollars, but I'll take twenty-eight thousand. Zlotnick knew it was worth that.

"So Yuri, you know this is a pawn shop and I can't give that much, even though I like it."

Yuri knew that she had stolen it and had better take what she could. She walked out of the pawn shop with eighteen-thousand dollars.

On the way back to the hotel, she phoned Chance.

Chance answered, "Hello."

"Hey Chance, I need to see you."

He responded, "Well, I'm at work."

"Well, you can stop by on your break, we really need to talk. I am at the Residence Inn on Deerwood Road, room 816; I'll see you at noon."

Yuri stopped by Victoria's Secret. She grabbed the freakiest camisole that she could find. She returned to her room, stashed her cash, showered with her body gels, and waited for Chance.

When he arrived, Yuri greeted him with the sexy outfit. She kissed him.

"Yuri, you know I'm getting married, and I never want to cheat on my wife."

Yuri said, "That's why I'm trying to see you now, before you marry her. I need you to make love to me one last night. Please, Chance."

Yuri rubbed his chest. As the bulge came into his pants, she unzipped them, and took it in her mouth. Chance had given in once again.

Yuri dreamed of making love to Chance all the time. She did not love him, but he knew every G-spot she had. After all, they had been fucking practically all their lives. They had fucked any and every kind of way they could. Chance let Yuri put toys up his ass, he also fucked her in the ass. The sky was the limit with their sex.

Yuri was still sucking Chance when the phone rang.

"Yuri, it's Shannon, I have to answer, SHHH."

"Oh, go right ahead."

As he talked to his fiancée, Yuri rode him like a cow-girl; he could barely keep his voice calm. Yuri gave it all she had. Her body was swirling as if she was playing with a hula hoop. She squeezed her muscles as tight as she could.

Chance uttered an unrecognizable sound, and said, "Look honey, I am very busy here, I'll get back with you soon. I love you."

Yuri instantly had an attitude and thought, 'he loves her... I'm fucking him intensely, you're fucking Me, loving My pussy!' "Is it good for you, baby?"

"Oh Yuri, it's so good, oh, I can't take it anymore. Yuri."

Yuri jumped off Chance and let him penetrate her mouth. She swallowed every lick of cum that came out, then she tongue-kissed him, so he could taste his own cum juices.

Yuri had a master plan. Now the game would begin. After resting, Yuri rode through her old neighborhood. She sat in front of her house. It looked lonely, just how it did when her mother and father had always been at work, when she was a kid. She looked at Chanel's house and smiled. The perfect family, she thought. That was where she spent many nights, being loved more by her best friend's parents than her own. She wondered if all of the sexcapades come from her not feeling wanted by her parents? Even though they had given her the world, they never had time for her. Love would have been better than any piece of jewelry or handbag she could ever receive from them. She wished she would have never seduced Eugene. Now her sexual urges were worse, and she didn't know what to do about it.

Yuri met Chanel and Marie at the Capital Grille, her treat. They had dinner and talked about the old school days. Marie was six months pregnant and in love. Marie asked Yuri to be the baby's godmother. Yuri was excited, of course.

"I will," she squealed excitedly. "And he'll have all the Polo gear, Gucci booties, and anything else I can find."

Marie said, "He doesn't need all of that girl, he just needs your love."

"Ha, he will have my unconditional love, plus all the finer things I have to give him," Yuri said.

"So, when do you leave, Yuri?"

"I leave Sunday evening, I've had such a wonderful time here, but this guy that I've been digging is coming in town on Monday. We went out once, but I'm really feeling him. I think I've found my soul-mate."

Chanel said, "Well that's great, Terrance will be here tomorrow night, so I can introduce you to him."

Yuri replied, "Sounds great. I'm a little exhausted, I'm gonna go back to the hotel and turn in early."

As Yuri was leaving she kissed Chanel on her head, and she rubbed Marie's belly. "Take care of my godson." With that, she walked away.

Yuri made it back to her room and immediately called Chance. "Hey Yuri, this is not a good time," Chance said.

"I just wanted you to know that I'm leaving on Sunday, and I wanted to see you one last time before I go."

"That's what you said the other day and I gave in."

"Chance, I need closure. You're the one that broke my cherry, the one I chose to give my virginity to. I've been in love with you all these years. The least you can do is let me have closure."

"Ok Yuri, but this is the last time I'll do this. I'm really trying to better myself, and I want to make my woman happy."

'Oh, you will,' thought Yuri. "See you at seven."

Friday could not have come fast enough. Yuri had been having a ball in her city, but could not wait to get back to Atlanta. She dressed in a Juicy Couture sweat suit, which fit her fat ass like a glove. Her waist line was small and every curve was perfectly put in the right place. She headed out to meet Chanel and her boyfriend.

"Terrance, this is Yuri," Chanel introduced them.

"Hello Terrance, it's my pleasure to meet the guy that has Chanel's head in the sky."

"Nice to meet you also, Yuri. Chanel worships the ground you walk on." Yuri smiled at her friend.

At the table, they ordered drinks. Two apple martinis, and a Coors Light for Terrance. "Chanel tells me that you're studying to be an architect."

"Yes, and when I graduate I'll go study in Dubai, and hopefully she'll accompany me."

Chanel looked at him with love in her eyes. As much as Chanel praised Yuri, Yuri despised the fact that all the good guys always went for Chanel. Chanel was smart, pretty, and still a virgin.

Chanel and Terrance made a great couple, he was light skinned, how Chanel liked them, good hair, and had a great body. He was definitely a jock. Yuri could not help but to look at the bulge in Terrance's pants, 'Damn!' she thought, if it's bulging like that while he's soft, it has to be huge. He's going to kill my friend when he fucks her.'

"Yuri, are you ok?" Chanel asked.

"Sorry, I was thinking about Atlanta, as usual."

"Well, Terrance and I will take you to the airport, what time do you leave?"

51

"Eight-thirty pm."

"We'll pick you up around six-thirty, ok?"

"Terrance, it was great meeting you!"

"Same here, Yuri."

"You better treat my girl right or I'll be looking for you!" Both girls giggled.

"I promise I'll treat her better than good."

Saturday morning, Yuri stopped by the pawn shop again. Zlotnick asked, "What you got for me now, Yuri?"

"Oh nothing, I'm going to do some sightseeing, and my friend wants me to take some pictures of Capitol Hill and all the tourist spots that we have around here. What kind of good cameras do you have for a few hundred dollars?"

"I have a Cannon Sure Shot, with a mega lens. It takes pictures and records, so you can have the best of both worlds."

"How much are you gonna to hit me for it?"

"It's a thousand- dollar camera, but for you, give me three hundred fifty dollars and it's yours."

"It's a deal, thank you Zlotnick."

"When do you leave, Yuri?"

"I leave tomorrow."

"Well Yuri, I hope to see you soon. Be good, and take good care of yourself in Atlanta."

Yuri drove around. She took some pictures of the White House; she drove to Howard and Georgetown to snap a few pictures. She took pictures of couples holding hands, women strolling in the park with kids in their strollers. She stopped by Starbucks and had a cup of hot tea, and took in the view of her city.

Yuri made it back to her hotel room. She ran herself a hot bubble bath, thinking, "Will make this a night to remember for myself and Chance."

Chance arrived, looking as scared as he was.

"What are you looking so scared about baby?" she asked innocently, as she hugged him tightly. Yuri was already naked, with two champagne glasses filled to the rim.

She handed one to Chance.

52

"Here, this should calm you," she said. "To new beginnings. I pray you and your wife will find all the love and joy that you so much deserve."

They toasted, Chance drank down the whole glass in one gulp.

After thirty minutes had passed, and two more glasses of champagne, Chance had his hands all over Yuri. He kissed and caressed her body like he had always done. He ate her pussy like he had never done before.

Yuri moaned and screamed his name, "Oh, Chance, I love you, don't stop!"

Chance took Yuri by her hair and slung her down on her knees, and put his hard erect dick in her mouth; he rammed it down her throat.

"Suck it, bitch, you don't love me. This is what you love, suck it."

Yuri liked how Chance was handling her. She sucked his dick professionally like she had done so many times since she was fourteen. Chance moaned and pulled her hair harder, he told her to climb on the bed. Yuri did as she was commanded. He fucked her uncontrollably; she loved the harsh treatment he gave her. He was rough and he came inside of her for the first time.

He was so aroused that he remained hard. She pulled the toy from under the bed while she was sucking him back all the way to life. While still sucking him she took the small dildo that was already lubricated and played with it around his ass hole. Yuri would always put her fingers in his ass. She had turned Chance into a stone cold freak. She took the toy and stuck it in his behind and fucked him with it, from time to time he played her freaky games.

She would always say "It's not a man fucking you baby, it's me, so that doesn't make you gay."

Tonight Chance took all four and a half inches, and seemed to really enjoy it. Yuri came just from watching the fake dick go in and out of his ass. She was a nasty bitch, just like he said! No other man had ever let Yuri fondle him like Chance did. Any other man she had would not even let her put her fingers by their ass. Chance was her sex slave and she did whatever she wanted with him.

He was like Burger King, 'Have it your way.'

After three hours of intense fucking, sucking, and all the other things they did, they showered.

Yuri said, "It's ten 'o clock, Chance, and I know your queen will be looking for you soon, and you turned off your phone."

Chance panicked, jumping out of the shower. He dried off as fast as he could, and put his clothes on, looking puzzled, as if he was coming out of a trance.

He acted as if he was returning from another world, "Bye Yuri it's been a pleasure, but we can no longer see each other. I'm gonna marry my fiancée and never cheat on her again."

Yuri said, with a smirk, "Have a nice life."

On the way to the airport Chanel and Terrance held hands the whole time.

Yuri thought, 'How is this nigga so in love, and hasn't even smelled her pussy?'

Still, they looked happy and Yuri was happy for her best friend.

Yuri was so glad to arrive in Atlanta. She had left her Honda at the MARTA station. When she finally got to her loft, she fell into her soft bed, that she had missed so much, and collapsed into a deep sleep.

Chapter 14

Yuri was so happy to see Shane. It had been two weeks since their date. Instead of going out, Yuri ordered in. They drank Grey Goose and pineapple juice. As business-minded as Shane appeared to be, he quickly took out the single Switzer Sweet, rolled the Cali Cush, and lit it up.

"Do you mind?" If she did, it was too late.

"No, I don't, I just never would have believed you smoked weed, in a million years."

"I don't, often, but when I have no appointments and a whole weekend, like I have now, I smoke; it relaxes my mind," he said as he pulled on it again.

 It smelled so good, like spearmint gum or something. Shane had gotten comfortable, watching the movie, and fell asleep. Yuri looked at his sexy face and body while he slept. He even had a light sexy snore. Yuri wanted kiss him; she imagined how she would freak him when the time came.

When Shane woke up, Yuri had showered and put on a sexy negligee. He looked around like, 'Where am I?' Once he sat his eyes on Yuri, he never took them off. He knew where the hell he was, and why he was there. As she walked to the kitchen, Shane undressed her with his sexy brown eyes. Yuri shut the refrigerator door. Shane was standing behind her. He kissed the back of her neck, slowly. Yuri relaxed her body and laid back on his chest. He reached around, caressing her perfectly perky titties. Yuri could feel him getting bigger and bigger against her back; she was automatically turned on. She felt the wetness coming on between her legs as Shane planted soft, sexual kisses down her back. Yuri squirmed, as the feeling sent electricity through her body.

She wanted to turn around and take over, like she always did, but tonight she would let Shane lead the way. Shane reached around while still kissing her neck. He rubbed the perfect strip of hair that was lining her pussy. Yuri squirmed like a snake. Shane took his two middle fingers and rubbed her clitoris; it was super wet then he stuck them inside of her. She was so wet it was over for the foreplay, now it was time to play. He turned her around and put his tongue down her throat. Yuri started unbuckling and tearing off Shane's pants and shirt. She wanted him so bad.

Shane tore the negligee completely apart with one pull, and he whispered, "I'll buy you many more."

He sat her up on the counter; he reached down on the ground to pull the condom out of his pants, while rubbing his big bullet up and down her clit. He made Yuri climax just from his magnificent foreplay.

He said, "Now I am going to fuck you like Mr. Marcus, right here, on your kitchen counter."

 He put the condom on without ever taking his eyes away from hers.

He said, "Damn, I want you! You are so damn sexy, girl."

He went up into Yuri slow, not knowing if she could handle all of his big love. He played with her, just pushing the tip inside, Yuri wanted to scream it felt so good, and he had not even put it all in, but the fat tip was pleasurable.

"Do you like that, Lil' Momma?" He asked.

Yuri's head was laid back on the cabinet. All she could do was shake her head.

She finally said, "I love it, baby!" Shane sucked on her hard nipples, as he went further and further inside of her. Yuri moaned and moved her hips to Shane's rhythm. She oohed and aahed, it was just spectacular!

Shane asked, "Now are you ready for me to fuck you?"

As he stopped his last gentle stroke, Yuri responded, "Yes, fuck me, daddy!"

That turned him on. Shane lifted Yuri up with his strong, muscular arms, and carried her to the wall, with his dick never slipping out of her. He fucked her standing up on the wall as hard as he could. Yuri screamed his name as loud as she dared. She did not care who heard. The neighbors would know his name. Yuri had been fucked in all kinds of ways, but never against a wall. Yuri screamed, and once again came. She did not just cum, she squirted.

He was totally turned on by that, and said, "I see you like this, huh? Now it's my turn." He lifted Yuri off his still brick-hard dick, and carried her to the couch. "Baby, spread your legs and bend over the couch."

Yuri put her big ass in the air. Shane stood back and admired the seductive view.

She was unbelievably wet, "Fuck me, Shane!" she screamed!

He dived back into her from behind. Shane stroked her hard, and Yuri gave him all the pleasure right back. She whipped her pussy around his dick; she tightened her pussy muscles around his hardness; she squeezed them and let them go several times, like a heartbeat.

Shane was completely turned on. He said, "Damn, girl, you gonna make me cum, it feels like you giving me head doin' that!"

She clenched even tighter, and thought, 'Just wait until I suck yo' dick.' His breathing got intense. "Please don't do that I can't take it any..." Before he could say another word, he went into a convulsion and released.

He pulled out of her slowly, feeling tired and sleepy. When Yuri came back from the kitchen with water, Shane had fallen asleep, right on the couch with the condom still on his now-soft peter.

Yuri was very pleased, and didn't even have to suck him to get him off. She laid on his chest and fell asleep right on the couch with him. When morning arrived, Shane was still holding Yuri in his arms.

She whispered, "I just wish this could last forever."

They laid in bed for the rest of the day. Shane never paid attention to all the phone calls that he had coming in. Yuri had cut her phone off the night before, not caring who called, because the only person that mattered, was the man she was with. They watched movies for the remainder of the day, made love, and fucked through certain scenes. Shane had a lot of stamina, and Yuri could handle all of it; everything he brought. Every time he felt between Yuri's wet legs he stood at ease. The evening came, and Shane had a meeting he had to go to. They showered and made love one last time. Every time she looked at his chocolate sexy face, they went at it again.

She kissed Shane passionately before he left and whispered softly in his ear, "Please don't forget about me."

He replied "You are mine now. I will never forget about you or this day; we are a team."

For the rest of the night Yuri could not get Shane off her mind. He was stuck in her brain. She thought about his black wavy hair, perfectly lined up, his deep dimples when he smiled. He didn't even have to smile for them to show. His skin as smooth as a baby's behind. He was so fine, and all she could think about was him. She still could smell the Tom Ford cologne that he wore, on her sheets, and she buried her nose in them. She thought most about how he made love to her, then fucked her, as he called it. She thought about the crooked hook on his tip that made her wet, she wondered when would be the next time they made love.

Yuri called Chanel and told her about her evening, she finally told her that she was no longer a virgin.

Chanel asked, "Didn't it hurt?"

"Well, kind of, but once he was inside, it was the best feeling that I ever felt."

Even though she had not been a virgin, it was the truth how Shane made her feel. It was true fire and desire!

Shane started doing everything for Yuri. The diamond earrings that her dad had given her for graduation were replaced with three karats. The 2008 Honda Accord was replaced with a 2015 Jeep that she looked at in a book for months. There were also endless shopping sprees.

Yuri had been sexing only Shane. Six months had passed and Yuri was being good. The new semester had started and Shane began to assist her with fees that her scholarship did not cover.

Yuri went out with Candice from time to time, but she wouldn't get at the guys that tried to make moves. Shane began to let Yuri go to California with him. He would take her to extravagant restaurants. Her favorite was Crustacean. She craved the Dungeness crabs.

57

They loved going to the beach, when they were in California, and could not resist making love there, as well. Shane had gotten a taste of Yuri's super head, and was sprung beyond measures. She would caress his hard dick, rub it, and suck it softly. While sucking, she would jack him off. She would put both balls in her mouth at once, and play a game with his dick, as if she was playing a harmonica. She slurped and moaned and yummed and hummed, until he exploded in her mouth. Shane had the sweetest cum that she had ever tasted.

Chapter 15

Chanel had called to tell Yuri the wonderful news.

"Chance is getting married in two weeks, on your birthday, and I know he will want his little sister there. You know you are our sister, Yuri."

Yuri said, "I am your sister, Chanel, but I leave for California on Friday, and I don't know if I'll be back before then. We usually stay a week or more. Shane has a lot of business deals, and I'm going to go relax on the beach. I love tanning."

Chanel replied, "Yuri, your ass don't no need a tan."

Yuri said, "It makes me look like I'm from the islands, and turns Shane on. Speaking of, where is Terrance?"

Chanel answered, "He's in Philly working on finals; he'll be here on Saturday and stay for the week. He's my date for the wedding."

Yuri asked, "Are you blushing, Nelly?"

"Yes Yuri, I'm in love, I almost lost my 'Virgin Mary', but when the passion got too hot, he backed off, because he loves and respects me."

"Well I'm glad you did the right thing, because I can't get enough of Shane." They both giggled.

"Well Yuri, you waited a long time, so it's ok, and you guys are going strong."

Yuri was glad that she had finally admitted that she was not a virgin. Even though her innocence went out the window a long time ago, she felt relieved; at least that she didn't have to lie to her best friend anymore.

Chanel said, "Well, if you don't make it, at least call Chance and wish him luck. After all it will be your birthday, so we'll be thinking about you."

"I will call, Chanel, I'm even going to send a gift. Is he still in the apartment on Seminole?"

"No, girl, they moved into a four bedroom, two-and-a-half bath. It is absolutely beautiful, and it sits on the lake in Bethesda. Their new address is 404 Lake Drive."

"Thank you Chanel, you know I love you so very much. Take care, and when you get married, I'll be right by your side. Tell your family I send my love!"

"Love you, Yuri. Smooches."

Yuri could not believe that Chance had chosen her birthday to marry that pretty Indian bitch. Yuri was hot as hell. She grabbed the phone to call and curse Chance out. She did not care how late it was, she wanted to give him a piece of her mind.

She thought to herself, 'I fucked him all my life, sucking and swallowing his cum, and he gets married on my fucking birthday?'

When she dialed the number a woman answered. She was so mad she didn't even care. "Hello, this is Yuri, may I speak with Chance?"

The voice on the other end said, "Sorry, there is no Chance here, I've had this number for over six months, and people are still calling for him."

Yuri replied, "Oh, sorry."

"No problem, have a blessed evening."

"Thank you."

Yuri thought, 'That bastard changed his number.' Then aloud, "I hate him. The motherfucker will never get married on my birthday!" Her cell rang and it was Shane. Yuri looked at the phone and let it just ring and ring.

All week Yuri got the gifts that Shane had promised. She got a gift every day until her birthday. The first evening started with dinner at Benihana, followed by chocolates and strawberries from Godiva. The second night, a Victoria's Secret shopping spree; she spent twelve hundred dollars on lingerie. On Wednesday, Shane gave her a beautifully wrapped box; inside was a David Yurman necklace and matching bracelet. Thursday came and Shane took Yuri for a helicopter ride from Atlanta to Savannah. They ate dinner on the pier on River Street. Yuri was having the time of her life. She kissed Shane. On the way back to Atlanta, she sucked his dick right in front of the pilot. She had no shame. Shane laid back and enjoyed the ride.

The weekend came so fast. Yuri spent Friday shopping for the Los Angeles trip. They would leave that evening. While shopping, Yuri grabbed Chance and his wife-to-be a gift. She had the gift wrapped. She selected the same beautiful colors as the wedding, Lilac & Cream. She prayed that his new 'wifey' would like the gift.

As Yuri was leaving the store, her cell phone began to ring. She slowed her pace to check the caller ID, and it was Candice.

She smiled and answered, "Hello Candice, what's up?"

"I was wondering if you were free for the next few hours. I know you're leaving tonight and I'd like to take you out to eat and give you your birthday gift, what time do you leave?"

"Yuri replied, "We leave on a redeye, so it's fine, I just have to meet Shane at eight o' clock. He's getting my truck washed, for what I don't know, I'm gonna leave it in the garage all week. He's just so clean. It's three-thirty, so you can pick me up at five-thirty."

Candice said, "Ok, I'll make reservations for six."

"Fine, I'll see you then, honey."

"Bye, Yuri."

When Candice arrived, Yuri was already waiting downstairs. Candice said, "I like that you don't make me wait."

"My mom always told me to be ready, especially if someone is taking you out," Yuri responded. They kissed and rode out.

Yuri asked Candice where she made the reservations at, because she was hungry.

Candice said "This spot called Ray's on the River, it sits on the Chattahoochee River, and the food is the bomb. I'm glad you're hungry."

"Yes, I am, I was about to eat when you called, but now I could eat a horse."

They laughed and sped up 75 North. When they arrived, the valet took the car. Candice grabbed the big Louis Vuitton bag out of the back seat. Yuri didn't know what was in it, but she knew it was Louis, they were seated immediately.

"Yuri, you see how crowded it is? This is why I always reserve tables, I hate to wait, and in here, you may never get called without a reservation."

They ordered spinach dip and apple martinis before dinner arrived.

"So Yuri, I see you've really been having fun with Shane."

"Girl, he is the best! I have fallen in love with him. I have all my money in the bank, even when he gives me money to shop with, I spend a little and put a lot up. I haven't paid rent since the day he stepped foot into the loft. You taught me well, Candice."

They both burst out laughing.

The waiter came to take their order. Candice ordered the roasted chicken with potatoes along with asparagus, and the prime rib with baked potato and broccoli for Yuri. They ate, and the food was delicious. Yuri was stuffed and could not eat another bite. The waiter came out with a few other waiters. Candice had already alerted them that it was Yuri's birthday. The small cake with candles was so cute. They sang Happy Birthday. After eating the cake, Yuri opened her gift. That moment made her feel very special. Candice had bought her a twelve-hundred- dollar Louis Vuitton bag, with the matching belt.

With tears in her eyes, she hugged Candice and said, "Thank you, big sis."

"No problem, it's nothing to a boss bitch." Together they laughed.

Candice asked, "So do you know what Shane is getting you?"

"Actually, he has been buying me a gift every day since Monday. He said they would keep coming until my birthday. I've been shopping all week. I have new furniture, shoes, clothes, just too much to name, he keeps spoiling me."

Candice said, "It's seven thirty, so we need to go, I want to stop by the Twist and have a drink."

"I'm supposed to meet Shane at eight."

Candice replied, "He won't mind Yuri."

Yuri said, "I'll give him a call."

Candice shook her head. "No you won't! He don't run everything."

Yuri smiled and agreed, "Ok, Candice, you're my big sis, and whatever you say goes."

They wrapped up at the restaurant, jumped in the Benz, and headed downtown. Candice was bumpin' Jeezy again. She loved all of his music.

Yuri commented, "You love Jeezy."

Candice nodded, "Yes, he goes hard, plus he and Q are very good friends. I'll have to introduce you."

"I'd love that, Candice."

Before they pulled to Twist, Candice said she had to be in Tennessee the following morning. She had met a high profile lawyer who wanted to spend the day with her.

She said, "We have sex for about ten to fifteen minutes, we talk the rest of the day away. I walk around his house with just my panties on, throwing this big ass, and he gets totally aroused. He's in his sixties and his Viagra keeps his dick hard, but it doesn't last too long."

They laughed.

Yuri asked, "So how much do you cash out on?"

"I'm gonna get five thousand dollars, plus gas."

"Damn, Candice, that is a nice check for one day."

"Yes it is, with no strings attached."

Yuri forgot to mail Chance's gift. "Candice, I had a gift to mail to DC, if possible could you please mail it when you get to Tennessee? I really don't want to carry it on the plane, and I want it to get there at least by Thursday."

"Ok, Yuri, I gotcha. I'll get it when I drop you off."

When they pulled up to Twist, Shane was standing on the curb, next to a 2015 S Class Convertible Benz coup, bright red with a big red bow sitting on top of it. His Aston Martin was in front of the car. Yuri's eyes lit up.

She exlaimed, "Candice you knew?"

"Yes, sis, I did, but that's what surprises are for! Yuri jumped out of the car, wrapped her arms around Shane, then took his face between her hands, putting her tongue down his throat. He returned the kiss passionately.

He pulled away for a moment to say, "Happy Birthday, Lil' Momma."

She said, "I love you Shane."

"Yuri, I love you, too!"

Candice stood there admiring the two of them, and then she began to admire the Benz. She nodded her head with approval.

"I have to go now Yuri. I'll use my key to get the gift." As Candice walked away she said, "Happy Birthday, I love you."

Chapter 16

The flight to L.A. was very quiet. Yuri sat in the first class seat and watched Shane as he slept. She was glad that God had put him in her life. He was so sexy, and at the age of twenty-eight, he was very wealthy. He had never sold drugs. His grandfather had passed when he was seventeen, leaving him a quarter of a million dollars in his will. Shane was an only child, and the only grandchild, on his father's side. Once he turned twenty-one, he received his inheritance. Instead of splurging and making poor choices with the money, Shane was smart and he invested in real estate. Because of those choices, he was now a self-made millionaire. He was a hard worker with an old soul. Yuri stared at her man until the stewardess began speaking, "Please bring your chairs and tables to the upright position." Shane was awakened by all the rumbling. The California lights were beautiful from the sky. Shane reached over and held her hand, as the plane began to land.

L.A. was cool at night. Shane took his suit coat and wrapped it around Yuri's shoulders. She loved the smell of the Creed cologne that mixed with his body. A car took them to the airport garage where his 2017 white Bentley sat. Yuri jumped in, feeling rich. They rode around listening to DJ Quick. Yuri had never heard it, since she was from the East Coast. Shane enjoyed listening to it, and he had it on blast. Once they got to the beach-front condo, Yuri showered and hopped straight into her bikini.

Shane said, "Damn, girl, every time I see you looking like that, I want to fuck you!"

Yuri replied, "Well, fuck me, daddy."

They fucked on the patio and then took it to the beach, stroking, not caring who watched. When they finished, they laid there and watched the midnight full moon.

It was a beautiful, bright Saturday morning. Yuri had held Shane all night, he turned over, kissed her, and stared into her eyes. She got wet just from the look that he gave her. She automatically started stroking him, until he gently erected. She took him into her mouth and sucked him hard, deep throating him. Shane went weak every time she did that. She took him down her throat, as if she didn't have tonsils.

Shane groaned, "Yuri!" While pulling her long hair, he went into convulsions.

Yuri pulled back so he would not cum. She hopped on top of him and stood up on her feet. She went up and down, down and up, on his hardness. Yuri was a control freak and always took advantage of her men. She sat down on his dick, with her famous tightening move. Shane had the 'I can't take it anymore' fuck face on. Yuri slid off of him and put it back in her mouth tasting her own sweetness. After four long strokes, Shane shook as if he was having a seizure, and deposited in Yuri's compactor. She was a walking garbage can of cum.

Shane just laid there. "Damn, Yuri, you take all my energy away from me." He added, "We have to get dressed and get out of here, or I'll fuck you all day."

Yuri smiled and said, "And I will fuck you and suck you all day."

The Bentley was waiting at the front door of the condo. Yuri had put on her Rock Republic shorts, Gucci flip flops and tank top. "Girl, whatever you wear looks sexy, but I love your birthday suit the best." Yuri smiled at Shane.

As they pulled up on Rodeo Drive, Yuri was happy, and ready to shop. "One week left until my birthday, and I am gonna enjoy all seven days until then."

Shane replied, "And I am going to spoil you until then, and after that, too. Now let's do some shopping."

First stop, Yuri bought a Christian Dior bag that she had seen in the InStyle magazine. The bag was thirty-one hundred dollars. The next store they got matching twelve-hundred- dollar Louis Vuitton bags to carry on the airplane. Shane stopped next in the Cartier store, picking up two pair of glasses; one pair buffalo horn, the other pair a wire frame. Next stop was the Gucci store, Yuri's favorite. She purchased two pair of sneakers, three pair of pumps, two hand bags and two belts. Shane also got two pair of sneakers, a pair of dress shoes, and a pair of loafers. He bought two hats and a belt, bringing the total to nine-thousand dollars in the Gucci store alone. Yuri shopped until she dropped.

Shane said, "I want to go back to the condo and make love to you until the weekend is over. You know, on Monday, I'll be very busy up until your birthday, so this weekend, your ass is mine. I'm sure you'll find something to get into for the week. There are a lot of things you can do here, like sight-seeing, ride a yacht, do the beach, whatever you want, Lil' Momma."

"I want you, and that's all, Shane." Yuri knew exactly how to charm her man.

They made love, and fucked the weekend away. Shane was gone before Yuri woke up. The day was gloomy; it looked like it was going to rain. Yuri decided she would go eat at Roscoe's Chicken and Waffles. They had not eaten there yet, this visit. It was one of her favorites, the number nine, three wings and a waffle. She sat and enjoyed the California scenery. Once she had eaten, she drove down Crenshaw, taking in the view. L.A. was so different from Atlanta and DC. She admired the palm trees. When it began to rain, she headed back east, to the condo.

She texted Shane on his cellphone. "Hey baby, I'm missing you, and if you were here, you know what I would do to you."

She laid on the plush couch; her phone vibrated. Shane had messaged her back. She smiled. "Hey, Lil' Momma, I wish I was there so you could do what you do! I'm trying to close on an apartment building on the Westside of L.A. It'll bring in a lot of cash, so when I'm done, you can do, what you do, boo."

She responded, "I'll do even more than that, baby, I have a new trick that Candice taught me, and I want to try it on you, lol! See you soon, baby."

Yuri watched T.V. for a while, and eventually dozed off.

She woke up to soft kisses on her lips. "Baby, you're finally back."

"Did you miss me, Lil' Momma?"

She said, "More than you know, daddy."

"I'm going to shower and then we can watch a movie."

Shane showered while Yuri stepped into her Victoria's Secrets. When Shane got out of the shower, Yuri returned with the Ace of Spades champagne. Shane was sound asleep. Yuri wanted to awake him with her wet tongue, but she decided to let him sleep. He was tired. She was a nympho. Shane had stamina, but Yuri was wearing him out.

She knew he had meetings to attend all this week, so she thought, 'I'll let him be.'

Yuri called Chanel. "Hi, BFF."

"Hey Yuri, what's going on, boo?"

"Oh, still out here in L.A."

"Will you make it out to the wedding?"

"I don't think so, Chanel, I don't think we're leaving until my birthday. Shane is swamped with work and I'm going to just lay around, but please send my love to your brother. I tried calling him, but his number was changed."

"Yeah, he changed it so all the sluts that he had calling would leave him alone. Chance is really in love, for the first time, and we're happy for him."

Yuri thought, 'If only Chanel knew he changed the number because of me, with his freaky dildo taking punkass." "I'm happy for him too," Yuri smirked.

"Well Yuri, I wish you could be here, the bachelorette party is Thursday night, and we have a stripper. It's gonna be off the chain. Chance is really going all out for this wedding. Shannon has really found her a good man, and she's a sweet woman. Since you've been gone, we hang out together a lot. She is heaven-sent."

Yuri felt jealous. "Well, don't let her take my place."

"Never, Yuri, you will always be my sister and best friend."

"I love you, Chanel."

"I love you more, Yuri. Be good, and tell Shane I said hello."

Yuri said, "Send my love to Terrance, talk to you later."

When the morning came, Shane showered and was out the door. He left a thousand dollars on the bar with a note. "Baby, buy you something nice. I didn't want to wake you, you looked so peaceful. Love, Shane."

Yuri wanted to get woken up, she liked freaking with Shane in the A.M. He really gave her all he had, like a morning workout.

Yuri decided to go sit on the beach. She grabbed her IPOD and pink backpack. As she looked out on the Pacific Ocean, there were beautiful surfers everywhere, people tanning, skating, and throwing Frisbees. Yuri wished Shane was there, but he was making the dough that she spent so much of. She grabbed her towel and laid out.

She dozed off, waking up to a deep sexy voice, "Hello is this spot taken?"

"No."

He laid his towel out. Yuri took off her Gucci shades to check him out. She put them back on and thought, 'Damn, he fine.' As he began to put sunscreen on his caramel skin, Yuri peeked, and it looked like he worked out every day and night. His body looked better than Shane's. He was well over 6' tall, skin perfect, light brown eyes and a sexy, manly ass, with two dimples on his back. He laid back on his towel, put on his Prada shades and earphones.

He caught a glimpse of her watching, as she tried to turn away.

"So what are you doing out here alone?"

Yuri responded, "Oh, just relaxing. My boyfriend is working, so I'm taking in the good sun."

He said, "Oh, ok, where are you from? You have an east coast accent."

"I'm from D.C., and you?"

"Born and raised right here in L.A. I'm a beach baby. I'm Cedric, and you are?"

She hesitated, "Yolanda, nice to meet you."

"So do you come here every day, Yolanda?"

"Yes, until I leave for D.C."

"Enjoy your stay."

"Thank you Cedric."

Yuri peeked out the corner of her eye and watched the nice bulge in his pants. Was he hard or was he just big beneath the shorts? Yuri had to pack up and leave. Cedric was a major distraction.

When she returned to the condo, she showered and texted Shane, "Hey baby, just left the beach. I wish you would have woken me, up, you know how I love to give it to you in the A.M. I miss you!"

Shane responded, "Lil' Momma, I wanted to give it to you in your sleep, but you were so peaceful, I had to let you be."

Yuri text: "I would have been peaceful had you woken me up and gave me what I needed."

Shane text: "I'll make it up to you tonight, its two dollar Tuesday at the House of Blues, I'll be home around seven so be ready. I'm meeting a few friends there at eight, I love you."

Yuri dressed in her new BCBG dress, Gucci shoes and bag. Shane could not take his eyes off of her.

"Yuri, you look so sexy right now, if this wasn't about money, we would not be going anywhere."

He grabbed her by the waist and gave her a lustful kiss.

On the way to the House of Blues, Anita Baker's 'Sweet Love' was playing on the car stereo. Shane sang along to the whole song.

"That's my girl." As young as he was, he knew all of the oldies.

When they arrived they went in, and Shane shook the two guys' hands. They looked as if they had lots of money. The smaller guy was with a plus-size woman, she looked to be about a thirty-four waist. She was at least a size eighteen to twenty, but very pretty. They seemed very happy and in love.

Interrupting her trance, Shane said, "These are my business partners, Mike and Tim, and this is Tim's wife, Cheryl."

"Nice to meet you all," Yuri replied. Yuri was checking Cheryl out, and the ring on her hand had at least four karats or better. The stone looked to be a perfect, colorless "D", and the setting was surely platinum. Yuri thought, 'One day I'll wear a rock like that on my ring finger.'

For the next two hours, Yuri listened to the guys talk business. She knew Shane would be working all week, but not to the extent that it carried on until the evening.

She was annoyed as she thought, "Cheryl must have money in on something because she's listening closely to every single word."

Whatever they were discussing, they all would take home two hundred thousand dollars each. Yuri was ready to go. When dinner was over, everyone seemed satisfied and tipsy. The papers had been signed, and the deal was sealed.

When they returned to the condo, Shane said, "Yuri let's take a shower together."

Yuri responded, "I would love to."

And with no hesitation, they showered. Shane was tired, but managed to give ten minutes of his good loving to her. Yuri wanted more once they got out of the shower. She sucked Shane, she pulled at his softness and anything she could do to please him. Shane had pleasured himself and not Yuri.

He said "Lil' momma, I've been working so hard to close on these properties, you know that I'm not trying to be so out of touch, but if I don't handle these deals, we won't be able to do the things we do. I couldn't pay for your expensive shopping sprees."

With that said, he fell asleep, leaving Yuri thinking.
She thought about how it was about to be Wednesday, in less than an hour, and Thursday was Shannon's bachelorette party. She remembered what Chanel said about Chance being in love with Shannon. For years he could not express his feelings to his family about loving her, she thought. We slept together for over five years. We did things to each other that we would let no other do, well he did, not me.

'I will fuck him again if it kills me,' she thought. 'If I'm not happy with this man, with all of this money, then Chance won't be happy either.'

Yuri woke up to an empty bed. Shane had slipped out of the bed once again. She was glad Wednesday had come. Shane's work week was just about over, and her birthday was three days away. She hoped to be back in Atlanta partying with Candice. L.A. was a beautiful city but no one was partying like they do in the ATL. Yuri decided to go back down to the beach. She wore her bikini with no cover-up today. She wanted to take in all the California sun that she could before she went back home. She laid her towel out in the exact same place as she had the day before. She put her earphones on, attached to her IPOD, and rocked to the sound of Jay Z. She pulled out her sunscreen and began to apply it, little by little, to her soft brown skin. As soon as she finished her legs, there was a tap on her back.

"Hey, Yolanda, you remember me?"

"Hello Cedric, of course I do. It was only yesterday. How could I forget?"

"I see you're here alone again, would you like for me to rub some of that on your back?" Yuri hesitated.

Cedric grabbed the bottle and rubbed it anyway. Cedric looked even better than he did yesterday. His golden brown tanned skin glowed. His cargo shorts fell off his hips, showing his masculine structure. He was shirtless and looking hot as hell. When he touched Yuri's back, it was electrifying. He massaged her like a masseuse. Yuri closed her eyes and was about to relax.

His smell was intoxicating. She felt thrilled, then tensed up realizing the effect his touch was having on her. She snatched the sunblock out of his hand, causing him to jump.

"Thank-you, she responded politely."

"No problem," he replied, feeling she was annoyed by him. "No problem, at all."

"Cedric, you must live around here?"

"Yes, I live right behind those houses, over there, in an apartment. I paint, and when I'm not painting, I'm right here, on this beach, in this very spot. Would you like to go get a drink with me, Yolanda? There's a bar up on the Marina."

Unsure, he asked, "Are you twenty-one?"

"Yes, I am," Yuri responded, lying as usual. They went to the bar and had a couple of Sex on the Beaches. Yuri had loosened up. They had a nice chat.

"So Yolanda, how long will you be in town?"

Yuri answered, "Oh, a few more days, I think. My boyfriend is working, so once his business is handled, we'll leave."

Cedric sighed, "I wish you didn't have a boyfriend, because you'd be hanging out with me."

"I am hanging out with you, now, and he wouldn't like that."

"Why wouldn't he?"

"Because you are really handsome, and he might be a little intimidated."

"Intimidated, huh?"

She said, "I really should go; I think I have had more than my share of Sex on the Beach."

"Yolanda, it was so good to see you, and I can say you are a real sexy woman, and your man is lucky to have you!"

"Thank you, Cedric, and it was nice seeing you again." Yuri grabbed her backpack before anything else was said or done. She was sweating and moist from Cedric flirting with her. When she returned to the high-rise condo, she showered and wished Shane would have been there. Cedric had got her almost drunk and most definitely horny. Yuri picked up the phone to call Candice.

"Hello Candice."

"Hi, Yuri."

"What's going on in the A?"

"Oh, not much. I've been offered a job at the Coca Cola Corporate offices, I start on Monday."

"Well, if Shane is still busy, I'm gonna to fly back on Saturday, because I want to go out for my birthday, and I would rather hang out with you."

70

"What's wrong, Yuri, you sound upset?"

"We shopped all last weekend, but Shane has been so busy that he hasn't paid me any attention."

"Yuri, you must understand, he is a business man and about making money, and you should be very happy that you have a young, fine-ass man that works as hard as he does."

"I know, Candice, but I've been out here just relaxing, and I've gotten bored."

"Yuri, all I can say is, don't nothin' move but the money. You don't have a new Benz for nothing, and ain't no tellin' what he'll have for you on your birthday. Just relax and enjoy your vacation, because you are so lucky to have it like you do."

"You know, Candice, you're right. I am lucky. I'm being selfish."

"Yes, you are. He has spoiled your young ass way too much! Well, girl it's 11:30pm, and you know I have to get my beauty sleep, so I'll see you when you get back. Oh, I mailed your gift, and it should arrive in D.C. tomorrow."

"Thank you Candice, I love you.

"Love you more, Yuri."

Shane trampled in after midnight. He was so tired,, he couldn't even make it to the shower.

Yuri rubbed his back and thought, 'What a hard-working, sexy man I have here.' She drifted off to sleep in his arms.

It was raining Thursday morning. Shane bought a fruit basket and breakfast from the restaurant on the corner. He read the paper, reviewing the stocks and bonds, and headed out to his office. Once again he gave Yuri $2,500.00.

"Lil' momma, go get something sexy for tomorrow. We will celebrate from tomorrow until your birthday."

Yuri was tired of shopping. There was nothing left for her to buy. She was shopped out and ready to go back to Atlanta. She had enough of the west coast.

When the rain finally stopped, Yuri went back to the beach. It was the only place that calmed and relaxed her. She went to the same spot, at the same time. She picked up her book and took in the blazing sun. She dozed off, and was awakened by the familiar voice.

"Hello, Yolanda, you're back in my spot," Cedric said.

Yuri smiled and shielded her eyes.

"Hello Cedric."

71

She thought he looked better every time she saw him. He never wore shirts, only cargo shorts and Nike sandals, showing his well-manicured feet. His hair shined in the sun with a perfect line.

"Can I join you?"

"It's your spot, isn't it?" They both laughed.

Cedric had a picnic basket today. "Do you care to join me? I made a little bit too much for just myself."

Yuri was a bit hungry.

"Sure I will, what are you having?"

Cedric pulled the linen sheet out, then he made two club turkey sandwiches with chips, strawberries, and grapes that were marinated in a bowl with some mango juice. They ate and enjoyed each other and found that they had a lot in common. Their meal came to an end too soon. "It was great and fun, thank you, Cedric."

He said, "That's not all."

He then pulled out a bottle of champagne. One of her favorites, 'Moet,' and popped the cork. After drinking the whole bottle, they were both laughing and talking clever.

"Yolanda I want to make love to you."

Yuri's mouth dropped. "I wish you could, but I have a...."

He took her hand.

"Look what you've done to me."

He put her hand on his erection. Yuri could not believe he had done that. He was big and hard, just the way she liked them. Yuri blushed and her whole face was flushed. She was wet.

"Yolanda, I apologize, you just do something to me, and I guess it's the champagne."

Yuri wanted Cedric and the incredible bulge that was in his pants.

He continued, "I can see the look in your eyes. You want me like I want you and my dick will not go down until you make it."

Ten minutes later, they walked into Cedric's one-, bedroom apartment. As soon as the front door closed, it was like Yuri and Cedric were animals, released from a cage. He slammed her up against the wall, as their tongues darted in and out of each other's mouths. They were kissing feverishly. His hands explored every inch of her body, like it was a fine piece of art. As they made their way towards the bedroom, their lips and bodies never separated. They were shedding clothing, piece by piece.

Yuri caught a glimpse of his dick, coming out of his shorts. It was love at first sight.

She thought, 'That shit is huge, and I can't wait another second to get all of that in my mouth.'

They had not quite made it to the bedroom. In the hallway by the bedroom door, Yuri dropped down on her knees and dispensed with the regular familiarities of kissing and licking first, the meet and greet. Yuri took that big mutherfucka in her mouth and deep throated it all, like the real bitch she was. She was spitting and slobbering all over that dick. All you could hear was her slurping and smacking and her eyes never left his. Trying to suppress a smile, Yuri was amazed at the pleasure she was giving Cedric, and he was looking like he was about to cry. Yuri slid his dick out of her mouth slowly and pulled him to the floor. As he laid down, Yuri climbed on top and sat on his face. She rotated her hips like she was listening to her favorite reggae song. His tongue danced in and out of her honey cup.

He groaned, "Damn baby!"

Yuri wanted to call his name, but she could not remember it.

She thought 'Fuck it, who cares!'

He mumbled and said, "Just don't stop."

Yuri was grinding and fucking his face. She melted in his mouth, and Cedric swallowed all of her juices. His whole face was wet. Cedric got up licking her juices from his lips. In one swoop he scooped her up off of the floor and laid her on the bed. Before Yuri could even blink, Cedric was turning her on her stomach, pulling her nice firm ass up on the edge of the bed. Her pussy was wet

He drove his dick in and out, as Yuri cried with pleasure. She was taking it all as she thought, 'This boy knows how to handle his business.' His strokes were long, hard and fierce, pounding her pussy out.

'OMG,' Yuri thought, 'This shit hurts so good. Just when she thought it could not get any better he slid his finger in her ass. Her pussy erupted like a volcano.

Cedric said, "Baby, this is the best pussy I've ever had." As he moaned, "I'm about to bust, baby."

Yuri thought 'I can't let this nigga bust all up in me.' Yuri jumped off his dick and wrapped her lips around it, savoring her own juices.

Cedric cried out, "You nasty bitch," just like she was!

Yuri thought and smiled, 'This nigga just don't know the half,' as she swallowed all of his semen.

After two hours of unprotected, forbidden fucking, Yuri knew she had to get back to the condo. She had lost track of time, horse-playing and having sex with a man she didn't know. As she put her clothes on, Cedric could not move from the bed. She said, "I'll see myself out."

"Can you at least leave me your number, Yolanda?"

73

She said "I will see you again," and walked out the door.

As the elevator door closed and she pressed the first floor, Yuri thought, "This is so wrong, but it felt so right." Her insides were still tingling. She could have fucked Cedric all night.

Yuri ran to the Condo and showered. She tried to get every last scent of his sex off of her. After she showered, she laid in the bath tub, soaking and scrubbing, in the hot water. Shane arrived at 9:00pm sharp. He showered and laid on the couch next to Yuri.

"Hey, Lil' Momma, what's wrong, you mad at me or something?"

"No baby, I'm just tired, the heat on the beach wore me out today."

"I'm sorry I've been working so hard. Tomorrow we'll have dinner and do whatever you want to do, but right now I have something in mind that I want to do." Shane kissed on Yuri's neck, she was tired and exhausted from fucking Cedric, but still got aroused.

She giggled and said, "Shane, I'm sleepy."

He ignored what she said and his hand went down her stomach, followed by his wet tongue. He put his fingers in her panties and felt her wetness. He planted small kisses all the way down, until he was at her clitoris. He gently made circles around her clit and stuck his tongue inside. Yuri opened up wide. He stopped for a second, to release her panties. He sucked her wetness, and in doing so, made a sound-effect like a vibrator.

Yuri fucked his face, as his tongue explored her insides. She could not hold back anymore, and reached an ultimate orgasm in his mouth.

"Damn, Yuri your pussy is sweet, hot, and juicy tonight."

He put on a condom and fucked Yuri like it was the first time.

"Damn baby this pussy is tight, what have you been doing, pussy exercises?"

She thought, 'If he only knew.'

He flipped her over and fucked her from the back. It was his favorite position, he smacked her ass as hard as he could.

Yuri moaned, "Ah Shane, ah shit, don't do it to me like this."

He slapped her ass again. "Whose pussy is this?"

"It's yours, daddy."

After pounding and pounding, Shane released, and his body went into convulsions. He pulled out slowly and laid down next to Yuri. They fell asleep with her head lying on his chest.

Yuri was happy that the weekend had come. One more day until her birthday. Shane had finished up early. It was all about Yuri, and her birthday weekend would be special. Yuri was looking exceptionally beautiful. She had on her True Religion Jeans, which fit her ass to a 'T'. She wore the Jadore tank top, with the Christian Dior bag, and 5" Christian Louboutin heels. She smelled like Dolce and Gabbana Light Blue.

Shane was also dressed to kill; Gucci down to the shoes. He watched Yuri walk to the Bentley Coupe. Her ass was so fat, waist small with a mean, fierce walk that said, "I am a bad bitch." He had caught him a trophy, and he loved every minute of it.

At dinner, they ate fried lobster tails, oysters, and brown rice with broccoli and cheese. The food was superb.

Shane had something to say, and in between controlling his portions, he said, "Yuri, I can't go back to Atlanta. We have a few more properties to close on, Tuesday, and I know you're looking forward to going home."

Yuri replied, "If you don't mind, Shane, I would still like to fly out tomorrow. Candice planned a party, and I really don't want to let her down. I could go, and that way I won't be a distraction to you."

"Lil momma, you are never a distraction to me. Only when you walk and throw your ass in those jeans, or when you are naked, or when you..."

Blushing and smiling, Yuri interrupted, "Stop it, Shane."

"Sure baby, you go, and when everything is all wrapped up here, I'll come running to you, my love."

"Thank you, Shane, I love you!"

"I love you, too."

June sixth had finally come; Yuri's birthday. Shane woke her up to breakfast in bed. The aroma of omelets with fresh diced vegetables, turkey bacon, toast, her favorite champagne, and a glass of orange juice.

She kissed Shane and whispered, "I love you. You are the best man I ever had."

He replied, "I thought I was the only man you ever had."

"You are," she lied flirtatiously.

She tore into the food. When she downed the mimosa, something almost went down her throat. She was shocked to see a five karat Cartier ring! She looked at Shane, lovingly put her arms around him, and stuck her tongue down his throat. He pulled back so that he could propose.

Speaking softly, Shane said, "Yuri, we have been together almost a year, and I've been thinking for a while now, I want you to be my wife. I can't imagine not waking up with you, or living without you. I know you're young, but I know that I do love you, and I want to spend the rest of my life with you."

Yuri was stunned. She knew she wasn't ready to commit to Shane for the rest of her life, and she couldn't forget what she'd done with Cedric. Yuri could not trust herself. But the other part of her didn't want to lose this rich, sexy, soft-hearted man. She also did not want to lose the opportunity of him sharing his world with her.

Shane interrupted her thoughts, impatiently "What do you say, baby?"

"Yes, I will marry you! I love you, Shane."

Shane said "I love you too, and for now we will not make any arrangements. But next year, on your 20thbirthday, you will be my wife."

Chapter 17

Yuri arrived at Hartsfield Jackson Airport, happy to be in Atlanta. She strutted through the airport with all new everything. She felt 'Boss Status.' Shane had laced her with everything she needed to floss for her birthday weekend. She commanded attention from the train to the exit. Candice was waiting at the gate for her. They got in the car and sped off. When Yuri turned on her phone she had six messages from Chanel. "Please call me, Yuri, ASAP." Next message: "Happy birthday, Yuri, where are you?"

Yuri was so happy to see her loft, after two weeks she just wanted to lay in her bed and relax, but it was her birthday, so she was getting outside. She had not partied in L.A.

T.I. was having a birthday bash and she would be at the party. After she showered, she called Chanel.

"Girl, it's about time you called, I've been blowing your phone up."

"Calm down, Chanel, I was on the plane, you sound devastated."

"I am, and everything is crazy around here."

"How was the wedding?"

"You will not believe, that's what all the drama is about. Let me tell you, to start it off, everything was going fine. Chance and Shannon was the happiest couple in the world. So on Thursday morning, Shannon said she was sick. We took her to the hospital, and that's when we found out she was eight weeks pregnant. We were all so happy. With all of that excitement, just when everyone was supposed to be on their way to the bridal bachelorette party, and with all of the congratulations on the baby celebration, she called it off. We thought it was because of the sickness that she was going through." Chanel sounded both frantic and confused all at once.

"Wow, Chanel, what does all of this have to do with the wedding?" Yuri listened, sounding puzzled, but looking mischievous.

"Girl, Shannon never showed up today. She left Chance hanging; we have been looking for her since last night. None of her family or friends have seen her. The police said we have to wait 24 hours to file a missing persons' report, and we have an hour and ten minutes until we can proceed with the report. Until then, we've formed searches and we've placed posters all around the city. Girl, Chance is going through it right now. His fiancée and his unborn child are missing!"

Chanel started crying, annoying the hell out of Yuri. She thought 'fuck Shannon and her baby,' but she put back on her caring voice, "Chanel, I'm sure she's ok, we have to think positive right now."

"Yuri, who would run off the night before their wedding, after they found out they were pregnant? It has to be foul play."

"I wish I was there, Chanel, you know, when you're hurting and need someone to lean on. Don't think the worst, they'll find her."

"I pray they will. Oh, by the way Yuri, Happy Birthday!"

"Thank you BFF. I have to go and get dressed because I'm going out with Candice. Oh, before I forget, Shane proposed to me last night, and I have a big rock on my finger."

Chanel was quiet and burst out crying.

Yuri said, "Chanel, what's wrong? Aren't you happy for me?"

"Yes, I am happy about your proposal, it's just, Chance was supposed to get married, and someone kidnapped Shannon along with my niece or nephew. It's just a bad day for my family."

"Everything will be ok, Chanel, you must trust God. I love you, now get some rest, and don't forget to pray."

"I love you more, Yuri, have fun."

"I'll check on you later."

Yuri thought about the gift that she had sent. Shannon must have received it. Yuri was almost sure of it. She smiled and got dressed.

When Candice arrived, Yuri was ready, looking hot as ever. She had graduated to the big leagues and her wardrobe now had a resemblance to Candice's. They both looked and smelled like money.

Candice glanced over at Yuri's finger and screamed, "Damn girl!"

"What, Candice?"

"What the fuck? When did you get that?"

Yuri smiled and responded at the same time, "Shane proposed to me."

"Wow, that's a rock! You are so lucky! He's a good man. Yuri, are you ready to settle down? You are so young!"

"I don't know, Candice, I only accepted because I was caught up in the moment. I do love him, but for now I'm going to take it one day at a time." Even though her mouth was saying that, Yuri was thinking, 'It is going down tonight, all the bosses are in attendance from all over.'

"Are you ready?" Candice asked.

"Hell yeah, let's get it."

Candice pulled up in the front of the Compound Night Club. The car clock read 12:40am. Candice thought, 'The perfect time'. The valet took the car. Candice walked to the front of the line, as usual. She approached the sexy African promoter, Alex, and he escorted her in. The word on the street was AG Entertainment ran Atlanta when it came to the party scene. Alex was the man. She was then shown to her VIP table by the waitress. That was followed by five bottles of Ace of spade, a liter of Grey Goose, pineapple, orange, and cranberry juices, along with four bottles of Voss water. Candice had it all ready and prepared, she knew that men would be sending drinks all night.

Taking in the scenery, Yuri said, "Wow, thank you Candice, I love you!"

"Don't thank me, Yuri. Thank your fiancé. He made all of this possible. He had it all arranged while you were on the flight here."

Yuri texted Shane. "Hey daddy, just arrived in the club, Thanx! You set it out! love you. Smooches! xoxoxo."

Two minutes later, a message came from Shane: "You are welcome, Lil' Momma, anything for you! Don't do anything I wouldn't do. Love you, too."

The party was bananas. TI did a small performance, Jeezy and Lil' Boosie did their thing, too. Everybody that was somebody was there. Yuri was half drunk and having a blast. Candice had started talking to a cat that she seemed to be feeling her. She never gave D-boys a chance. Yuri tried not to even look at the other guys, but it was so many fine niggas, what could she do?

After two more drinks, Yuri was loose. The dude that she had been checking for all night finally walked over and approached her.

"Hey sexy, what's up with you? I see y'all over here, ballin'.""

"Hey, how are you?"

"I'm cool now that I've met you."

"You been with the girl over there all night. She cool with you all over here?"

"I'm the man; I do what I want to do. I fuck the cow, while she holds the head."

"Oh yeah," Yuri smirked.

"Yeah, you goin' with us tonight?"

"Us, who's us?"

"Me and her."

"Ha, I am not following you. Are you serious?"

"Yep, she loves seeing this big python slide in and out of another woman, it turns her on."

Yuri looked over at the pretty, olive-skinned woman. Her hair was long and glossy. Her eyes were deep, dark and serious. She looked Yuri's way and gave a nod of acknowledgement.

Yuri thought, 'Am I drunk, or is he really serious?'

He was dead serious.

Yuri said "I'll let her watch, but this is gonna cost you. I need money for shopping."

"Just say that you wanna get paid."

"Well yes, I want to get paid, I usually want no less than $500, but since she's watching, I want a stack."

"You got it, baby."

Yuri was drunk, but she managed to get the words out. "And for the record, it's my birthday, so you better fuck me right."

Yuri told Candice about the conversation with the guy.

"Yuri, you just got engaged yesterday, you sure you want to do something like this?" She was half pleading with Yuri to change her mind.

"Girl, it's my birthday, plus he said he got a stack. You know I ain't turnin' down no green."

"Yuri, be careful, because you're drunk."

Yuri ignored Candice, and began to dance to the music, shaking her fat ass, and moving through the crowd toward the couple. As she walked away, she said, "Candice, I will be just fine."

Once they left the club, Candice dropped Yuri off at the Twelve Hotel, near her loft. Yuri was drunk as she walked into the residential Hotel. Men were everywhere. They tried talking to her. She swung her hips as seductively as she could, to the elevator, punching in the 21st floor. Yuri was greeted by the woman, at the door. As Yuri stood at the threshold of the room, she could see him stepping out of the shower. Her eyes did not leave his body.

The woman interrupted her thoughts and said, "Come on in and makes yourself comfortable."

Yuri walked over to the love seat.

The woman said, "We didn't catch your name."

Yuri said, "Yolanda, and now that we have established names, I need what you said you were going to give me."

The guy moved in closer, he was just out of the shower and lost his towel, with it falling to the floor. He did not have a python like he said, but he was a nice size, not too big, and most definitely, not too small. The woman handed over the stack that was promised.

He approached Yuri and said, "Now get naked."

80

Yuri came out of her dress, leaving only her Gucci pumps on. He began kissing on Yuri's breast, her nipples were hard. With her breast cupped in his hand, he whispered, "Happy Birthday!" Yuri was aroused and so was the woman. He pushed Yuri to the bed and kissed all over her body. Yuri closed her eyes and let herself go.

She felt the woman's touch: it was soft. Before she could open her eyes the woman had taken the lead and slid her tongue into Yuri's wetness, at the same time, while he sucked her nipples. Yuri wanted her to stop, but it felt so good. She did not stop her. The guy stood back and watched as his girl took Yuri down. It was supposed to be the other way around. Yuri was drunk, the feeling was incredible. She moaned and bucked. The woman ate her pussy like Chance, but even better. Yuri was sweating, and wet as hell; Yuri screamed. While the woman ate her pussy, he slid his dick in his girl from behind. Yuri had never had a threesome. At this moment, she was having fun. The woman licked and sucked on Yuri until she had an orgasm; the best one of her life.

He pulled out of his girl and pulled out another rubber, put it on, and stuck his dick in Yuri. The woman positioned her body to suck on Yuri's nipples, and then she worked her way to her lips and kissed her passionately. While he was fucking Yuri, he finger-fucked his girl. Yuri was lost in her thoughts and in the moment. 'They must do this a lot because they have a routine,' Yuri thought.

He said to his girl, "Do it to her one more time, and I'm gonna cum."

The woman went back down on Yuri. With the same condom still on, he ploughed into his girl's pussy, and began fucking her hard from the back. The harder he pounded, the fiercer she ate Yuri's pussy. The woman let out a scream and came all over his dick. She was still slurping all over Yuri's pussy.

Yuri was going crazy and he was still erect. He took off the condom, and he put his whole dick in Yuri's mouth.

He whispered, "Kiss it."

Yuri, did more than that, she sucked him hard and strong. He grabbed her head and made love to her mouth, and he released down her throat. Yuri laughed, laying there between the couple. Everyone was breathing hard from the spectacular threesome. Her heart felt like it would come out of her chest. When they were asleep, Yuri slipped into her dress, quietly, washed her face, and walked home. Feeling good as ever, she never remembered either of their names.

As she thought to herself, 'I should have got their phone number.'

Well at least hers.

Chapter 18

Chance laid around the house. It really was a blue Monday. The police had not yet found his fiancée. All he could think about was his unborn child. Chanel and their parents stayed by his side. His mother made him some hot tea and offered him some Xanax, to help with the anxiety attacks that he was having. Chance laid there with Shannon's wedding dress as a cover. They had searched Saturday and all day Sunday for Shannon. The police said there had been no signs of foul play, but they would keep looking.

Terrance had returned from Philly on Saturday night. He felt so bad for Chanel; Chance had become his partner. He had become something like a brother-in-law. Terrance arrived to be by his girl's side. On the wedding day, Terrance was going to propose to Chanel, but now everything had fallen apart. When Chanel saw the Maxima pull up, she ran outside and hugged her man.

She cried and asked, "Why is this happening to my family?"

He hugged her tightly, putting her hair behind her ear and said, "Chanel, everything will be alright, don't think the worst. God will take care of them."

"If God will take care of them, how could he even allow something like this to happen?"

"Nelly, we are never to question our Father's doing, he would not bring us into something that he will not bring us through. Trust Him and He will make all things work together for the good."

Yuri slept all day. She missed the entire Sunday, and half of Monday. Between the liquor and the threesome, she was beat. Shane called, Chanel, and her dad, Mike called, too. To hear from her dad made her think of her mother. It had been a year, and Barbara still would not speak to Yuri. She totally disowned her. Even Barbara's will had been changed. Barb would have rather left her money to a total stranger before she left Yuri one dime. Yuri prayed that one day her mother would forgive her.

Yuri called Chanel first. Terrance answered her phone. "Hello?"

"Hi, I'm calling for Chanel."

"Hi, this is Terrance, and who may I say is calling?"

"This is Yuri, is Chanel around?"

"Chanel is sleeping, and I would rather not wake her. She had been up since Saturday, and we finally got her to sleep."

She asked, "How is Chance doing, do they have any good news yet?"

"No, the police are doing all they can. Chance is a train wreck, he's not responding to anyone. It's just crazy around here right now."

"Can you please have Chanel call me as soon as she wakes up?"

"Sure Yuri, if anyone can brighten her day, you can."

"Thank you, Terrance, and I know you do the same for her."

"Have a good evening, Yuri."

"You too, Terrance."

"Oh before you hang up".

"Yes, Terrance?"

"I met your mother today. She came by and brought a pot roast, and you look a lot like her. She was so kind to lend her support."

"That's good, Terrance. My mom is a great person, and she loves Chanel's family."

"I'll have Chanel call you when she wakes up."

"OK, Terrance." Yuri wanted to cry, she was glad that at least someone had seen her mother, and that she was ok.

Barb was a woman with pride. Not even what she had seen, with Eugene and Yuri could break her. If anything, it made her work harder on setting people free that were innocent. Yuri thought about how good her mother's pot roast used to be, how tender it was, and how soft and good the red potatoes in it were. Even the carrots were delicious; the gravy was seasoned to perfection, brown and thick. It was one of Yuri's favorite meals.

Yuri wanted to call her mother again, but she knew she would not get an answer. Yuri finally did something she hardly did; she fell to her knees and prayed.

"Dear Father God, I am coming to you in the only way I know how, I know I don't get on my knees enough, but tonight I need to talk to you. If you are listening, please forgive me for my sins, only you know them all, I need my mother in my life, Dear God. I know she hates me right now, but you, and only you, can take the hatred out of her heart. I am her only child, and I need her more than ever. Please don't let anything happen to her, or myself, before we reunite. Father, I know I have to stop doing the selfish things that I do, like cheating on Shane when he gives me so much. This is why my mom hates me so, because of my cheating. Father God, please take the cheating and that sexual demon away from me. Please Lord, take the lust out of my life, and Lord, bless Chance, and wherever his fiancée and child may be, just let them be alive. I am asking you to do all these things in the mighty name of Jesus, Amen."

Yuri got up, climbed into her bed, took two Tylenol, and drifted off to sleep.

The pounding on the door startled Yuri. "Who is it?"

83

"It's me, Shane, open the door." Yuri opened the door and Shane grabbed and kissed her tightly. "I have been calling you for two days and when you didn't answer, I jumped on the first thing smoking. You scared me, Yuri."

"I'm sorry, Shane, I just drank a bit too much on Saturday and I've been asleep."

"Damn, it's Tuesday, Yuri, don't ever do that shit again." He hugged her close. It actually felt good to know that Shane cared so much.

"Shane, I thought you had to close on those properties today."

"Tim and Cheryl are there and they are great negotiators, I couldn't have cared less about those properties, Lil' momma. What I care about is right here." They laid in the bed for the rest of the day, cuddling and getting some good rest.

Shane and Yuri were awakened by the phone ringing, Chanel was calling. "Hey Chanel, how are you feeling?"

"I'm rested, but not feeling any better. My brother is a total mess, and we still don't know what's going on. We've hired a private investigator because these damn DC police act like because there was no foul play and her suitcase was gone, that they can't help us. Terrance said he told you that your mom came by."

"Yes, he told me."

"I don't understand how you guys were so close, and not once since Gene left, have you come to see her."

"Chanel, it was like she hated the world after whatever happened with her and him."

"Yuri, she loves you though, and she appears very happy being single. She went to London and Brazil last month. She said she is enjoying herself and exploring the world."

"I'll visit her soon. I prayed for all of you, Nelly," Yuri replied trying to change the subject. What Chanel had told her about her mom being happy, made her feel awful, but she had to just suck it up

"Thanks Yuri, let's pray my brother doesn't end up in a nut house."

"Is he that bad, Chanel?"

"Yes girl, that bad."

"Keep me informed if you guys get any news."

"Ok Yuri, talk to you later."

Shane wasn't eavesdropping, but he overheard everything Yuri said to Chanel. He said, "I heard you talking about your mother, I would like to meet her one day, so when I can't get in touch with you, I can call her."

"You will meet her soon."

"Have you even told her that you're engaged?"

"Yes, she knows, and she's very happy for us." Lying straight through her teeth, she continued, "I also told my father, and he wants us to come visit him in Miami. I was mad that he remarried, but I came to realize he and my mom were just not happy together because now he is very happy; and my little sister is gorgeous."

She was trying to take the conversation totally away from her mom. She had not told her dad anything either, but she would. Knowing how Shane liked to travel, he might just pop up and say let's go to Miami, even though Mike would not mind. She still told Shane a lie.

Shane said, "I go back west on Thursday, would you like to come?"

"No, I'm gonna stay around here, to clean the house and just do some reading. School starts August 14th, and I'm getting ready now. I have a lot of paperwork to fill out, and I want to stay focused."

"That's great, Lil' momma, and I'm proud of you. So what do you want to do tonight and tomorrow?"

"First of all, I want to do you, daddy!" They sexed Tuesday night away.

Shane woke up to breakfast in bed. It was not the best, but Yuri tried hard. Since Shane only ate seafood, she cooked shrimp with cheese grits, wheat toast with a glass of orange juice. If it wasn't good, you would have never known, because Shane ate every last bite.

"Thank you, Lil' Momma, I see you are stepping your game up," he complimented her.

"Yes baby, and I have a roast simmering in the crock pot for dinner, we can stay in all day and play."

Shane grabbed Yuri. "I love you, girl."

"I love you, babes."

On Thursday, Yuri dropped Shane off at the airport, they kissed and cuddled. "Thank you for the dinner last night. Oh, and most of all for the dessert."

Yuri smiled. "Your dessert was even better; I still taste it." She licked her lips.

He grinned. "I'll see you on Monday, and I'll call you when I land."

"Ok, baby I love you."

On the way back home, Yuri phoned Chanel. "Hey sis, how is everything going?"

"A little better, Yuri. The private investigator we hired said he had some leads, and he doesn't want us to get our hopes up, but he thinks we should have some news tomorrow. Chance finally got out of bed, he hasn't taken a shower since last Friday."

"Wow, it's Thursday."

"Right, so imagine how he smells." Yuri tried to imagine, but could only smell his fresh body scent that she was so familiar with.

Yuri said "Well, I'm glad he's coming around, Chanel."

"So am I, it's been a long week for all of us, and Shannon's family, even though I think her cousin Tammy knows where she is. I told the PI to stay on her because something about her seems suspicious. I smell a rat, and when my mind tells me something, I know it to be right."

"Yes, Chanel, you are pretty much always right, except for the time you told us to cross the creek because the water was low, and you, Marie, and my ass almost drowned."

Chanel burst into laughter and responded, "We are all alive, and I did say we wouldn't die." They both laughed.

"Chanel, if you need me, or something comes up, don't hesitate to call. I love you, Nelly."

"I love you, too, Yuri. Talk to you later."

Yuri then called Candice. "Hey sis, what are you up to?"

Candice said, "Girl, I'm on my way to Barbados with the attorney from Tennessee, I'll return on Monday. What are you doing, Yuri?"

"I just dropped Shane off at the airport, he went back to California until Monday. I guess I'll be going out alone this weekend."

"Have fun, because I'm about to spend a lot of this man's money. I'll hit you up when I get back in the states."

"Bring me a souvenir."

"Will do, lil' sister, and Saturday, Q's boy, Mardy, is throwing a party for his boy at Diamonds of Atlanta. If you want to go, I'll have them put you on the guest list."

"Please do, I like the Body Tap. It just won't be the same without you."

"Aww Yuri, you know how to Boss up, have fun."

"You too, Candy." They giggled

Yuri decided not to go out on Friday. Saturday, she went to the Underground. Candice would never go there because she said it was too hood for her. When Yuri walked in, all eyes were on her. It felt different going out alone, but like Candice had told her "Boss up," and that is just what she did. She found one empty seat at the bar, ordered her trademark Apple Martini, and checked out the scene. The DJ was playing all the hottest and latest music; Atlanta music, along with Rick Ross, and Lil Wayne. When Jay-Z came on Yuri got up and danced all alone, just like all the rest of the girls, she was in her own zone. She liked the hood club and after one more drink she headed out to Diamonds of Atlanta.

She pulled up to the door and the valet greeted her. "What's up, little Yuri, where's Candy?"

"Oh, she went on vacation."

"It must be nice," he replied. Yuri walked to the door, was greeted and immediately allowed in. When she entered, she walked around. She went downstairs and all the strippers were on the stage.

She went to see Q and his people. They were like, "Hey, Yuri." They were excited to see her.

Yuri said, "Hi Q, how are you?"

"I'm good, and you look good, girl!"

"Thank you Q."

"Yuri these are my niggas from Tennessee. Tim is getting married next week, so he's doin' it big like a single man this week."

"Congratulations," Yuri said.

"Thank you, Ma," Tim responded.

"So Yuri, you came out alone?" Candice had obviously not told him she was going to Barbados. "Well you're good with us. I

I'll make you a drink, or if you want, champagne, take your pick." He waved his hand at all the liquor to choose from on the table.

"Thanks Q."

After four drinks, Yuri was almost at her limit. She got up and danced like a stripper with the other ladies that were in Q's VIP section. Q said, "Yuri, you better stop shaking yo' ass in front of me, before I get turned on."

Yuri responded, "Shut up Q, your ass is drunk!" At that moment her conscience told her to leave. 'Yuri, you are drunk, go home.'

Yuri downed another drink and told her conscience, "Go fuck yourself."

Yuri was having a ball, and she was not ready to leave. Within the hour, Q had his hands all over Yuri. He was grinding on her ass, Yuri's dancing made Q stand at attention. She already knew he had good sex. Candice bragged about how he screwed her for hours, and how nasty he was, how he had mean head game, and that he was working with six inches.

When she saw Candice's friend Passion watching, she stepped back and gained her composure. She started dancing on one of Q's boys. Q saw what was going on and saw Passion being nosey. He popped another bottle of Ace of Spades and toasted her. Yuri knew she was wrong, but she just was a natural born slut.

Q was about to leave, he had his boy give Yuri a note, and it read: "Meet me at the Double Tree Hotel right off Cobb Parkway. It will be our little secret, and no one will ever know. If you don't tell, I won't. I've been wanting you, and I know you want me. Room 339, I'll be waiting."

Yuri stayed around the club, playing it off, getting more numbers. Yuri thought about how 'freaky' Candice said he was. She said she could do all kinds of freaky shit to him, and he liked it. She wondered was he as freaky as Chance could be, and she was ready to find out.

At 3:45am Yuri pulled up to the Double Tree. Her conscience told her, 'Don't do it, go home.' Totally ignoring her conscience once more, she knocked on the door. Q opened it, still drunk. He said, "So you showed up, I see."

"I guess, because I'm drunk."

"And I guess, because you want this dick. Come here, Yuri." He took his clothes off, lifted her short skirt and immediately went into her, no foreplay, no kissing. Just mad fucking. Yuri liked how rough he handled her. At some points he was rougher than others. Candice was right, Q, was a monster.

Yuri got so caught up in the moment that she thought about Chance. She took two fingers and tried to slip them into Q's ass, Q pulled out of her.

"Bitch, what are you doing?" he yelled at her unpleasantly surprised. "I am no fucking homo,. Don't you ever!"

Q slapped her hard in the face. He grabbed her by the hair.

"Come here, bitch, suck me until I cum in your mouth. "

Yuri became sober quickly.

He threw her on her knees and said, "Suck it, or I'll call Candice right now and tell her what we're."Yuri starting sucking his dick. He power drove it in her mouth. She could not even suck it, but he grabbed her head and fucked her mouth. He screamed, "Suck it hard, harder, bitch!"

She started crying, she prayed and asked God what had she gotten herself into.

After Yuri couldn't make Q cum, he flipped her over and went straight into her ass with no lubrication. Q spit in her ass and beat her asshole to the core.

He hit her and hit her ass as hard as he could saying, "Is this what you want, bitch? I'm a gangsta, bitch, now you take this dick in yo' ass."

Yuri cried, "Please stop, Q."

Q said, "You are a sick bitch."

Q ignored Yuri's plees and he penetrated deeper and deeper, in and out of her ass. He pulled out of her with force.

"Now, bitch, get yo' trick ass out, now, and go fuck that fag whos ass you be stickin' your fingers up!"

Yuri, without hesitation, got dressed and left the room. She jumped in her Benz and sped off thinking, 'If only I would have listened to my first mind.' She could not call anyone. She cried all the way home.

When Yuri got to the loft, she sat in a hot bath. Her ass was burning. It felt torn from Q's penis. She laid in the tub feeling dumb, and was wondering what made her even want to sleep with Q. Even more, what was she thinking, putting her fingers in his ass? She stepped out of the tub. When she looked in the mirror, her eye was slightly purple. Q had smacked her so hard he turned the whole right side of her face bluish-purple. She thought, 'What will I tell Shane?' He was coming back on Monday from his business trip.

What would she tell Candice? She knew Q wouldn't tell, but her eye did not look good.

Yuri woke up late that Sunday morning. Her body was in so much pain. She grabbed some Ibuprofen from the cabinet. She went to the bathroom and checked herself out in the mirror. Her eye was worse. She sat and could not stop crying. After a few hours of applying ice, the swelling went down. She didn't want to leave the house like that. Yuri did not want people to see her that way. Yuri came up with a story, and she rehearsed it, so she could have it perfect for Shane. The lie was, 'She had gone to the mall and was pulling into a parking spot that another lady was pulling into. When she would not move, the other woman sucker punched her in the face.' That was her story and she was sticking to it. Yuri stayed in the rest of the day, she didn't want to step foot out of the house.

Chapter 19

Monday morning, Yuri got up and showered. The swelling on her face had gone down, but her eye was still slightly blue. She got dressed and went down to Planned Parenthood because of a light discharge she was experiencing. After she was seen, she was told that she had been exposed to Chlamydia. She was prescribed antibiotics for seven days. Q had not only humiliated her but he burned her too!

The doctor advised her, "No sex."

She was thinking, 'How am I going to pull that off?' Yuri called Shane and said, "Hey baby, how are you?"

"Hey, Lil' Momma, busy as hell out here."

"I thought you were coming back today?"

"I was, but I might not make it, actually, I may not make it until Thursday, are you mad? "

"No baby, handle your business, I'm not going anywhere, just waiting on my man."

"Ok, Lil' Momma, I have to go, but I'll call you later."

"Ok Shane, I love you."

"I love you, too." When they hung up, Yuri sat there for a moment, staring at the phone. Yuri was so happy that he had to stay. This would give her more time to recover from the damage to her face, and her STD.

Yuri went back home and called Chanel. "Hello Nelly, how are you, girl?"

"I'm ok, actually, I'm on my way to Virginia to Shannon's cousin's house. I told you I thought her cousin, Tammy, knew something more. She led the private investigator straight to an aunt's house."

"Is Chance with you?"

"No, Shannon won't talk to anyone in the family but me. I hope I can talk some sense into her, because he loves her so much and he's done nothing wrong."

"Chanel, I hope everything goes right for you all."

"Thank you. Yuri, how are you?"

"I'm ok, just sitting around the loft, wishing Shane was in town."

"I feel the same way about Terrance." They giggled.

"Well, call me when you get some good news."

"Ok Yuri, I love you."

"Right back at you, Nelly, bye."

Yuri ordered pizza and vowed not to leave the house. Her butt was still hurting, and she still had a vaginal discharge, and a black eye. She needed rest. Yuri took two sleeping pills and slept like a baby. She slept Monday away. Sunrise, Tuesday morning, the phone woke Yuri from her sleep. It was Chanel. Yuri picked up the phone half asleep.

"Hey Chanel, you must have good news."

"Actually, no. I saw Shannon and we talked."

"So is she ok?"

"Yes and no, and when I get to Chance, I hope he'll be ok."

"What's wrong, Chanel?"

"Shannon had an abortion, and she told me not to tell Chance until we were face to face."

"Wow, are you serious? Why?"

"She didn't tell me the reason why. Anyway, I'm on my way back to the city, and when I sit down and speak with Chance, I'll know what all this is about. My parents were so happy that they were about to be grandparents, and now I have to tell them this."

"I am so sorry, Chanel, I hope Chance will be ok when you break the news to him."

"Me too, Yuri, he has already been so down and depressed, imagine what this will do."

"I'll be praying that everything will go ok, Chanel. I'll call you later."

"Ok, love you, Yuri."

"Love you too, Chanel."

Yuri's conscience began to surface again.

'You horny, selfish bitch, you know exactly why she killed her baby.'

She tried to block it out, but it would not get out of her head. She turned on her IPOD and drowned out the things she was thinking. Yuri finally got dressed and left the house, she put on her dark Gucci shades to hide her eye. She went into the mall to get a foundation that would blend in with her skin, just in case Shane arrived earlier, she would be prepared. After purchasing the make-up, Yuri grabbed a cappuccino at Starbucks. She sat in the middle of the mall watching the people go about their merry way, and she sipped from her cup, lost in thought. Yuri decided not to sit any longer, wasting time, she needed to be on the move.

As she was leaving the mall, she almost bumped into Troy. Yuri was stunned to see Troy with a woman that looked a total mess. She had big shopping bags. He looked at Yuri and walked past her like he never knew her at all. Yuri thought, 'Damn he could have at least spoken, but maybe his ugly-ass bitch would have been jealous,' just like Yuri was. Yuri had nothing to do, so she went back home.

The day had been going so slow. She had not heard from Candice. She must have stayed another day. Yuri thought. At least with everyone gone she would not have to tell the truth about the mall incident, well, the story she made up. Yuri made a sandwich and took a long nap.

Two hours later, through her nap, Yuri was awakened by her phone. "Hey, Chanel."

"Oh, Yuri!" Chanel cried into the phone overwhelmed with emotion.

It terrified Yuri. Chanel was a calm person, but Yuri could hear in her jittery tone.

Yuri sat up in the bed. She could hear fear and panic in Chanel's voice. "What's wrong, Chanel?"

Chanel said, through her tears and pain, "We, we", crying harder, "We found Chance dead!"

Yuri jumped up off the bed, tears rolling down her face. She screamed "No, Chanel, No!! Don't say that."

"It's true." They both cried. "I hate whoever did this to my brother!" She screamed as she cried.

"Did what, who killed him Chanel?"

Chanel could not breathe or talk. She said "I'll call you back, Yuri, my mother is trying to get through on the other line."

"Ok, call me right back, I'm gonna book a flight for first thing tomorrow."

"Ok, Yuri." Just like that, Chanel was off the line.

Yuri cried ferociously. She wondered why someone would kill Chance. He was a kind man. Chance would not have harmed anyone. He did not do drugs, smoke or even do the clubs, and now he was dead. Yuri called Delta Airlines and booked a flight for Wednesday morning. She was all alone and wanted someone to hold her. The thought of Chance holding her came to mind. She remembered all the days and nights they had spent together. She realized that she did love Chance, after all, and not only for sex. She called Shane and told him the bad news. He told her he would be there for her and that he would meet her the following day in D.C. He made arrangements and his flight would arrive an hour after hers. Yuri cried and thanked him.

"Lil momma, you don't need to thank me. You said he was like a big brother to you, and I know you love Chanel and her family. Stay strong, baby. I love you, and I'll see you tomorrow."

92

Yuri wished she could call her mother; she wanted to talk to her. She began to pray. Even though this was a bad ordeal, she prayed that her mom would be there for her, and even comfort her. It had been a whole year.

Yuri thought, 'What if she embarrasses me in front of Shane? What would he think?'

She had told him how close they were, even though she knew that Barb had written her off, and out of her will. Barb had even gone as far as getting everything that reminded her of Yuri out of the house. She remembered the talk she had with Chanel, when she told Yuri that her room was completely transformed into an office. Her mom's bedroom had new furniture as well. Yuri never forgot that conversation because it hurt so badly. She also thought about Chance telling her he loved her. Between someone killing Chance and her mother disowning her, she did not know which one she was crying about. She felt weak; her day could not get any worse. Yuri packed her clothes and pulled out her three pictures of Chance. She stared at them and cried uncontrollably. The day could not have gone any slower. Yuri finally decided to call Chanel again. It was evening, and she hoped everything had calmed down.

"Hey, Chanel, how are you doing?"

"Hey, Yuri, not good, but Terrance is here with me now."

"How are your parents doing?"

"Mom is in total shock and has not come out of her room, and Daddy is just trying to hold us all together," Chanel sniffled.

"So Chanel, do they know who did this to him?"

"Oh, Yuri, I didn't tell you earlier, I was so distraught! No one killed him, Chance hung himself." Yuri dropped the phone and cried like a baby.

Yuri got herself together, picked up the phone, and Chanel said, "That's the part that is so hard for Momma to believe. He left a note and told us not to cry, that he was better off dying with his unborn child." Chanel paused, "This is Shannon calling, Yuri, I'll have to call you back."

"That's ok Chanel, get some rest, I'll see you in the morning."

"Do you need us to pick you up at the airport?"

"No, Shane is flying in, also, and we'll rent a car. Sorry you have to meet under such terrible circumstances."

"That is fine with me, good night Yuri."

"Good night Chanel, I love you."

Yuri was out-done with what she had heard, and knew it was her fault. She thought about the last time she and Chance made love, and how she put the two ecstasy pills in his glass. She

93

remembered how he took all four and a half inches of the dildo, without complaining, not even knowing the video camera was taping every single sick act she had done, while she played Cat Woman in the black dominatrix body suit. Now she was glad she had worn the suit, because her body was covered from head to toe in latex. She knew Shannon had seen it. She mailed it attention to Shannon. She didn't know it would cause Chance to kill himself. She did not want him with Shannon, but she damn sure did not want Chance dead by suicide, either. Yuri cried until she fell asleep.

Chapter 20

Yuri arrived in her city. It felt good to be in D.C., just not under these circumstances. She sat in the BWI Airport, at the Starbucks, and waited on Shane's plane to arrive from Los Angeles. She could not wait to hug him.

She looked at the rock on her finger and said, "I really have to change."

Shane arrived, and they met at the Avis rental car office. Yuri ran and held Shane tight. She cried just from seeing him. Knowing someone was there for her made her emotional.

"Baby, don't cry, everything will be alright."

" It's so sad Shane, and the worst part is, no one killed him."

"Really, what happened, Yuri?"

"He hung himself."

"He killed himself? Damn, what kind of problems or issues did he have? Black folks just don't kill themselves like that."

Yuri stopped and said, "Shane, please just let it be, I can't take talking about it anymore."

They got in the Escalade truck and drove over to Chanel's parents' home. When they arrived, Yuri looked next door; Barb's Volvo wagon was in the driveway. Yuri knew she would at least have to see her mother before she could go see Chanel and her family.

Yuri asked Shane, "Are you ready to meet my mother?"

"Of course, I've been waiting for a long time," he replied.

Yuri's heart was beating rapidly as she walked up on the porch. She rang the doorbell. After two rings Barbara opened up the door. She looked at Yuri. "Hello, Yuri," she said, not at all excited.

"Hello mother, I've missed you." Yuri hugged her, leaving Barb nothing left to do but to return the hug.

As much as Barb despised her daughter, it felt good to hug her only child.

While standing outside, Barb finally said, "Come on in." Yuri introduced Shane. Barb treated him with kindness. She sensed a genuine heart with Shane. Yuri was just happy Barb let them in; it was a huge burden off her back. They talked about the wedding, and how Yuri had gotten into college, but the main topic of conversation was Chance.

Yuri asked, "Have they found out anything?"

Barb answered, "All I know is, Chanel went to speak to him, and a few hours after she left, it happened. She won't tell the police what they talked about, or anything. Chanel and Chance's fiancée, Shannon, are keeping something from us, according to her mom. I guess time will tell, or maybe it won't." Barb asked, "So where are you guys staying?"

"At the hotel on Virginia Street."

"If you were married, you could have stayed here, but I don't condone shacking."

Barb was lying and making excuses. Yuri knew her mom was letting her know that she was not welcome.

"Well, I have one of my pot roasts with carrots, and red potatoes in the oven. You guys want to walk next door so we can see the family? They are having such a terrible time, so please don't ask any questions."

Barb took the roast out of the oven to carry next door. Shane politely took it out of her hand, being the gentleman that he was. Barb looked into his gentle eyes and felt sorry for what he was putting himself through with her scandalous daughter.

Yuri was so glad to see Chanel; they hugged and cried for what seemed like forever, but for about five minutes. Terrance and Shane had heard much about each other and they shook hands. They agreed to 'just let them be. Terrance took Shane and introduced him to Chanel's dad, Mr. Brown. Mr. Brown appeared to be calm, but you could tell he was trying his best to be strong for his family. Mrs. Brown had been in her bedroom, ever since losing Chance, and had not come down. Chanel asked Yuri if she remembered Shannon. Yuri hugged Shannon and extended her condolences. She thought, 'If only I had not done what I did, she would be married and carrying their child.' Marie entered the room with her newborn baby and this was too much, too soon, for Shannon. Shannon burst into tears and ran out of the house. Chanel and Terrance went running after her.

Yuri was eager to introduce Shane to Marie. "Shane this is my other best friend, Marie, and my godson, Mason."

Yuri gently took Mason out of Marie's arms.

"Wow, he is so beautiful." Yuri said. Cooing to the baby, "I am going to buy you everything." She then hugged Marie speaking softly. "We have to help Chanel through this, Marie."

"I know, I've been here since she called me yesterday. I just can't believe it, Yuri. This is just not right. What was going on in his mind?"

Yuri said, "I guess we'll never know."

Chanel told Yuri that they had to head to the funeral home and finish the arrangements. She needed to go with her father because her mother just could not get herself together and face it. Yuri told her, in the meantime she and Shane would go back to the hotel, and they all would meet up later. Yuri looked around and admired all the pictures and trophies. All of this was a part of Chance. She kissed Mr. Brown, Marie, and her godson. Yuri and Shane said their farewells and left to head to the hotel.

Yuri laid in Shane's arms and slept the afternoon away. When the sun went down, they got dressed and returned to the Brown's residence.

Chanel had made the service plans with her dad. Yuri asked, "When is the service?" "

"It's this Saturday. We don't want to waste any time. We want it over and done with. I have to prepare Momma. She has to come out of that room. She can't go on like this, she has totally isolated herself, and now she's blaming herself. She hasn't eaten one bite of food. Everyone has been so kind, and prepared good delicious food, but Mom won't eat or speak to anyone. Pastor Wallace has been in with her, but he has made very little progress. Dang, Yuri! I just don't understand! Why us? He was only twenty-five years old. He had so much to live for!" The tears would not stop flowing, "Who would have thought Chance would have ever hurt himself?" Yuri grabbed Chanel and hugged her; they embraced each other and cried. "I just need for these two days to go well, and we can bury him next to my grandmother."

"Is there anything that you need me to do?"

"No Yuri, thank you, just you being here is all I need, and by the way, we have a lot of family arriving tomorrow and Thursday. The only thing I have to do is clean to prepare for them."

"I'll help you, that's the least I can do. Shane and Terrance can get better acquainted and grab a beer while we prepare for your family and reminisce on the good ole times."

Chanel smiled through her tears and said, "Sounds good to me, Yuri."

The room was dark, and Yuri's heart was racing. As she sat up in bed, she was sweating profusely, she looked around the room and Shane was sound asleep. She jumped up and checked the bathroom, kitchen, and the door to the suite. Her dream seemed so real that she was still frightened. Yuri took a moment and regained her composure, to dwell on the dream. She dreamed that she was making love to Shane and Chance kicked in the door of the hotel. He dragged her out of the bed and Shane did nothing to defend her. He just laid there laughing, in a dreadful tone. Chance never spoke, but the anger in his eyes said it all. He took her to the bathroom and tried to drown her, pushing and pulling her head in and out of the toilet. Yuri screamed, but Shane only laughed, telling Chance to dunk her more and more. Chance grabbed her and choked her, almost taking the life out of her. Just when he was about to throw her off the 19th floor balcony, she woke up.

Yuri got back in the bed slowly, and put her arms around Shane. She tried to fall asleep again before the sunlight would begin to creep in through the curtains. Yuri could not have been asleep more than two hours when the early morning call came through. Yuri thought, 'Who the hell would be calling my phone at 7:38am?' She eased out of bed and crept to the bathroom, careful not to disturb Shane.

"Hello?"

"What's up, Yuri."

"What's up sis, how are you? I was wondering when you would be back in town."

"Oh, really?" Candice asked.

"Yes."

"Are you around, Yuri? I wanted to come and see you."

"No, there was a death in the family, and I'm in D.C."

"What?" asked Yuri. She was confused by what Candice had just stated. "Sorry to hear that, but if you were here, it might be two."

"What?" asked Yuri.

"Bitch, you know exactly what I am talking about." Yuri's heart dropped. "Q told me every fucking thing. While I was gone, you helped yourself to what was mine. We are not just lovers, but homies and friends. I just can't believe how you would do that shit," said Candice.

Yuri interrupted, "Candice."

"Candice, my ass, bitch, you listen to me and listen good, or I will tell Shane all about your rendezvous with Q, and how you got the dog shit fucked out of you in your ass, and I will tell him all about the threesome on your birthday, and Troy, too. I am just letting you know to stay the fuck away from Q, and stay far away from the club! This is your only warning, and if I see your little ass, or if Passion sees you, we're going to whup your ass! She told me not to trust you, and I gave you the benefit of the doubt. Bitch, you didn't get one cent, and got fucked like a slut. I bet you won't try and put your finger in another real nigga's ass. Now go find the faggot you did that to, because the niggas around here not cut like that."

Tears rolled down Yuri's face. She tried to speak, "I am so sorry, Candice, I was drunk."

"Is that the only fucking excuse you can come with? Stay drunk, ho, and stay the fuck out of my way. And oh, thanks to you, and because of that messy shit you did, I have a new '17 Range Rover, thanks, bitch!" Click.

Yuri sat on the stool, in the dark, thinking. If Chance hadn't been enough to break her heart, now Candice. Yuri had betrayed everyone that loved and cared for her. She looked in the mirror, crying, and wondered, 'What is it about my endless need to be so damn freaky?'

Shane walked into the bathroom, startling Yuri. "Are you ok, Lil' momma?"

"Yeah, I'm ok. Losing Chance is just hitting me so hard, and I feel so bad about him not being here anymore."

98

"You can't beat yourself up over it, this was no one's fault, it was a decision he made, and now we all have to live with that."

"I hate it when people say that! Maybe it wasn't his choice, Shane. We don't know for sure what was going through his head the day he decided to take his own life. God allows tragedy to happen, to bring us together, and to make us all stronger."

It was Saturday, and the funeral was slowly progressing. Mrs. Brown, Chanel's mother, sat in the front row of the Church. Even though Chance wasn't religious, Pastor Wallace agreed to do the service because Mr. and Mrs. Brown were members of Southside Baptist Church. Mr. Brown held onto his wife and brought her comfort. Chanel was looking great and held herself together, trying to appear strong, even though this was killing her inside. Terrance and the family were right beside her, with Shannon on the other side.

Shannon could not keep her composure; she let out a cry so loud, "I should have never done it! Why Lord, why?"

Everyone stared and looked at her sadness, shaking their heads. heavy-set woman approached the pulpit. Her voice rang throughout the church, piercing every soul as she sang a familiar song, 'His Eye is on the Sparrow.' Mrs. Brown fell to the floor. Half the church cried with her. It was such a sad moment.

Chance looked as if he was just sleeping so peacefully. The mortuary did a good job concealing the scar on his neck. The pastor preached from the book of Ecclesiastes, Chapter 3. The sermon was 'Everything has its time and season.' He gave everyone a better outlook on death.

Yuri could not help but observe all the faces of the people that had come to pay their respects for Chance. Yuri looked around and saw Eugene sitting in the back pew. He still looked really good and she was glad that he was ok. She felt another pair of eyes on her and she was right. Barbara was watching her every move. Barbara made sure Yuri knew she was watching, and as soon as Yuri acknowledged her mom, if looks could kill, Yuri would be dead. Barbara rolled her eyes and never looked her way again.

After the service, everyone left the church. It seemed like everything was moving in slow motion. Yuri and Shane walked over to Barbara after the burial; they both gave her a hug. Barb did not want to be hugged by Yuri, but she did anyway.

As they embraced she whispered, "I only did this for the Browns. I hope I never see you again."

Yuri's heart was broken, but she gave a fake smile so neither Shane nor anyone else would notice her mother's rude farewell.

Yuri said, "Bye, Mother." Barb walked away and did not look back.

Everyone met back at the Brown's. There was so much food; it was like going to a buffet. After dinner, Yuri played with her godson, Mason. She gave Marie one thousand dollars to get whatever the baby needed. Yuri, Marie, and Chanel made small talk until the sun set.

"Tomorrow, we're going back to Atlanta. Shane has been here a few days too many, and he has a lot of work to do, and I think I'm gonna find me a job, at least part time, while I will wait for school to start."

"That is a good idea, Yuri," Chanel said, "I love my job here at Saks Fifth Avenue. I can finally get the clothes you wear at half price." They laughed.

"I'm going to go back to the hotel and pack because we leave early in the morning. I love you guys."

"We love you more, Yuri." They all hugged.

Chapter 21

On the plane ride back to Atlanta, Shane slept and Yuri looked out the window, dazed. All she could think about was how she and Candice had words, and now she was kicked out of the circle. She was no longer able to walk up in the strip club. The VIP girls loved Candice, and they would most definitely want problems with Yuri. They never liked her anyway, but on the strength of Candice, she was ok with them. Now all of that had changed. She knew one day Shane would ask about Candice. She was the only person she hung out with in Atlanta. Now Yuri was friendless.

As the plane arrived, there was a sense of relief to have departed from D.C. It had been five long days of mourning. Shane grabbed their luggage and walked toward the car service that was waiting.

"Lil momma, on Tuesday I have to fly back to Los Angeles, I've been gone too many days and they need me. Will you be ok, baby?"

"Yes, baby, I will, I'm gonna try and find employment."

"In that case, we have two whole days to do whatever we want."

"I just want to lay around the house and cuddle with you."

"I couldn't ask for anything better." Shane kissed and held her all the way to the loft. As they pulled into the driveway, Shane said, "As a matter of fact, take your bags in and let's go to my house. Yuri smiled, without hesitation, as she followed his command.

As soon as Shane unlocked the door, Yuri could not contain her enthusiastic exploration of Shane's six bedroom, five thousand square foot home. His house was on the south side in the countryside of Fayetteville, GA. There were only six other homes within a few miles of each other. Shane smiled as Yuri's eyes lit up. "When we are married, this is where we'll live with the five children we're going to have," he said with a big grin.

"Shane! Are you crazy?" And they both laughed.

Yuri thought she had never seen a home so beautiful. "Who designed all of this?"

"I did, with a little help from my mother's designer." The fireplace stood over 15'.

The center attraction was a beautiful painting that would be considered a masterpiece, hanging above. Yuri could not take her eyes off the painting.

She was interrupted by Shane starring at her and saying, "I'll turn on the air, and then we'll light a fire."

"It's summer-time, Shane."

"Honey, I know that, I just want you to see how beautiful it is, and it will relax you. Come on, you've had a rough week, let's relax together." Yuri did not want to resist. He leaned down to kiss her.

Shane pulled a few things out of the freezer. He had everything in order. "Who does the shopping, and is your meat fresh?"

"The maid keeps me stocked, and throws away what isn't good, so just in case I come in town, I'll be able to prepare my meals. Are you ready to help me cook lunch?"

"Sure, baby."

Making eye contact with Yuri, Shane gave her a naughty smile and said, "Lil momma, you will be my dessert, right in front of the fireplace."

The two days with Shane were the best for Yuri. She wished it could go on, but Shane had to go out west and she would return to the loft. She knew she would be bored, but she was all alone. She could not call Candice, she had snaked out the only friend she had in Georgia. She could not go to her normal party spots. These were all the places that Candice and all of her girls would hang out. She did not want to run into any of them or Q. As she thought about what to do, she couldn't help but think about Q and how he looked so clean but was so dirty, walking around carrying a disease. She was glad that Shane wore condoms. Even though she had finished the antibiotics and was now cleared, she didn't want to ruin anything with Shane.

Yuri laid around the house for the next few days. As soon as Friday came around, she was ready to hit the streets. She was tired of talking and two-waying Shane. She needed some excitement. She decided to go back to the club at the Underground. It was a mixed crowd, with some fly guys and girls, some broke niggas and hoodrats. She liked the atmosphere, and knew the people she hung around would never come to a spot like this. They would call it a 'Slum Club.'

Yuri was dressed in her Rock & Republic capris, Chanel sneakers, along with her Chanel bag and Chanel belt. Even with sneakers on, she would be one of the flyest chicks in the club. She took the big five karat rock off her hand, thinking she might get robbed. She walked straight through the club to the VIP section. Everyone was waiting in the twenty- dollar line.

She thought, "They are corny. Damn, they are slum for real. Ten more dollars would get them straight through the door."

When Yuri walked in, she checked out where she could post up. She went and sat at the bar, just like the last time. Instead of ordering an Apple Martini, like she did when she was at an upscale club, she ordered a Long Island Ice Tea. She sipped it slowly, as she leaned and rocked with it. A Dem Franchise Boys song played. Yuri was an east coast music fanatic, but Atlanta was turning her out with the dirty south music. As she leaned and rocked, the nigga with the dreads danced behind her, he had a mean lean. He dipped with it and Yuri laughed and broke it down on him. The whole club leaned and rocked. It was like watching something on Soul Train. Pastor Troy came on as soon as Franchise Boys went off. 'No No Play in GA' came on, and everyone was really feeling it. Yuri did not know what it was, but it had the club totally crunked.

After a few more songs and dancing, she finally took her seat and dread-head walked up and said, "Hey shawty, what's yo name?"

"I'm Yuri, and yours?"

"I'm Uno, Shawty." Yuri was drunk and burst into laughter in his face. "What's funny, Shawty?"

"You just talk so different and fast, I can tell you're from here."

"Showl am, I'm a Grady baby, shawty, born right down the screet." She could not stop laughing, and Yuri felt the need to correct Uno, and said, "Screet is street."

"Where yo' man, Shawty?"

"He is in California."

"I wish I could be yo' man, you new 'round here, cuz I ain't never seent you."

"I come here from time to time, it's cool."

"Yeah, this my patna spot, I be up in hea."

Yuri said, "Man, I really can't understand your talk."

Uno responded, "I get dat from y'all outta-townas a lot, you gonz buy me a drink, Shawty?"

"Buy you a drink?"

"Yeah, niggas trick off so much you ain't use to a real nigga askin' for one. I'll buy the nex round."

"Ok," Yuri said, ordering a Long Island.

She sipped a little, and hit the dance floor, and talked.

"He's kinda cute," Yuri thought.

His lips were sexy as well, not too big, plump and luscious even with his horrible grammar.' The scar on his face that ran slightly under his eye almost to his lip, made him look mean but sexy. He looked like he could have been a problem child that fought all the time as a kid, however, Uno favored future and had a mean A- Town swag. He kind of sounded retarded to her, but he was cool, with his dreads hanging to his shoulders, and was clean. He wore Levi's 501 Jeans and a white tee, with a colorful pair of Jordans. Yuri wondered what he drove, or if he even had a car. After they danced, Uno bought the next round, and they partied the night away.

One more Long Island and Yuri was ready to go home. Uno said, "You sho you can drive, Shawty?"

"I'm not drunk, I can hold my shit."

"I'm gone walk you to yo' car." When they got to the car, Uno said, "Damn Shawty, you ridin' clean! Yo' mane must got that bag?"

"He's good," Yuri said. "Uno, I had fun tonight, and I will see you again soon."

"Damn, Shawty, I can get dem digits?"

Yuri thought, 'I'm not giving this dumb sounding sucka my number, but there was something about him that turned her on. It may have been the Long Islands: after sizing him up, it could have been the bulge in his pants. She crossed her arms and leaned back.

" I'll be back on Friday and we'll hang out, this is my new spot."

"Aight Shawty, be careful, I see you lata."

"See you, Uno."

Once Yuri arrived home, she showered and wished Shane was in town. The Long Island Ice Tea had taken its toll on her. She texted Shane, "I love you," and was fast asleep. Yuri woke up the next morning with a bad hangover. She thought about Candice, as she drank some ginger ale and took two aspirin. She wished she could have been at the strip club last night. 107.9 announced it on the radio all night. She knew it was where all the ballers probably were. Nonetheless, she enjoyed hanging out with A-town Uno. She thought of his voice and laughed at how many times he used the word 'Shawty'. She was just glad she had someone to hang out with. For the rest of the weekend, Yuri relaxed around the house. She called and checked on Chanel.

"Hey Chanel, how are you?"

"I'm ok, just trying to prepare myself for school next month, and I've been going through some of my brother's things trying to figure something out."

"Can I help you with anything, Chanel?"

"No thanks, Yuri, it's nothing much. I just need closure and I'll be fine."

"How are you and Terrance?"

"We're doing great.

He had a few beers too many last weekend and came on to me. He was a little upset when I turned him down. He yelled and said that he was tired of waiting. He even had the nerve to tell me that he had so many bitches throwing him pussy that I'm lucky he loves me. Girl, I was a little scared, but I knew he was drunk and just wanted sex."

"Chanel, you don't think Terrance is messing around on you? "

"No, I don't think so, why do you ask?"

"Because he's a man, and a man in college, and you know what goes on in college. You're about to be a sophomore, everybody is running around fucking. It just so happens that the 10 percent that still are virgins, you're in that group. I'm not being funny, sis, but trust me; your guy is handsome, and if you're not giving it to him, then somebody else is. I just don't want your heart broken, so don't put all of your trust into him."

"Ok Yuri, I have my guard up, and like I said, my husband will be the one to bust my cherry."

"I heard that Chanel, I wish I would have waited, I'm glad that you're still holding out."

"Yuri, I have to go now, I'll talk to you later."

"Ok Chanel, peace."

Yuri laid on the couch and thought about Terrance cheating on Chanel. She did not like the fact that he went off on Chanel. She thought to herself, 'He's lucky that I'm not in DC, because if I was, I would have driven to Philly to catch his ass.' She no longer liked Terrance. She knew Chanel had fallen in love with him, for sure. She let it go and went to bed.

Shane had been in California working hard. He was running from L.A. to Sacramento and Arizona, buying foreclosed apartments. Shane asked Yuri if she wanted to come, anytime he knew he couldn't get back to Georgia for weeks at a time. Yuri declined, because she hated business meetings and staying at the condos and hotels in the places they flew to. Most women would love that life, but not Yuri, she wanted to party and chill at her own spot.

Yuri had been going to the Underground a lot over the summer. School was about to start and she would get into her studies. She hung out with Uno a lot, as well. She learnt that he had just traded his Crown Vic with the Snickers Candy bar paint job, in for a late model GMC truck. She thought, "thank goodness." She wouldn't have wanted to be caught dead in that. It was cute back in the days, just not now.

The more Shane stayed out of town, the closer Yuri drew to Uno. All the hoodrats and average chicks liked Uno. At the club, he was a slick talker, even though he could barely talk. Yuri always made fun of the way he spoke.

After a month, Yuri gave in to Uno, but instead of the Intercontinental Hotel or the Twelve, Uno took her to the Holiday Inn. Yuri thought, 'Damn, I used to stay here with Momma and Daddy, when I was twelve.' She didn't complain to Uno about it. Uno made her forget what kind of hotel it was, it could have been the Super 8 as far as she was concerned. Uno had stamina. Uno could screw all night. Uno brought Yuri to multiple orgasms, over and over again. He could screw so long that Yuri would have to carry K-Y Jelly with her. Yuri liked how Uno would tell her to stick her fingers inside herself and lick them. The only thing Yuri did not like sometimes, was how she sucked him for at least an hour and could not make him cum, only leaving her jaws aching. With his big foot-long, she wondered how this thin nigga have so much dick, it was bigger than his body.

Yuri was liking Uno's sex so much that she started spending Shane's money on him, trying to dress him like she wanted. Instead of Jordans, she bought him Gucci and Louis Vuitton sneakers. The more he sexed her, the more she paid. Uno even began to stay at the loft.

He would say to Yuri, "Put that nigga's shit up when I come 'round, I don' wanna see pitchers or nothin'."

Yuri did just what Uno told her to do. Uno did not try to pay a light bill, but he had rules.

When Shane came in town, Yuri totally stopped staying at home. She would tell Shane that she wanted to stay at the big house in Fayetteville, so she could get used to it. He never felt any kind of way about it, and was happy she wanted to be there. Shane loved Yuri and Yuri was falling in love with Uno's uneducated half a pound, four and a half ounce selling ass.

Uno would even tell Yuri, "Break up wit dat nigga, you my Shawty, he jus' the bank."

Yuri would say, "I love him, I just like your sex."

Uno said, "I like yo's, too, and I nee' you a lil' nastier."

That's when Yuri found out how Uno could stay hard so long. He was an ecstasy pill poppin', geeked up fool. He even got Yuri hooked on pills, too. Yuri had gotten sprung on the pills.

Once school started, she began missing classes, sleeping all day from coming off pills all night. Uno turned Yuri out. He had her sleeping with him, and strippers, and whoever else. He even let other men fuck her, and made them pay, and split the money with her. Yuri was headed for self-destruction with Uno. Shane had begun to sense that Yuri was acting strange. He told her that he was going to stay in Atlanta the whole week and he wanted to stay at her loft. Yuri cleaned up and told Uno he would have to stay away. Uno told Yuri he would need one thousand dollars to buy his drugs, and he would chill at the trap house for the week. Uno did not even have a spot of his own. He was twenty-five and still living in Mechanicsville with his momma.

Yuri loved ecstasy so much, that without them, her mood was shitty. Shane loved her so much, that he didn't care how she acted.

When Shane wanted to make love to Yuri, she would say, "Just fuck me and let's go to bed."

She made him cum as fast as she could, and prayed that she didn't call him Uno. As good as Shane could make her feel, Uno made her feel double the pleasure of him. She thought about the girls that Uno would have go down on her, and he even made her eat some of them out. She could not stop thinking about Uno.

To get Shane to leave, she called Chanel and she asked how things were going in D.C. "Fine, Yuri, how are you?"

"I'm ok, just been relaxing with Shane all week, and that's been good."

"Tell him I send my love."

"Chanel said hello, and she sends her love, baby."

Shane said, "Hello Chanel, right back atcha."

"How's Terrance?"

"He's ok, I just been into my books, Yuri, I thought about what you said, but he doesn't show any indications of foul play."

"Well that's good, because this man over here better never cheat on me!"

Shane laughed, "I am all yours, Lil' momma, just don't cheat on me."

At the moment the line of Yuri's phone was clicking. She looked at it and played it off. It was Uno, and he knew that Shane was around. It was Friday, and Shane had been around the whole week. Yuri knew Uno must have taken a pill and was feeling cocky.

Chanel said, "Yuri your phone is clicking do you need to get that?"

"No, actually, I was going to come and see you tomorrow, and maybe come back here Sunday night. I haven't seen you since the funeral."

"That sounds great. I have my apartment by the campus now. Terrance will be here tomorrow morning, so if you're cool with the three of us hanging out, then that's fine.

"It's cool with me, Chanel."

After Yuri hung up with Chanel, she went over to Shane and said, "Shane can I please go see my BFF and take my godson, Mason, shopping?"

"Sure, baby, I really need to fly out anyway, I just missed spending time with you, girl, and I can't have anyone take my place."

Yuri called Chanel to tell her the news. "Hey, Chanel, I guess I will see you tomorrow, peace.

Shane said, "Since you're leaving tomorrow, let me leave something on your mind."

They made love half the night. Yuri blocked Uno, and everything else, out of her mind, and sexed her fiancé like she used to.

Chapter 22

When Yuri arrived in D.C., at the airport, Terrance grabbed her bags and gave her a welcome home hug. Chanel ran around the car and they hugged like they hadn't seen each other just 3 months earlier. Chanel loved Yuri and the feelings were mutual. Chanel had made reservations at their favorite restaurant, and the treat would be on her and Terrance. Marie and Mason met them there. Mason was now six months, and as handsome as ever. Yuri bought him a pair of Gucci baby booties and a new Kenneth Cole baby bag. She slipped five hundred dollars to Marie and told her to buy him some clothes. Marie said, "You have to stop spoiling him like you do."

"He is my Godson, and if I got it, he's gonna have it. Shane gave me three thousand dollars last night, just for today and tomorrow."

Terrance whistled, "It must be nice."

"It's ok, well it's better than ok, I can't wait to spoil my baby like that."

Chanel looked at Terrance and smiled, with love in her eyes. Yuri thought, 'What a perfect couple.'

Terrance and Chanel were splitting the two-hundred dollar dinner ticket. Yuri snatched it up and insisted on paying. That was the reason Shane gave her the money, to spend on her friends. After dinner Marie had to take Mason home to put him to bed. Chanel, Terrance, and Yuri went to the apartment. On the way Chanel asked, "Does your mom know that you're here?"

"I called and she didn't answer."

Lying, Chanel said, "She has been home a lot since the funeral. Whenever I stop by to check on my momma the Volvo is in the yard."

Yuri thought about how Barb had caught her looking at Eugene. 'It wasn't like it seemed,' thought Yuri, 'I looked back and there he was.' She said "I'll call again later."

Chanel pressed, "We can go by there before we get home, if you want."

Yuri said, "I'll just see her tomorrow."

When they arrived at Chanel's apartment, Yuri showered and called Uno. "Hey, Shawty."

"Hey Uno, what you doin'?"

"I'm at the scrip club, and this chick sittin' on my dick since you not."

"Don't talk like that!"

"Girl, please, where you at? Still with that lame-ass nigga?"

"No, I'm in D.C., I came to visit my friends."

108

"Shawty, when you comin' back?"

"Tomorrow. That was the only way that Shane would leave. I think he knows I'm cheating on him."

"He should, the way I be stretchin' tha' pussy out."

"Shut up, Uno."

"Shawty, I ain' seen ya since las' week. I 'm gone tear yo' ass up tomorrow night." Yuri smiled and could not wait.

"Ok, Uno."

"Aight', Shawty." They both hung up.

When Yuri got off the phone, she heard Chanel and Terrance having a light-weight argument. She felt he was too sexy not to be cheating. Shane was fine as hell, too, but he didn't cheat, so why did she feel Terrance was? She knocked on the bedroom door.

"Chanel is everything ok?"

"Yes, I'll be there in a second."

Chanel came out of the room; they sat talking and watching movies until four a.m. They slept on the couch, like they did when they were children. When Yuri woke up, Chanel had left. She ran to Publix for some fruit and breakfast food. Yuri peeked in the crack of the bedroom door. Terrance was still asleep. She got a face towel and showered. Before she got out of the shower she felt she should put Terrance to the test, just to see where his mind was. She needed a towel to dry herself with. She called out for Terrance. "Terrance, Terrance!"

"Yes?" He answered, groggily.

"I'm sorry to wake you, but I didn't grab a towel, can you get me a big towel please?"

"Yes, Yuri," he mumbled. When Terrance walked into the bathroom, Yuri was standing there ass-hole naked.

"I'm sorry, Yuri."

"Why are you sorry, Terrance? Don't be. Come here and bring the towel." Yuri grabbed his hand, and placed it on her breast, and asked softly, "Don't you like that Terrance?"

As she watched the bulge grow in his pajama pants, Terrance snatched his hand back and said, "No, I don't like that, I love my woman and you're her best friend, please don't ever come on to me again!"

As he stormed out of the bathroom, Chanel walked through the front door, with a look of astonishment on her face. She could not believe what she was seeing. She dropped both bags of groceries.

Yuri put the towel around her, fast. Chanel said, "What the fuck is going on?" The entire time she was waiting for a response, she watched Terrance's penis go from hard to soft.

He began, "Baby, she…"

Yuri interrupted and cried, "He just walked in here and grabbed my breast." Tears began to flow down her face.

Terrance was shocked. "She's lying!"

"Shut up Terrance," Chanel screamed, "How could you do this to me? How dare you try my best friend."

"But Chanel, she's lying!" Yuri continued to shed more insincere tears.

"I knew I couldn't trust you and think that you would wait on me! I was a fool! Please, just leave, Terrance." Chanel yelled, pointing to the door.

Terrance said "But Chanel, she, please, I love you!"

"Terrance, if you don't leave now, I'll call the police."

Terrance was full of anger, and could not believe what was happening.

He walked slowly over to get his suitcase, leaving the house with his head down, thinking, "I wish she would listen to me, if she only knew how much I love her."

Terrance got in his car and sat for a minute thinking how he could get Chanel to just hear him out, and then drove away.

Chanel ran and got the robe off her bedroom door; she wrapped it around Yuri and hugged her as they cried together.

"I am so sorry, Yuri, I guess he was tired of waiting on me for sex, but why did it have to be you that he came on to, right here in my fucking apartment?" Chanel continued through her tears. "He knows I just lost my brother and I was depending on him to help me through this, Yuri, I am just cursed! When it rains it pours."

"No, you're not, Chanel. God has a way of revealing things to us before it gets any worse."

"Yuri, I should have listened when you told me that Terrance was probably messing around. If he tried to sleep with you, my best friend, he is for sure screwing someone. That is why I am going to wait for God to send me my husband, and he will be my first," Chanel cried, shaking her head, and continued, "Just to think, I almost gave in to him. He has scarred me for life."

110

"Chanel, don't feel like that, because one day you are gonna find the man of your dreams, and he will never cheat on you."

"I have to lay down, I'm tired and my head hurts, this is too much for me. I'm sorry, I was going to cook us some breakfast, but my appetite is gone, and my heart is hurting too. You know, Yuri, I'm glad I came in when I did. I'm glad he didn't rape you."

"Me, too, he did have me a little scared. "

"Sorry, sis," Chanel said.

"Me, too."

Yuri had worked her charm again. Her conscience was talking to her again.

"You are a mean, selfish bitch. Because your nasty-ass is so unhappy, you don't want Chanel to be happy, either. Is there anyone you don't do wrong?"

Yuri actually thought she was protecting Chanel. She only felt bad about knowing that Shane was a good man and she had accepted his proposal.

Yuri thought, "If only Chanel's timing wasn't off, I wouldn't have had to pretend that he came on to me."

Chanel finally woke up, and realized that she had slept the morning and afternoon away.

Yuri walked into the room with eagerness and suggested, "Let's get dressed and do what girls do best when they're upset."

"And what is that?" Chanel asked.

"Shop! I am taking you shopping. We can go to Saks and use your discount. Now doesn't that sound good, sis? Get dressed; we can't just sit around here all day. Let's get moving."

Chanel rubbed her eyes and removed the blankets. She sat on the edge of the bed while Yuri opened up the blinds and let the sunlight in.

Chanel stretched, and with a slight smile on her face, balanced her feet on the floor, then said, "Let me get ready."

"That a girl," encouraged Yuri.

When they arrived at the mall, the first stop was Starbucks. They each ordered a coffee cake and caramel macchiato. They then strolled through the mall, chatting and window shopping. Yuri stopped to buy two BCBG dresses. They hopped over to Kenneth Cole. Yuri bought a watch and shoes.

Chanel was thinking, and then said to Yuri, "Wow, Yuri, Shane will really love the watch and the shoes."

"I know Chanel, he loves jewelry, clothes, and shoes. Saks will be our last stop."

Yuri found two pair of True Religion jeans and one pair of Seven for all mankind. Chanel had two pair of Trues, also, and a sexy black dress made by Ralph Lauren. The discount that Chanel got from working there made it even better. They went to the cologne section. Yuri purchased a $240.00 bottle of Silver Mountain Water Creed. With Chanel's discount it took fifty dollars off of the original price.

Chanel said, "Yuri, you really are spoiled."

"It's Shane's money, so I spend a little on him, too."

"You just spent $800.00 on three items."

"Yeah, he deserves it," said Yuri

"He is a good man, I wished Terrance would have been, and things would have turned out differently."

Yuri saw the pain in Chanel's eyes. "Enough about Shane, we are going to the Mexican Restaurant to eat, and drink a pitcher of margaritas."

"Yuri, you know I don't really drink."

"Then just have one frozen margarita and that's it. Deal?"

"Deal."

As they were on their way to the restaurant, Chanel's phone was ringing non-stop. She looked at her caller ID and it was Terrance. She immediately pressed the button to send him straight to voicemail. He continued to blow up her phone so she made sure he couldn't leave a message. She called her service provider and changed her number. In a matter of minutes, he could not get through.

Sitting at the table, they chatted about their lives, and the upcoming events with school approaching.

Yuri said, "Chanel, I'm going to get you a ticket to Atlanta for next weekend, you need a vacation. When was the last time you were out of the city? Was it on my 13th birthday, when we went to New York?"

"No," said Chanel. "Remember when I went to Florida with my family, and me and Chance played on the beach the entire time?"

"That was a family vacation, what you need now is a relaxing vacation, before you hit the books. So what do you say, Chanel? Atlanta?"

"I guess, Yuri, what about my clothes?"

"You just bought three new outfits and you already know we're going to shop when you get there."

"Ok, I'll go."

"Trust me, Chanel, you need to get away. You'll feel so much better. When we get to the airport tomorrow, I'll pay for your ticket."

Chanel placed her hand on Yuri's arm and said, "Thank you, Yuri, ATL here I come!"

Yuri was happy now that she had got rid of the man that Chanel was deeply in love with, knowing that Chanel cared about her. It made her feel good to have her best friend in her pocket. The next day, Yuri got to the airport, paid for Chanel's ticket, and left for Atlanta. She was glad that Chanel had agreed to come join her in Atlanta the following weekend. She sat in her seat, leaned her head back, and thought about Chanel and Terrance.

Yuri was gone for only one day, but it seemed like a week. She had not seen Uno all week. She called him immediately.

He answered, "Hey, Shawty, you back?"

"Yep, what's up, Uno?"

"D's nuts tha's what, you wanna kiss dem?"

Yuri laughed and said, "You are crazy."

"Did you bring me somein' back?"

"Me."

"I already got you, Shawty, don' play wit' me," Uno said.

"Yes, boo, I got you something."

"Well, when I leave the Trap I'll be through, so get tha' pussy ready fo' daddy."

"Ok, boo," she giggled.

As planned, at 11:45pm, Uno pulled up, music on blast. He did not care that people in the neighborhood had to go to work. Yuri was sleeping, and the music startled her. She pretended she had been waiting up for Uno.

113

Uno walked in and his eyes looked the size of fifty cent pieces. His eyes were so big, Yuri knew he was on ecstasy, and she might be sucking on his big dick half the night. The first thing Uno thought about, before he gave Yuri a hug was his gifts.

He said while hugging her, "Wha' you brin' me back, Shawty?"

She responded, "I told you, me."

"Damn girl, I see that, and you look good, gimmie some shugga." Yuri reached up and kissed him softly on his lips. He asked, "Wha' is that? Come 'ere." Uno took her head and put his tongue down her throat. "Damn girl, you dun made ma nature rise." He pulled his pants down. "Come her, Shawty, kiss it. Do you miss 'im."

"Yes, Uno." Yuri and Uno couldn't keep their hands off each other. He almost didn't make it through her giving him foreplay with her tongue.

Uno moaned, "Damn, I missed you, girl."

He turned sideways so he could play with her wet pussy. Once his fingers were inside, Yuri got her rhythm and sucked Uno just the way he liked it.

"Damn, girl, you mus' 'ave missed daddy, you suckin' it like a vacuum, 'bout to suck a nigga up. Damn, girl."

Yuri liked when Uno talked to her and expressed his pleasure. Uno fucked her mouth for over thirty minutes. Her jaws were worn out. She could make Shane or any other man cum in less than ten minutes, but with Uno, it took patience and time. He wanted to savor the moment. Yuri climbed on top and rode him.

He moaned, "Damn, you wet, gimmie me tha' pussy, ride dis dick, who pussy is it?"

"Yours, Uno, yours," she screamed.

After riding Uno, he said, "You know the only way to make me cum, go get the lube."

Yuri returned with the K-Y Jelly. She rubbed it all over Uno's hard, stiff dick. She laid on her back lifting her legs, giving him access to enter her ass. Uno did not like to fuck her in her ass from behind, he thought that reminded him of some gay ass shit. He went in from the front. Yuri took it all, as he entered her ass slowly. They got into a rhythm, back and forth, and Yuri was feeling all of Uno. The pain was a good pain. Uno knew where to touch her. He went easy, in and out, touching her clit until they both came.

Laying there, trying to catch their breath, Uno said, as if he had been thinking for a moment, "Now where my shit, Shawty?"

Yuri jumped up, out of the bed, to go get the gifts. As she walked away, Uno smacked her on the ass.

"You gone make a nigga fall in love with yo' ass."

Yuri smiled as she walked away. She was already in love. Yuri came out of the closet with the Kenneth Cole bag, along with the small Saks bag. Uno opened his gifts, checking and admiring the watch and shoes. He took the fake watch that was purchased at the Korean store at the Underground off, and replaced it with the Kenneth Cole watch. He could not get over the shoes. He was impressed.

"Damn Shawty, you got good taste."

Yuri was actually tired of seeing him dressed in that colorful attire that he wore. She was transforming him and dressing him the way Shane would dress. Shane was a fly guy. Uno was an urban wearing cool- dressing kind of guy. Next he pulled out the $240.00 bottle of Silver Mountain Water Creed. He sprayed it on.

"This shit smell good, Shawty."

Yuri said, "I know, look how much it cost."

Uno looked at the receipt and said "Damn, girl, I was mad when I had to pay $50.00 fo' tha' Polo Black I got. I see you really fellin' a nigga huh."

"Yes, I am feeling you, Uno."

Uno burst into laughter and said, "Wit' yo' east coast soundin' ass."

Yuri laughed and countered "With your country talking ass." Yuri smiled and said softly, "Uno, baby, I'm tired, are you coming to bed?"

Uno was gathering his bags and responded, "Naw, Shawty, I gotta get back to da Trap. If I leave now, I can make at leas' $2,000.00 a' for da mornin'. I'm out, I'll call ya tomorra'."

Yuri tried to hide her disappointment. Uno had done what he came to do. He satisfied her, got his shit, and left.

She got up behind him, locked the door, and went to lay in the bed.

Her conscience began to speak, "Bitch you must be stupid, what kind of fool are you? Your man makes two hundred thousand dollars for just setting up a deal, and you're in love with this fuck nigga whose daily goal is to make only two thousand dollars. What the fuck is your problem, you letting dick control your life?"

Yuri blocked her thoughts. The only thing she knew was that Uno made her feel good, and for her, that was all that really mattered. She could not get over the feelings that she was having for Uno. She felt like she was catching feelings for this nigga and falling in love. What could she do?

On Monday, Yuri got up and began her day, running errands, taking care of her business. She stopped off at the Whole Health Food Store. She grabbed a few items, and things to freeze for

115

Chanel that she liked to eat. She purchased enough for the next two weeks so they would not run out of food. After leaving the store, Yuri picked up her cell and called Shane. He answered, and was happy to hear her voice. Shane had been really busy working, and negotiating deals, but Yuri was always on his mind.

He said "Hey, Lil' Momma, I'm glad you called. I miss you."

"Hey baby, I miss you too, how are you?"

"I'm ok, I'm out here in the valley, I just closed on some townhomes. I'll be in town on Thursday, I can't wait to get some loving."

"Baby, Chanel will be arriving here on Friday morning, so can you take us to dinner Friday evening?"

"I can do that, baby, anything for you, Lil' momma."

"I love you, Shane."

"I love you, too, talk to you later."

Yuri was happy that Shane was coming home. She never told Chanel about Uno, and her plan was not to. When Yuri exited off the freeway, she recognized Candice at a stop light behind the wheel of a new, black Range Rover with the strut kit on it. She was pushing it! Passion was sitting in the passenger seat. They glanced over, noticed Yuri, and turned the corner. Yuri turned off in the same direction. The light had changed and now they were right beside her. Yuri had the top dropped. Passion let the window down and threw a chocolate milkshake that she was drinking at Yuri and screamed, "You hoe ass bitch!" They laughed and drove off.

Yuri's hair and car were drenched in chocolate shake. She thought to herself, 'I need to move, because Candice shops and eats down here, and I don't know if she's stalking me, or if she's down here doing her thang.' After all, that's how Yuri found the loft, from shopping with Candice.

Yuri went home, showered and cleaned herself up. She had to be flawless at all times. She wished every day that she had not messed around with Q. She really never wanted to sleep with him.

She called Uno, "Hey, Uno, where are you? I want to come see you."

"Hey, Shawty, I'm ova her off 20 and MLK. Come through and stop at da liquor sto'e and grab some Switzer Sweets an' a fith a Hennessy an' a Coke."

"Damn, Uno, is that it?"

"Nope, I need a packa squares."

"You know I hate when you smoke cigarettes, if you don't quit they're going to kill you."

"I gotta die a somethin', come on."

"Ok, I'm on my way."

Yuri stopped at the store and grabbed everything that Uno requested, even the cigarettes. When she pulled up, the guy that Uno bought his dope from was sitting there. He drove a red G Wagon. It was the only new car that sat outside. The rest of the cars were Crown Vics and old beat up Chevys that Uno's boys drove.

Uno called Yuri over, "Come here, Spida, this my Shawty, Yuri, she from D.C., mane."

"What up, Yuri?"

"Hello Spida." Yuri could tell he was not from Atlanta. His accent was different. He was nice-looking, heavy set, brown skin, with a deep voice.

Uno said, "Where da stuff from da liquor sto'e, Shawty?"

"It's in the car."

"Go git it."

As she walked away, Spida said, "Damn, nigga, you doin' it like that? I'm used to one of your bankhead rats pullin' up, nigga you got a dime."

"I told you folk."

"Man, lemme fuck her."

"Naw, nigga, tha's my good pussy."

"Nigga, I'll give you five hundred jus' to let me fuck that pussy. It ain't been no problem before, I fucked all yo' other bitches."

"Five hundred?"

"Yeah, five hundred, nigga."

"Gimmie a thousan' and I'll see."

As they were negotiating their fees, Yuri walked toward them.

She said, "Here, baby."

"Thanks Shawty. She come through always fo' a nigga."

Spida could not take his eyes off Yuri. He loved what he saw, and wondered why a chick like her, with a Benz, and as fly as she was, wanted to sit around a dope house, with a broke ass nigga like Uno. Uno was averaging about $3,000.00 a week, he had a weed, pill and liquor habit. He kept money for a new outfit, only for the weekends, so he could look good for the club and re-up on the money.

117

Spida said, "I'm out, I gotta make this money." He jumped in his ride, turned up his music, he was bumpin' Gorilla Zoe 'Hood Nigga,' and rode out.

"Ma nigga like wha' he seen, I got a trophy."

Yuri blushed, she liked that. After an hour of sitting, watching fiends come in and out for crack and pills, Yuri was ready to go. The weed and cigarettes gave her a terrible headache. Uno's weed smelled like someone was burning trash in the woods.

Yuri said, "Walk me to the car; I'm going home to lay down."

"Can I come lay wit' ya lata?"

"I guess."

"You guess? Wha' da fuck ya mean?"

"Yes, Uno, you can come, I was going to tell you that Shane will be back on Thursday, and I probably won't see you until Monday or Tuesday."

"Damn, tha' fuck-nigga always poppin' up."

"Uno, he's my fiancé."

"He ain' shit but a fuck-boy, he yo' trick."

"Whatever you want to call him, he will be here."

"Well 'fore he come, I'm gone beat tha' pussy up. He should already know somebody be up in it. Tha's how weak tha' nigga's work is, sucka."

"Uno, get off of him."

"You takin' up fo' tha' sucka?"

"No."

"I'll call ya when I leave here lata on, an' don' ya eva take up fo' tha' nigga in my face."

"Uno, you are draggin' it out."

"I'm fo' real, Shawty."

"Ok, baby." That was a relief for Yuri. Now she could enjoy her time with Shane and Chanel, without any interruptions from Uno.

Chapter 23

Shane arrived on time, as usual. All day Tuesday and Wednesday, Yuri cleaned and made sure everything was in order. Yuri made sure that there was not a single trace of a man lingering in her house. She opened windows, and used the sanitizer. It was difficult to air out the smell of cigarette smoke and the smell of that dirty, dirty weed that was left behind by Uno. When she finished, you would have thought Merry Maids had come through.

Yuri purchased a few more things from the grocery store. She bought things that she knew Shane enjoyed, such as his favorites, Coors Light and Backwoods. She could not wait to smell the good California Chronic that he smoked. Yuri was unsure how Chanel would react to the marijuana smoke. Oh well, it was her house, and her fiancé paid the bills.

Standing at the threshold of the door, he looked as good as ever. Shane walked in, set down his bags, picked Yuri up, and twirled her around, kissing her.

"Damn, girl, I missed you," he said appreciatively.

Yuri responded with a hug in return, tighter than ever, and said, "I'm so glad you're home."

Shane replied, "Baby, after October, I will be all yours until New Years, I'll work from the office here. That means we'll have a lot of time together." Yuri's heart dropped.

"That's great," Yuri forced.

"We might have time to make a baby."

"Shane, you know I start school in two weeks; we won't be having kids anytime soon. I'm already behind a semester."

"Baby, that's why you should have gone to summer school, you would have been caught up, and we'd have time to make our baby." Shane sat Yuri on the bed and fell on top of her. "Damn, Yuri, you look sexier every time I see you."

"And you look more handsome every time I see you."

"Thank you, girl," he whispered, pulling up her skirt at the same time. Yuri's body became tense, but after looking into Shane's deep brown eyes, his smile revealing his deep dimples, she let loose and went wild.

Shane and Yuri did a move that they never tried, 69, and pleasured each other all at once. Yuri sucked Shane's dick like she had done when they first met. Shane always pleasured Yuri well.

Yuri lifted her legs and screamed, "Uno," and then she caught herself and instead said, "Oh no, oh no, damn, Shane, I am about to cum."

Shane never heard the name that Yuri called. She made it all better, swallowing her words right down with his cum. They laid together for a while and talked, and then showered and laughed, and talked some more.

"So what do you and Chanel have planned?"

"We are going to the spa as soon as she arrives tomorrow, getting manicures and pedicures. Then, we'll wait on you, so you can feed us."

Just listening to Yuri got Shane aroused. He was hard again; hard as a brick. He was faithful to her and never thought about, or slept with, other women. Shane was all business until he got with his girl.

Shane repeated, "I can feed you, huh?" Yuri gave him her seductive eye. "I want to feed you, Lil' Momma, come here and eat this dick."

Yuri was right back sucking on Shane. They did things she loved to do. Shane fucked Yuri from the bed to the floor, even on the balcony, and they didn't care who had a view.

Chanel arrived, as planned, and Yuri picked her up in the Benz with the top dropped, their long hair blowing in the wind. "Yuri, I love your car, this makes my Impala look like shit."

"Girl, don't be ridiculous, your Impala is clean. We are both riding new booties."

"New booties?" Chanel asked, "Girl, where do you get all this slang-talk from?"

"I live in the A."

They laughed, flying down interstate 75north. They exited at Lenox Road, right near Candice's house. Yuri prayed that she would not run into Candice, especially after the other day, with the throwing of the chocolate shake on her, acting much like a kid. As the episode flashed across her mind she thought, 'Some bitches never grow up.'

Yuri and Chanel were able to meet their scheduled appointment time at the spa. They sat in the sauna until the masseuse arrived.

Yuri asked, "So Chanel, how was your week?"

"It was very different, because I usually talk to Terrance all day and all night. Even when I'm at work, we DM'd each other. Yuri, I wish he had not come on to you. I feel like a fool."

"Chanel, you shouldn't feel like a fool, at least you found out before you lost your virginity to him."

"Girl, he been going by my parents' house and all, Momma said she wanted to speak with me about the situation, but I didn't have time to stop by, so I'll see her on Tuesday, when I return."

After their time at the spa, Yuri treated them to manicures and pedicures. She called Shane and told him that she was short on cash. He agreed to meet her at the bank. Shane made a deposit of $80,000 from one of his foreclosed properties that he sold. He withdrew $7,500.00 and gave Yuri $3,500.00. "This should be enough for us to spend for the weekend."

Yuri grabbed the money and said, "Thank you, baby. I love you."

"I love you, too." "I'm going to grab an outfit, and I'll be at the loft around 7:30pm."

"Ok, baby, I'll see you later."

Chanel said, "Damn, I wish I had someone to love me. Yuri, he is a great guy."

"Yes, he is, that's why I'm going to marry him."

Before they left for dinner, Shane ran into the loft and grabbed his bottle of Creed. He shook it to get his last squirts out.

After he got what was left, he tossed the bottle in the trash and said, "Man I love that cologne. I'll have to get another bottle."

Chanel wondered if he used a lot of the cologne, because Yuri had just purchased him a bottle last week. Chanel kept quiet and said nothing.

At dinner, Shane poured the $200.00 bottle of Merlot, and they toasted to a new and improved school year. Yuri's phone interrupted the moment, but she ignored it, and it continued to vibrate. She finally opened her clutch to see that it was Uno. Why was he calling? He knew she had company and that Shane was at home. He was so damned disrespectful. Shane asked Chanel about her sophomore year of college. That was Yuri's opportunity to bust a move to the restroom, to powder her nose. Walking swiftly to the ladies' room, Yuri found an empty stall and called Uno.

She whispered, "Uno, what's up? You know I told you I was coming to dinner with Shane and my best friend, and we're at the restaurant now."

"You been givn' that lame-ass nigga my pussy?"

"Uno, stop it."

"Answer my question."

"Uno, he's my fiancé."

"The way you suck this dick, I can't tell tha', shit."

"I just came on my cycle."

"What does tha' mean? I fuck you like tha' all da time. You betta not fuck him no mo."

"I won't, Shane ain't like that, he don't like bloody pussy. I have to go, Uno."

"You gone make this shit up to me, Shawty."

"See you later, Uno."

When Yuri arrived back at the table, the waiter was bringing the main course. Shane asked, "Are you ok, baby? You were gone awhile."

"Yes, I'm ok. You know it's that time of the month and I had to take care of my business."

He whispered, "I'm glad I got it in last night, I was just in time."

"Me, too, baby."

Shane said, "Yuri, Chanel was telling me she ended her relationship with Terrance, for career purposes. Why didn't you tell me?"

"I'm sorry, Shane, I didn't bring it up because I really didn't think it was important, and I really didn't think she wanted anyone to know." Yuri and Chanel glanced at each other and shook their heads. This was their secret, and neither Yuri nor Chanel would tell.

After dinner, Shane asked if they wanted to go bowling with his friends. He also mentioned to Chanel that he had a friend that he thought she should meet.

"You are a very sweet woman, and Mark would really be a good man for you." Shane continued, "What do you think, you want to give it a try?"

"Sure Shane, I don't mind, I'm keeping my options open."

Yuri was not the least bit interested in what they were talking about, because Uno had called a dozen times, and she was distracted. "I have really bad cramps, and would be bad company, so Shane, go ahead and take Chanel, and you guys can drop me off at home."

Chanel asked, "Yuri, you sure you don't mind?"

"Of course not, I'll get some rest for tomorrow and be ready for shopping. After all, I really do need to rest and get my strength up so I can shop 'til I drop!"

Shane and Chanel dropped Yuri off at her house. Yuri didn't have one ounce of concern that Chanel would try her fiancé. Chanel was nothing like her. She was loyal, and a virgin, and she knew that Shane was in love. Yuri showered and called Uno.

"Uno, what is wrong with you tonight?"

"Shawty, you been ignorin' my calls."

"No Uno, I've been busy."

"When I call Shawty, I wanna talk. I don' like waitin' on ya. You my ho, an' when tha' fuck-boy come in, he jus' take ova."

"Uno, let's get something straight, I am not your whore, and why are you always talking shit about him? Are you jealous?"

"Naw Shawty, I ain' no jealous nigga, I'll rob tha' nigga."

"Why are you talking like that? You must have been drinking that Hennessey again."

"Sho'e did, an' abou' to go fuck these two bad bitches, since you so busy an' ain' got no time fo' a nigga."

"Uno, you are so disrespectful."

"An' you not? You ova there playin'wifey. I can' wait till tha' nigga gone to put dez nuts in yo' mouth. You on punishmen', an' by the way, don' even call me when he gone. I got bitches waitin' in line, an' you wanna put a nigga on the back burner, like I'm a hoe-ass nigga."

"Uno, Uno?" Yuri couldn't believe he hung up on her.

Chanel and Shane made it back to the loft from the bowling alley. As they walked into the house, they were chatting about their evening. "So, Chanel, did you like him?"

"He was cool, but I could not get over the southern accent." They laughed.

Yuri walked in and said, "Yeah, they can't speak correct English." She thought about Uno, as she made the statement. She thought about Uno's ebonic slang.

Chanel said, "Yuri, he called me 'Shorty' a million times."

"No, Chanel, he called you 'Shawty'." They all laughed in harmony.

It was Saturday and raining. Chanel and Yuri still kept their plans to go shopping. Yuri gave Chanel $1,000.00 of the $3,500.00 that Shane had given her. Chanel, said "I'm going to go to Express and BeBe to shop, because those shoes that you buy, Yuri, are way over my head. I want those shoes from Saks, that are on sale for $250.00, plus an additional forty percent off, with my employee discount."

"That sounds good, because tonight we are getting out!"

Their first stop was the Underground. Yuri had not heard from Uno. She had called him and texted him; he was acting crazy. She just wanted to see him, and even introduce him to Chanel, so he would know how she felt.

As they were sitting at the bar, sipping on their first round, Uno walked in and strolled past Yuri and Chanel.

123

Chanel said, "Damn, he smells good. I know that smell."

Yuri knew it, too, from smelling the Creed on Shane, but she said nothing.

Chanel continued, "Look at how that chick who's with him is standing. Is her butt real?"

"I'm not sure," Yuri responded, feeling jealous. "I know one thing, that bitch looks super-cheap with those Citi trend jeans, and those man-made material shoes."

They laughed, "You can't tell her shit."

"Her man is flossing her," Chanel commented. Yuri was not intimidated, now if her clothes would have been on Yuri's level, then maybe, but a bitch with fifteen dollar jeans would never get the satisfaction of thinking she was fly. The girl was also funny looking, her big ass was all she had.

Uno acted as though Yuri was invisible. After listening to a few more songs, Yuri told Chanel, "Now let's go to where some real rich niggas are."

Chanel was ready to go to the loft, but she wanted to hang out, too.

She thought, "I'm on vacation; I might as well have fun."

Chanel and Yuri ended up at the Compound. This was Yuri's old stomping grounds. Yuri knew this was Candice's hang-out spot, too. Candice hung out there for the exclusive parties. Either way, it was off the chain. Yuri paid the valet. They walked through the VIP line; she paid $100.00 a piece for them. Chanel looking around, taking it all in, and said, "These clubs are expensive."

Yuri responded, "Well, not really, if you want to stand in the $20 line, over there, you can very well do that; I choose not to. I like the fast lane." The $20 line was down the street. "Here in the ATL we Boss up, Shawty."

"What?" Chanel asked, and they both laughed.

"When you go through lines like we just did, they call it 'Bossing up'."

They walked to the VIP area. Chanel liked this club, the ambience was totally different from the club they had just left. Men tried to get at her and enjoyed her company. Chanel danced and even gave her number to the tall, sexy guy that had sort-of a resemblance to Terrance. After the club, they ate at the Waffle House and retired for the night. The weekend had come and gone so fast.

It was Sunday morning and Yuri woke Chanel. She wanted to attend Pastor Creflo Dollar's church. Chanel attended church as often as she could. Yuri, on the other hand had not been to church in as long as she could remember. Chanel was happy and relieved to accept the invitation. They got dressed and Yuri called Shane to ask if he wanted to go, as well. He said, "Yes. I'll meet you ladies there. You know I don't live too far from the church. Call me when you guys get close, so we can all sit together."

As they waited in the long line to get into the church parking lot, Chanel smiled, admiring the gold dome on the mega-church that said <u>World Changers</u>. Shane was looking good, dressed in a Hugo Boss suit. Yuri sighed happily, in silent admiration of her man, and how fly he was, and he always smelled good, too. Yuri and Chanel were looking the part of church-going ladies. They toned down their outfits to suit the environment. They all made it to the inside, the church was huge. They took seats somewhere in the middle. Pastor Dollar spoke from the book of St. Matthews 5:28 about lust. Yuri thought, 'He doesn't know me, but he is totally talking about me.' At that moment it seemed like everybody knew her sins, and she felt like all eyes were on her. She snapped out of her thoughts and began to listen to the pastor preach.

The one thing she did like about what he was saying was, "Blessings are coming your way."

It was now time for the church offerings. When the collection plate passed through, Shane reached in his wallet, and gave Yuri and Chanel each a $100.00 bill.

Yuri looked at the money before she dropped it in the collection plate and thought, 'Damn, why not just give ten or twenty dollars?' Then she thought, 'The pastor just said that your blessings were on the way.' Everyone had an appetite after the service, and agreed that they should grab a bite to eat at Spondivit's. Shane went in with Chanel and Yuri on his side. The host approached Shane and asked "How many will be dining today?"

"Three."

"Come, follow me." Sitting at the table, Yuri, Shane, and Chanel looked at the menu, picked out what they wanted, and chatted, until the waiter came to take their order.

While they waited, Shane said "I've been working on this deal here in town, and if it goes well, you will be very happy, Lil' Momma."

Yuri pressed, "Tell me now."

"I don't want to get your hopes up too high, just pray."

Then he looked over at Chanel and added, "Chanel, I'm glad you got us up to go to church."

Chanel said, "Shane, it wasn't me, it was Yuri who woke me up to get dressed and go."

With a look of surprise, he smiled at Yuri and nodded "Well, lil' momma, I am impressed. Thank you."

Yuri smiled and Chanel said, "Church was good. I enjoyed being with my best friend and her great man."

"Thank you. When do you leave, Chanel?" Shane asked.

"Tomorrow evening. I have to prepare myself for school; this will be a good year for me. Before I start, though, I have a few loose ends I need to take care of for my brother."

Chanel put her elbows on the table and leaned her head in her hands.

Shane said, "Chanel, if there is anything you or your family need, please do not hesitate to ask. Yuri and I are here for you."

Yuri moved toward Chanel, hugged her tightly, and whispered, "Everything will be ok." Chanel shook her head in the 'yes' motion.

Shane asked, "So, do you ladies want to hit the streets tonight and celebrate this last weekend together before school starts, because when school starts, the night life will be over, Yuri."

Yuri responded, "Yes, baby, we want to get out and have some fun."

Shane said, "Jay-Z is having an after-party at the 'Velvet Room' and I've paid six thousand dollars for a table, so you ladies be ready."

Yuri said, "Ok Shane, but there's a pair of shoes I wanted, and they would be perfect for tonight. Can I go and pick them up, please?"

"Why are you begging, Lil' Momma, I got you." Yuri kissed his dimple on his cheek. "How much are they?" He asked.

She answered, "They're sixteen hundred dollars."

Shane whistled, "They must be red-bottoms."

"You know it, daddy," she giggled.

Before Shane pulled off in the sparkling clean Aston Martin, he gave Yuri the Unlimited American Express Card.

He said, "Grab Chanel a pair of shoes, also. I'll call my man, Walter. I want you to grab that new Diamonte print Louis belt for me and if you like one of the wallets that he put to the side, grab that, too."

Yuri said, "Ok, baby, I'll do that. Oh, and since Chanel works at Saks. We'll use her discount to help your pockets."

Shane smiled, this time showing both his dimples and looking sexy as ever. He added, "One more thing, I need another bottle of Creed."

"Ok baby, I love you."

"I love you, too." Yuri sped off, looking and feeling rich.

As they were pulling out of the parking lot, Chanel commented, "He must use a lot of cologne."

Yuri remembered the bottle that she bought for Uno and she did not respond, turning the music up. She now had Uno on her mind. One more day and her monthly cycle would be over. Yuri knew Shane would never sleep with her while she was on, but Uno didn't care, he enjoyed bloody sheets. Yuri was getting horny just thinking about Uno, but she couldn't call him.

The mall was packed. Everyone knew about the Jay-Z concert and after-party. All the rich niggas and fly chicks were front and center. Yuri got her shoes, she also purchased Chanel a pair of $800.00 Louboutins.

Chanel smiled and said, "My first pair of red bottoms, and they'll probably be my last."

Yuri had several pair, but still preferred her Guccis. The Christian Louboutins were tall and felt high as hell. The Guccis, she wore them like she had on sneakers, no matter how tall they were.

Yuri grabbed Shane's new belt and one of the three wallets that Walter had laid to the side for Shane. Walter was considered Shane's personal shopper and was always compensated with a nice commission. Yuri thanked Walter and went home with all the bags, including the Creed cologne and a bottle of perfume for her. She glanced at the receipt and smiled.

"What Yuri?" Chanel asked.

"I saved $1,800.00, the total went from $4,500.00 to $2,700.00." Yuri gave Chanel $500.00 from her bag.

Chanel said, "Thanks, girl, what is this for?"

"Thank me for what?"

"Just for being my friend and always being here for me."

"If you didn't have the discount, I would have been out the $500.00 anyway, so take it and pay your rent, or whatever you want to do with it."

"Thank you, Yuri, I love you so very much, and nothing will ever come between us."

"Let's chill and get ready for the party tonight, I'm about to show you how to really Boss up, Chanel." They both laughed.

Yuri and Chanel were dressed to kill.

Shane called and said, "We're on the way."

His boy from L.A., who owned the club on Peter Street, drove his big black Phantom. Chanel smiled when the car pulled up. The girls were dressed to impress. Yuri had on the red-bottoms that she recently purchased, a short Moschino dress, silver accessories to match her Prada clutch, and the Cartier engagement ring. All that together made her glow. Chanel had on her BCBG dress and the accessories she had gotten at Saks with her discount. Her Louboutins complimented the dress. The girls' hair was flawless, the Dominicans made sure of that. Their manicures and pedicures were perfect for the hot August weather. They both walked toward the Phantom, asses sitting firm, heads held up high, looking like the stallions they were.

When they got to the club, it was something that Chanel had only seen in the movies. Yuri saw the excitement in her eyes.

"That is the same look I had in my eyes when I came here for the first time," Yuri said to Chanel.

When they made it to the front of the club, the Valet parked the Phantom. Once at the door, the sexy African who was always at the door, at all the parties, greeted Shane and his boy Hassan. The security guards that Shane rented for the night escorted them in, as if they were celebrities, pushing everyone out of the way, placing them at their VIP table. Chanel felt stardom in her life. Yuri was used to it. Everyone was in attendance. Jay-Z had done it like no other. Ace of Spades were being popped everywhere.

Chanel told Yuri, "Had we not been in VIP, I would never have wanted to be here."

They were packed in like sardines. When Yuri glanced down into the stuffed crowd, she spotted Uno. His eyes were as big as a full moon. She hoped and prayed he stayed his distance and would not make trouble. She then noticed Candice. She was with Passion and a few more of the strippers from the club. Q stood in front of them, entering into their section. Candice looked and rolled her eyes. She whispered in Passion's ear and pointed at Yuri. Passion gave Yuri the finger. Yuri turned away not telling Chanel anything about Candice's presence.

Jay-Z finally appeared with his entourage. Beenie Siegal, Memphis Bleek, SwitzBeatz, Missy Elliott, and every other celebrity was in the building. Jay-Z walked out singing 'Change Clothes.' The crowd went mad. He rapped, "I got 99 problems, but a bitch ain't one." Jay-Z had the club turned up.

Chanel had to excuse herself to go to the restroom. The hired security guard pushed his way to the front of the line. Chicks cursed and hollered, but there was nothing they could do. Once Chanel walked out of the stall, she saw Yuri against the wall with a female talking trash to her. Chanel thought it was maybe because of how they cut the line. All Chanel heard, when she came out, was the female calling Yuri a 'stank bitch.'

Chanel ran over to Yuri. She was a good girl, but she would fight with and for her friend at the drop of a dime.

The female said to Chanel, "If you knew better, you would do better, this bitch is a snake and if I was you, I would run before you get bit." The female looked at Yuri and said, "Bitch," with hatred in her eyes.

As she exited the restroom she smushed Yuri in her face, almost knocking her to the ground.

Chanel asked Yuri, "What the hell was that all about, and who was that?"

Yuri answered, "I don't know, I think she has me mistaken for someone else."

"Well whoever she thinks you are, she hates her." Yuri's heart was beating fast and she was glad that security was waiting at the door. She was even happier that Candice did not bust her out in front of Shane or Chanel.

As Yuri was walking out, before entering back into the VIP area, Uno grabbed her arm. Chanel was puzzled, "He was the same guy with the girl, at the Underground club," she thought.

He whispered in Yuri's ear, "You gone make this shit up." Yuri snatched away like she didn't know him. Uno grabbed Chanel and said, "Hey Shawty, I sho' wish I could get to know you betta."

Yuri looked back, hating how Uno was acting. Chanel pulled her arm away from him and walked away, into VIP. She told Yuri, "We saw him the other night, with his girl, now he's grabbing my arm, trying to push up on me."

Yuri said, "He's a nobody, that's why he's way down there, with the rest of the wannabees." Yuri had had enough, and was ready to go, before Candice or Uno caused any other problems. Shane's boy popped his last bottle, and they left.

"The club was awesome, Yuri, I won't have to party again for a whole year, and I love the picture we took with Jay-Z. I'm blowing it up and getting it framed."

"I'm glad you had fun, Chanel."

When they arrived at the loft, Shane walked them to the door. "Chanel, it was great hanging out with you. Hopefully, I'll see you before you leave."

"I really had a wonderful weekend with you and Yuri, Shane, I bossed up!" Shane and Yuri laughed.

He kissed Yuri. "I love you, lil' momma, I'll see you tomorrow after my meeting."

"I love you, baby," Yuri replied.

"Thank you Hassan," both girls sang out in unison.

"Good night, ladies." Hassan had on a wedding ring, and not once did he try to push up on Chanel, or anyone else in the club.

Chanel thought, "I guess there are loyal men in the world after all."

Her man, Terrance, had just been unfaithful to her. She thought about him, and wondered what he had going on, since they were apart. Had he forgotten about her? Was he in a new relationship yet? She missed Terrance, but had never given him the opportunity to explain. The girls were tipsy and tired. They had popped more bottles than Jay-Z could rap about. Their feet were in pain from dancing all night in five and a half inch Louboutin heels. They sat on the couch, rubbing their feet, talking about the extravagant evening they had.

"Yuri, I've had a spectacular time. Now I have to go home and straighten some things out. There are still a few details that are bothering me about Chance's death, and I won't sleep until I figure them out."

"What is it, Chanel? Is there anything I can help you with?"

"No, it's really nothing, if I need you though, I will surely let you know. I may just call that guy that I exchanged numbers with," Chanel giggled.

"Chanel, you only liked him because he resembles Terrance."

"He did favor him, but I liked his conversation, and he was really laid back."

"I think you should call him. It won't hurt to try. Chanel, you deserve nothing but the best." They sat on the couch chatting until both of them fell asleep right where they were.

Shane rang Yuri's phone early. She was tired, and feeling bubbly from all the champagne she had the night before. "Hello?"

"Nothing comes to a sleeper, but dreams," Shane said, "Get up and meet me on 15th Street in forty-five minutes."

Yuri said, "That's like really quick, Shane, can't it wait?"

"No, it can't wait and I don't think you want it to wait. Get your butt up, its right around the corner from your loft. Get here, and bring Chanel, also."

Chanel didn't want to get up either. She jumped straight in the shower. She threw on her Victoria Secret's sweat suit. Yuri wore her Juicy Couture sweat suit that fit her ass to a T. When they arrived on 15th Street, they spotted Shane's Escalade in front of the townhomes. Shane was conversing with a man in an Italian suit. They shook hands, the guy walked away, jumped into a 745 BMW, and sped off. When Chanel and Yuri got out of the car, Shane laughed. "What's funny?" Yuri asked.

"You guys are. I see this weekend has really taken a toll on both of you. You guys were looking like super models last night, hair whipped and now y'all both have snatch-back pony tails." He laughed, "Now that's how you party!"

Yuri was annoyed and tired, "Why did you get me up, Shane, so you can joke on me?"

"Actually, not, I woke you up to see this."

"See what?"

"Your new townhome, it's brand-spanking-new; all you have to do is sign on this dotted line, baby, and it's all yours."

Yuri turned around and looked at the townhouse behind her. It was a three bedroom, two and a half bath, tri-level home.

"Are you serious, Shane?"

"Sign on the line, and as I said, it's all yours, paid in full, no mortgage, just taxes every year. I know that you can handle that." Yuri kissed Shane, took the papers, and signed. Chanel smiled, as well. She was happy that her best friend had a good-looking, smart, young and rich man. She thought, 'Who could ask for anything better?'

They went inside Yuri's new home. It was beautiful, the kitchen was all grey granite, with black appliances to compliment the granite. The laundry room had a Maytag front-loader washer and dryer.

"Wow, Shane, this is beautiful!" Yuri screamed with excitement.

Shane said, "I figured, I pay nearly two thousand dollars a month, on your rent in that small ass loft. The contractors that were building this went bankrupt and couldn't finish, so you know me, I sprang into action. We went down to the state building, with a lot of others, and we bid on it. Guess who won? Yours truly…me! I paid sixty-two thousand dollars. It could have gone for two hundred thousand dollars. So we did good."

Yuri asked, "So when can we move in?"

"ASAP; you better hurry up because I am not paying the rent in the loft for September, so if you don't want to pay it, I think you should pack up."

Yuri hugged Shane. "Thank you so much, baby. I'll start packing today." She hugged her man and put her tongue all the way down his throat. "Shane, you are a blessing."

"And so are you, Lil' Momma."

She said, "You are the best!" Just like she used to tell her mom.

Yuri dropped Chanel off at the airport. They gave each other a big, long hug. They kissed each other's cheeks.

"I love you, Yuri! Thanks for everything that you've done for me this weekend. Really, you made me feel like a princess, because you are most definitely a queen!"

They laughed.

"Don't mention it Chanel, it's all from the heart." Yuri went inside her Louis Vuitton bag, took out five crispy one hundred dollar bills, handed them to Chanel, and said, "Please give this to Marie for Mason; kiss both of them for me. Tell Mason that his godmother loves him very much!"

"I will, Yuri, and thank you once again. See you later, sis."

Chapter 24

School had begun again. Yuri had settled into her new townhome and Shane returned to California to buy more property. Yuri was back to giving Uno all of her time, but Uno's pill popping habit had gotten out of control. His moods changed like the weather, he had started treating Yuri just like he treated the ratchet chicks he always messed with.

Uno had lost a pack of pills that he was supposed to be selling, and he knew that he couldn't cop anything else from Spida until he paid off his debt. Spida had let Uno slide so many times. Once, Uno owed him two thousand dollars for a four-and-a-half of soft cocaine. Another time, Spida let him slide when he owed him for a couple of pounds of weed that he had let him hold. Uno was always fucking up, but Spida knew he was a good dope house boy and he always made it up to him. Uno finally called Spida to tell him that he thought the chick that stayed the night with him had burnt him for the pills. Spida told him to stop slipping and laying up with bitches that still be stealing from him.

Uno said, "Folk you know I'll pay you back, jus' let me hold some 'til I come back up."

"I'll give you a full pack, but you have to let me fuck oh girl, like I been tryin' to do for the pas' few months."

"Mane, come on, it gotta be somethin' else I can do, fam."

"That's it, homie, and if you don' wanna to do that, I can' help you. You'll hafta jus' find another plug." Uno knew that he had burned every other plug, and he would not be able to cop from anyone else in the city. None would even let him spend his money with them, let alone front him. Spida was his only source.

Uno called Yuri up. "Hey, baby," Yuri answered.

"Hey, Shawty, I need you to come holla at me. You not on yo period is you?"

"No, why? Do you want some, baby? It's not like you care if I was bleeding or not," Yuri said giggling.

"Shawty, for real, I need ya to handle somn' fo' me."

"Where you at, Uno?"

"I'm at the Trap spot."

"Ok, I'm on my way."

Yuri pulled up, Spida's G Wagon was sitting in the drive way. She got out of her Benz, looking sophisticated as ever, head held up high. She knew she was bad, and no one could tell her different. She walked in the door, bringing a breath of fresh air into the house. The aroma of Creed perfume lit the whole house up. Spida breathed in her scent as his eyes lit up with lust; his tongue hung out of his mouth like a dog in heat. Uno was in the backroom and he heard Yuri come into the house. He told her to come to him. She walked in the room, and for a trap house, the bedroom was very clean and comfortable. Yuri stepped in and Uno told her to sit on the bed next to him. She sat, looking her boo straight in the face.

"What is it Uno?" Yuri asked.

"I hafta pay off this debt, and I need yo' help. I ran into a few problems and now I'm in a bind, I messed up som'n and I hafta take care of my supplier."

Yuri asked, "How much do you need, Uno? I have a few thousand just sitting at the house."

"It's not that simple Shawty. My folks won' take the money from you 'cuz he know it ain't from me."

Yuri replied, "What the hell does it matter where the money came from, as long as it's given to him? I am not understanding this at all. So what does he want you to do?"

"He wants," he hesitated. "He wants you, Shawty."

"Me? Are you fucking crazy, Uno?" Yuri yelled.

"Shhhhh, naw I'm nah crazy. It jus' my las' alternative. I love you, Yuri, an' if you love me, you do this fo' me."

"You love me, but you are giving me an indecent proposal!" She screamed. "And then it's your fat, greasy-ass supplier that we are talking about."

"Shawty, I jus' need ya to do this one time fo' me and I'll neva come at ya sideways again."

Yuri was pissed, "Hell no, I will not do that!"

Uno used reverse psychology. "WELL THEN GET THE FUCK OUT OF HERE, BITCH!" he screamed. "You don' love me, 'cuz if ya did, you would do wha' the fuck a nigga need ya to do!"

Tears streamed down Yuri's face as she walked out of the room. "Don' eva come back, Shawty, oh even pick up yo' phone to call a nigga!" Uno said.

Yuri turned around. "But I love you. Uno, don't do this to me."

"You doin' it to yo' self. If ya love me then jus' help me out dis one time, baby. Please Yuri, I'll make it up to ya, I promise."

Yuri kept her head down and agreed to sleep with Spida.

Uno exited the room and a few seconds later Spida strolled in, already erect. Yuri was disgusted just from seeing the print in his pants. She screwed a lot of strangers but never did she think that she would be sleeping with someone that the man she loved had sold her to. Spida looked at Yuri lustfully.

"Get naked, Sexy," he said, "I wanna to see yo' sexy body." Yuri hesitated, then started undressing. Once she was naked, she stood in front of Spida, feeling totally humiliated. Spida said, "Turn around and dance, bounce that ass for daddy."

Yuri growled "You are not my fucking daddy!"

"Well shake that ass, baby."

Yuri turned around and barely shook her ass. Spida was still turned on. He turned Yuri back around to face him and grabbed her perfectly round titties, then sucked on them. Yuri was sick to her stomach, feeling as if she would vomit right onto his head. Spida unbuckled his belt, unzipped his pants, and pulled them down to his ankles. Yuri looked at the small bulge and became really nauseous. His small dick barely bulged out of his boxers. Spida said, "Suck on it, baby," as he tugged and pulled on it, like it was so big.

"Hell no!" Yuri yelled, "Never will I suck on that little motherfucker! Uno said I had to fuck you, and that's all I'm doing!"

Spida prodded, "I have five hundred dollahs fo' yo' pockets, come on, girl."

Yuri replied, "I have a thousand dollars for your little dick ass, if I don't have to fuck you," as she stood there, naked.

Spida liked Yuri's slick mouth, he loved a woman that was sassy, talked the talk and walked the walk. He was totally turned on. Spida pulled a condom out of his pants pocket, he grabbed Yuri, turned her around, and tried putting his small baby dick inside of her. Yuri's pussy was as dry as a desert and would not get wet. Her pussy usually got very wet, but she just could not turn on the faucet for Spida. Spida spit on his hand, put the spit onto Yuri's clitoris, and he pushed inside of her. Yuri cried, as he hunched her over. Spida moaned and he called out her name. He called her baby, he even said, 'I love you', as he smacked her ass. He fucked as if he was in paradise.

After four-and-a-half minutes of what Spida would call 'gangsta love' came to an end, Spida came.

Yuri was so happy that it was over, she thought, 'Not only was his dick small, he came quick.' This was a great thing for her. Spida pulled the condom off, threw it in the trash, and walked out of the room, as if he was 'The Man.' The way he smiled when he walked into the front room, everyone would have thought that he did excessive damage.

Yuri put on her clothes. She ran past Uno, out of the house, saying not one word. She sped off, in tears, she was totally pissed. If there was one thing that Yuri hated, it was small dicks!

"Spida's dick takes the cake," she thought.

It had to have stopped growing when he was a toddler. Her godson Mason's dick was larger than Spida's!

Yuri went home and ran into her bathroom; she showered until there was no more hot water. Uno had been ringing her phone nonstop from the time she ran out. For the rest of the evening, she ignored all of his calls. The next day, Uno showed up at the house. He beat and beat on the door; he knew that she was home because her Benz was parked outside. The neighbor looked on as he pounded. Yuri knew that she would have to open the door, because the neighbors knew Shane, and she didn't want anyone to see Uno acting a damn fool, so she finally opened the door.

"I'm sorry, Shawty. Forgive me, please. I love you, Yuri, and I needs ya in my life." He kissed her neck. When that didn't work, he started taking off her clothes.

"Stop, Uno! I am not in the mood for your bullshit!" Yuri screamed.

"But I want you, Shawty." Uno pulled up Yuri's gown and pushed her onto the couch as he spread her legs open. Yuri automatically became wet, because Uno made her have a waterfall all the time. No one could get her pussy wet like Uno, not even Shane.

Uno sucked on her pearl and did his famous buzz, with his tongue hitting against her clit. Uno ate Yuri like she was breakfast, lunch and dinner. After making her cum twice with his tongue, he then pleasured her with all of his love. Yuri could fuck Uno's over-sized penis all day and night, riding doggy-style, sideways, on the couch, on the table, on the bed, on the floor, it didn't matter, as long as he was sexing her.

Chapter 25

Yuri had started getting blocked calls, someone had been playing on her phone all week; she wondered if it was Candice. She even wondered if it was Uno, because they had not been all that into each other since the incident with Spida. Uno had been real messy lately. He even let one of those sorry-ass skanks he messed with get her number out of his phone. He probably was on those pills or had come down off of a high. When he came off of a high, he would sleep for a whole day. Whatever the reason, the chick had Yuri's number.

Yuri was watching her back, because just a few days ago, she had been awakened by screeching tires driving off crazy. She ran downstairs and opened the door, to see if she could catch what kind of car was going down the street. She looked down, and there was a pretty peach and brown box, sitting on the steps.

Yuri looked around and thought, "Maybe it was Shane, and he doesn't want me to know he's in town yet."

Instead of taking the box into the house, Yuri opened it right where it sat. Once the box was opened, she moved the soft wrapping paper and jumped back, almost falling over the rail. The rattle snake's head came out, hissing at her fiercely. Yuri snatched her hand back, scared to death! She hated snakes, and now someone was messing with her, using a snake! Who would do this, she wondered? She kicked the box into the grass and watched the snake rattle away, looking slimy and scandalous. The only person that she could think of now was Candice, because she had called her a snake on a couple of different occasions. She thought, 'Candice doesn't even know where I live', but it wouldn't be hard to find, and Yuri's car always stayed on the street.

That was the only defect about the townhome, was that Yuri did not have a garage. There was no private parking anywhere. Uno's boy, Spida, had seen Yuri leaving and stopped, only to get called every version of little dick mutherfucker that she could possibly come up with. It could have been him stalking her since he had got the pussy. Yuri knew that she also slept with the woman down the street's sexy husband, and had gotten caught. Yuri had snaked out so many people, she didn't know who to blame. Her conscience said, 'Bitch you are a snake, and someone is going to give you a taste of your own medicine!' Yuri shook the thought out of her mind. She knew that she had to keep a closer look on her surroundings.

Yuri had fallen all the way in love with Uno. He was back up grinding with his 'Crown Royal' bag of money. She was the bread winner and he saved his hustling money and lived off Yuri's money. When he finally reached ten thousand dollars, he thought he was rich. He wanted more.

He went to Yuri and told her, "Look, Shawty, I ain' gonna lie to ya, but my goons been followin' ya man when he in town. They know when he go to the bank an' drop his paper off and all!"

Yuri begged, "Uno leave Shane alone, he's a good person."

He rebutted, "All you gotta do is let us know when he's takin' his cash to the bank, and I'll take care a the res'. I'm only gonna get one lick, an' I won' botha him no mo'."

Yuri said, "I can't do that, he's my fiancé."

Uno replied, "You don' even love tha' nigga, an' if you don'wan' tha' nigga hurt an' kilt, you'll let me get tha money the easy way."

Yuri begged, "Uno most of his money be checks. The most cash he ever deposits is fifteen to eighteen thousand, from the rent he receives at his apartment building, on the third of the month."

Uno continued, "Oh, I know 'bout tha' buildin' on North Avenue tha' he rent out. The rent ova tha' is high and a lot of 'em in dare's D-boys. So I also know they is payin' cash. Tha's why I said tha' price."

"Uno, that's some petty shit. Why would you rob someone for a few thousand dollars?"

Uno asked, "So ya gonna tell 'im 'bout me afta ya been fuckin' me fo' damn nea six months? Wha' he gonna say bout tha' when I tell 'im I cum in ya every night when he in L.A., an' he still wearin' rubbers? When I tell 'im every detail abou' where we fuck in da townhome he bought fo' ya. How I walk 'round puttin' my nut stains agains' tha' thick, big blue robe a his afta I fuck ya on tha' new shit he bought ya?"

"Uno, you're not playing fair," Yuri said, with her voice trembling.

"Bitch, ya neva have playt fair, so who he gonna believe, you or me? I'm jus' sayin' Shawty, lemme get 'im one time. I'm not gonna hurt 'im. I'm jus' gonna take da cash. I won' even carry a gun. He can keep his money orders an' checks. I jus'wan' the cash, I promise, baby. I won' hurt him or you. I love ya, Shawty. Put it dis way, I din't hafta tell ya 'bout us followin' 'im."

"Uno, do whatever, just don't hurt him. He is a good person."

Yuri thought next month she would have to let Shane or Uno go. The ten or twenty thousand that Uno wanted to take from Shane was like millions to him. That would be her good-bye present to Uno, if she left. Shane had already told her that in October he would be in Georgia for good, and not travel to L.A. anymore. She decided that she would tell Uno the best time to rob Shane would be October 3rd. Shane would be picking up rent and dropping it off to the bank. She thought this would stop Uno from blackmailing or snitching her out.

School had started and Yuri kept her mind on her books. She prayed that Uno would just die, or disappear, although she loved him. Uno had gotten out of hand. The ten thousand dollars made him turn into the devil for money was the root of all evil. Uno wanted more and he wanted it fast. Uno made sure that he sexed Yuri down, every time, slurping up all of her juices. Every time they sexed, he made Yuri feel alive and loved. He had her mind play tricks on her.

Chapter 26

Yuri had not spoken to Chanel in over a month. If she was not working at Saks, she was at school. Chanel was working on her bachelor's degree and nothing could stop her. Chance was doing the same when he killed himself. Yuri called Chanel,

"Hello Yuri," Chanel said cautiously.

"Hey, Chanel, how are things going?"

"Ok, I guess, I'm as good as I'll get," Chanel said curtly.

"What's wrong, Chanel?" Yuri questioned.

"I've just been cleaning out Chance's things, and…" she paused. "It's hard, difficult and confusing. I'm just trying to connect the dots. It's not making any sense, Yuri."

"Well, Chanel, only God knows, so don't tear yourself down, because you'll only breakdown."

"Like I want to breakdown someone about my brother," Chanel said with anger. "Look, I gotta go, I'll talk to you another time."

"Bye Cha…" as she hung up on Yuri.

Yuri walked outside, and it was a pleasant October morning. She left early for school so she could get her usual morning Starbucks' cake and cappuccino.

As she approached her car she noticed the long scratch that read, "Snake Bitch." She was pissed as she went to the driver side to get an assessment on the scratch and noticed that both tires were slashed. Yuri looked down the street for the vandal. As she watched, her neighbor whose man she had seduced on the porch was smiling devilishly.

Yuri screamed, "Bitch, let me find out that you did this to my car, I will beat your ass!"

The neighbor retorted, "Bitch, fuck you and your car. I see that I'm not the only enemy that you have!" She laughed and turned to go into her house.

Yuri stormed back into the house to call AAA. There would be no school today. Yuri spent the day at the repair shop. She called Shane to tell him about the tires, but wouldn't dare tell him about the paint. Not to raise any suspicions about her enemies, she offered the shop owner five hundred dollars extra to sand and paint the car the same day. She was desperate to get the car back quickly, because Shane would be back in town by the end of the week. She had to make sure he didn't see the "Snake Bitch" that someone had scratched into her paint. She knew that this would raise too many unwanted questions.

Yuri wanted to know who was taunting her. As she sat in the small waiting room at the auto shop, she thought about the choice she would have to make between Shane and Uno. She knew that she could make a life with Shane and that he really loved her. Uno, on the other hand, was a bad boy but she thought that she could eventually smooth out the rough edges. Besides that, she loved his big dick. He could make her body respond in ways that it never had before. As she was lost in her fantasy life with Uno, the phone rang to bring her back into a cold reality. "Hell....?" Yuri cautiously answered the phone.

"Hey, Shawty, ya ready ta do dis?" Uno asked her, excited about his plan to come up.

"Uno, baby, this is a really fucked up idea. I feel terrible about doing this to Shane. He is such a good person. Can't we figure…"

Uno cut her off, "Yuri, if ya really love a nigga like ya said, you'll do dis fo' yo' man."

"Uno, you know that I love you but there is some other shit going on in my life too. Please don't ask me to do this to Shane." She lowered her voice and walked outside to talk more privately. "I know I don't feel the same way about him that I do you but he has taken care of me. I don't want anything to happen to him. He is a good person. I don't want him hurt…."

Uno cut her off again, "Ya don' love tha' nigga do ya? Bitch, ya jus' love tha' cash he kick ya down wit. Tha' nigga ain' shit. No real mofo would let his bitch be home so much alone. Come on gurl, tha' nigga probly got some chick he stickin' in Cali. Tha's why his punk-ass always outta town."

"You are wrong! Shane would never do that." Yuri sounded confident on the phone.

"Shawty, ya don' know wha' tha mofo be doin' when he gon. Look, ya gonna give me tha' shit fo' Friday or am I gonna hafta fuck it outta ya? Cuz ya know I can. Besides I know tha' man's routine. Wit or wit'out ya, I'm gonna hit 'im on Friday, at the apartments bafore he go to da bank."

"Look Uno, I have a better idea, he has a house in Fayetteville. How about I make him take me there for dinner and you could pretend it was a home invasion robbery. He has a safe and I know that he'll have more money there, since he will be just coming back into town on Friday. He'll have to go around and collect all the rents from the other properties, as well, and won't be able to get to the bank until Saturday."

Uno became interested in the new plan, since it meant more cash.

Uno said, "Yeah? Go on, this is da kinda of shit I like. A gurl tha' kin think like a nigga."

Yuri continued formulating her new plan, "When we get there, I'll call you and pretend you're my girlfriend, Chanel. Just be ready for the call, and you can slip into the garage before he closes it. Shane is a stickler about keeping his cars in the garage. When we go into the house, you can come in and pretend to hold us both up. That way it will look more real, and I can't be implicated."

Uno smiled on the other end of the phone, "I like dis plan. I may hafta fuck the shit outta ya tonight, Shawty. Ya gonna let me git up in dat shit tonight?"

"Yeah, I might," Yuri responded softly. "But you gotta promise not to hurt Shane."

Uno replied, "Yeah aight, whatever. Where ya at now?"

"At the auto repair shop, getting new tires and a new paint job."

"Paint job? Yo ass wasn' in no accident?"

"No, some dumb muthafucka thought that it would be funny to slash my tires and write 'Snake Bitch' on my Benz."

"Oh snap, tha's fucked up."

"Yeah, and if I find the bitch, that's what I'm gonna do, fuck her up!"

"Yo Shawty, ya say 'her'; how ya know it's another female?"

"It's probably some dumb bitch, whose man I fucked. I can think of a few jealous chicks."

"Yeah right, I know ya dun some scandalous shit, but tha's how I like my chicks, down an' dirty. So it sound like ya need someone to fuck ya real good tonight so ya kin relax an' handle yo' business. Fortunately, I'm da nigga fo' da job."

"Yeah, that's right Uno. I'm sure you can make me forget my worries. I'll call you when I get home."

"Lata, Shawty," Uno hung up the phone. A second later the phone rang again.

Yuri answered, "Damn, you can't wait?"

"Huh?" Chanel said, confused, "Yuri, this is Chanel."

"Oh I'm sorry; I thought you were someone else." Yuri played off the mistake.

"Shane, I hope, talking like that." I called because I know the last time we spoke I was kind of short with you. I'm sorry, but I had a lot on my mind. I've been in D.C. for a few days, going through Chance's stuff," Chanel paused, "Well, I really need a break. I am thinking of coming down to Atlanta this weekend, and I was hoping I could stay with you. I booked a flight for Friday evening."

"Oh, Chanel, you're my best friend, of course you can stay. I have plenty of room. You know Shane bought this big-ass townhouse. He'll be coming home on Friday, so I can stay with him and you can get some rest."

Chanel hesitated, "Do you mind picking me up from the airport, also? If it's inconvenient, I can take a cab. I don't want it to be a hassle. I'll only be in town until next Tuesday. I have to be back here for class and work."

"Of course I'll pick you up, and it's really no trouble. See you on Friday."

"Thanks Yuri, I'm happy you're okay with it."

"Bye, Chanel," and as Yuri hung up the phone she remembered that Uno wanted to hit the house on Friday. 'Fuck', Yuri thought, 'how am I gonna do this? Chanel may complicate the situation, so I may need to call Uno back.' As she was distracted by the potential problems of Friday's events, the manager from the auto shop came outside.

"Ms. Jones, your car is ready and looks brand new. The scratch wasn't through the paint, so we were able to buff it out."

Yuri thought, 'Damn, that was an expensive buff job, but fuck it, as long as Shane won't be asking questions. This was too close for comfort. I have got to be more careful.'

Yuri dragged herself through the door and looked at the answering machine for any messages. The light blinking was unusual, because everyone called her on her cell. She went to the machine and pressed play. "Bitch, I'm going to fuck you up and make your life a living hell, like you made mine. Snake bitch, I hope you liked your present."

Yuri's conscience went into high gear. She wondered who could be taunting her. The voice was a computer generated voice. She couldn't tell if the caller was even male or female.

"Fuck," she screamed.

A moment of panic ran through her until she looked at the time and realized that within an hour Uno would be there to blow her back out. The problem of the answering machine's message seemed like the least of her problems.

An hour later, relief came as Uno was at the door with his sexy swag. She knew that Friday would mean that she had chosen Uno over Shane. She hoped that decision wouldn't come back to haunt her. As she pulled him through the doorway, she began kissing him deeply. He was a little shocked at her response to him, but he figured that she had chosen him over ol' boy. He knew that the night was on and poppin'. He slammed her down on the floor, stripped her, and began to eat her out like she had never been eaten before.

As she tried to squirm, to get away from cumming too quickly, Uno said, "Dis is how ya like it, baby."

Yuri couldn't keep her desire for him secret. She moaned and licked her lips as her body went straight to heaven. He shoved his fingers into her wet pussy.

"Yeah, Shawty, ya ready."

He pulled down his pants and boxers and led her to the couch and made her get on her knees. She caressed his big dick and began to suck. She felt power when she made a man moan and say her name. Uno was feeling her rhythm and then made her get up and lean over the back of the couch. With one hand on her ass, and the other on his dick, he pushed it gently into her wet pussy. When

141

he was entirely inside, he began to fuck her, slowly at first. He knew that this would drive her crazy. Yuri liked it rough, and wanted only big dick niggas inside of her.

What Yuri didn't know, was that Uno had taken some X, and he was gonna be up in her pussy all night. He had to sex her in a way that she would be completely loyal to him. He had figured out her weakness, and he was definitely her kryptonite. Yuri had fallen for Uno because of his dick game and his swag. She tried to show him the finer things of life that she experienced with Shane. However, it was the grimy part of Uno that attracted her, like a moth to a flame. He kept her off-balanced. She knew that he could be her downfall. He was the only man she couldn't control with her body. What scared her even more was that he knew this as well. The night continued with wild animal sex, and when both of them were spent, they laid together in her bed.

"Uno, you love me?" Yuri asked softly.

"Ya know me, Shawty." Uno said, without admitting any feelings. "So ya gonna do dis 'ome invasion shit on Friday? I got my end set up, I jus' need da address an' da call."

"Yeah I know but please don't hurt Shane," Yuri pleaded.

Yuri woke up the next morning when the sun peaked through the curtains in her bedroom. She turned, expecting Uno to still be in her bed, but he wasn't there. When she got up and went through the house, she realized he was gone and had collected all his stuff as well. He was like a fucking ghost. She sighed, because she wanted to fuck again. She looked down at her cell phone, sitting on the kitchen counter, as she went to get some coffee. TWO MISSED CALLS on the screen of the phone. She decided to see if Shane had left her a message.

"Hey, Lil' Momma, I know you miss me. I need you to make a run today, before I get home. Could you go over to the apartment this morning and pick up an envelope from my manager? I need to get the money in the bank Monday. I'm not sure if I'll have time to spend the weekend with you, because I have to get back to Cali on Tuesday for a meeting."

Yuri stood there smiling as she listened to the message.

"Beep...'Snake bitch'...Click." Yuri was becoming unnerved by her stalker. She started to make a mental list of who this mystery caller could be.

The phone rang as she held it. It startled her, so she answered tentatively, "Hello?"

"Hey, Lil' Momma, you alright?" Shane asked.

"Yes, baby, now that you're talking to me. I miss you so much. I thought that I would make dinner for you on Friday when you come home."

"That's nice, but I kinda wanted to go straight home from the airport. We could get breakfast on Saturday morning."

142

"Uh," Yuri stuttered, "How about I come to your house and bring dinner? That way we can both relax. I'll pick up the envelope you want, from the manager at the apartment, and bring it when I come."

"Oh, I forgot I asked you to do that. Are you sure it's not a problem? I'm not sure if I can get back to put the money in the bank before five. I'll put it in the safe until Monday."

"Shane, I don't mind at all."

"Just be careful, Yuri. That is not the greatest of neighborhood and it's a lot of cash."

"Shane, quit worrying. I'll be fine. I'm just going to the front office to get the deposit. What can happen? I'll be cautious and careful. I love you and I miss you."

"I love you, too, Lil' Momma. I'll see you tomorrow night." Shane hung up the phone.

Yuri looked at the cell screen and noticed the time, 7:59am.

"Shit, I gotta go to class. I'm almost late." She ran to the bathroom for a quick shower and got ready to go. As she walked out the door, she thought about how yesterday morning started, and prayed it would be a better day.

As Yuri drove to school she was preoccupied with the upcoming events of Friday. She continued to have uneasy feelings about whether or not she should set Shane up, to let Uno rob him. She was almost remorseful about the whole plan until she thought about Uno, and the sex last night. She also had a flash-back about what Uno said about Shane being in Cali so often. Shit, he was just coming home tomorrow, and had to go back next week. She made it to class and sat with a million ideas running through her head listening to the professor. She knew Shane was serious about her, but did he really trust her? He had never really confided in her about the nature of his business dealings in California. She thought about the possibility of another woman with Shane. She also thought about whether or not Uno really loved her, or was just using her. Her thoughts returned to the time that he used her to fuck off a debt with Spida. She began to get madder as she remembered that time. Then she started to think about the mystery caller, the person taunting her. She had done so much to so many. She couldn't begin to think about whom the person was and what they wanted to do to her.

"Fuck it, and get in line," she said out loud in the class.

"Excuse me, Ms. Jones, did you say something?" Professor Daniel asked.

"Oh, I'm sorry, I was just thinking about my car..." Yuri got up to leave. "I'm sorry. I just had a very bad day yesterday. I guess I'm a little preoccupied."

"You may go, Ms. Jones. There is no class tomorrow so I'll see you on Monday."

That morning, Yuri woke up in a cold sweat. She looked at the clock on the table next to the bed. It was only 7am but nonetheless, she had a sense of dread about the upcoming events of the night. She decided to call Chanel to see what time her plane would arrive that evening.

"Hey, Chanel, it's Yuri. I was just checking to see what time your plane was coming in."

"Hi, Yuri, I think my plane gets in around 9:30pm. If you can pick me up around 10pm that would be great."

Yuri thought that sounded perfect. It would give her enough time to get there with the money and have him open the safe for the robbery. This way she would even have an excuse to leave, and Uno could hit the place when she was nowhere around.

"Yuri, if that's a problem, I can take a cab," Chanel interjected, interrupting Yuri's thoughts about her plans for the evening.

"Huh, I, no Chanel, I will be there to pick you up at ten. There's no problem. I'm looking forward to seeing you tonight."

"Thanks girl. I gotta pack now. See you at 10pm tonight."

As Yuri laid in the bed, she tried to go over the events of the last few days in her mind. She knew that this robbery was wrong, but she had to prove her love to Uno. She began to believe that maybe all these trips to Cali that Shane made were to see another woman. As that seed of doubt began to grow, the callous and cold-blooded side of Yuri started to awaken. She wondered why he was going to Cali two to three times a month. Until now, she never thought about it because it was her time, when he was away, to do whatever. His time away meant she could spend hers with Uno. However, now she was more curious about the trips. She also knew that he came home with a lot of money after each trip. She remembered that once she saw him open his suitcase after a trip and there was at least sixty thousand dollars in cash in the corner of the suitcase. She hadn't felt comfortable about asking about it so she had just left it alone. Whenever she asked about what type of business he was in, he was always vague and just said 'real estate.' Shane never talked about his family or his friends. It seemed that she knew nothing about him. He knew things about her that she had told him when they were making love. He was definitely her knight in shining armor. She began to wonder how she could do this to him. He had been nothing but kind and generous to her. Her conscience had a way of showing up at unwanted times.

But as much as she cared about Shane, she was really in love with Uno. He was the type of dude that she could not control or manipulate. He knew her game, and he wouldn't fall. It was a challenge for her with Uno. She didn't know if he loved her, but she sure knew that he was sexing her the way she liked and her body responded automatically to Uno. She was also captive to his thug side. She could tell he was rough, but not deep into the game, and that made him less dangerous. She began to dream about Uno as she dozed off to sleep again. Her dream was interrupted by the phone ringing.

"Hey, Lil' Momma, how are you doing?" Shane said on the phone. "You miss me yet?"

"Of course, I miss you, baby," Yuri said, as her body had an involuntary reaction to the thought of Uno. "I can't wait until you get here tonight."

"I can't wait to see you either, Lil' Momma." Shane hung up. He called right back, "Hey, Lil' Momma, I forgot to tell you that the deposit is waiting for you to pick up at the apartment building. Mr. Neese is the manager, just go and ask for him. I'll get the money from you tonight."

Yuri was curious, "How much is it?"

"It's about twenty or thirty grand."

"Wow that is a lot of money, you sure it's safe?"

"Yeah, just look around before you go into the building and then go straight home."

"You know that would make a great shopping spree," Yuri joked.

"No shopping," Shane rebuffed. "Home. I'll take you shopping if you want to go." Shane laughed, "I'm sure that my credit cards have a much higher limit. This money is for my business."

Yuri secretly smiled, "So what exactly is your business?"

Shane replied, "Well, real estate, of course. I can't tell you that much on the phone."

"Why?"

"You never know who might be listening. Why are you so interested in knowing about my business?"

"I don't know, maybe I need to get into the business as well," Yuri laughed.

"Trust me, the money is good but it is not easy being me," Shane had a serious tone, "Look, I just wanted to remind you about the pickup. I have to get ready for my meeting this morning. I am meeting clients at 7am."

Yuri looked at the clock, forgetting Shane was in California. "It's 8:30am."

"So I have an hour and a half. I better get a move on. I'll see you this evening."

"I love you, Shane."

"I love you too, Lil' Momma." Yuri hung up, and five minutes later the phone rang again.

"Shane, if you don't stop calling, you're gonna miss your meeting." There was a pause at the other end.

"Snake Bitch," and the phone disconnected.

All of a sudden, a cold chill covered her. She realized that the caller was going to continue to taunt her until there was a more serious threat. Yuri was scared, but what was she going to do? She has no idea who this person was. She couldn't go to the police. What would she say? I made some bitch mad because I fucked her boyfriend. She knew that eventually she'd have to face the person, and she would deal with them at that point. Right now, she had to get the money for Shane. This would eventually be the money that Uno would get. She thought for a moment about just handing the money over to Uno and not going through with the silly home invasion plot. Then she began to wonder how much more money was in the safe. Yuri's greed took over. She wanted all the money.

Later that evening, Yuri began to primp and prep. She wanted to be irresistible to both Shane and Uno. She knew that she would be fucking one, if not both of them that night. She put the money in the center console of the Benz when she picked up the cash earlier. She was wearing a short black dress that was fitted to her body. The five inch Giuseppes stilettos reminded her of the dancers at the clubs. She would privately strip for Shane and Uno later on. She got wet just thinking about it. She wondered what it would be like to have a threesome with the two men she loved. This thought excited her even more. She decided that she would go without panties to Shane's house, so she could get a quickie in before she left for the airport. Shit, the airport!" She thought about what the Virgin Mary, Chanel, would think if she knew, and decided that panties must go into her purse.

It was 8:30pm when she arrived outside Shane's house. The traffic was light for a weekend in Atlanta. She saw the light on downstairs and knew that Uno was close behind. She called him before she left, verified the plan and told him that Chanel coming in tonight would give her an alibi. She asked him to call her at nine, so she could pretend in front of Shane that she had to go. Then, as she went out of the garage, Uno could come in and hide. He would go in and rob Shane after he went to the safe. Yuri said that she would distract him enough that he wouldn't close the safe. There would definitely be no struggle. She wanted to make sure that Shane didn't get hurt. She knew that she had to string both of them along as long as possible. She couldn't give up either one. Shane had the money, and Uno had the sex. This was the best of both worlds and she wanted to protect it. Yuri dialed Uno once more.

"Are you near, I'm going in now."

"Yeah, Shawty, I see tha' Benzo. I'm gonna call ya in 20 minutes. Tha' way ya kin be sho tha' nigga got tha' safe open. Once ya outta there we'll go in. Ya think ya kin handle yo' biz in twenty?"

"I don't know, but I'm sure as hell gonna try. You know, it's not like fucking you, Uno. You have my body so trained, it only takes me five minutes to cum with you."

"Well, Shawty, ya do this fo' daddy an' I'll have a big 'prise fo' yo' ass tonight." Yuri got wet just thinking about the idea of fucking both of them, again.

She got out of her car and adjusted her dress. Knowing that she had on no panties had her a little self-conscious. She saw Shane standing at the front door, smiling. He was in for the night. He was wearing a pair of flannel plaid pajama bottoms and no shirt. His sexy abs were the first thing she noticed about Shane. She thought about how she was going to be sore tomorrow, because she was gonna fuck both of her niggas tonight.

Uno watched her from the street as the door closed. Uno stealthily moved to the side of the garage, and patiently waited for the mark to be alone.

After twenty minutes, he called, time's up, Shawty. My turn to fuck wit tha' nigga's money."

Yuri made her excuses to Shane for the abrupt departure, explaining that she forgot Chanel was coming into town.

She walked hurriedly out of the garage below and yelled back "Just close the garage door."

She saw Uno slip in on the other side of the car and crouch down, out of sight. By the time she got to the car, the garage door was going down. Her heart fell as the door closed. There was no turning back. She just hoped that Shane would give up the money with no problems. The safe was still unlocked when she went out. She didn't give him enough time to close it. It looked like he had a million dollars in there. She knew that it wasn't that much, but to her surprise, he had lots of cash, a few gold bars, and some jewelry. She hoped that Uno would know to clean out the entire safe, and not just the cash.

She went home and quickly showered. It was ten minutes to ten. She had to pick Chanel up in a few. Thank God the traffic was light and she was close to the airport. The only trace of her evening with Shane was her smudged makeup, and the nervousness she felt knowing that Uno was robbing him. As she made it around to the Jet Blue terminal to pick up Chanel her phone rang.

"Hello, I'm almost to the terminal. I see you now."

As Yuri saw Chanel waiting, she tried to maneuver through the cars. The voice on the phone was a man's voice.

"Yuri, I need ta see ya." Yuri, recognized the voice as Uno's but he sounded panicked.

"What happened Uno? What's wrong?" Yuri was panicking, too.

"Look, Shawty, I need ya ta come ta my crib, NOW!" As he said that, Chanel was opening the car door and motioning for Yuri to pop the trunk for her bag.

"Listen, I can't talk now. I'll call you back when I get to the house."

"Bitch, don' hang up." Uno screamed into the phone, as she disconnected.

"Hey, girl" Chanel said as she kissed Yuri on the cheek, getting into the car.

"Hey Chanel," Yuri quietly replied, as her stomach churned, thinking about what the problem Uno may have had while he robbed Shane could be. "What's wrong Yuri, you look like you're worried about something."

"It's nothing, Shane just got back in town and I wasn't able to spend a lot of time with him. He's always gone."

"I'm so sorry, Yuri, if I ruined your evening with Shane. Why didn't you tell me, I could have taken a cab from the airport and waited for you to come home. Why don't you get dressed up and

147

go back over there, when you take me to the house. That way you two can have a night cap," Chanel said with a devilish grin. "I won't expect you until morning." She winked at Yuri.

Yuri smiled and thought maybe that was the way she could get away to meet Uno. "Okay, you don't mind though?"

"Of course not! You deserve a night with your man." They pulled up in front of the townhouse and Chanel got her bag out of the trunk. Carrying a small rolling bag and a laptop case she walked into the house. "I like what you've done to the place, Yuri."

"Yeah, I'm trying to make it my home. I just wish Shane were here in town more so that he could spend time here, as well."

"Shane's a good dude Yuri. Don't go overstepping your boundaries. I'm sure there is a good reason for him to spend his time in Cali. Didn't you say he was in business out there?"

"He says he has a few clients that are very selective about what type of real estate they want, and where they want to live. He used to live there and still has a lot of connections."

"Hey, look Yuri, I'm fine, and I'll get familiar with everything here. You go over to be with your man. Call him when you're on your way. Don't worry about me. I'm tired from the flight, so I'm just going to bed."

Yuri got back into the car after quickly freshening up. She called Uno. The phone went straight to voicemail. Then she tried to call Shane. His phone rang and went to voicemail, too.

She called Uno's phone four more times, and the last time she left a message, "Shit, Uno, what is going on? Why are you doing this to me? Answer the fucking phone. I'm on my way there, to your spot."

She tried Shane's phone one more time. There was a male voice that answered but it was not Shane's.

"Hello?" The officer on the scene answered the phone.

"Hello, who is this, where is Shane?" Yuri's voice was panicked. She knew that something went wrong with the robbery.

"Mam please calm down. May I ask, to who am I speaking with?" said the officer.

Yuri replied "who is this?"

"I'm Detective Wallace." "I am with the Fayetteville Police Department".

Now Yuri was petrified, she started to cry feeling sorrowful. "Please tell me what happened!" He coaxed expertly, "Are you a family member?"

"I'm his fiancée, Sir. Please tell me what happened!"

"Maam all I can tell you is he has been transferred to Grady Memorial."

"Hospital!" Yuri shrieked, "What happened to him? Is he hurt? Please don't tell me he's dead. I'm his fiancée!" Yuri began to sob uncontrollably and pulled over to the side of the road.

The officer tried to comfort her, and told her that he had been shot in a robbery that evening. "When was the last time you saw Mr. Mitchell, ma'am?"

"Uh, I was coming over to see him now," Yuri lied, omitting that she just came from his house a few hours ago.

She didn't want the suspicion pointed at her. The officer asked her to meet him at the hospital, to take her statement, and fill her in as to what happened.

Yuri made it to the hospital lot in record time. She was amazed that she hadn't gotten a ticket, as she sped through the streets of Atlanta. She bolted to the paramedic entrance, right behind a gurney carrying a gunshot victim. She was trying to peek, to make sure that it wasn't Shane under those sheets. The man being wheeled in was the same size as her man. She couldn't see the face because it was covered in blood. As she tried to compose herself and keep from throwing up, a small middle-aged black woman in scrubs came up to her, and prevented her from going further into the inner portion of the ER.

"May I help you ma'am?" the nurse asked as she positioned herself in front of Yuri.

"I'm looking for my boy…my husband. He was shot this evening and the…"

"Name?" the woman abruptly cut her off.

"Yuri Jones," she said quietly. The nurse looked over the top of her glasses. "Your husband's name is Yuri Jones?" She quickly looked at the board behind the desk, "We don't have a Yuri…"

Yuri cut her off, "I'm sorry, his name is Shane, Shane Mitchell; my name is Yuri Jones."

"Oh, I see…" She glanced at the board again. "I see here he's in surgery. You'll have to wait over there until the doctor comes out. He can give you more information. You can have a seat."

The woman pointed to an overcrowded waiting room. It was a typical county facility, too many people, too little staff. Yuri thanked the nurse and went to sit in a corner, to avoid the crowd of people. She got a can of coke and a bag of potato chips.

A man dressed in uniform approached her. She assumed that it was the Detective that she had spoken to on the phone earlier that evening.

"Hello, I'm Detective Alberto Ramos, I was sent here to wait for you, Ms. Jones. My partner, Detective Wallace, was the one you spoke with on the phone."

"Hi Detective," Yuri tried to look calm, but it was a futile attempt. She was upset and intrigued by the Detective. He was about 28-30 years old with an olive complexion. He had dark brown eyes and jet black hair. He was about six feet tall with a muscular build. She could see by how the uniform fit that he might be worth checking out later. But now she had to concentrate and keep her cool.

"You can call me Yuri." She smiled and almost blushed.

Detective Ramos motioned for her to sit, as he took a seat next to her.

"I'm sorry about your boyfriend. He was shot twice; once in the stomach and the second time, I think, was near the neck or head. I'm amazed that he's still alive. There was a lot of blood at the scene."

Yuri was shocked and began to cry. "Oh my God, I didn't know that it was that bad! When the nurse said he was in surgery, I assumed it was not too bad."

The detective continued to give her details of the robbery, and asked her questions. She pretended not to know the answers, since she told them that she wasn't at the scene. She tried to sound shocked at the details. She was distracted by Detective Ramos's dark brown eyes. She thought about what it would be like if he handcuffed her and took her in the back of his car. Trying not to flirt too much, Yuri tried to mix crying with concern. The only real emotion that she could muster was guilt.

She was anxious to talk to Uno and find out what the fuck happened after she left Shane's house. She continued to look at the door, expecting the doctor to emerge and give an update on Shane's condition. She saw Spida come through the waiting-room door. He was wearing a devious grin and looked her dead in the eyes, looking at her like 'I know your secret, bitch.' Spida sat across the room and watched her. She tried not to blurt out the wrong thing, but the unspoken hate between them was unnerving. Detective Ramos turned around to look at Spida, then decided to go over and talk to the nurse again, to get an estimate of how much time it would be before he could question Shane directly. As the detective left, Spida got up and walked over to Yuri.

Before she could get a word out, he grabbed her by the arm and said, "We needa take dis outside."

"What the fuck are you talking about?" Yuri raised her voice and became indignant.

"I think ya betta lowa' yo' voice befo' ya go ta jail," Spida taunted her. He pulled her up and snatched her outside. As he cornered her, "Look, yo' little boyfriend ain' as squeaky clean as ya think."

"Who, Uno?" Yuri retorted, "Don't you think I know that..."

Spida interrupted, "No, bitch, Shane."

Yuri Became upset about the way she was being spoken to and burst out, "You don't even know Shane! He's way cleaner than you, muthafucka. Besides, you haven't told me why you're here?"

"Shane, of course; that's my fam."

150

"What are you talking about? You don't even know Shane."

"Ya dumb ass bitch, he my cuz. Din't he eva talk 'bout me?" He looked ashamed, "He din't tell ya tha' he had a cuz here in Atlanta?"

Yuri looked puzzled because she didn't remember Shane really talking about any family.

"Yeah", Spida nodded, "I know both a the niggas ya fuckin'." He looked down at her breasts and fondled them. "Ya gonna have a third nigga to fuck if ya wanna keep tha' pretty little ass outta jail."

Yuri tried to act dumb.

"Don' gimme that dumb shit, Baby, I gotcha dead right. Jus' think of it as insurance. Ya know. Ya fuck me an' I'll insure tha' I don' tell my poor ol' stupid cuz 'bout his girl, or turn yo' dumb ass punk boy-toy into da police. I'm sure I could think of a few things we could do." He grabbed her crotch. "I want some more a this sweet pussy, like I had las' time."

Yuri doubled over, sick, and started to have dry heaves. She couldn't even imagine having to fuck Spida again. The last time she did it as a favor to pay a debt for Uno. This time, she would have to do it to save her own ass. "When do we have to…"

"Anxious to git down, I like dat; don' worry, baby, we'll have plenty a time. Now give yo' Spida-man a kiss." He forced himself on her. She was resistant and stiff at first, then became limp in his arms. She knew that this was something she had to do.

She heard people coming over to where they were standing. She broke away from Spida's embrace. Detective Ramos had just come out of the doors and didn't see Spida kiss Yuri. He walked over to the two of them standing there.

"You must be Mr. Mitchell," holding out his hand to shake Spida's hand. "We spoke on the phone. Like I told Ms. Jones, I mean Yuri, Mr. Mitchell is still in surgery, and the word from the OR is that he is comatose, as well."

Yuri began to sob, both happy that Spida couldn't tell Shane about Uno, and sad that her man was comatose. She still didn't know what happened at the house. She needed to get away from both of them to call Uno. She excused herself from in front of both men.

"I need to call my girlfriend, Chanel, to come here and wait with me."

The men both nodded and she walked over to her car, in the lot, to have some privacy. The first number she dialed was Uno's cell. As it was ringing, she got impatient and angry. It went to voice mail. She hit the end button and tried to call 5 more times. Each time ringing and going to voicemail. On the seventh call she left a brief message to call her back.

She hit the steering wheel of the car, "Fuck! Where the fuck is Uno?"

151

She decided to call Chanel. "Hey, girl," Yuri was choked up. "I'm sorry it's so late, but I need you to come to the hospital."

"Hospital?" Chanel screamed in the phone, "What happened, are you okay? Is Shane…"

Yuri cut her off and gave her the one -minute version of what happened, minus the information about Spida. "I need you to come and sit with me. He is supposed to be out of surgery in another hour. I just want to see him. Then we can go home."

"I don't have a car, though. Is it far? I'll take a cab and I'll drive us home."

"I'm sorry that this is such a hassle. Thanks for being a great friend." Yuri paused, "I wish I was a good friend…" she stopped. "Just hurry up, please. I don't want to be here alone."

"I'll be there for Shane and you."

Forty-five minutes later, Chanel came through the ER door and saw Yuri alone in the corner. There were detectives at the front desk but she knew that it was Friday night at the county.

"Chanel," Yuri cried, and got up to hug her when she saw her come through the door. "Thank you for coming. I'm going out of my mind waiting for the doctor to come out. They came to the door ten minutes ago and told me he was going into recovery and the surgeon would be out in a minute to talk." Yuri choked back tears, "It feels like I've been here an eternity."

Chanel hugged her and walked her back over to the corner of the waiting room. "I know. This is what we felt like when Chance killed himself. Waiting for the news was the most difficult part."

"Oh Chanel, I'm sorry. It hasn't been that long." Yuri said hugging her friend. Spida walked over to the two of them. "He's out of surgery," Yuri said coldly to him, and cut her eyes.

"I know." Spida turned to Chanel and in a charming voice, "Hi, I'm Samuel, Shane's cousin. He was right about you. You are very pretty." Chanel blushed and Yuri cut her eyes at him.

"Samuel…" Chanel is cut off.

"Spida, tha's my street name. Ya know how it is. Only close friends an' fam know my real name."

"Okay Spida, nice to meet you. I'm sorry about your cousin. He is a real nice dude and I hope they catch the people that did this."

"I'm sure they'll catch someone," Spida replied.

The doctor came through the door and beckoned the family to come into the conference room.

They all sat down. Dr. Levy sat at the head of the table and said, "Sorry about having to meet in this space but all of the consultations rooms are being painted, JACHO review next week. Anyway, Mr…" He pauses to look at the chart in his hand, "Mr. Mitchell is a lucky man. The first bullet grazed the spleen and we had to remove it to stop the bleeding. There was a second gunshot to the neck that went near the spinal cord. We put him into a medically induced coma so that he could heal. We don't think there will be any permanent damage, but we'll know more in the morning."

"You mean he could be paralyzed?" Yuri asked quietly. She began to weep at the thought. She couldn't believe how wrong this entire evening had gone. Her conscience began to get the best of her.

Chanel tightened her hand and leaned into Yuri saying, "I'm sure Shane will be okay. He's a fighter. Don't worry."

Dr. Levy interjected, "We won't know the full extent of his injuries until he is weaned off the pain medications. Right now, it is best that we keep him comfortable."

Yuri asked, "Can I see him, Dr. Levy?"

"Only for a minute. The family can go in one at a time. I don't want him to be over-stimulated right now."

"Can he hear us talk to him?"

"Yes, he's not in a coma, just sedated heavily."

Yuri got up to walk into the recovery room and Spida went behind her.

"I'll just wait here for you to return, Yuri," Chanel said.

Yuri nodded and gave Spida an evil look. He smiled and enjoyed her sense of discomfort. He held the door open for her to go in front of him.

"Afta you," Spida nodded.

"Thank you," Yuri said coldly, and cut her eyes as she passed him.

Chanel noticed the tension in the room, but thought it was because Shane had been shot, and Yuri was tired.

Yuri walked into the room where Shane was in recovery and saw him on the gurney. He had tubes and lines coming out of his mouth and the sides of his chest. There was blood all over the sheets underneath him. She had a rush of nausea that came over her like a tidal wave. It took everything she had, not to cry and throw-up at the same time.

Spida walked over to Shane nonchalantly and looked down at his face. He tried to act like he was choked up, but secretly was glad that he was in this position, for the heartache he had caused him. He knew that he must be cool so as not to raise any suspicion. Yuri was convinced that Uno was hiding and not answering her calls because he had something to do with the shooting. She was shocked to find out that Spida was Shane's cousin, but had no clue that he was around during the robbery.

Chapter 27

Yuri finally got out of bed at 12 in the afternoon the next day. Her head was splitting. She still had not been able to get in touch with Uno last night. She was anxious to know all of the details of the robbery. She knew that it must have been bad because he still had not answered his phone. She looked over to the side table to see if Uno had called. She saw that there were two missed calls, at 4:00am and 4:30am. She thought it had to be Uno because what other fool would call at 4:00 in the morning? She began to listen to the message and when she heard the message she dropped the phone and began to cry.

"Snake bitch, you see, you can't treat no one right."

Her conscience went into overdrive. She began to feel guilty about Shane being in the hospital. She didn't know what she would do if Shane couldn't walk or, God forbid, didn't make it. She didn't have anyone to talk to. She thought, if she told Chanel she would judge her for all the mistakes that she had made. She also despised Spida and didn't know what he knew about her part in the home invasion robbery. She knew that Uno had once used her to pay off a debt, so how did she know that he wouldn't throw her under the bus to implicate her in the entire thing.

She thought, "I've got to get it together. Where the fuck was Uno?" The phone rang and it startled her.

"Hello?" Yuri answered cautiously.

The voice on the phone was computer generated. "Snake bitch, now your boyfriend is fucked up. That should have been you in there." She hung up the phone. She lay down and put her head under her pillow; she began to weep. Chanel walked into the room and saw Yuri crying.

"Yuri, what's the matter?"

"Oh, Chanel, nothing is going right. Shane is the nicest person I have ever met and now he's lying in the hospital and may never walk again. He may even…"

Chanel cut her off, "Don't even think like that. Shane is going to get better and he will be walking out of the hospital in a few days."

"Yeah, that sounds good, Chanel, but what if he doesn't? I don't know what I'll do if he dies. I feel so guilty."

"Why would you feel guilty? You weren't even there. You had nothing to do with it. I'm sure that Shane was just a random target. I think that we should pray for his recovery."

"Pray, man, I am too far gone with God. He doesn't like me, and he never has, otherwise my life would never have been this fucked up."

Chanel looked puzzled, "I don't know where or when you think your life got fucked up. Your mother was the nicest person I have ever known. She was a successful attorney until Mike left her. She was always taking care of you. I don't know how you thought your life was dysfunctional.

154

Your momma bought you and gave you everything. She never denied you anything. You had the best clothes, best shoes, and had a wonderful education. She took you all over the world. I think you're having a pity party. You need to snap out of it. Don't forget, we grew up together, and now you have a wonderful man who loves you, spoils you and needs your support and prayer. So don't give me that 'God don't answer prayer's shit. You need to get down on your knees right now. This is not for you, Yuri, and this is not about you. This is about Shane and him getting better."

Chanel dragged Yuri out of her bed and onto her knees. Chanel bowed her head. Yuri looked at her.

Chanel began to pray, "Dear Father God, We come to you and ask you to heal your child, Shane. He is a good man and didn't deserve to be shot. Heal his body completely. We thank you, God, that the healing has already begun. In the mighty name of your son, Jesus Christ, We thank you, Amen."

Yuri mumbled, "Amen."

"Now Yuri, get up and get dressed. I made some food downstairs. You haven't had anything to eat since early last night. I know you must be starved."

"Yes mother," Yuri smirked.

Later that day, they decided to go to the hospital. Even though Yuri wanted to see Shane, the uncertainty of the previous night's events had her exhausted. She threw on her sweat suit and a tight T-shirt to go to the hospital. Chanel put on her casual jeans and her Howard University sweatshirt. She pulled her hair back in a bun and as they were looking in the mirror, Chanel began to smile. Trying to lighten the somber mood. Chanel reminded Yuri of when Shane bought the townhouse, and woke them up to come see it after they partied the night before. She spoke about how nice he was and that he truly loved Yuri. She was happy that Yuri had found someone to love her. She knew that Yuri was hard to deal with and hoped that Yuri would be just as good to Shane.

Yuri thought about how happy she was, and why she ever needed to get involved with Uno. She knew that she could have had a great life with Shane that he would have eventually married her, and wanted to have kids, once he settled down. He treated her like a queen. She had to just ask and it was hers. He laid the world out on a silver platter for her but she was drawn to Uno like a moth to a flame. Uno represented something dangerous, something forbidden. She felt excitement and guilt at the same time. Yuri knew that she should have never started anything with Uno.

Snapped out of her daydream, Yuri said, "What?"

Chanel was looking at her strangely before she said, "Nothing, Yuri, you just seem to be a thousand miles away. Is there something else going on that you want to talk about?"

"Just anxious to talk to Shane, I mean see him, and know that he's okay."

"Okay, let's go," Chanel said, as she walked out of the house behind Yuri.

Chapter 28

Yuri and Chanel walked up to the nurse's station on the floor that Shane had been moved to. The nurse looked up and said, "Only one person can go in at a time."

Chanel nodded, "Go ahead, I know you need to see him. I'll go sit in the waiting room. I'll just peek my head in to see him, before we leave. Take your time."

"Are you sure?" Yuri asked. Chanel nodded as she turned and headed for the waiting room.

Just as Yuri turned into the room, Candice headed out of the same room. "Bitch, what the fuck are you doing here?" Candice asked Yuri with a glare.

"What the fuck are you talking about? He's my fiancé. Why are you here?"

Candice laughed "Fiancé, that's a joke. Bitch, you fuck everybody. I wish I had never introduced you to Shane. I know you must have had something to do with this. Bitch, you are a snake and no one is safe around you."

"I didn't have anything to do with this and I'm just as concerned about getting Shane better, just like you." Yuri added, "I can't help it if I have a man and you don't." Candice slapped the dog shit out of Yuri; before she could retaliate, Spida walked into the room. He grabbed Yuri's hand in mid-air positioning himself between the two women.

"Now ladies, y'all have to control yourselves. Dis is a hospital. Ya jus' can't go 'round slappin' people, Candice."

Candice glared at them and walked out of the room toward the waiting room. Once she was in the waiting room, Candice broke down and started to cry. She was concerned about the health of her friend, Shane. He was in a coma now, and in her mind, she knew that Yuri was the cause.

Chanel sat in the corner of the waiting room and saw that Candice was upset. She saw the tissue box on the table and offered her one.

"Thank...You..." was all Candice was able to get out, through the tears, as she took the tissue.

Chanel recognized her but didn't know from where. "Are you going to be okay?"

"Yeah, just my homeboy that I grew up with is in there, shot, and his girlfriend is a snake bitch. I could kick myself for ever thinking that she was a good person to introduce him to. She has so many other men on the side, and she's acting like she is a 'goody-two-shoes' girlfriend, like she is so concerned and so loyal; that's bullshit. She is nothing but a two-faced lying hoe; I hate her!"

Chanel tried to soothe her. "Calm down, being this upset isn't good for anyone. I know that because my friend was shot last night too. You have to pray and ask God to heal your friend and if possible your relationship with your other friend."

Candice turned and got up.

"Thanks," she said bluntly, "but with friends like Yuri, I don't ever need an enemy."

With that, Candice walked out of the waiting room, toward the elevator. As she disappeared into the elevator, Chanel was able to place the angry woman. She was the female who had the fight with Yuri in the bathroom, at the club. Chanel began to wonder why Yuri would lie about knowing the woman; especially when she was the person that had introduced her to Shane. She also wondered what Yuri had done to make the woman hate her so much now. She continued to watch for Yuri come out of Shane's room. After about an hour, Chanel got hungry, and went down to the cafeteria.

She was sitting by herself when a tall man approached her and asked if he could sit down. She looked puzzled for a moment and then realized it was Shane's cousin, Samuel.

"Hi Sam....I mean Spida, I almost didn't recognize you today." Chanel smiled.

"Hey, how ya' doin' today? You look fresh in doze jeans, gurl," Spida flirted.

"Thanks," she blushed, "How is Shane doing? Is he responsive yet?"

"Don' worry, my cuz is strong. He'll be okay. We got good genes. The doc said he responsive to pain or whatever."

"Well, it sounds like he's getting better. I'm glad to know that, because Yuri is going crazy at the house with worry."

Spida said, "Hey, I have an idea, why don' I come and pick da two a ya up in da mornin' aroun' ten, and take ya to Glady's fo' breakfas'."

"You don't have to do all that, Spida."

"I know that, but I wanna take ya out." He smiled at her, "I mean da two a ya out. Besides, I know dat ya mus' not be eatin' well cuz a Shane. At leas' I kin feed ya, at leas' one good meal. On top a tha', I'm kinda feelin' ya."

Chanel responded, "I don't mind, but I can't answer for Yuri. I felt like you and Yuri weren't exactly friends, from your last meeting."

"Yeah, well maybe we din't git off on da righ' foot. Ya know, Shane bein' shot an' all, but I hope tha' don' mean ya won' go out wit me."

"Well, I think you seem to be nice enough, I will still ask her to come along."

Spida joked with her, "Oh, so ya don' trust to be alone wit me? You need ya gurl ta be dare?"

"No, but you asked us to go to breakfast."

"Oh, I git it. You mus' 'ave a man at home so ya hafta 'ave an alibi."

157

"You sure have jokes," Chanel laughed, "If you wanted to know if I had a man, all you had to do was ask."

"Well...." Spida waited for the answer.

"Well, what?" Chanel paused and thought about Terrance, then thought about Terrance with Yuri.

"No, I'm kinda in between right now."

Spida was surprised, "Baby gurl, ya so fine ya should 'ave a line a niggas jus' followin' ya."

"Not quite a line, my last boyfriend cheated on me so...."

"So he a fool. Tha's okay. His loss, ma gain," Spida smiled and continued, "So ya gonna lemme take ya ta breakfas' in da mornin'?" Spida thought an x-rated thought. "Or, we could start tonight wit dinna an' keep da night goin' 'til breakfas' in da mornin'."

"Spida, now you're moving a little too fast," Chanel scolded.

"Well, can' blame a nigga fo' tryin'. Seriously, I'll pick you an' Yuri up in da mornin' fo' breakfas' if ya want."

He handed her his cell number.

"Don' lose it. If ya change ya mind abou' dinna, jus' call me."

He grabbed her hand and kissed it like Prince Charming. "I'm gonna check on my cuz. See ya tomorra."

A few minutes later, Spida walked into Shane's room. "Hey, Baby Gurl, any change?"

Yuri snapped back at him, "Who the fuck you think you're calling 'Baby Gurl'?"

"Oh, now we gotta be all formal an' shit?" Spida looked at her with surprise. "Afta all I've done fo' ya?" Spida retorted, "Don' forget I know ya lil' game, nasty bitch. Ya may be able ta fool ya gurl Chanel, but ya can' fool Big Daddy."

Yuri started to laugh, "Big Daddy? You're more like Little Boy." She made a gesture to indicate the little dick that Spida had.

Spida responded back, "Yuri, I'm gonna hafta teach ya ta like lil' dick muthafuckas, cuz I'm gonna have dis dick in yo' mouth an' pussy fo' awhile."

"What are you talking about? Shane is my man. I'm not ever going to fuck you."

"No? Well if ya wan' Shane ta continue ta be yo' man, an' ya not go to jail fo' his shootin'.... Ya not only gonna fuck me, ya gonna suck me an' like it," Spida smiled devilishly. "Do I nee' ta remin' ya that I know ya game? So if ya wanna keep playin' it, ya gonna play by my rules."

Yuri's face became flushed, and as she tried to hide her fear, she knew that Spida had some information about the robbery, and her involvement. He saw that he now had her attention, and grabbed her arm.

"I think ya nee' ta take a break, I'll meet ya in the parkin' lot in five minutes, understan'?"

Yuri nodded and thought about Chanel, "But what will I tell Chanel? She's in the waiting room and she'll see me leave."

"No worries. I jus' lef' her in da cafeteria downstairs. Five."

Spida left Shane's room. Yuri looked over at Shane and couldn't believe that Spida was about to blackmail her. She got nauseated and ran into the bathroom to throw-up. She stopped to look in the mirror and knew that she had to do this to protect her man. She never wanted to hurt Shane. Now she felt that she had no other choice.

Chapter 29

Five minutes later, Yuri was sitting timidly, in the back seat of Spida's black 750LI. He looked at her, expectantly as he unzipped his pants and pointed at his dick.

"Daddy need some tension relief. Come on, Baby, lemme see some a doz skills tha' I been hearin' 'bout. I know tha' pussy wa' good, so lemme feel tha' mouth."

She looked down into his boxers and saw his dick now, in full light. It was a little over the size of a baby's penis. Maybe about 3 inches, fully erect. Yuri only dealt with niggas with big dicks. The smallest that she could remember was about 6 ½ inches, and she only dealt with him, because it was curved like a banana and could hit her G-spot. This nigga's dick wouldn't even fit in her hand, let alone her mouth. She became sick at the thought.

He looked at her and wondered what was taking her so long to start. He didn't want to lose his erection.

"Wha's takin' ya so long ta start, Bitch? We ain' got all day." He grabbed her head and shoved it onto his dick. "Lemme see dem skills." He leaned his head back as she began to give him head.

Yuri was sick and knew that in order to keep her secret she would have to keep Spida happy. She wanted Shane to wake up, but couldn't help thinking that if he was in a coma, Spida couldn't tell him. She wondered what would happen when he did wake up. She continued to be distracted by the thought of Shane while giving Spida head. She could hear him moaning. Then all of a sudden she tasted salty cum in her mouth.

"Shit," Spida yelled as he came in her mouth.

He held her head down to his dick as she was choking for air and relief. She spit the cum out of her mouth, all over the upholstery of the back seat of the car. He opened his eyes and looked, "Fuck, Bitch, wha-tha-fuck do ya think ya doin'?"

"I don't swallow," she said, with tears in her eyes. She was nauseated and ashamed that her life had come to this.

"Well, ya betta learn ta swallow, Bitch. Ya gonna get a lotta practice."

He reached under the seat and grabbed a towel to clean himself up with. Then he handed her a piece of gum.

"Here, I don' think ya need ta go back in dare wit ya breath smellin' like dick. I think I saw a toothbrush in Shane's bathroom. You kin freshen up upstairs. I'll be in contact wit ya."

Spida got out of the back seat, looked around to make sure that no one was looking, and walked over to the other door to open it for Yuri to get out. He offered her his hand, to help her get out. She slapped it out of her way and got out of the car, fuming. She went stomping back to the hospital entrance.

"Layta, Yuri," Spida taunted, then got into the driver's seat and left the hospital.

Yuri was almost in tears when she got into the elevator to go back up to Shane's room. She cautiously looked for Chanel, and hoped that no one noticed that she was missing. She got to the room unscathed and went into the bathroom to fix herself up. As she looked into the mirror, she saw a broken version of herself. She began to cry uncontrollably and wondered where it all went wrong. How could she have gotten in so much trouble and put herself in this position? The thought of Spida sickened her and she threw up again in the toilet.

As she stood there, looking in the mirror, there was a knock on the bathroom door. She heard Chanel's voice from the other side,

"Yuri, are you okay?"

She came out of the bathroom wiping her eyes, "Yeah, I'm just tired and stressed."

"Where did you go? I came up here looking for you a minute ago."

Trying to make up a quick excuse, Yuri replied, "Uh, I just had to go outside for a minute."

Chanel said "Oh okay, before I forget, I saw Spida in the cafeteria and he invited us to breakfast in the morning."

"What? Yuri yelled, "I'm not gonna....." She stopped mid-sentence.

Chanel was confused about her reaction. "Why don't you like Spida? He seems like a nice guy. We talked and…"

Yuri cut her off, "I'm sorry I didn't mean it like that. I'm just concerned about Shane and I really can't think about having any fun or going out. If you want to go, that's fine. Count me out."

She hoped she was able to hide her disdain for Spida. She had to play it cool if she wanted Spida to keep her secret. She just hoped that Chanel wouldn't get too friendly with him. She wanted Chanel to be with her, and support her, while Shane was hospitalized, and it was bad enough that she had to see Spida here, she didn't want him coming over to the house, as well.

"Look," Yuri said calmly, "I have had a lot to deal with over the last 48 hours. I'm tired and don't want to fight with you. Please, can we go home now? You and Spida can have breakfast in the morning, I'll sleep in and we can come here in the afternoon."

"But you need to eat also, I'm worried that you aren't eating. Shane needs you to be healthy, not broke down from not sleeping or eating. We'll go, and bring you some food back, in the morning. That way, you get the best of both worlds. You can sleep in and eat some good ol' chicken and waffles," Chanel smiled at her.

Not wanting to fight, Yuri agreed and begged her again, "Can we go now?"

She looked over at Shane and walked to the head of his bed. She looked at him so helplessly and began to feel tears fall on her cheeks. She felt so guilty about everything. She remembered that the doctor said to talk to him normally, and that even though he might not respond, he would hear what she said. She leaned over him and kissed him gently on the forehead.

She squeezed his hand, "I love you, I am so sorry." As she was leaning down she felt his hand squeeze hers back. She jumped up and pointed at his hand. "He... He moved... Chanel... he's waking up. He squeezed my hand. I felt it."

Chanel ran out of the room to get the nurse or doctor. The nurse walked in and looked, "What's going on in here? What's all the commotion?"

Yuri said excitedly, "He moved, he moved and squeezed my hand!"

"Oh dear, I'm sorry, that was probably a reflex movement. He is still comatose."

Yuri stated to the nurse, somewhat combatively, "I know what I felt, and I know that he is getting better."

The nurse, not wanting to start an argument, patted Yuri on the shoulder and said, "I pray that he is getting better, dear. That's all we can do right now is pray."

She turned to walk out of the room and Yuri cut her eyes at her.

Yuri went back to sit by Shane's bed. "Chanel, you can go on and pick me up later. I want to be here when Shane wakes up."

"Yuri, the nurse said that it was a reflex..."

"I don't care what she said, I feel that he is going to wake up soon and I want to be the first one he sees." Yuri made a motion for Chanel to leave the room. Chanel turned and walked out.

She stopped at the doorway and said, "I'll be back later to pick you up, okay? I'll bring you some dinner. Yuri, you need to eat." She continued out the door before Yuri could say no to her offer.

Moments later, when Chanel reached the entrance of the hospital, she saw Spida in the parking lot talking to a man. They looked like they were arguing. The other man looked frustrated, threw his hands in the air, turned and left. He got into a Corvette and left the parking lot.

Spida looked around and saw Chanel. He walked over to her and tried to look unconcerned about the encounter that Chanel had just witnessed.

Chanel smiled and asked, "What was that all about? Who was that guy you were arguing with?"

"Oh him? He nobody. Jus' one a my associates who wanna git mo' money, but I refuse. He mad cuz I wouldn' give 'im a raise. Ya know how hard it is ta fin' good help," he laughed and put his arm around her. "So, are ya gonna take me up on my offa fo' dinna?"

"Well, actually, I was going to call you and see what your schedule was like. Yuri is up there with Shane. He moved and she thinks that he maybe waking up soon."

"Oh, really," Spida said, surprised by the potential improvement in his cousin's condition.

Chanel said, "You don't sound too happy that he's waking up."

"No, it's na tha', I hafta to be hones' wit ya. I'll tell ya da story ova dinna, deal?"

Chanel's curiosity was peaked, "Deal."

Twenty minutes later, they drove up in Spida's black 750LI BMW to the front of Justin's Restaurant in Midtown, ATL. He let the valet park the car and met Chanel on the sidewalk in front of the restaurant. He offered his arm like a pure southern gentleman.

She accepted his arm and giggled, "Mr. Spida."

He smiled, "I may be hood but tha'don' mean tha' my momma din't teach me no manners."

She laughed, "Well, Sir she taught you well from what I can see."

They entered the restaurant and sat over in the corner booth. After a few minutes, when they became more comfortable with each other, more personal questions began to be asked.

Spida started with "So, wha's the deal wit you an' Yuri? How long y'all been knowin' each otha an' shit?"

"We grew up next door to each other. I was always studying and wanted to go to college. Well Yuri, she has always been about the boys and now, men. Until Shane of course, she seemed to have settled down, from what I can see. She's not like the old Yuri."

Spida looks at her suspiciously and said, "Really?"

Not sounding too convinced, Chanel said, "Well, I hope she's not the old Yuri," remembering that Shane was Spida's cousin.

"Ya know, it hard ta change a leopard's spots. No worries. Me an' Shane ain' exactly close deez days. We ain' been close for a long time."

Chanel, still curious, asked, "If you don't mind my asking, what is up between the two of you?"

"Me an' Yuri, or Me an' Shane?"

"Well, now that you mentioned it, both. I thought there was some tension between Yuri and you when we first met."

"Well le's jus' say our firs' meetin' wasn' at the hospital, an' I think she was a lil' surprised to find out that I'm Shane's cuz. As far as me an' my cuz, our beef goes back ta high school. He da the

163

good one, ya know; good grades, always athletic, Mr. Popula, neva got in no trouble, or should I say neva get caught. Me on da otha hand, I wuzz a thug. I barely went ta school, I could git da grades but I was too bored an' worried 'bout makin' money. Both a us growed up kinda poor, but his momma worked an' taught us how ta save an' survive. My momma wuzza party girl, taput it nicely. I guess I was aways jealous a cuz even though his momma kinda raise me afta my mutha wuz kilt.

Ma' had owed a small time drug dealer petty change, got on the wrong track and started smok'n crack. We were living in Detroit back then. When she died, I moved to L.A.

It became a competition between us from then on. We wuz livin' in California an' he start ta do things ta show Moms wha' I wuz doin' wrong. Firs' it wuzza healthy competition, ya know; grades, school stuff, an' then it start wit da girls." Spida, kind of embarrassed, had never really talked to anyone about his past. He felt comfortable with Chanel, though. She continued to listen intently about his youthful indiscretions. "Anyway, there wuz dis one girl tha' I wuz really diggin' an' I had told him abou' huh cuz I was a thug an' had my grind on, but my cuz wuz really the Casanova a da family. I wanted ta take huh out, but din't know how ta ask. The nex' thing I know, Shane an' huh wuz hookt up an' he wuz datin' huh. He took huh to da prom an' I wuz so pisst tha'....uh.... I start a small fire in da broom closet, which made everyone drencht from da sprinklas, an' dat ruin da prom."

Chanel asked, "Did they know you did it?"

"Nope, faulty wirin'. "Spida smiled. "I think Shane knew, but he try ta tell me tha' she ask him to da prom an' he wasn' tryin' ta steal my girl. We had a beef 'bout it an' I wouldn' listen. We been like bruddas growin' up 'til my ma died."

Chanel put her hand on his hand and continued to listen to his story. She looked like she understood his pain.

"Ya know, you da firs' person I eva tol' this to. It hurt so bad when I wuzza kid an' afta my mutha died, I jus' din't wanna feel any mo' pain. I drop outta high school in my senior yea' afta da fire. I decided ta use summa dat anga in da military. I joined the Marines an' wen' ta Afghanistan."

"Military?" Chanel asked, surprised about the story Spida was telling.

"Spida wuz da name I got in da Marines. We was in a small bunker in da desert an' they had some big ass spiders tha' I was 'fraid of. Afta killin' dem tarantula-like muthafuckas, da guys thought tha' would be a good nick-name fo' me. It stuck, an' when I come back here and start my business, it gave me some street cred, ya know?"

Chanel laughed, "So you and Shane were mad at each other over a girl?"

"Well, nah any girl. She an' I hooked up afta tha' an' I wuz gonna marry huh. When I tol' huh tha' I was a virgin an' wanted to wait 'til we got married, she laughed. She tol' me tha' she wanted to know wha' the package wuz like before she would say yes. I was real subconscious 'bout my uh..." he took a deep breath and blew it out, "my penis..."

164

Chanel sucked in some air and frowned, she could see the devastation in his face. "Don't tell me she laughed at you?"

Spida was embarrassed and nodded, "So ya see, I have ova-compensated wit my hood rep an' makin' money. I don' know why I'm tellin' ya all dis, Chanel."

She just squeezed his hand and continued to listen to his story.

"So, I 'ave made it a point ta get back at my cuz anytime I could. Yo' girl, Yuri knows dat, too. Tha's why she uncomfortable. I know tha's yo' girl an' I know tha' my cuz is crazy in love wit her. But the fact is, she a ho. Point blank, bottom line."

Chanel wondered, totally stupified, why would Spida say that.

"Samuel, Shane is Yuri's first love, he broke her virginity. After I came a few months ago, before the shooting, I saw how much he loved her and I had hoped, for her sake, that Yuri had grown up and could love him for the man I saw him to be; but I wasn't sure she was capable. She's not a hoe, she's just young and immature. Don't be mean, Spida."

After a few hours of dinner, Chanel realized that it was late, and she hadn't heard from Yuri. She had forgotten to call her and let her know that the car was still in the hospital parking lot. She had told her that she was going to dinner, but the time had gotten away from her.

"Oh my God, what time is it?" Chanel asked.

"Seven fitty, almos' eight," Spida replied.

"Oh shoot, I forgot to call Yuri. What is she going to think?" Chanel said.

"She a big girl, jus' call 'er now an' ask 'er do she wan' anythin' ta eat from here. We only fiteen minutes away from da hospital."

Chanel turned, got her phone out of her purse, and dialed Yuri, "Hello Yuri, it's Chanel... Yeah, I'm here eating with Shane's cousin.... Is there any improvement in Shane's condition? Well, we're only a few minutes away. Have you eaten anything....? Do you want us to bring some dinner there to the hospital?"

Chanel mouthed 'no' to Spida.

"Well before I forget, the car is still in the parking lot. You can leave anytime. I'm with Spida and he's going to drop me off at home." Chanel listened, then frowned. "Of course, I'll be okay with him. I'll call you if I need you. Don't worry, he's been a perfect gentleman. We are having a great time. Don't worry and uh, don't wait up. I'll see you in the morning. Good night." Chanel hung up the phone before Yuri could admonish her for being with Spida.

He looked at her and said "Well tha' means we don' hafta be home 'fore midnight, Cinderella. I know a few spots if ya like ta go."

Chanel responded, "I'm sorry, I didn't even ask if you had plans. You don't have to take me..."

He cut her off, "Are ya crazy? I wuz hopin' tha' she wouldn' send the posse out ta bring ya back! I haven' had dis much fun wit anyone in a while. Le's git outta here an' we kin go ta dis otha spot I know."

Chanel looked down at her clothes, "I'm sorry, I'm not really dressed for the evening. I didn't bring any club clothes, either."

"No worries, le's go."

Dinner was over. Chanel thanked Spida for the meal as they waited on the valet to bring the car. Spida admired Chanel's curvaceous ass, he fantasized about fucking her and Yuri together. Yuri would ride his dick, while Chanel would sit on his face. He thought about Yuri's aquafina flow. She had some of the wettest pussy that he had ever had. His dick became hard just thinking about it. He snapped out of his trance once Chanel said the car was waiting. He was embarrassed, and hoped Chanel hadn't noticed the bulge in his pants. The way she looked at him, he wondered if she could read his mind. If she only knew the nasty thoughts he was daydreaming about.

The next twenty minutes, in the car, they enjoyed the music and didn't have too much conversation. He pulled up in front of Lenox Mall and gave the guy a twenty dollar bill to just keep the car parked out front.

"Come on, le's see if we kin fin' some party clothes fo' ya." Spida smiled, helping her out of the car.

"Oh, Spida, you didn't have to do all this. You could have just taken me home. The dinner was more than enough. I really don't need anything," she said.

"Nonsense, besides we only have a few minutes, tha' way we don' hafta be here fo' hours. Ya know, how ya girls like ta do it." Forty-five minutes later they came back to the car with four or five bags of designer clothes, shoes and accessories. "I like da way ya shop, straight an' to da point," Spida laughed.

"Helps when you know your size, and what looks good," Chanel winked at him, "But I really think we should go by Yuri's house. I need to change, and I feel guilty that I'm not sitting with her at the hospital."

"Look, if ya wan', I come get ya at midnight, tha' way ya have a few hours ta check on Yuri. I wish you'd stay da night wit me, though."

Spida had hoped she would, but he didn't know that Chanel was a virgin. He thought he would get lucky that night. After all, she was Yuri's friend. Yuri was a ho, and Candice was a ho as well. He thought if the price was right, dinner, club and some fly gear, he might get lucky, yet he felt there was more to Chanel and he wanted to know more about her.

166

Chanel responded, "I don't do the sleep-over thing with any guy, unless he's my man." Changing the subject Chanel added, "You know where Yuri lives?"

"Yeah, I pass't by dare a few times," Spida said. When they pulled up to the townhouse, he pressed, "Chanel, I sure hope I kin git ta know ya betta."

Chanel replied, "Well you seem like a nice guy, but I'm not looking for a serious relationship right now. I know we'll see each other at the hospital until Shane gets better, but I'm also in school. My professor agreed to email my assignments, so I won't get behind. I think I can hang out tonight, but after that, I won't have too much time to play."

"Well, I'll take what time I kin git wit ya. Look, there be no pressure if ya don' wan' ta go out layta. I kin take a rain check. I know tha' you mus'be tired." He looked down at his phone. "Listen, I think, I'm gonna pass on da club tonight anyway. I hafta take care o' some business now. I'm sorry. But I got ya an' if ya need some mo' clothes an' want ta shop mo', I gotcha on dat too."

Chanel smiled and gathered her bags out of the back seat. She leaned through the driver's window and kissed Spida on the cheek.

"Thanks again for dinner, it was wonderful. I appreciate your buying the clothes, I'll give you..."

Spida cut her off, "It was my pleasure and you don't owe me anything."

She walked off and he waved 'bye' to her. He watched her get into the house and sat there in the driveway, fantasizing about fucking her. He drove to the hospital, thinking about Yuri, because he was horny as hell.

Chapter 30

Spida walked up to the hospital with pussy on his mind. He walked into Shane's room and Yuri was still sitting by the bed. She had fallen asleep in the chair next to Shane's bed, with her sweatshirt off. Under the sweatshirt she had on a low v-neck T-shirt. He walked around her and started to fondle her titties. When she felt him grope her, she moaned dreaming about Shane. Spida grabbed more firmly and slid one hand into the front of her pants. When she felt his hand there she jumped and woke up.

She saw Spida behind her and screamed "Stop it, bitch."

Spida said, "You da bitch. Quit screamin' 'fore the nurse come in. I nee' ya ta gimme some pussy, cuz I'm horny." He grabbed his dick and said, "I nee' ya ta suck me." Yuri became disgusted at the thought. Spida said, "The nurse walk out as I wuz walkin' in, so we got abou' twenny o' thirty minutes 'til she make huh nex' round. Come 'ere." He pulled her over to him.

"Are you crazy, muthafucka?" Yuri yelled.

"No, but you a ho an' if ya don' do what I wan', I guess I kin holla at one a da detectives lookin' fo' my poor cuz's shoota."

Yuri cried, "What do you want from me, Spida?"

He stuck his hand back down her pants and fingered her, "This wet pussy is what I want."

As Spida pulled down her pants, he smiled and looked over at his cousin's unconscious body. He said "This is fo' you cuz, since ya can' fuck 'er, I'm holdin' ya down."

He stuck his dick in Yuri's raw pussy, while still holding onto her titties, and stroking her. He directed her body where he wanted it. She stood there bent over stiff, like a blow-up doll.

Spida said, "If you don' wanna have the nurse catch us, ya betta throw tha' pussy like a quarterback an' make me cum."

Yuri did as she was told, and tightened up her pussy, because she didn't want to get caught in this position. She fucked him like he wanted to be fucked. Spida started to moan and call Yuri's name. Yuri began to talk to him, to speed up the process.

She said, "You love me, don't you? Tell me you want me, it's good for you, mutherfucka, ain't it?"

Spida replied, "I love this pussy!"

Well, give me that dick and cum, baby," she said, trying anything to make him release.

Spida was going crazy, he was on the verge of cumming and snatched his dick out of her pussy.

"Las' time ya wouldn' swallow, dis time ya gonna swallow my cum," he said menacingly.

He shoved his dick in her mouth and made her suck him, as she got down on her knees. Ten more minutes had gone by and Yuri felt like it was almost time for the doctor or nurse to come in. Spida didn't care. He was not stopping until he was satisfied. Yuri started to really suck on him, and he held onto Shane's bedrail. He was moaning and holding Yuri's head down, almost to the point of her not being able to breath. She was so angry, she wanted to bite his little dick off and flush it down the toilet. It was small enough to go down with no problem. She sucked and sucked. She did one of her tonsil tricks making Spida just about go into a seizure. He released in her mouth and made sure she swallowed every single drop of cum.

"Good girl," he whispered, "Uno said dat you wuz da bomb!" He looked over at Shane and said, "Tha's why all you niggas is in love wit dis ho. She got good pussy an' give good head." He looked at Yuri and continued, "I wunda how tha' ass feel?"

Yuri was disgusted and ran into the bathroom, throwing up. She was thinking that she had not thrown up this much in her entire life. Not only was Spida's dick small but his cum was salty and sour. It was nothing like Shane or Uno's. It was nothing like anything she had ever swallowed. She just wanted Spida to leave. He looked into the bathroom after she was in there for a minute.

"I'm leavin', look out fo' my cuz." Spida laughed and added, "I can' wait ta fuck both you an' ya girl, Chanel. Tha' will be the bes' treat of all."

Yuri snapped back, "You little-dick bastard, leave my best friend out of this! She is innocent and knows nothing about this! She's a virgin. What you're trying to do won't happen. I'm tired of you threatening me! Whatever your bitch-ass is going to do, do it, because I'm done!"

"Ok Yuri, 'ave it yer way. A virgin, huh?" Spida replied, "I migh' jus'hafta pop tha' cherry." He walked out of the room, smiling, with a devilish conniving look on his face.

Yuri began to cry after Spida left the room. She wanted to kill him. She hated his guts. Her mom had always told her to never use the word 'hate'but Yuri hated Spida with a passion. She went back to Shane's bedside. She kissed him on his forehead, "You deserve a better woman than I am. I need you to wake up Shane, please wake up," she whispered in his ear.

A few minutes later, Chanel walked into the room, and watched her best friend holding her man's hand, looking so sad. Ten minutes earlier and she would have caught Yuri with a dick in her mouth. She walked up on Yuri and rubbed her back.

"Yuri, let's go home. It's late, and tomorrow there's another detective that wants to talk to you."

Yuri was wiping her eyes, "What did you say?" She was preoccupied with the recent events with Spida.

Chanel said "Another detective, Reginald Wallace, called the house and said he had some more questions for you. He wants to talk to you tomorrow afternoon. He sounds much nicer than the other detective." Yuri kissed Shane, knowing that she needed to rest. She got up, looked back at him, hoping tomorrow he would be awake when she came to visit, and left with Chanel.

Chapter 31

Once back at the townhouse, Chanel ran a hot bubbling bath for Yuri. She sat on the side of the tub while Yuri laid there in a daze.

"Yuri, may I ask what's on your mind?"

Yuri snapped out of her thoughts. "Chanel, just everything. I have a fucked-up life."

"Why would you say that?"

"We'll talk about it tomorrow. Right now, I would just like to lay here and soak."

"Okay Yuri, I'm going to bed. We'll talk tomorrow." Chanel got up to leave the bathroom, and gave Yuri her privacy.

Yuri was awakened at six a.m. by an unknown caller. She wasn't going to answer, thinking it was probably the person taunting her. With all that she had gone through in the last few days, she was not in the mood for ignorance so early in the morning.

"Hello," she said, tired and irritated.

"Hey, Shawty, I nee'ta see ya ASAP." She jumped up as she heard his voice,

"Uno, where are you? Where have you been? What happened the other night?"

He cut her off and said, "I can' talk on the phone. Look, meet me at da gas station on University Avenue in thirty."

He hung up. Yuri tip-toed down the stairs and out the door, making sure not to wake up Chanel. She had the sweats she slept in on, and flip flops. She jumped into the Benz and headed south on 75. When Yuri arrived, she didn't notice that Uno had been sitting there. He was no longer in the GMC Truck. He was in a new Corvette.

Yuri got in and they sped off. He was looking around to make sure that he wasn't being followed. He drove like a NASCAR driver, making sure he wasn't being tailed.

"Damn, Shawty, I missed ya."

When they pulled up to an apartment building, Uno circled around and then parked. They walked into a sparsely furnished apartment. Uno started kissing her and undressing her. At the same time, she was pulling off his shirt. She unbuttoned his pants and looked up at him, as she kneeled at his feet like a sex slave. Yuri wanted him as bad as he wanted her. She looked at his big dick as if she had just won a trophy. She kissed around the tip and put both hands on it, tugging him to a full erection. Once she had his full attention, she began to suck him like she had never done before. She tried to put Uno's whole dick down her throat.

"Damn girl, ya missed daddy didn' ya?" Uno whispered, trying not to cum too quick.

Yuri never responded, just continued to keep on giving the best head of her life. It felt so good that Uno knew she was about to make him explode. He pulled her up and took her over to the queen-sized bed, sucked on her neck, and then kissed her breast.

"I wanna feel tha' pussy!" Uno said, as he opened her legs.

He slid only part of his pole inside Yuri. She let out an 'awwww' of relief; she pulled her legs back as far as she could go. He slid the entire length of his long-john into her, as he did a sex-push up inside of her. Yuri screamed as Uno went all the way inside of her. It felt as if it had been an eternity since they were together. Uno long-stroked her slow and easy. It was the first time that Uno had really made love to her. He sucked her neck, leaving his passion bite on her. They French kissed, they did every position that they could, and after forty-five minutes of lovemaking, Uno came inside Yuri. They laid there, holding each other.

After twenty quiet minutes had passed, Yuri asked Uno, "Why is everything so crazy now? I've been going nuts not knowing what happened to you. I thought you told me you wouldn't hurt Shane. Now he's in a coma in the hospital. Spida has been making it all worse. He's been making me do the unthinkable. I wish you wouldn't have involved him, now he's blackmailing me and treating me like some nasty slut bitch! If you wouldn't have had me fuck him, I would not be getting this treatment."

"Yuri, I didn' tell tha' nigga nothin'. I didn' know tha' he was yo man's cousin 'til we wuz in da house. Spida knew tha' you was his cousin's girl. Tha's why he wanted ta fuck ya so bad."

"But why did you have to shoot Shane? You said that you weren't going to even bring a gun."

"I didn'. When we was downstairs, it was crazy cuz the safe wuz open. I was gonna hit 'im wit a wood board ta knock 'im out, but 'fore I wuz able ta knock 'im out, he look up an' say 'Samuel', so I look like 'who da fuck is Samuel'? I wuz confused 'til Spida pull his gun an' start ta tell 'im tha' he wuz tired of sellin' his drugs an' bein' beneath 'im. He go on ta tell 'im that he want all a da money an' da business. He start talkin' abou' all dat Shane took from 'im they whole life. So tha' nigga Shane started talkin' shit an' tellin' him dat he couldn' help dat he couldn' satisfy his bitches, an' dat his girl chose him ova Spida." Uno continued the story, "I knew dat dist be some family shit tha' didn' involve me, so I start ta load up da cash, cuz they be on some otha shit. Afta I grab abou' seventy thou'outta da safe, tha's when Spida say some shit abou' you. Shane got pissed an' start to charge at Spida. I ran fo' da door an' tha's when I heard the gunshots. We wuz in different cars, so I bounced."

"So Spida shot Shane?" Yuri asked, stunned.

"Hell yeah he did! I damn sho' didn', doz niggas was trippin', an' basically it be abou' a bitch."

"You said you only got seventy thousand dollars, was there was much more left?"

"Hell yeah, Shawty, dare be like two-hundred thous' to three hundred thous' or mo'. So dat fuck-nigga Spida had to take da res' 'fore the police come.

"Well, he acts like he knows that I set it up. He has made me his sex-slut," Yuri cried. "I hate him!"

"Shawty, I tol''im you knew nothin''bout the hit. From da looks of it, you didn' even know tha' yo' man be a D-boy. Tha' nigga got dem bricks an' pills on deck."

"I had no idea," Yuri said.

"I know dat, an' Spida knew dat from da beginnin' cuz I got dare ta hit da rent money. It be Spida tha' set us both up, cuz he be workin' fo' Shane."

"I see you've been spending money too, Uno. You have to lay low. There's this Detective Wallace who is asking questions. He wants to speak to me soon. Spida is acting like the concerned cousin and there is no telling what he will do to save his ass. He's always at the hospital and everyone is feeling sorry for him, even Chanel."

"From da conversation tha' I ova heard, Spida be jealous a yo' boy Shane, an' he wan' 'im dead so he kin take ova his whole empire. Damn, Shawty, yo ass didn' know yo' man be tha' rich?"

"So what do we do now, Uno?"

"Shawty, we hafta stay away from each otha."

"But I love you, and he's making me suck his dick and fuck him."

"Shawty, you jus' hafta play da game righ', 'til I kin figure somethin'out. I hafta fine out where he put da res' a dat cash. If ya help me do dat, then we kin bounce an' git outta here fo' real. Like some Bonnie an' Clyde shit."

Yuri hugged Uno and cried, "I love you, Uno, please make all of this go away!"

"Don'worry, Shawty, I will. I promise."

Chapter 32

When Yuri arrived back home, Chanel was sitting on the porch with Spida, looking scared. She jumped up and ran to the car.

Yuri asked, "What is Spida doing here?"

Chanel pointed to the large picture window in front that was broken. "That's why."

"Damn!" Yuri screamed.

"I was in the shower and that's when I heard a crash. It sounded like a shot from a gun at first, then the crash as the window shattered," Chanel explained. "I dropped to the floor and called your phone. When you didn't answer, I called Spida and he came right over."

Yuri looked over at him and rolled her eyes. She thought that he probably came over because he was around the corner and was the one who broke the window. She wanted to spit on him.

Chanel said, "There has been so much going on that I didn't want to call the police. I was really scared, Yuri."

"I'm sorry, Chanel, I think it's time for you to head back to D.C."

"I won't leave you here alone, Yuri. I gave you my word on that. I mean it."

Yuri looked at Spida and said, "Thank you for coming over Spida, but I think you can leave now." She was disgusted at the sight of looking at him.

"Tha's okay, cuz I 'ave already called someone ova ta fix it."

"Thanks," Yuri said coldly, "but you didn't have to do that. I could have taken care of it myself."

"Tha's the leas' I could do fo' ma girls," said Spida. I'm gonna look in on ma cuz since I'm in da neighborhood." He looked in the direction of Chanel, "I'll see ya layta, Chanel." He looked toward Yuri and grinned, "A pleasure, as always, Yuri."

Yuri's blood was boiling. She was pissed thinking about how he busted her window, and was now using Shane's money to pay for it to be fixed. She remembered what Uno had told her earlier.

"Just play the game and he'll get his. Don't worry, every dog has his day."

Spida would get his sooner rather than later if Yuri had anything to do with it. Spida left just after the man came to repair the plate glass window. Spida paid him to do the job, then took off.

Once Spida was gone, they walked into the house. "Oh Yuri, the detective called. He wanted to know if it would be more convenient to meet here, at the precinct, or at the hospital.

Here's the number, give him a call," Chanel said as she handed Yuri the phone number written on a small scrap of paper. Yuri looked at the number and took a deep breath. She dialed the number and in two rings the detective answered.

"Detective Wallace, how may I help you?"

"Yes my name is Yuri Jones, I'm returning your call. I assume it is in regards to my fiancé Shane Mitchell, and the shooting."

"Yes, Ms. Jones, I've been waiting on your call. How are you doing?"

"I'm okay, just praying that Shane will be okay."

"I wanted to know if you could meet me and talk in person. I have a few more questions to ask you about that night. You know, when a robbery takes place, anyone that was in contact with Mr. Mitchell becomes a suspect. If possible, it would be easiest for me to speak to you down here at the precinct."

"Actually Mr. Wall..." Yuri begins. Detective Wallace interrupted her to correct his title. "Detective Wallace, sorry, I was hoping that we could meet at the hospital and speak there. I haven't been there yet today, and I'm trying to get there as soon as possible. I could meet you in the cafeteria."

"That's okay with me, Ms. Jones. Say about one o'clock?"

"That's fine. I'll meet you at one in the cafeteria." Yuri hung up, and looked at the phone in her hand thinking, 'I hope he doesn't ask too many questions. Yuri showered, getting her mind and thoughts right about the events that occurred last Friday night. She knew that she could not stutter, or say the wrong thing to incriminate herself in the robbery. Her story would have to be consistent with the one she told Detective Ramos. Even though he had been a total asshole, she gave him the lies she had.

Yuri checked her watch and it was exactly one o'clock when she walked into the cafeteria at Grady Hospital. She thought that if Shane knew he was at Grady, he would be pissed. Grady was for the poor and unfortunate. Shane would always say when riding by on the interstate, 'I wouldn't be caught dead in that hospital.' He was more of a Cedars Sinai type of nigga. Now Yuri knew something else about Shane; he was a drug dealer sitting on a million dollars or better. She thought about the safe in California that she had seen in his condo there. She knew that was his main safe. If the one in Atlanta had almost four hundred thousand, how much was in the safe in California? She came out of her thoughts and remembered that Grady had one of the best trauma units in Atlanta; they specialized in gunshot and stab wounds.

Yuri bought herself some hot tea, sat down, and waited for the detective to get there. When she spied a tall, thirty-ish gentleman in khaki slacks and white shirt, she knew that must have been Detective Wallace. She thought 'Damn, I thought the Spanish detective was cute,' but Reginald Wallace was totally her type, judging by the dick imprint in his pants. Detective Wallace was a young guy in his thirties, about 6'1", tall, dark chocolate skin tone, and sexy as hell. He favored

174

Idris Elba, the actor. He was very well groomed and looked nothing like a typical cop. Most of the men that were Atlanta police looked like normal guys anyway. As he approached her, he had a serious face, but his slight smile that was warming. As he spoke, Yuri began to melt. "Hello, Ms. Jones. I am Detective Wallace. May I have a seat?"

"Sure," Yuri said, looking like she had a school girl crush on him.

"I have the statement you gave on the night of the robbery; I just have a few more questions about the night Mr. Mitchell was shot."

Yuri began to explain how she had been with Shane earlier that night, but left because her best friend had arrived in town. She also told him that while she was headed back to Shane's house was when she received the call about the shooting. As she talked, Detective Wallace admired her beauty, and couldn't take his eyes off her. He thought to himself, if she wasn't a suspect, she would be a chick that he would date. He was single and dating a few women, but none of them had her sex-appeal. Yuri had on a super tight pair of Rock and Republic jeans and a bustier, hugging her size 36C cup with her breasts filling it out well. Her 5" Gucci pumps sealed the deal. She knew that her outfit, and the way that it fit her body made him take some pressure off of her during the interrogation. Detective Wallace liked what he saw, but he kept a lid on his feelings. He was trained to show no emotion.

He then asked Yuri, "So you never made it to Mr. Mitchell's house?"

"No, I didn't," Yuri paused, as she thought about her last statement.

"Well, I'm sorry to say that we found a condom in Mr. Mitchell's trash, and we're having it tested for DNA. Do you know if your fiancé was seeing someone else?"

Yuri became irritated now thinking about if he really had someone in California. Duh, who would tell their woman that they were dating or fucking another woman? "Sorry if I struck a nerve Ms Jones, I have to ask these questions to compl…" He was about to finish his sentence as Spida walked up.

"I see you've met Yuri."

"Hello Samuel, how is your cousin doing?"

"He still in a coma, but dey say he may be wakin' up soon." He looked at Yuri. "Look wha' he got waitin' on 'im when he wake up. I'd wake up if I wuz him," Spida said, playfully, looking at Yuri.

Yuri looked at him and rolled her eyes. The detective sensed her tension. They had never said anything to each other but the body language said it all. Yuri's whole demeanor had changed. He wondered what their beef was about. He thought if he was Shane's cousin, these two were definitely not friends. The word enemy was written all over Yuri's face.

\

Chapter 33

While Yuri spoke with Detective Wallace, Chanel stayed upstairs with Shane. She had just stepped out to call her mother in the hallway. When she returned, Candice was in the room. She walked in without Candice realizing she was there. Candice stood by the bed, almost in tears, and looking at Shane.

She spoke softly, "Hey Shane, I just stopped by to check on you, homie. Shane, please wake up."

Chanel had her hair differently, wearing no make-up, and had glasses on. Candice had not even noticed that she was the same female that she had run into twice before, at the club and the hospital. Candice acknowledged Chanel in the room, but continued to whisper to Shane.

"It's me, Candice, I have so much to tell you. I wish…" She stopped and through tears continued, "Please just wake up, Shane. I am so sorry." Candice reached down and kissed the palm of his hand and looked up at Chanel. She smiled and said,

"Please take care of my friend." Candice left the room and never looked back.

Chanel wondered why Candice was saying that she was so sorry. Did she have something to do with Shane's shooting? She was about to start doing some investigating of her own. Chanel felt so bad for Shane lying there. She didn't want him to die, for Yuri's sake. This made her think about the nasty bitch on the video tape, she wished she knew more. She wanted to know who destroyed Chance's life.

Hassan walked in and said, "Hello, Chanel."

She responded, "Nice to see you again, Hassan. Sorry it's under these circumstances. The last time we were all together, I was hung-over for two days."

Hassan laughed, "How is my boy doing?"

"He's still sedated; hopefully things will turn around soon."

"Where is Yuri?"

"She had to speak with one of the detectives handling Shane's case."

"Well, I was going to tell her that his parents are flying in today. They'll be here about four o'clock. They had no idea that any of this had happened. They caught the first flight out from Cali when they found out."

"His cousin Samuel has been here everyday, I wonder why he never called them to let them know about the shooting?"

"That's a whole other story, Chanel. I can't go into that with you now. So he has been here?"

"Yes, every day since it happened."

"I wonder who told him, because they were not actually on the best of terms."

"Yes, I know, Sam... Spida told me."

Hassan walked over to Shane and whispered, "My brotha, you can't die. I need you, and we have a lot to straighten out. You're a soldier. Now, fight and wake up."

Hassan turned and walked out of the room. He was trying not to cry in front of Chanel, but he was hurt about all that had happened to Shane.

It was about two-thirty and Detective Wallace was finishing up his interview with Yuri. She made Spida leave because she didn't want him to know what they talked about.

Detective Wallace finished up his question with, "Are you and Samuel good friends?"

Knowing that she couldn't really lie, she responded, "No, not really. I don't know him like that. We have never really hung out or anything. I didn't know Shane had a cousin, here in Atlanta. I guess there is a lot I didn't know about Shane."

"Well, Ms. Jones, if you hear anything or find out anything, please don't hesitate to call me."

Yuri stood up and said, "It was a pleasure meeting you," as she flirted with him.

"The pleasure was all mine, Ms. Jones," the Detective flirted back. As she walked out, she looked over to the table that Spida was sitting at and rolled her eyes at him. He smiled and thought 'I can't wait to fuck her in that fat ass.'

When Yuri went back up to the room, Hassan was just leaving. He spoke, and she smiled.

"Hello Hassan, how are you doing?"

"I'm okay. It just hurts to see my boy lying there like that. He's a fighter and a man of God. Oh, before I forget, his family from California is on the way here."

"On their way here, as in to Atlanta, or here, as in to the hospital?" Yuri asked fearfully. She had never met Shane's mom and didn't want this to be the way they met.

Hassan continued, "His mom is hysterical because she just found out today."

"I'm sorry, Hassan, but all I know about Shane is Shane. I probably shouldn't have accepted his proposal without knowing one single family member. I didn't even know he had a cousin here, in Atlanta, until I met Spida in the hospital."

"It's not your fault, Yuri. We will talk later." As Hassan walked away, he thought to himself that he always had bad vibes about Yuri, but never pushed because Shane loved her. He knew from the past that Spida couldn't be trusted.

Chapter 34

Spida received a call while sitting in the cafeteria, still daydreaming about Yuri. He looked down at the phone and saw 'UNIDENTIFIED CALLER' on the screen.

"Speak," Spida said trying not to be conspicuous.

"We needa talk man," Uno said, nervously on the phone, like he was being recorded.

"Yo, ma man, wha's goin' on?"

"I say we needa talk today, nah tomorrow, nah nex' week. Today at five."

Sensing the fear in Uno, he tried to go along. "No worries ma man, I'll be there."

"At da spot, Spida, five o'clock. Don' fuck wit me, man, be dare." Uno hung up the phone. Spida looked at his watch and decided to go up to see his dear cousin Shane.

Meanwhile, up in his hospital room, Yuri was waiting for Shane's parents, who were on their way up, according to the nurse. She looked nervously at Chanel, but knew that it was too late for her to go anywhere. Even if she were able to leave, leaving now would just raise more suspicion.

The door to his room flew open and an older lady, who was about sixty, but looked thirty years old, rushed into the room and went straight to the bedside.

She began to cry uncontrollably saying, "Shane, Shane what have they done to you? Who did this to you?"

An older gentleman, about 65, stood behind her, gently touching her arm saying, "Jimelle, calm down. It's going to be okay."

She glared at him and snapped, "Look at him, Clarence. How can you say he's going to be okay? We don't know if he'll be able to walk or talk again. He's so helpless lying in this bed."

Trying to take control, Clarence told her to have a seat as he pulled a chair by their son's bed. She sat down, but was still tearful.

"Jimelle, I know that the doctors are doing all they can to get him well. Shane is going to be okay."

She had concentrated only on her son, and did not realize that there were other people in the room. She searched everyone to look for a familiar face. She saw Chanel and Yuri in the corner, just staring at her. She could tell that one of them must be the girlfriend. She looked at Chanel and saw that she was dressed casual, yet conservative, and figured she must be Yuri, Shane's girlfriend.

She got up and walked over to them and said to Chanel, "My dear, I'm so sorry that we had to meet under these circumstances. Shane has told me a lot about you and you are as pretty as he said," as she extended her hand to shake Chanel's.

Yuri, slightly embarrassed and irritated by the mix up, extended her hand to Mrs. Mitchell. "Mrs. Mitchell, I'm Yuri Jones, your son's fiancée."

Jimelle looked at Yuri as she shook her hand and couldn't believe that her son would fall for such a woman. She looked at her outfit and judged that she was a whore or a gold digger! She could not hide her distaste for Yuri.

She exclained in disbelief, "Fiancée? Dear, did you say fiancée? Shane never said anything about asking you to marry him. When did this all occur, the night he was shot?"

Yuri came back with much attitude, "Well, ma'am he did ask me and we are getting married as soon as he gets better. I didn't know that he consulted his mother for decisions like that."

Jimelle huffed, and was quite insulted, "Well, I never...."

Yuri was ready to jump down her throat and retorted, "And with that attitude, you never will..." She was cut off by Chanel.

In a calming tone Chanel said, "Why don't we give Shane's parents some time alone with Shane. We're sorry Mr. and Mrs. Mitchell. We know that you came a long way, and we'll be outside if you need us." Chanel pulled Yuri out of the room before she had a chance to start again. Chanel continued, "Come on Yuri, let's go down to the cafeteria."

Yuri glared at Shane's mother as she left the room. Under her breath, she said, "Bitch" as she walked by her and left out with Chanel. Once out in the hallway, and more than an earshot from Shane's room, Chanel asked, "What the hell is your problem?"

"My problem? That bitch started it. Looking me up and down, questioning if Shane really proposed to me or not."

"Yuri, that is Shane's mother and obviously neither you nor anyone else let them know that their son was shot and lying in a hospital."

"Yeah, but I didn't have any numbers or anything to call. They found out and they are here now, aren't they?"

"You know the world doesn't revolve around you all the time, Yuri. You need to be a little more concerned about other people's feelings. It is not always about you," Chanel scolded her, pissed that Yuri always only thought about herself.

"I guess you're right about that, but she started in on my clothes. What's wrong with my clothes? I have a t-shirt and jeans on."

"The clothes you have on are for the club, not for the hospital. Go look in a mirror and I think you can answer that question. Give the woman a break, Yuri. She just walked into the room to find her son almost half dead." Chanel shook her head and stepped into the elevator, nearly knocking Spida down.

"Hey, pretty lady. Where ya goin' so fast?"

"Chanel, wait up." Yuri, seeing Spida, decided to get into the elevator and take her chances with Chanel's scolding versus talking to Spida.

Spida shook his head, not understanding why Chanel and Yuri were fighting, and said under his breath, "Women."

He walked into the room almost in a jovial mood saying, "Hey cuz, wuzz up. Ya wake yet?"

When he got inside the door he realized that he had made a huge mistake.

"Samuel, what…" Shane's mother said as she looked up and saw him come into the room. "Hey Aunt J an' Unc, wha's goin' on? It's been a while since…"

Jimelle cut him off mid-sentence, "Oh no, don't Aunt J and Unc us! Why didn't you call us when Shane was shot? We just found out today. I can't believe that you would treat us like that, Samuel. After all that I have done for you! I raised you like my own, and you treat me like this? You boys were so close growing up. I can't believe that you would act this way towards each other. Samuel, you should be ashamed of yourself."

Spida had his head down, because there was no use talking to his Aunt Jimelle when she was acting like this. "But…"

"Besides, I know that your mother was no good, but I raised you and gave you everything. How could you? How could you do…"

"But…" he was trying to get a word in. "Aunt J, I tried ta call ya when he got shot, but there was no ansa, an' this wuz somethin' I didn' wanna leave on da answerin' machine." He kissed her. "Ya know I love ya. I 'preciate everythin'ya eva done fo' me. 'Sides, who ya favorite nephew?" Spida smooched in her ear real loud. She stopped fussing and began to cry.

"Now see what you've done," Mr. Mitchell told Spida.

"Hey Unc, ya know I didn' mean ta make 'er cry. Look, I been here every day watchin' ma lil' cuz. I'm jus' as concerned 'bout him gettin' betta too."

They all sat down by the bed and began to talk about Shane and Spida being children and all of the good times that they had together.

After about an hour or so had gone by, the doctor came in to make his rounds. He spoke to Shane's father because he was a retired military doctor, and understood the terminology well. He also understood that his prognosis was guarded, but there were small advances that Shane was making daily, in his recovery. Dr. Levy told them that he was still sedated heavily, to be able to heal the other areas of his body. They would be withdrawing the medications used to sedate him in another week or two. They had also been weaning him off the ventilator. Shane was responding, and soon could be breathing on his own. After speaking for another few minutes, Shane's parents thanked Dr. Levy for his time, and asked when he could be moved. He told them that it would be awhile before they could do that safely. They were concerned about his care in a County Hospital, and didn't know about Grady's reputation. Dr. Levy assured them that Grady was one of the best trauma hospitals in Atlanta. He also told them that he was on staff at Emory too, and if they wanted to move him anywhere, that would be the best place for their son. He told them that he would be in charge of his care if they decided to move him. They thanked him again, and said they would be in touch. The doctor left the room.

Jimelle looked for Samuel and noticed that he was gone. "Where did Sam go? He was just here before Dr. Levy came in."

"Jimelle, you know how that boy can't sit still. He's in the streets somewhere. He got a phone call, and that was it. He walked out, and that was the last I saw of him. I'm sure he'll call you later, when he gets a chance."

"I just can't stand it when he or Shane does that. It makes me worried that they're doing something wrong. I can't believe this day. My baby shot, my nephew doesn't tell me, and that woman thinks she's marrying Shane... Over my dead body!"

"Don't say that, Jimelle, I'm sure she is charming in her own way."

"Charming, my ass..." She turned to Shane, kissed him on the forehead and said, "Baby, you need to wake up, Momma's here. I love you, sweetheart. Don't you do this to me."

She buried her head in the pillow and wept softly.

Shane's father stood behind her. Shaking his head, he whispered, "Son, I hope you wake up too."

Chapter 35

Spida pulled up at 5:45 pm, late as usual when it came to dealing with Uno, but this time he had a real excuse. Running into Shane's parents was not only unexpected, but a meeting he would never look forward to either. When he walked into the room, Spida was smoking a blunt.

Uno could smell that good Cali weed and said, "Let me pull on dat Backwood mane, ma mind all fucked-up." Uno pulled a long drag on the blunt, getting straight to the point with Spida.

"Look mane, why you didn' tell me tha' you and dat nigga wuz fam? Tha's why ya wanted ta fuck ma Shawty so bad."

Spida said, "An', she nah yo' Shawty. She everybody bitch, includin' mines now." Uno wanted to take his pistol and smack Spida upside the head, but he wanted to know about the cash and where the rest of his cut was.

"Spida, we had a'greemen' tha we'd split dat wuz in da safe. I took sevenny thou', an there had da be ova three hun'red thou' lef' in da safe. I seen it wit ma own eyes."

"Actually, Uno, it was nah money at da bottom. There wuz three o' fo' kilos a cocaine. So it made it look like mo' money den it wuz. I took a hundred thou' an' the kilos."

"Whaddaya mean, three o' fo' keys? Ya dunno wha' ya took, nigga? In dat case ya owe me fifteen thou' mo dollas an' two bricks, nigga."

"I don' owe ya shit, nigga, cuz you bitched up an' ran outta da house."

"Mane, yo' ass trippin'."

"Ya coulda grab wha' ya' wanted. Ya think I would take a penitentiary chance a getting' outta Fayetteville wit shit fo' ya?" Uno knew that Spida was right. He did run, but he also knew that Spida was lying about how much money was in the safe.

"So wha' da fuck ya mean, nigga? Ya gonna cut me outta ma own deal? I bought a 'Vette wit summa da money an' I only got thirty thou' lef'."

"Nigga, you mean to tell me you bought a muthafuckin' car 'fore ya bought a house?" Spida laughed. "I'll work a deal wit ya, I'll let ya git two a doz birds fo'dat thirty ya got lef'. Den ya kin work off one fo' me."

Uno screamed, "Nigga, I ain' ya fuck boy. I wan' da res a ma cut!"

Spida said, "Take it o' leave it, nigga. Gimme a call when ya ready ta git dis paypa. Righ' now my dick is hard an' I think I'm gonna fin' yo' Shawty ta suck it." He laughed and left the house. Uno wanted to pull out his nine and pop Spida in the back of the head.

Spida pulled off and called Yuri. When she saw the number, she automatically became annoyed. "What the fuck do you want?"

182

"Summa dat sweet, tight black pussy ya got."

"Fuck you, Spida, leave me alone!"

"I'll leave ya'lone, bitch, since ya wan' me to, I guess I'll let ma cuz's folks in on our lil' secret. Hoe, I'll let all ya skeletons outta da closet. Ya know ma aunt say she hadda bad taste in huh mouth 'bout ya an' I change huh mind. But if ya don' wan' any a dis dick, I guess I jus' head back ta da hospital an' enlighten dem on a few things."

Yuri started crying, she cried a lot lately. "Why are you doing this to me, Spida?" As Chanel walked up she heard the last part of the conversation with Spida, and she rubbed Yuri's back, startling her. "I have to go," Yuri told Spida.

"I think ya betta make up a good story ta tell ya frien'cuz I'll be pullin' up ta git ya in thirty minutes, an' if ya don' git in da car, I'll park, go up dat elevata, an' tell ma aunt an' uncle 'bout tha' slut bitch tha' their son is tryin' ta marry, an' the accomplice ta'is shootin'. Oh an' not ta mention how ya be eatin' up dis dick." Yuri hung up the phone.

Realizing something was up, Chanel asked, "What's wrong Yuri; what did Spida say that has got you so upset?"

"He said that his aunt was feeling bad vibes about me and that he changed her mind."

"Yuri, she's just going through a lot right now. I am sure that she'll come around. Do you want to go home and relax so they can come get some time in with Shane?"

"Actually, I'm going to grab a cup of tea with Spida and see if we can reconcile our differences. At least he did take up for me."

"I think that's a good idea, Yuri, at least go say good-bye to his parents."

"Fuck his parents! Well, his mom anyway."

"Yuri, stop acting like a little bitch." Yuri had never heard Chanel talk to her like that; she had never called her out of her name.

"I'm sorry, Chanel, but I just can't face them again right now. Can you, please?" Chanel turned and walked away.

As Yuri stood there, her phone rang, "Hello?" The line clicked. "That stupid asshole is playing on my phone!" Yuri screamed.

The nurse looked at Yuri, wondering was she going crazy. She asked "Ma'am are you ok?" She had seen Yuri so much the past week she knew that her mind wasn't right.

Yuri screamed, "No," as she exited the hospital. She ran out just as Spida was pulling up. Seeing him made her sick to her stomach. He let the window down, "Damn girl, you's righ' on time, git in."

183

Yuri looked around, not noticing Detective Wallace getting out of his regular car. He remembered he had questions for her. Then he thought he remembered Yuri saying she was not on good terms with Spida. "Why would she be in the car with him?" Detective Wallace said aloud to himself.

Detective Wallace went up to the room, Chanel was leaving out.

"Hello, Ms. Brown, how are you?"

"I'm okay, Detective. And yourself?"

"Just trying to solve crimes."

"Well, I pray you solve this one."

"I really think I will. I saw Yuri leave with Samuel, do you know if she is coming back?"

"I doubt it, Detective. Shane's parents are in the room and Samuel defended Yuri, so she's just going to have coffee and talk with him, so they can be friends."

"That's good, I guess. I'll talk to his parents, you have a nice day."

"You do the same, Detective."

As Chanel walked away, Detective Wallace thought that she was smart and beautiful, something that he was never attracted to. Even though he was on the right side of the table, he still liked females that gave him a challenge. Strippers, waitresses, he even had a woman who sold marijuana with her sons. He could not break away from her because the head she gave was powerful. He admitted he was tongue whipped by her. Snapping back, he thought that Chanel had given him a good enough reason not to think anything about Yuri leaving with Samuel.

Spida pulled up to the Georgian Terrace Hotel. Yuri was upset,

"Damn, Spida, you would pick a hotel right in the heart of the city that me and Shane used to come to. You just keep torturing me."

"I am 'bout ta torture tha' pussy righ' now. Here da key, it's room 339. Lemme git dis call, Shawty," he laughed.

Yuri got out of the car while Spida answered his phone, "Wha' nigga?"

"Mane, I wanna do wha' ya said I kin do," Uno said, speaking in codes.

"I see ya changed ya mind fas'."

"Mane, when kin I git da shit?"

"Dude, it won' be today, I 'ave a date wit yo' ho." He chuckled, An' tomorra I'll be wit ma fam. Shane's folks came in ta' town, an' I'm takin'dem ta dinna. Dey migh' leave on Sunday. So we migh' kin hook up den, on da otha han', I don' move like dat on Sundays."

"So you tellin' me fo' days or mo', mane?"

"Yeah, lil' nigga, quit lettin' tha' money burn yo' pockets, if it ain't all there, then I don' wan' it, so chill. I hafta go. I got some good pussy waitin'!" Spida hung up and laughed.

Spida got to the room, Yuri was still dressed. He asked, "Why ya nah nekked?"

She was hot. He started undressing her. As Spida sucked on Yuri's titties, tears dropped down her face. Spida didn't care. He told her that the salt from her tears made her titties taste even better. As he undressed, he took her hand and made her jack his little dick. Just the touch of Yuri's hand gave him an erection. Once he was hard, he told her to suck it before he fucked her. Yuri told him that this would be the last time, and she meant it. Before she could put her mouth on it, her phone rang. It was Uno. She didn't care what Spida said, she answered.

"Hey, Uno!" Yuri said sadly.

"Hey Shawty, where ya at?"

"I'm," before she said another word Spida snatched the phone.

"Nigga, wit me, didn' I tell ya I ha' a date. Ma dick is hard an' ya not'bout ta spoil ma fun. She kin holla at ya layta, afta she get deez nuts off huh jaws." He hung up. Yuri wanted to kill him, she wondered what kind of nigga was Uno that he would allow this to keep happening. Now she was questioning his gangsta.

Spida interrupted her thoughts when he shoved his dick in her mouth.

"Suck it, nasty bitch!" He screamed. Yuri's reflexes kicked in and she bit Spida's dick as hard as she could. Spida took his fist and cracked her right on the head. She fell to the floor.

Yuri was unconscious for a few minutes. When she came to, Spida had already fucked her, and came inside of her. As she looked at Spida, she saw triples; he was getting dressed.

When he opened the door, he said to her, "I'm sho yo ho ass kin git a lift home. See ya, an' I wouldn' wanna be ya."

As Yuri sat on the floor waiting for the dizziness to fade away, she called Uno. His call had been the last call that came in. That made it easier to call him back. "Wha'?" he answered.

"Uno, Spida just hit me so hard in my head, because I didn't want to suck his dick. I need a ride from the Georgian Terrace," she cried.

"Bitch, you shouldn' a lef' wit 'im."

185

"You told me to play the game with him! I was following your instructions, trying to make you happy. Like I said before, had you not put me in your money situation, with you and Spida, this shit wouldn't be going on!"

"Look, Shawty, I jus' foun' out my mane Shawty be pregnan'. We celebratin' so I can' come now. Ya righ' by yo house. Catch a taxi, an' I'll hit ya up layta."

Yuri felt betrayed, and all alone at the same damn time. She wondered how he could tell her something like that at a time like this. She threw on her clothes without trying to clean up. Outside the hotel, taxis were waiting. She jumped in one and went home. When Chanel got there, she told Yuri that she had decided to stay at the hospital with Shane's parents. She told her how nice they were and how his mom sent her apologies for being so rude. She also told her that Detective Wallace had shown up looking for her, and how he saw her pull off with Spida, just before he could speak to her.

Yuri asked, "What did he say to Shane's parents?" Chanel told her that he said whoever it was who shot him, followed, or waited on his arrival, because of how they came in when he drove into his garage.

Chanel looked at Yuri, "Why do you have a knot on your head, Yuri?"

"As I was getting out of Spida's car I reached back in to thank him and hit it on the door."

"It looks like it hurts, let me get you some Tylenol, because from the looks of it, you hit it pretty hard." Chanel came back with the Tylenol and hot tea. "Take this, you really need to rest, I'll lay right here and watch you snore."

"Thank you, Chanel, I love you."

"You better, Yuri."

Yuri slept the day away. When she woke up, she realized she had missed three 'unavailable' calls. She knew it couldn't be anyone but her enemy/stalker. They did not get to call her a 'snake' or 'bitch' because she hadn't answered. She wondered who it was taunting her; they really didn't have a life, to run around doing the childish things they were doing. Her conscience kicked in, 'If you weren't so hard up for a big dick and a smile, you'd be fine.' "Shut up!" She screamed.

Chanel ran into the room, "What's wrong, Yuri?"

"Sorry, Chanel, I think I was dreaming."

"Yuri, Shane's parents leave tomorrow, Spida is taking them out. I think you should go up to the hospital and apologize to his mom; after all, you guys will be getting married when Shane wakes up. You don't want to start off having a bad relationship with his mom; it will only make it worse for the two of you."

"Okay, Chanel, I'll shower and put something more suitable on to go see her."

"Thanks, Yuri, that would be nice. I'll get dressed so we can go."

When Yuri walked into the hospital room, Shane's mom hugged her. "I apologize that I was rude Yuri, it's just hard to see my son lying there and then, you know, he hadn't told me about you. But I must admit, even though he didn't mention anything about an engagement, he did tell us a couple of weeks ago that he wanted to fly us here for a surprise. So I guess that surprise was you."

"I also apologize, Mrs. Mitchell. I was rude and not thinking at the time, it was only a misunderstanding, and it will never happen again."

"Thank God that's over!" The women laughed. Shane's mom let Yuri know that they would be leaving to handle their business in California, and when they returned, Shane would be moved to Emory Hospital. They also told her that they would then stay in Georgia, until he was well.

Yuri knew that his mom would be hell.

She thought, 'What if Shane never wakes up?' He was breathing on his own, but still in a coma. She wanted Uno anyway, as sad as she felt about Shane's shooting. She still loved Uno. She was glad that Uno was not the one who had done the shooting; Spida's pussy ass did it.

Chapter 36

Mr. and Mrs. Mitchell met everyone at the hospital. Spida, Hassan, Yuri, and Chanel all held hands, while Mrs. Mitchell led a prayer. Somehow, Yuri ended up holding Spida's hand. He fingered her palm, while his aunt prayed. Yuri snatched her hand away, making everyone open their eyes.

"Amen!" Mrs. Mitchell said. As she looked to see what the disturbance was about, she noticed the look on Yuri's face. "Are you okay, Yuri?"

"Sorry everyone, Spida, I mean Samuel must have been thinking too strongly about something, and squeezed my hand really hard."

Spida looked dumbfounded. "Sorry Aunt J, I had a moment. Sorry Yuri."

"Well, we have to be going," Mr. Mitchell said. "We have to return the rental car, then go through this busy Atlanta airport. Hassan, it is always a pleasure to see you."

"Likewise, Sir, and Mrs. Mitchell, you stay beautiful."

"Thank you, Hassan," she said, nice and calm. "Samuel, we will be back Tuesday evening. Look after your cousin and if there is any type of change, please call me."

"I will Aunt J, I love ya. Unc, look out fo' ma aunt."

"I always do Sam. Yuri and Chanel it was great to meet you ladies. Please look after Shane."

"We will see you both next week. Have a good trip."

Spida woke up, bright and early to the Monday morning sunrise. The stripper that laid next to him was still sound asleep.

He thought to himself. 'I hafta stop gettin' drunk an' payin' deez hoes fo' pussy.'

He got up swiftly, got dressed, and left the two hundred and fifty dollars she asked for on the night stand. He decided to go sit at the hospital and visit Shane before anyone else showed up, to have some alone-time with his cousin.

Spida arrived at 7:00am. Grady was swarming with homeless people, inside and out. He now understood why his aunt and uncle wanted their son out of this grimy hospital. He got on an elevator that was musty and overcrowded. He was wishing he would have taken the stairs instead. When he reached the room, Shane's nurse was coming out.

"Hello, Mr. Mitchell, I see you're here early today."

"Yes ma'am, how my cousin doin'?"

"I just cleaned him up and everything is still the same, but he has really improved. It is a miracle that he is breathing on his own. God really favors him."

"Thank ya ma'am, yeah, he a blesst man." Spida walked into the room thinking about what the nurse just said about Shane being blessed and favored. He was very aware of his being the favored one, and despised him for that. He was favorable with the women, favorable with the teachers, and God had even favored Shane, and blessed him with a much bigger penis than Spida.

He thought back to when they were kids and they would pull out their wee-wees to see who could pee the farthest. Shane would ask, "Sam why your thing so little?" Shane and the other boys would laugh at him, causing Spida to have very low self-esteem at a young age.

Spida stood by Shane's bed and he started talking to him.

"Man, I wish it would a neva come ta dis, but cuz ya brought this shit on yo' self. All ma life I been ya big cuz, but ya made me feel small. Ya took ma dope plug." He started getting angry, talking louder and louder. "Ya stole ma bitch, ma plug, an' everythin' dat I had, nigga. Ya," and before Spida could say another word, Shane's eyes came open.

Shane struggled to look around. Once he laid eyes on Spida, he reached out, trying to grab him. This sent Spida jumping back scared. Spida was about to run to get a nurse, then realized that Shane could identify him as the shooter. Instead, he ran back toward Shane and grabbed a pillow from under his head, ready to suffocate him. Shane grabbed his arm, as the machines began to go off. Spida managed to hold the pillow over Shane's face, suffocating him. He pressed down as hard as he could, trying to kill him once again. Shane scratched Spida's arm, fighting for his life. After a few seconds of struggling with Shane, the nurse came in. Spida snatched the pillow back. He put it behind Shane's head, as if he was only trying to elevate him. The nurse noticed that Shane's eyes were big with fear, as he gasped for air.

Spida screamed, "He woke up, I didn't know what to do and I couldn't leave his side."

"That's fine. The machine went off at the Nurses' station and alerted us of his movement. I'm sorry Mr. Mitchell, you'll have to step out now, because he seems very upset. I'm calling Dr. Levy, and they will inform his parents and his fiancée that he has awoken. Sorry sir, you have to leave. We have to calm him down, so we can get his vitals."

Spida paced the waiting room, wondering if and when Shane could talk, would he tell on him. Just as he had done when they were kids. Shane always told.

The nurse came into the waiting room, "We have him stable, Mr. Mitchell. We had to put a trach in because he had trouble breathing again."

"Can I go see him now?" Spida asked anxiously.

"I'm sorry no one is allowed in right now. We have also informed Detective Wallace that he is awake. He's on his way." Spida walked over to look out the window. Standing with his hands in his pockets, he watched the cars zoom by on 75. He had to come up with a plan, and quick.

189

Not quick enough, he was startled by that annoying voice, "Samuel, may I have a moment?" Spida was instantly nervous, and it showed.

Speaking under his breath, Spida said, "Wha' da fuck dis pig wan'?"

Confused, Detective Wallace responded, "I'm sorry, did you say something Samuel?"

"I be talkin' ta ma self, Detective. Wuzzup?"

Detective Wallace walked over toward Spida. He wanted his presence to intimidate Spida, and it did. They sat in the family area.

Detective Wallace began, "Samuel, I know you are his family, however, Ms. Jones had not even known you before the shooting. She claimed she didn't even know that he had a cousin here. I know this is not a good time for these questions, but I'm trying to put together all the pieces to this case."

Irritated, Spida replied, "Whazit ya nee' ta know, Detective?"

"Well, you were the first one to arrive at the hospital. How and when did you find out that Mr. Mitchell had been shot?"

"Well," he stuttered, looking all over the place, he clenched and unclenched his hands. Not knowing what to say, Spida rambled, "I, um, ran inta' Shane earlier tha' day, an'..."

Before he could finish, Detective Ramos interrupted, "Detective Wallace, excuse me for a minute, I need to speak with you, outside, please."

Detective Wallace glanced over at Spida and noticed how nervous he looked, "Hold that thought, Samuel. I need to take care of this."

Breathing a sigh of relief, Spida responded, "Yeah, I'll be righ' here waitin'." Spida could not wait until the detectives were out of sight, so he could be out like Casper and get ghost.

Chapter 37

Yuri drove as fast as she could to the hospital. It took her approximately eight minutes to get there from her house. Chanel told her to slow down, but Yuri paid her no mind. As they approached Shane's room, they heard Detective Wallace talking to his partner.

"Hello Ms. Jones and Ms. Brown."

"Hello Detectives," they both acknowledged the detectives at the same time. Yuri tried to walk past the detectives and go into Shane's room, but Detective Wallace stopped her. "I'm sorry Ms. Jones but no one is allowed in his room at this time. After he woke up, he seemed upset, which made things a little complicated right now."

"Was anyone with him when he woke up," asked Yuri?

"Yes, his cousin Samuel was here with him. I have not seen or heard from him since we spoke, a little after he was kicked out of the room by the nurse." Yuri wondered to herself if Shane acted so hysterically because he remembered what happened when he was shot.

Detective Wallace asked his partner and Chanel if he could have a word with Yuri, alone. Detective Ramos invited Chanel to the cafeteria while Detective Wallace and Yuri went to the family waiting area.

"Yuri," he said calmly, I'm not sure if you know this, but you gave my partner and me conflicting stories. Because of that, you are still a suspect in our case. You told Detective Ramos that you had not been at the scene, and you had not been with Shane, but you were on your way to see him when you got the call. Which story is true, because you told me that you had been with Mr. Mitchell earlier that day, and you left because your friend was arriving in town. The only similarity is that you got the call on your way back." He looked up from his notes, "Don't fuck with me, Yuri. I will have your ass locked up quicker than you think."

Yuri started crying, "Detective, I was scared and confused."

Yuri walked toward the detective, breaking down, giving him no other option than to hug her. He looked around to make sure that no one was watching them. He wanted to back away and push her off of him; however, the $240.00 bottle of Creed perfume, mixed with Yuri's natural sweet body scent had him mesmerized.

He snapped out of it quick, "Ms. Jones, I know you're hurting about this, but you have to tell me the truth, ok?"

Sobbing, Yuri managed to respond, "Detective, please, just let me get my thoughts and mind right, I am emotionally drained from all of this. You have to understand."

"Ok, Ms. Jones, I will give you until tomorrow morning, then we have to talk. Mr. Mitchell's parents will be in town tomorrow evening and I have to assure them that I am closer to solving this case. Speaking of solving this case, I need to find Samuel. I have some unanswered questions for him. Get your mind right, because I want the truth tomorrow."

"Thank you, Detective," Yuri whispered, through her fake tears.

Spida left the hospital and was pacing back and forth at his trap house. He was thinking about Shane, and what he was going to tell the police about the confrontation. Only thing Spida was sure of, was that Shane wouldn't mention the drugs. Spida realized that he needed to get rid of the dope. He had over one hundred and fifty thousand dollars in cash, plus the four kilos of uncut cocaine that he had stolen. He knew that he could go to Uno and trade him the two kilos for the thirty thousand dollars he'd offered. With that, Spida would go into hiding. He also thought of giving Uno the other two kilos to work off, and pay him another thirty thousand. With two hundred thousand dollars in cash, Spida knew that was enough for him to hide out and relax while he waited to find out how Shane would react. Spida grabbed a fifth of Remy Martin VSOP and drank on it, as if it were water. He put the kilos into a Louis Vuitton duffle bag and called Uno.

Uno answered on the first ring, "Wuzzup, mane?"

"Nah much, I be tryin' ta see if ya still got all a dat an' is ya ready ta make da move?"

"Yeah, nigga, now. Mane, we kin git togetha when traffic die down. I'm out in Alpharetta wit ma Shawty an' it won' be 'till lata, mane. Seven o'clock, nigga. No lata." Uno hung up, leaving Spida talking to himself.

Finally, at a quarter to six that evening, the doctor let Yuri and Chanel into Shane's room. He was highly sedated, but he was awake. Yuri and Chanel stood by his bedside and prayed.

Chanel led the prayer, "Father God, we would like to give you thanks for bringing Shane back to us. Father, we never doubted you. You showed up when you knew the time was right. We thank you for your mercy and your grace. Please heal his body and return his health to the way it was before. Thank you Father God. In Jesus' name we pray, amen."

When Chanel finished praying, Yuri asked if she could have some time alone with Shane. Chanel left the room to give them some privacy.

Shane looked at Yuri as she started talking, "Baby, I'm so sorry that this happened to you. I wish you would have told me you had family here." A tear slid down Shane's cheek. "Shane, I promise, baby when you get better, I will not stand in the way of your happiness. You deserve someone much better than me." Shane tried to sit up and reach for Yuri, but he was too weak.

Before Yuri could react, her phone rang. It was Uno calling. Yuri could not even give Shane thirty minutes of her time without being interrupted. She answered quickly, "Hello?"

"Wazzup, Shawty? Wha' ya doin'?"

"I'm at the hospital with Shane. He woke up today." She went into the bathroom to step away from Shane.

Uno sounded furious. "He what!"

Yuri continued, "He woke up and Spida just so happened to be in the room with him. After he woke up and saw Spida, Shane had a panic attack and the nurse put Spida out. I hope Spida don't bitch up, and in the end, snitch you out."

"Tha' nigga betta not, be on dat bullshit. I wuz callin' ya ta tell ya tha' I be meetin' Spida lata. How he be lookin' today? I wanna know if he got his mind righ'."

"Actually I didn't see him. The detective said he wanted to ask him some questions, but he got distracted and Spida was gone."

"Well tha' splains why he tryin' ta hook up wit me so tough."

"What are ya'll hooking up for, Uno?"

"I'll holla at ya bout it when I sees you lata. Love ya, Shawty. Hold it down up there." Yuri whispered, "I love you too, Uno."

When Yuri walked out of the restroom, she found Hassan standing at Shane's side.

He was talking to Shane, "Hey, my brotha, I am so glad that you are ok. I can't wait until you can talk so you can tell me who did this to you. We'll handle them. I promise, those niggas got it comin'." Hassan heard someone behind him and turned around quick, with his hand already reaching for his nine, "Yuri, you almost got shot."

"Sorry, Hassan, I was using the restroom. I didn't hear you come in."

"Well, how's he doing, Yuri?"

"He looks as if he wants to speak, but he's still heavily medicated. I think I'm going to sit here with him for a while, hoping he'll come around."

"Me, too." Hassan sat down next to Shane's bed and continued, "How is the investigation coming along?"

Yuri was caught off guard, "Oh, I assume its progressing. The detectives were here earlier."

"And what did they say?"

"I don't know they were talking to Spida. I've been in here with Shane the whole time."

Hassan noticed that Yuri seemed a little nervous but kept going, "You know, Reginald is my high school buddy, and he owes me one. I saved his sister at one of our high school football games. The captain of the football team was gonna rape her. Anyway, Regi promised, whatever I needed, he would always come through for me. I already got him working on finding the niggas who did this, so it's just a matter of time."

193

Hassan leaned back in his chair to get comfortable. Before Hassan could continue, Shane started moaning. Hassan jumped up, almost yelling, "Shane, Shane, can you hear me?"

Even though Yuri was on edge, she played the part, "Shane, baby, are you in pain? Do you want me to get the nurse? Talk to me, baby."

Hassan interrupted, "Come on, man. I got so much to tell you."

Shane tried opening his eyes, he mumbled, "Sam."

Confused, Hassan turned to Yuri, "Did he just say 'Sam?'"

Yuri knew exactly why Shane would say 'Sam', but she couldn't admit it to Hasaan. "I don't know I couldn't understand him."

"I know that's what he said." Hassan turned to Shane, "Relax man, don't try to talk. If you're trying to say that Sam had something to do with the shooting, blink your eyes twice." Hassan didn't notice the worried look on Yuri's face when Shane blinked twice. He was too busy getting mad. "I should have known that scandalous, jealous ass nigga had something to do with this shit!"

Yuri tried to cover the shakiness in her voice, "Why do you think that, Hassan?"

"The same reason why you never knew about him. Shane didn't fuck with Sam. He knew Sam could not be trusted. Think about it Yuri, how was he the first one to be here at the hospital? It just doesn't make sense. That nigga better not show his face here again, I will kill his ass! Better yet, let me call Regi and tell him to go ahead and arrest his ass, before I get to his ass first!"

Yuri told Hassan that she was going to find Chanel. She left the room and immediately dialed Uno.

"Wuzzup?"

Yuri tried to whisper, "Shane just said 'Sam.' What's even more fucked up is Shane's best friend, Hassan, was in the room with us, and he heard him. Hassan is friends with Detective Wallace and he's calling him, because he owes Hassan a favor. You need to do something, and fast, because Spida is hot as hell right now!" Yuri noticed Chanel getting off the elevator, coming toward her. "I have to go." She hung up without giving Uno a chance to say anything.

Chapter 38

Spida already knew where to meet Uno. Anytime they dealt with weight, they met at Uno's ex-girlfriend's house. They could give her a couple hundred dollars to go shopping, and her ass was gone all day, without questions. Being the hood rat that she was, she didn't even notice that they were playing her. Spida pulled up in his truck, with the duffle bag sitting next to him. He told Uno to meet him at seven; it was now almost eight.

Furious, Spida said to himself, "This nigga nee' me an' he got me here waitin' like a bitch. Fuck 'im, I'm goin' ta sell dis shit ta da lil' cats down on Peter Street."

He turned his truck and started to pull out. Out of nowhere, Uno showed up, smoking a blunt.

"Wha' da fuck be wrong wit dis nigga? He bout ta have all dis work wit 'im an' he smokin' in da car? Maybe I should jus' sell 'im two kilos." Spida knew Uno was a fuck-up.

Uno jumped in Spida's truck, interrupting his thoughts, "Wazzup, mane?"

"Wha's crackin', Uno? Where da paper, so I kin coun' it an' git the hell outta here?"

"Mane, where da fuck da bricks, firs'? I don' trust anyone righ' now."

"Nigga, dey righ' here. Plus, I'll give ya two days ta git ridda two mo' fo' me."

Uno didn't agree. "Nigga, you owe me two!"

"I don' owe ya shit, nigga, ya coulda got dem yo'self, but yo' punk ass ran like a bitch."

Uno pulled out his pistol and aimed it right at Spida's head, "You a bitch! You fuckboy."

Before Spida could react, Uno shot him dead in the head, like he always wanted to. Uno made sure that he had a silencer screwed on, so no one would hear the shot. Spida slumped over, causing his horn to blow.

Uno shoved him off laughing to himself, "Fuck nigga neva paid attention ta da gloves I always wore fo' situations like dis. Uno made sure to snatch the twenty five- thousand dollar tarantula chain, while steadily talkin' shit and searching Spida, "Fuck-boy, ya shoulda gave me wha' wuz mines."

 He snatched the fifty thousand dollar Rolex off his arm, and took the four thousand dollars in cash that Spida had in his pocket. He almost forgot the Louis Vuitton duffle bag, but snatched it up with a smile on his face. He looked around, to make sure no one was watching, and jumped out of the truck. The tow truck driver, who was his friend, hitched the truck and rolled off, just as he was paid to do.

Chapter 39

Yuri was awakened by her loud cell phone ringing. She had not talked to Uno, and knew that he may have been coming down from one of his late night binges. He liked to party all night on ecstasy.

"Hey, baby."

It was not who she expected.

"Baby? Sorry Ms. Jones, were you expecting Mr. Mitchell? Is he talking already?"

Yuri didn't know what to say, "Um," she was interrupted by her other line beeping. "Detective Wallace, will you please hold on a minute, I think that's the hospital calling." She clicked over, hoping it was Uno. "Hello?"

The computer generated voice said, "Bitch, you're dead!"

Yuri clicked back over, "Sorry, Detective, it was a wrong number. What can I do for you?"

He hesitated to answer, but asked if he could meet Yuri at the hospital within the next hour. Yuri told the detective that it was too early, and she would appreciate if he would meet her at her house instead.

He agreed, "That would be fine, Ms. Jones, I will see you at eight-thirty."

Yuri rushed to the guest room to wake Chanel.

"Chanel, I have to meet with the detectives around the corner at Starbucks. Will you please go sit with Shane at the hospital until I get there?"

She did not trust Spida around Shane. Even though she was sure that she didn't want to be with Shane, she did not want Spida to hurt him.

Chanel got dressed and asked Yuri if she should take a taxi.

"No, Chanel, take my car. The detectives are going to pick me up, and I'll have them drop me off at the hospital when we're done. Thanks, Chanel."

"No problem, Yuri."

By the time Detective Wallace arrived at Yuri's house, she had already showered. She was wearing a robe with a sexy Victoria's Secret bra and thong. When Yuri let Detective Wallace in, he noticed her expensive taste in furniture. He knew that Shane was into real estate and figured he must have bought Yuri anything she wanted. What Detective Wallace didn't know, was that drug money paid for everything. Yuri offered the detective some coffee. Detective Wallace could not take his eyes off of her, as she shook her ass, and disappeared into the kitchen. The scent he remembered smelling at the hospital began to overcrowd his brain. As Yuri sat the coffee down on the table in front of him, her robe came slightly open, exposing her lace bra. He quickly turned his head, as he reached into the briefcase to collect his notes, "Okay, Ms. Jones, let's get started."

Yuri dropped her robe. "Yeah, let's get started, Detective."

Detective Wallace turned his head, "Ms. Jones, please put your clothes back on."

Yuri seductively said, "Make me, Officer. I've been looking at you ever since we spoke at the hospital, I've never been fucked by a police officer. Now, handcuff me, and fuck me hard."

Detective Wallace didn't know what to say, he was sweating and looking around nervously, "Ms. Jones, what are you trying to do?"

Yuri stepped closer to him, "I am trying to give you what every man wants. Don't be shy, Detective." Yuri noticed how nervous he was, he was loosening his tie, while breathing very heavily. "Come on, Detective." Yuri straddled him while he was searching where to put his hands. He smelled that scent again, her Creed perfume that no man could resist. Without thinking twice, his hands were all over her body. He helped her out of her bra and began sucking on her nipples.

"That's right, Detective, I knew you wanted this the whole time."

She reached down and unzipped his pants, pulling out his erect dick, she was not disappointed at all. It was exactly what she liked. She wasted no time putting her lips around it. The detective couldn't do anything but moan in pleasure as he grabbed her hair. Yuri loved the way his smooth dick fit perfectly in her mouth. He rubbed his fingers through her hair enjoying just about the best blow job he had ever had. What started as a scheme was turning out to be something Yuri enjoyed. Before the detective could fill her mouth with his warm cum, he reached out to grab a condom. Yuri rose to her feet, almost smiling, about ready to climb on his rock hard dick. He grabbed her, bent her over the couch, and entered her from behind; Yuri couldn't help but scream out in pleasure. She was throwing it back, and he was matching her thrust for thrust.

"This is what you wanted, Yuri." Yuri thought to herself, 'I got him exactly where I want him.' The detective was ready to bust, feeling Yuri tighten her muscles around him.

"Yeah, Detective, fuck me," Yuri didn't even get to finish before the front door swung open.

"Yuri, I forgot my… " Chanel gasped, she could not believe her eyes. Detective Wallace was fucking Yuri. Yuri could not move quickly enough. Chanel was in shock as she witnessed Detective Wallace pull his big dick out of Yuri. She didn't even give them a chance to get dressed. "What the fuck is going on? You are supposed to be helping find out who shot Shane, not fucking his fiancée while he's laid up in a hospital!" Chanel did not give the detective a chance to respond, "Yuri, you knew exactly what you were doing. You sent me out of the house, you knew you were not going to Starbucks, this was your plan all along."

After scolding them, Chanel grabbed her wallet, which she had forgotten. Yuri tried to stop her, but she snatched her arm away, "I don't know who you are anymore!"

When Chanel walked out of the house, Detective Wallace put his head down and apologized to Yuri, as if he was the one who started it. He knew they were both dead wrong for what they had done. Yuri responded, seductively, "Why are you apologizing, baby?"

She walked back up on him. Standing on her tippy toes, she kissed his neck.

"The damage is done, she's gone, and I want to make you cum." She rubbed his dick and it sprung back to life, ready to finish what they had started.

They fucked for twenty minutes as hard as they could until they both exploded with sparks. Yuri grabbed a hot towel and wiped off Detective Wallace's dick. She was nowhere near done with him. She then kissed and sucked the tip of his dick. Detective Wallace did not know what kind of spell Yuri had put on him, but he knew that he was catching feelings.

Chapter 40

Chanel arrived at the hospital to find Candice and another female standing at Shane's bed. Shane looked at Chanel and smiled, he lifted his arm so she could hold his hand. Chanel smiled and grabbed his hand. She turned her attention back to the two women.

"Hello ladies, I'm Chanel."

"Hello, Chanel, my name is Candice and this is my friend, Passion. Shane is our boy, and we came to check on him. Are you his new girlfriend?"

Candice asked Chanel, with a confused look on her face.

"No, my best friend, Yuri, is his fiancée."

"Your face looks so familiar, and I think I know from where. Were you with Yuri and Shane that night at the Velvet Room?"

"Yes, that was me, and I remember you too."

Chanel, can we step outside and talk for a minute, if you don't mind?"

"No, not at all," Chanel turned Shane, "I'll be right back, I promise."

Once they stepped out of Shane's room, Candice turned to Chanel, "So you're her best friend from D.C.?"

"Yes, that would be me."

"I remember your brother was getting married. I was the one who mailed Yuri's gift to him and his fiancée."

"Oh, really, that's funny, because I don't think he ever mentioned receiving it."

"Well, someone must have, because Yuri insisted that I send it certified from Memphis. Anyway, how are the bride and groom doing?"

Chanel looked down with a sad look on her face. She took a deep breath. "My brother is deceased."

Candice was stunned, and wished that she hadn't even brought it up, "I am very sorry to hear that, Chanel." She hugged Chanel, feeling her pain, "Are you ok, Chanel?"

"Yes, it's just still hard to cope, when I think about him."

"If you don't mind me asking, what happened to him?"

Chanel took another deep breath, "He hung himself a few days after the wedding was supposed to take place."

Candice was instantly sorry that she had asked. "I'm so sorry, may God bless his soul."

Chanel changed the subject, "Candice, why are you and Yuri no longer friends?"

Candice sighed, "Let's go sit over here, Chanel, this may take a minute."

"Sure, I have nothing but time," Chanel couldn't help but think about Yuri and Detective Wallace and what she had witnessed.

"Chanel, you remember that night that I shoved Yuri's head?"

Chanel smiled, "Yes how could I forget?"

"Well, when Yuri first arrived here in Atlanta, we met on Clark's campus and we just clicked. So when she went back home and came back, I let her stay with me for a while."

"Yes, she told me about that."

"Anyways, she had met my boyfriend, Q. Well, I went on vacation to the Bahamas, and she helped herself to him, and he told me what happened. Would you believe that she tried to fuck him in his ass with a toy? He was not having that, so he beat the shit out of that bitch. I'm sorry Chanel, but your friend is a snake." Before Chanel could say anything, Candice continued, "She mentioned to me that you and her mother thought that she was a virgin. Girl, she has been fucking since middle school. That girl had everybody fooled." Chanel just sat there, listening, not knowing what to say. "Chanel, I'm sorry to say this, but I wouldn't doubt if Yuri had something to do with Shane getting shot. Anyway, why isn't she here with her fiancé?"

Yuri stepped out of the elevator and noticed that Chanel was sitting with Candice. She quickly walked over to them, stepping to Candice, "Bitch, what the fuck are you doing here?"

Candice jumped out of the chair, with her fist balled up, and punched Yuri in the face, before Chanel could even stand and get in between them. Candice wasted no time, "Snake bitch, because I can."

Yuri reached around Chanel and slapped Candice as hard as she could, "Bitch, I am tired of you."

"Well, do something about it," Candice responded, trying to step around Chanel. While Candice was trying to get to Yuri, Passion walked out of Shane's room. She realized what was going on, and snuck up on Yuri from behind. She cold cocked her twice, with two strong punches to her head making her fall.

Chanel screamed, "Stop! You guys are not going to jump her!"

As Yuri got up off the floor, a nurse walked by. The nurse thought to herself, "This chick has a lot of shit going on."

She did not alert security because she figured it was just a family misunderstanding.

200

Candice turned to Passion, "Let's get out of here, before I catch a murder case on this snake punk bitch."

Yuri screamed, "Stop playing on my phone, bitch! Grow the fuck up."

Candice responded, "Quit fucking everybody's man, ho! I cannot wait until Shane is strong enough to know about all the fucking you have done. Even after the night he proposed to you! Your ass came back here and had a threesome! Let's go Passion."

As they walked away, Passion turned to Yuri, "Watch your back, bitch."

Yuri walked over to Chanel, "I am so sorry, Chanel."

"For what, Yuri? You should be in there asking Shane for forgiveness." Yuri tried to hug Chanel but she moved back out of Yuri's reach. "I hope you get it together, Yuri. Since you moved here, it seems like Satan has gotten into you. May God be with you."

Chanel turned to go back into the room with Shane, leaving Yuri to think about what she just said.

Yuri just sat there, rubbing the knot in the back of her head that Passion had planted. She thought about the talk that she had with Detective Wallace. She was not going to jail for anyone. If someone was going down, it was going to be Spida. If Spida decided to rat Uno out, Uno would have to deal with Spida himself. She took a long deep breath and went into Shane's room.

Yuri noticed that Shane looked much better. The nurses informed Yuri that the trach was going to be removed on Thursday. They also mentioned that Shane's parents were scheduled to land that evening, at 6:30pm. Yuri rubbed Shane's head, and assured him that everything would be fine. He laid back and closed his eyes.

Chapter 41

Yuri drove away from the hospital, tired after putting on a show for Shane's parents. Shane's parents asked Yuri if she had seen Spida. She told them that she had not seen him since Sunday, when they were all at the hospital together. The nurse mentioned she had seen Spida talking to Detective Wallace the day before, but he had not returned since. They all knew that Spida was known for his disappearing acts, so it was no big deal.

Driving down the freeway, Yuri called Uno, "Wazzup, Shawty?"

"Why haven't you called me, Uno? I've been worried about you."

"Cuz I been tryin' t handle things so we kin be straight. Plus, ya know ma Shawty be pregnant. She been havin' a nigga on lock."

Yuri hated hearing him call another woman 'his Shawty,' and she instantly felt stupid for loving Uno like she did. "Baby, Chanel went to eat with Shane's parents, and I told them I couldn't go because I needed some rest, but I really wanted to see you."

"Where ya at, Shawty?"

Yuri got excited, "I am passing 14thStreet, about to get off at my exit."

"Come ova here ta 85 an' North Druid Hills, turn lef' an' I'll meet ya at da Panera Bread, ok? See ya in ten minutes."

Yuri pulled up and saw Uno sitting in his Corvette, looking sexy and rich. She thought it was funny how a car could change someone's appearance. Yuri got out of her car and climbed into Uno's.

He instructed her firmly, "Lock yo car, we goin fo' a ride, Shawty."

While Yuri was admiring his 'Vette, Uno fired up a blunt. Yuri noticed that Uno's weed smelled like Shane's and Spida's weed, not knowing that Uno had taken the ounce of weed from Spida after he murdered him.

Yuri asked Uno, seductively, "Where are we going?"

"Up 85, I ain' got ma dick sucked in da Vette yet." Uno pulled out his already hard dick and continued, "I wan' ya ta be da firs' ta do it."

Uno's dick was like a magnet to Yuri. As soon as he pulled it out, she could not resist; she went straight to work. Uno loved Yuri's head and every time she deep throated him, he accelerated on the gas, getting up to over a hundred and ten miles an hour. Yuri made him cum and swallowed it all. Uno was having a hard time catching his breath.

"Damn, Shawty, das wha' I'm talkin' 'bout. Ya know, no one kin do it like you."

Yuri laid back in her seat; as long as Uno was satisfied, so was she.

Uno got down to business, "So, wha's goin' on at da hospital?"

"Shane is much better. His parents got back in today, and Thursday they are taking his trach out. I think he is going to tell on Spida. The detectives know that there were two people in the house, because the neighbors witnessed two separate cars leaving. The detectives also said Shane had hair and skin under his fingernails. Some of it was probably mine, and some of it had to have been Spida's. They said they were sure there was a struggle."

Uno interrupted, "Yea, tha's when dem stupid niggas be fightin' ovada gun an'da's when I git da hell outta there."

"Uno, did you get with Spida yesterday? His aunt and uncle have been looking for him. The detective was talking with him, but he left for a minute, and when he came back, Spida was gone."

Uno was quick to lie, "I seen 'im yestaday. We made a few moves an' tha' nigga rolled out."

"I don't know what is going on Uno, but my gut is telling me that you need to stay the hell away from Spida."

"Don' worry Shawty, I hear ya." Uno smiled and thought to himself, 'I sho am gonna stay away from dat nigga. He a'ready six feet unda, where I pay dem niggas ta bury 'im'.

Chapter 42

Thursday seemed like it would never come. It was time for Shane's trach to be removed. Before his parents or anyone arrived, Hassan showed up.

He walked up to Shane's bedside, "Look, my brotha, we have to talk, and I want to run this down on you now while you can't talk. Just listen and don't get upset, because you know the machine will sound off, and the nurses will be quick to come. You feel me bro?" Shane nodded his head 'yes', completely understanding. Hassan continued, "Well the day Yuri and I was here, you came out and said 'Sam,' right?" Shane shook his head 'yes'. "When you said Spida's name, I knew that he had something to do with this, right?" Shane shook his head 'yes' again. "Well, to make this not so hard on you, I didn't do anything to him, but I had offered a hundred- thousand dollar hit on him. Man, there was four hundred thousand dollars worth of money and dope in your safe, and half of it was mine, so I couldn't let that nigga get away with it. I called the little soldiers in Mechanicsville and told them that they could get the money, once they delivered Spida's bitch-ass to me, alive. Well, they couldn't deliver him alive because the mutherfucka that ran up in your house with him, killed him, and paid them to bury him."

Shane did not know how to feel, he knew Spida was grimy, but he was also family. All he could do was shake his head. Hassan noticed that the look on Shane's face was sadness. "I found out who he paid to bury him, and I got them niggas to deliver me the body, so I could let Regi in on what was going on. Regi is the detective that's handling your case. Anyway, Tow Truck Mike was supposed to bury the body ten feet underground. He was paid twenty-five thousand dollars, but I paid the nigga twenty-five more to hand over the body, and forget the whole situation. My people also told me that the dude that did the robbery with Spida and the murder had been fucking with Yuri for a while now."

Shane started getting angry and Hassan noticed.

"Well that's all I am going to tell you, man. You're getting upset. I'm sorry to tell you like this. I am going to call Regi and let him know what is going on, and let him know where to find the body."

As Hassan stood to leave, Shane grabbed a pen and paper and started writing, "Man, I want to know everything about this nigga."

Hassan sighed and sat back down, "His name is Jessy Johnson but they call him Uno. He is 25 years old and from Mechanicsville. That's how I got up with him so fast. Word is the nigga is scandalous. He was living with his momma until recently. Seems like he hit this lick and he been hiding out. He has a baby momma that lives in Marietta. I was gone have her ass hit up, but my heart ain't like that. I'm not gone let that sucka take me all the way out of my character. But I'm gone fuck him up, if Regi don't catch him first."

Shane wrote, "Tell them niggas we offering one hundred and fifty thousand for him, dead or alive."

Hassan nodded, "I got you, bro. What you want to do about your bitch? I knew that ho was a snake bitch since the beginning."

Shane was quick to write, "I will handle her." Hassan knew that Shane was in love. He wanted to blow the back of Yuri's head off, but on the strength of Shane, he let it go.

Chapter 43

Yuri got dressed and ready to go to the hospital. She had been receiving more and more prank calls, they were driving her crazy. She went into the room to wake Chanel. Once she opened the door, she noticed that Chanel was gone.

She pulled out her cell phone and called her, she answered in a good mood, "Hey, Yuri!"

Yuri instantly wondered what Chanel was up to, "Hey, Chanel, I was just about to go to the hospital, and wanted to ask if you wanted to go with me, this morning?"

Chanel was quick to respond, "Actually, Yuri, I'm pulling up to the hospital with Shane's parents now. They called and asked if we wanted to go eat at Glady's Knights' with them. I tried to wake you, but you were sound asleep."

Even though Yuri was a tad bit bothered by Chanel going to eat with Shane's parents alone, she answered, "Ok, I'll be there soon."

"Well Yuri, you know, the trach comes out this afternoon at one, so you have a few hours."

"I am getting dressed now. Alright Chanel, my other line is beeping, I'll see you soon, bye." Yuri did not even give Chanel a chance to say 'bye.' she clicked over, "Hello?"

"Yuri, where are you?" Yuri was surprised to hear Detective Wallace's voice. "I'm at home, Detective. What's wrong?"

He screamed into the phone, "I am on my way to you, do not leave!"

Yuri was wondering why he was so anxious to talk to her. She hoped that he had not found out about her knowing who robbed Shane. She had just snuck out with Detective Wallace the night before. He didn't mention anything to her then. As Yuri was looking out the window, she noticed Detective Wallace's car speeding toward her house. Once he made it in front of her townhome, he jumped out of the car. He was looking around, cautiously, as he made his way to her door.

Yuri opened the door, expecting the worst. Detective Wallace wasted no time, "You better tell me everything you know, right now! If not, my partner, Detective Ramos, will be the one to interrogate you, and if you lie to him, he will lock your ass up. I will not be able to help you then."

"I told you Reginald," Yuri tried to act like she had told him everything.

Detective Wallace, aggressively grabbed Yuri by the neck, shoving her hard against the door, "Don't play with me Yuri!" You already have me mixed up. I should have never slept with you."

Yuri hugged him and rubbed his back, "Calm down, baby. I will tell you everything, but please tell me what you know."

Falling into Yuri's trap, Detective Wallace responded, "Well, as you know, Hassan is a buddy of mine from way back, who saved my sister from some ignorant niggas, so I owe him. Anyways, he just told me that the dude that you are fucking, Jessy Johnson, is the one who did this to Shane. He also found out that he killed Samuel, and paid to have him buried. Well, Hassan paid the niggas to unburry the body, and I am supposed to come across the body in a couple of hours, to crack the case. So you need to tell me what you know Yuri, because he shot Shane and now he killed Samuel."

Yuri put her head down and whispered, "Uno did not shoot Shane."

"Well, who did?" Detective Wallace was glad to finally get Yuri to open up to him.

"Spida did. They went to rob Shane. I didn't know that Spida was Shane's cousin. He wanted to be with me so bad that he used me and Uno to get to Shane. I did sleep with Uno, but I never told him to hurt Shane." Yuri couldn't stop the tears from falling, "Spida is dead?"

Detective Wallace started to feel bad for Yuri, "Yes, and your boy toy did it. Now I have to figure this out to try and save your ass."

Yuri hugged the detective tight. "Please don't let me go to jail. I need you, baby." Yuri started kissing him. She began pulling at his belt, instantly causing him to get hard. Yuri whispered in the detective's ear, "I think I'm falling in love, Officer."

She noticed how passionately he kissed her, and she couldn't help but think to herself, 'got him.'

He undressed her and they fell onto the floor. He reached in his pants, pulled out a condom, and made love to Yuri. She had worked her magic on him, again. He could not resist Yuri, because she made him see stars every time she made him cum. When they finished, he laid next to Yuri. He could not believe that he had violated all the rules. He let his emotions get the best of him. Yuri had stolen his heart.

Now that he knew her secret, he could not let anything happen to his precious Yuri. He was going to protect her as best he could. He would make Uno confess to the murder and the robbery. He was sure he could, because Uno had been to jail, so his DNA would not be hard to get. His boys in the homicide unit would make sure his prints were found all over the murder scene. Then and only then could he have Yuri to himself.

Chapter 44

Yuri cleaned up and went to the hospital, feeling guilty. Hassan had told the detective that he knew she had something to do with Shane's shooting. Detective Wallace tried to convince Hassan that Yuri was set up by the men, to get next to Shane, and that she slipped, by sleeping with Uno.

Yuri called Uno before she arrived at the hospital. Uno answered, "Bitch, wha' yawan'? I hear' ya say somethin' tada police."

Yuri tried to speak, "I," but Uno was quick to interrupt. "Bitch, stop lyin.' Don' call me no mo.'"

Yuri started to get mad, "I won't call you, Uno. But you have to know that the guys you had do that to Spida sold you out, now listen."

Uno knew she had to know something, because he never mentioned anything about Spida, "I'm lisenin'."

"The dude you paid to bury Spida's body delivered him to Shane's boy, who is cool with Detective Wallace. I tried to tell them that you did not shoot Shane, but in a few hours they'll be looking for you, to question you about Spida."

Uno shouted, "Shit! Fuckin' wit ya got me all fucked up!"

Yuri shouted back at him, "Me? I told you not to do it, but your broke ass would not let it go. Then you pulled Spida's scandalous ass in, now that's what fucked you up."

Uno laughed, "We don' hafta worry 'bout Spida, he won' be a problem. Look, I can' hang 'round here an' wait fo'dem ta find me. I'm gone hafta roll out for a while an' lay low. I'm 'bout ta throw dis phone out an get outta town."

Yuri couldn't help but sound desperate. "I love you, Uno, what about me?"

"Wha bout ya, Yuri? Figure it out like I hafta."

He hung up on Yuri before she had a chance to say anything. Yuri could not stop the tears from falling. She did not want to go into the hospital, but she knew they would be looking for her. She knew if she didn't show up, things would look worse.

As Yuri walked into the room, the trach was being removed. All eyes were on her, yet she couldn't look anyone in the face, guilt was written all over her. Hassan looked at her with pure hatred, but kept his mouth shut to keep the peace, for now.

Mrs. Mitchell hugged her future daughter-in-law, "Baby, everything will be okay. Soon all this will be over and you two love birds can get married."

Once the trach was out, Shane said, "I love you Momma." Jimelle rubbed his head and kissed him, "I know baby, I know."

208

He turned and looked at Yuri, she could not read his expression, but noticed his eyes had fire in them. Shane asked everyone if he could have a moment with his fiancée. He looked at Chanel,

"Chanel, thank you for being here for me, I appreciate it."

Chanel was surprised that Shane knew she had been there the whole time.

Everyone exited to give Shane time with Yuri. Shane started, "What's up, Lil' Momma?"

Yuri was trying to stay calm, "Not much, baby, just waiting on you to wake up."

Shane couldn't help but smile, "Have you really?"

"Yes, Shane, why would you say that?"

Shane was quick to respond, "Because while I was asleep, or whatever the fuck they called it, I heard all kinds of shit. You fucked my cousin, right under my nose, Yuri!" Shane started to get upset but continued, "You fucked the nigga that robbed me with Spida too! Why would you do that to me, after all I've done for you?"

Yuri did not know what to say, "It wasn't like that, Shane."

Shane didn't even let her finish, "Then what the fuck was it like, Yuri?" Yuri was afraid to answer. Shane continued, "Look, I want to know where that nigga is, or do you love him so much that you won't say?"

Yuri now had tears in her eyes, "Shane, I don't know where Uno is."

Shane was getting even more upset, "So you're telling me that you helped him rob me and steal my money, but you don't know where his is? What the hell did you get out of it, some dick? They told me that the nigga don't even have shit. Come on, Yuri. He's still living with his momma! That's the kind of sucka you wanted to deal with? Now I know why Candice had been trying to get at me so bad, because you are a snake bitch, just like she said."

Yuri tried to talk but was sobbing, "I'm sorry, Shane. I love you."

"You don't love me, Yuri. You never loved me, you loved my money. Then you tricked it off with another nigga."

Yuri was getting herself together, "I'm sure you know about Spida, too. Spida blackmailed me and made me sleep with him. I didn't know that he was your cousin."

At that point Shane was sure that Yuri did not know that Spida was dead, but she did know. Shane changed the conversation, "You find that nigga and tell me where he's at. The townhouse, the car and the ring are all in your name, they're yours, but it's over between us, Yuri. I can't take anymore lies from you!"

Yuri was quick to come back, "Speaking of lies, Shane. You are the biggest drug dealer from Atlanta to L.A.! When were you going to tell me that? What if something happened to you? They would have been asking me questions. What was I supposed to say?"

Shane was getting upset all over again, "That's just it, Yuri. You could not have told them anything, leaving you innocent of phone calls and a big conspiracy case. I was protecting you, Yuri! I see you did not do the same for me."

Yuri put her head down and did not even try to say anything. Shane looked away, "I will let you hang around for a while so my parents won't get to thinking the worst about you, but once they're gone, so are you. It's over Yuri; I could never trust you again. Can you please go get my mom?"

Yuri tried to say something, "But Shane…" Shane looked at her with a deadly stare and a scandalous grin, "Get out, bitch, now!"

As Yuri walked out, Shane thought he would give her some time to think about their conversation.

Yuri left Chanel at the hospital, she needed time to herself. She was driving home, crying. It seemed as if her whole world was tumbling down on her. She had no one to call. She remembered that Detective Wallace had given her a secure line to call, so she called him. He was quick to answer, "Hello, Yuri."

Between sobs, Yuri managed to whisper, "Regi, I need to talk, can we please meet somewhere."

"Yuri, I'm on the clock."

Yuri interrupted with desperation in her voice, "Please Detective, it's really important."

"Ok Yuri, I'll try to wrap this up quickly, then I'll call you soon, so we can meet somewhere."

Yuri was impatient, "Will it take long?"

Someone reported a body, and I have to work on getting it identified. After I handle this, you will be my next priority."

"Thanks Regi, I love you."

He paused, with a smile and responded, "I am falling in love with you, too. I'll see you soon."

Chapter 45

The evening news came on and the body had been identified, but no name was given, until they could find a family member. The following day, Detective Wallace walked into the hospital with the homicide detective. Before they entered Shane's room, they heard someone walk up behind them. Detective Wallace turned around, "Hassan Muhammad, is that you?"

Hassan played along, "Yes, it is. Reginald Wallace? A police detective?"

Detective Wallace laughed, "Yes sir, it's me, the one and only." They greeted one another with the old school handshake as if they had not seen each other in years. "So what are you doing here Hassan?"

Hassan replied, "My good friend is lying in that room. He was shot a few weeks ago."

"I've been working on his case. He is a lucky man."

Detective Wallace was the only one who knew that he meant he was lucky to have Yuri, not so lucky to be alive.

"So what brings you here today, Regi. I mean, Detective?"

Detective Wallace smiled, "Well actually, I have some news to deliver. I need to speak with Shane Mitchell, or one of his relatives."

"His parents are in the room I'll get them for you."

"When Shane's parents exited the room, they all greeted each other. The Detective asked for them to have a seat, Mr. Mitchell sat next to Hassan; however, Mrs. Mitchell decided not to sit down. The Detective tried again, "Mrs. Mitchell you might want to sit down for this."

Mrs. Mitchell responded, "No, I don't need to sit down. My son has awakened and there is nothing else that can break me down. Now, what is it?"

The homicide detective continued, "I would rather you sat, but since you won't, we were called to the Chattahoochee River, where we found your nephew, Samuel Mitchell, shot and drowned."

Jimelle fell to the ground, she could not breath. Her husband picked her up, "What happened?" Clarence asked, being strong for his wife.

"All we know right now is that he was shot and the person who moved the body put an anchor on his leg, and threw him into the river. We will need you to come down to the station to identify the body. Well, maybe you, Mr. Mitchell, I don't think your wife should see him like this, right now."

"Ok, she'll stay here and I'll go with you." He kissed his wife and left with the detectives.

Once the detectives left with Clarence, Jimelle and Hassan went into Shane's room, and told Shane about Spida. Even though Shane knew that Spida had betrayed him, he still felt bad. He hugged his mom and tried to comfort her. Spida was like her son as well. She had taken care of Spida most of his life. Now she would fly him back to California or Detroit for a proper burial. If his mom would have anything to say, Spida's final resting place would be Detroit.

Chanel came into the room after the family had cried, prayed and were all feeling better.

She hugged Shane's mother, "I am so sorry, Mrs. Mitchell. May God be with you."

She looked over at Hassan who did not show any remorse; his face was the same as before they received the news. She went over to the bed and hugged Shane, "I am so sorry this happened."

Shane responded with no emotion, "It's life. When you are in the game, either it will make you, or take you out." He looked at Chanel and smiled, "You just always remain the sweet, kind, and respectful young lady that you are. God has something bright for your future."

Chanel smiled and hugged Shane again. "Well, now that I know that you're ok, I am going to return back to D.C. this weekend. I've been taking all my courses online, and I'll be glad to get back to class, to get a better understanding. So I'll visit these last few days, and then it's back to the Brick City."

Shane smiled at her, "Thank you for being here, there were days when I was asleep but I could hear you read, sing and pray for me. You better call Tyrone one day, girl; you were doing your thang."

Chanel blushed with embarrassment, "Thank you, Shane, I will check on you tomorrow."

She gave everyone a hug before she left.

Chapter 46

Detective Wallace met Yuri at his apartment. Before Yuri could get comfortable, he asked, "What is it, Yuri?"

Yuri answered, nervously, "Shane knows a lot, and now I'm scared that he may have a hit out on me."

She was interrupted by her ringing cell phone. Yuri noticed the caller was 'unknown' and a scared look came across her face.

Detective Wallace noticed, and snatched the phone. "Let me answer, Hello?"

The computer generated voice screamed into the phone, "Bitch, you are dead!"

Detective Wallace did not get a chance to say anything before the caller hung up.

Yuri cried while Detective Wallace held her.

While caressing her hair, he tried to comfort her, "I promise I won't let anyone hurt you. But you have to let me know where Jessy is so I can bring him in, for the murder and robbery."

Yuri was quick to defend Uno, "But he didn't shoot Shane."

Detective Wallace interrupted, "He may not have pulled the trigger, but he was there. I have also received word that they have a one hundred and fifty thousand dollar hit out on him and I need to catch him, before they get a hold of him. So if you want to help clear your name, you have to set him up and bring him to me, ASAP."

Yuri was in love with Uno, but she loved herself more. She asked, "So, if I get him to you, what if he says that I was involved?"

"Baby, I will make it like you were never involved in anything. You have to trust me, Yuri. I want us to be together and have kids." At the mention of having kids, Yuri got sick to her stomach. She had the sharpest pain she had ever had before.

"Ok, I'll call Uno today, and ask him to meet me somewhere."

Detective Wallace smiled, "The sooner the better."

Before Yuri left, she stripped down and gave Detective Wallace the best five minutes that he could have wanted and asked from her. She made sure that he would stick to his word. She whipped her pussy on him, turning him into her love slave, just like Chance was at one time.

213

Chapter 47

Chanel wondered when Yuri was going to come home. Chanel had been trying to call her all day and she was not answering. As she packed, she thought about home, and how she missed her parents. She wondered what Maria and Mason were doing. She knew that Barb had started seeing someone about her drinking, and she wondered if she was following up. She also thought about what Barb had told her about breaking up with Terrance. She wished that he was still around and could hold her right now.

After Candice told her Yuri slept with Q, she wondered if Yuri had played her too. She never gave Terrance the chance to explain, or hear his side of the story. She knew that if love came her way again, she was not going to lose it. After Chanel finished packing, she decided to drive over and see Shane. When she arrived, Shane's parents were leaving. They told her that they had made arrangements to ship Spida's body back to California.

The nurses let Shane know that he would be able to make Spida's funeral. He was getting released on Friday, and the funeral was not going to happen until the following Monday. Shane was relieved, because he had been in the hospital for over a month now, and he was ready to get back to real estate, and his undercover drug dealings.

He greeted Chanel, "Hey Chanel, what's going on?"

With a smile on her face, Chanel replied, "Hello Shane, I see you're getting out of here."

"Yes Chanel, and I would like to thank you for sticking around and helping nurse me back to health."

Chanel felt weird about him saying that to her. "It was all for Yuri. Speaking of Yuri, did she come back up here?"

Shane was quick to respond, "No, I haven't seen her since she left."

Chanel felt uncomfortable, "Oh, sorry Shane."

Shane just smiled, "Sorry for what, Chanel? I'm fine, but are you ok?"

Chanel smiled back, "Yes, I'm ok."

Shane was not sure he believed her, but he changed the subject, "So when does your plane leave?"

"I leave Sunday evening at six."

"Well, I know you and Sam had become friends, and I wanted to know if you'd like to fly out to L.A. with me next Saturday to attend his funeral with me?"

"I would, but the plane ticket that I bought was non-refundable."

Shane interrupted her, "Don't worry about the ticket, if you go with me, I'll buy you another ticket home."

Chanel got excited, "That sounds great! Yuri, you and I will have fun in California. I have never been to..."

Before Chanel could finish Shane said, "Actually, Chanel, Yuri won't be attending. I really don't think her and Sam really hit it off."

Chanel was a little shocked, "Well, I think I should speak with Yuri first. I don't know how she would feel about my flying with you alone, well, not alone on the plane, but you know what I mean."

"Actually, we would be alone. I chartered a jet to take us. I'll be fresh out of the hospital, and a commercial flight will be too crammed for me. Just let me know, Chanel."

Chanel did not know what to say, "I'll let you know. Do you need anything before I leave? I'm going to the house to unpack my things."

Shane smiled, "All I need is a hug."

She walked over and hugged him, "I'm glad you're ok, because you are really a good guy. Yuri is very lucky," she kissed him on the forehead and left.

Chapter 48

Yuri called Uno, but the phone service had been disconnected. She didn't know how she would find him, but she did know where his mom lived. She decided to go to his mom's. She knew Uno loved his mother, and would eventually stop by to see her. Yuri spent the whole weekend casing the spot. She never answered Chanel, or the unknown numbers. She concentrated on catching Uno. After Sunday evening came, Yuri had not slept or bathed. She realized that maybe Uno was not going to show. She decided to go home.

Chanel was happy to see Yuri, "Look at you. You look a mess, where have you been?"

Yuri was exhausted, "I don't want to talk about it, Chanel. I just want to shower and sleep."

Chanel decided not to question her. "I'll make you some tea while you shower."

"Thank you, Chanel." Yuri showered and laid down while she sipped her tea.

Chanel laid next to Yuri on her bed, "Yuri, would you mind if I went with Shane, to California for Sam's funeral?" Yuri did not say anything. She just gave her a thumbs up, so Chanel continued, "Why won't you just come to Cali with us? You don't have to go to the funeral. Just ride out there with us."

Yuri did not get a chance to answer, she was sound asleep. Chanel just covered her up, turned out the lights, and left her to rest.

Tuesday morning, Yuri woke up and realized that she had slept a whole day away. She arose still feeling tired. The weekend of not sleeping, in the car, had worn her completely out. She went downstairs and found Chanel washing clothes. She had cooked lunch.

"Hey girl, you finally woke up?"

Yuri yawned, "Yes, and I'm still really tired."

"Really, well, have a seat; I cooked us lunch. Have some orange juice, I squeezed it fresh this morning." Once they sat down, Chanel turned to Yuri, "So Yuri, why haven't you been to the hospital to see Shane? His parents have gone back to make preparations for Sam's funeral, and I think he needs you there."

Yuri did not even think about it, "I just feel like since he woke up, he hasn't been acting the same. He's changed, so I wanted to distance myself."

Chanel looked a little confused, "Well, I think you should go see him. You know we leave for the funeral on Friday."

Yuri almost choked on her orange juice. "Who is we, Chanel?"

"I told you the other night, before you fell asleep, that Shane asked me to go to the funeral with him. He knew that Sam and I had become friends. I asked if you would mind."

"Oh, I don't remember, but that's fine, Chanel. I don't mind at all. Are you coming back after the funeral?"

"No, I'm going to fly back to D.C., and get myself back in order. I've stayed here in Atlanta way too long."

"Thank you for being here, Chanel and I'm very sorry about the incident with Detective Wallace. I don't know what got into me. He came onto me, and I was weak. Please accept my apology." They hugged. "I'll get dressed and you can drive me to the hospital, Chanel. I don't feel too well, but if it will make you happy, I'll go."

Chanel shook her head, "It's not to make me happy, Yuri. It's to make your fiancé happy."

"Ok Chanel, I'm going to get dressed."

As Yuri showered her conscience kicked in, "Why are you about to go to the hospital, when you know the man does not want to see you. Save yourself the humiliation and chill."

Yuri paid her thoughts no mind.

Chapter 49

When Yuri and Chanel walked into Shane's room, Candice and Passion were talking to him. He was sitting in his chair looking as if he had never been shot. He was wearing new pajamas and a polo robe, looking sexy as hell. Everyone stopped talking and looked at Chanel and Yuri.

Chanel broke the silence, "Hello everyone, are we intruding?"

Shane was the first to respond, "Of course not, Chanel."

Candice interrupted, looking Yuri up and down, "You're not, but she is."

Yuri got defensive, "No, bitch, you are the intruder. Why are you all over my man, giggling and shit?"

Candice jumped out of her chair, "Bitch, he's not your man anymore, and he's my boy. I wish I hadn't hooked him up with your ratchet hoe ass!"

Shane jumped between them, before they could swing on each other.

"Ladies, please, Candice, it was good to see you. We'll catch up when I get back in town. Passion, you be good at the club."

Candice had to respect her boy, "Ok Shane, you be safe." After Candice and Passion hugged Shane, Candice turned to Yuri, "Bitch, I am going to get at you one day. Oh, and I made sure Shane knew about Q, and the night he proposed to you." Candice laughed and rolled her eyes. Before she walked out, she turned and hugged Chanel, "Stay true to yourself, girl. Please don't let that bitch rub off on you. That girl is poison."

Once Candice and Passion left, the room was quiet. Chanel broke the silence once more, "I am going to grab a cup of coffee. Would you guys like anything?"

Shane did not take his eyes off Yuri, "No thanks Chanel, we good."

After Chanel left, Shane did not give Yuri a chance to say anything, "Yuri, why are you back up here?"

"Because I love you and I just can't walk away like this."

Shane laughed, "Oh, you love me, but you ran off and fucked Q. You love me, but you had a threesome on the same night that I proposed. Damn, if anything, it should have been with me, and the chick that I pick to do all that with. You don't love me! You love that nigga!" Yuri could not say another word; she knew he was right. She did love Uno. Shane continued, "I just hope you are not around when my boys find him, because I don't want you getting shipped back home in a body bag."

Yuri's throat dropped to her heart, "He did not shoot you Shane."

Shane was getting mad, "How do you know, bitch? Oh, you mean to tell me you know what happened? I tell you what, Lil' Momma, if you don't want to get on my bad side, I better not see your face around here again. I mean it! Now get the fuck out and stay away from me. You do not want to see the other side of me come out."

She had tears streaming out of her eyes, "But Shane…"

Shane interrupted, "Do not push me, Yuri! It's over, done, finished."

Yuri ran out of the room. She did not see Chanel in the cafeteria, so she started walking. She hugged herself, wishing Uno were there for her. After all, if it had not been for her falling in love with Uno, she would not be in this predicament.

Yuri stopped just outside and the hospital, holding on to one of its pillars for support. The tears running from her eyes lessened as she tried to compose herself. Passers-by were already staring. The last year of her life played before her like an old black and white film. She could not pin point exactly where she went wrong. Everything just seemed a chaotic spiral downwards.

"All I wanted wass to be happy," she sniffled to herself as she wiped her eyes with a tissue from her purse.

She left the hospital and for the first time in a long while, didn't know what to do next.

Chapter 50

Wednesday morning, Yuri was back on the lookout for Uno. Instead of sitting by his mother's house, she sat by his spot. After three and a half hours of sitting, a late model Impala pulled up. Yuri ducked so she would not be noticed, in the small neon she rented for her stake out. Uno jumped out of the car, looking around cautiously, as he entered the house, with a Glock 17, fully loaded and cocked in his hand. Uno looked around as he entered the house. Yuri grabbed her cell phone to call Detective Wallace. She would rather him be locked up, because she knew that once Shane got to him, there would be a closed casket.

Detective Wallace answered on the second ring, "What's up baby?"

Yuri whispered, as if someone was listening, "Detective, I am on Hardwell and MLK, and Uno just walked into the house. He has someone in the car, so I know he won't be long. Matter of fact, he is coming out now."

"Put me on speaker and try to follow him, but stay as far behind as you can."

Yuri put on her shades and floppy hat, "Ok."

Uno sped off, Yuri stayed a few cars behind.

"We're going past the colleges, looks like to 20. Oh, no, we just crossed under 20. Now he's turning left, by the West End Mall."

Detective Wallace knew exactly where she was, "I am eight minutes away, Yuri, stay with him."

"I am."

Once they pulled up to the light, a car sped around Yuri. Two men in face masks popped out of the back and passenger seats, as the driver got next to the Impala. The gun-play began, as Yuri shrieked, "Oh no!"

Detective Wallace imagined the worst, "What happened, Yuri? What's going on?"

Yuri screamed into the phone, "They're having a shoot out! Hurry up, Detective!"

"I'm almost there."

One of the masked men had a shot gun, and the other had a fully automatic 45, knocking holes in Uno's car. Uno and his passenger returned fire. Cars were wrecking as if they were getting hit by stray bullets. People were trying to run for cover, but no one knew where the bullets were coming from. One of the shooters in the other car got hit, and the car started to drive off, but Uno and his passenger did not stop firing at the car. Yuri ducked down after a bullet hit her car. When she looked up, she saw Uno's car speed off. The other car did not move. She then noticed the driver climbing out the window with blood everywhere. The passenger in the front lay dead. Everyone heard the sirens in the distance, but no one moved. Yuri didn't know what to do. When she looked around, she saw police cars swarm in from everywhere. She heard Detective Wallace screaming, "Yuri! Yuri!"

She jumped out of her car, "I'm over here, Detective."

When Detective Wallace ran up to her, he noticed how shaken up she was, "It's okay, Yuri, I'm here. Nothing is going to happen to you. Where is Uno?"

Yuri was crying, "I don't know, probably dead like everyone else."

When Detective Wallace looked around, he noticed there were a lot of innocent bystanders caught in the cross-fire. He saw the paramedics helping a woman who was kneeling next to a little girl who had been shot. There were already at least three bodies covered with sheets.

Detective Wallace shook his head, hugging Yuri, "It's okay, Yuri."

Yuri could not believe her eyes, everything had gone wrong. She knew that Shane had sent someone to kill Uno, and she had to watch it happen.

Detective Wallace pulled Yuri's face to his, and looked her in the eyes, "Go home, Yuri. You don't need to see all this. I'll call you when I hear something."

Before Detective Wallace could walk away, he got a call on his radio, "We just found the other vehicle wrecked on University. One victim DOA, we need paramedics."

Yuri cried harder, she knew it was Uno. She saw he was having a hard time keeping the car on the road. Yuri felt sick to her stomach. She felt that she had not only lost Shane, but now Uno. The man she truly loved was gone.

Yuri watched the five o'clock news, "We have some breaking news. A deadly shoot out! So far we have confirmed four dead, one child, four years old; Destiny Bryant was shot dead by a stray bullet. Police are still working on identifying the other victims. Once we get that information, we will relay that information to you."

Yuri turned the television off because she could not bear anymore. She sat on her couch with her face in her hands. She was sobbing, "Why, God? What am I supposed to do now? Please help me."

Chapter 51

When Shane was released from the hospital, before he headed to the airport, he stopped by Hassan's. He was going to pick up the half-a-million dollars that Hassan had collected for him since he had been down.

Shane gave him dap and some brotherly love, "Man, I am glad you're my partner. Any other nigga would have run off with my cash as soon as I was shot, hoping that I would die. But you, my man, straight loyal."

Hassan nodded his head, "You already know Shane, it's death before dishonor."

Shane asked, "Speaking of death, I saw the news, what's up with that situation?"

Hassan smiled, "It's been taken care of."

Shane knew exactly what he meant. "Thank you, man. I have to go pack, so I can head out to the west. My money is waiting on me." Shane still had over a million dollars waiting for him in Cali.

Shane and Hassan shook hands, "I'll holla, homie."

"Fo' sho'."

Shane made sure that Spida's funeral was a good one. There were more older people than younger ones in attendance. Spida could never keep a woman, because of the size of his penis, and he never kept homeboys, because he wanted everything to go his way. The military had messed Spida up. All Shane could think was that he was a big nigga with a small ego. Chanel sat next to Shane. Even though she had only known Spida for a little over a month, she still cried. Shane's mom took it the worst. After the funeral service, Shane did not want the driver to take them to the military base where Spida would be laid to rest.

He took Chanel to Crustacean's, his favorite restaurant in Beverly Hills, on Santa Monica Boulevard. Chanel had never had Vietnamese-French seafood. The floor was made of a fish tank. The ambiance was remarkable.

When the server approached the table, he recognized his regular customer, "Hello, Mr. Mitchell."

Shane smiled, "Hey, Angelo. What's going on?"

The server smiled back, "I've been good, Sir. Where have you been lately, Mr. Mitchell?"

Shane always kept his whereabouts to himself, "Oh, I've been out of the city for a while. I'm back, and I'm hungry too."

The server laughed, "Our special tonight is a blackened grilled Mahi-Mahi, served with mushrooms, red potatoes, and asparagus."

"Sounds good, Angelo, but I'll pass."

"Yes Sir, would you like your usual meal, and a bottle of champagne?"

"Of course, you got it, man."

Angelo left, and came back with a bottle of Perrier and Jouet. Chanel admired the beautiful flowered bottle. She felt awkward being with Shane, alone, in such a romantic setting. She wished that Yuri would have come along with them.

Shane noticed the uncomfortable look on Chanel's face, "So Chanel, have you made reservations to leave yet?"

"Yes, this has been a great weekend, here, in Los Angeles. I loved Roscoe's Chicken and Waffles. It was much better than Glady's Knights'. I also loved the Santa Monica Pier, those jet skis were so much fun. Other that the fact that we were here for the funeral, I had a wonderful time. When Chanel looked up, the server was laying out their meal. Chanel could not believe her eyes.

When she saw the Dungeness crabs, she exclaimed, "And this seals the deal! Whoa Shane, this looks great."

Shane smiled, "Wait until you taste it. It tastes so much better than it looks."

Chanel ate until she could not eat another bite. For dessert she had the apple pie with French vanilla ice cream. It tasted better than any French vanilla ice cream she had ever had. When the six hundred and fifty- dollar tab came, Chanel felt guilty for tasting all the appetizers on the menu knowing that it was only the two of them. "Oh God, Shane, I am so sorry. I didn't know this place was so expensive. The food was great, but I would have settled for Red Lobster."

Shane chuckled, "This is cheap, considering what I usually eat. When someone takes you out, Chanel you never worry about the price. Unless you see him adding up what he is about to spend, before he orders. That's when you worry, or just walk out before him, so you won't get embarrassed."

They both laughed. They were feeling the effects of the champagne they had been drinking.

Chanel noticed Shane looking into her eyes, she blushed, "Shane, I am full and tired. I need to go to my room so I can lay down."

"Ok Chanel, let's go." Shane dropped a two- hundred dollar tip on the table for the server's awesome, on-point service.

Walking out, Chanel spotted Angelo, "Thank you so much, you were the best."

Shane shook his hand, "That's why I always ask for him when I come here."

They pulled Shane's Bentley Coupe to the front door. He dropped the top and headed north on the I-10 freeway, back toward the Hollywood hotel.

Chapter 52

Yuri had been at home all weekend, feeling sick. She was glad the weekend was almost over. She was tired of the prank calls she had been receiving every day. She could not sleep; she laid in bed thinking of Uno, and the terrible shootout she witnessed. She wondered how Spida's funeral went, but she did not want to call Chanel. She was surprised Chanel had not tried to call her.

Yuri woke up Monday morning feeling even worse. She decided to get dressed and go to the emergency room. She told the nurse that she had been having dizzy spells, and that she was under a lot of stress. The nurse went through all the normal procedures. She checked her blood pressure, temperature, and asked for a urine sample. She told her that the doctor would be in soon to go over the results with her.

Yuri laid back and rested her head on the pillow. She heard something and looked up. As she looked up she saw Shane entering the room.

Shane was crying, "Yuri I am so sorry about how I've been treating you."

Shane got down on his knees and begged for her forgiveness. He went on to tell her how beautiful she was and that he still wanted to marry her.

"Yuri, I want you to have my children and I want us to be a family."

Yuri jumped up from the bed with tears in her eyes, "Yes Shane, of course I'll marry you! I'm so sorry about everything, too. I'm so happy to see you! I love you, and I never want to lose you again."

The doctor came into the room, interrupting Yuri's dream, "Hello, Ms. Jones."

Yuri sat up, "Hello, Doctor."

"So, how do you feel?"

"Not so well, I've had a lot on my mind. I think I've been too stressed lately. Is everything okay?"

The doctor smiled, "Oh, everything is fine. You might want to try and avoid all stressful situations, because you're five weeks pregnant, Ms. Jones."

Yuri almost fell off the bed, "Pregnant?"

"Yes Ma'am, congratulations." Yuri started crying. The doctor was confused, "What's wrong? Are you ok?"

"No! I can't be pregnant! What am I going to do?"

The doctor did not know what to think, "Ma'am, we have a counselor you can speak to, if you feel you need some counseling."

224

Yuri gathered her things quickly, "No, I'm ok."

She left the room, paid her co-pay, and left.

Yuri sat in the car, crying, holding her stomach. She knew that something was wrong with her body. She felt drastic changes in the last few weeks. She started sobbing when she thought about whose baby it might be. She remembered about how Spida had hit her that day at the hotel and knocked her unconscious. She woke up feeling his thick cum seeping from between her legs. There was also a possibility that it could be Uno's. Even though they never used condoms, she had yet to get pregnant; thereby leaving her to believe that Uno was shooting blanks. Yuri could not believe that as tiny as Spida's dick was, he was the one to get her pregnant. She knew it had to be just her luck.

She drove home in a daze, seeing nothing. It was a relief when she saw her house but the car might as well have been on autopilot and Yuri a passenger because she remembered nothing of the journey. Her mind was preoccupied with the idea of being a mother. With all that had happened, she did not quite feel ready but she had decided it was Uno's baby so abortion was not even an option for her.

She had lain on the couch intending only to rest her feet before she showered for bed. Her stomach felt too full of turmoil to eat and exhaustion was nibbling away at her feet. As she contemplated what she would do next, sleep came over her and dreams of Uno and a lttle baby girl filled her mind.

She smiled and a little as she slept.

Chapter 53

Yuri woke up to the sound of gunfire that riddled her house. She fell to the ground and laid there until she heard the tires screech off.

She crawled to the phone and called Detective Wallace, "Regi, I need you. Someone just shot up my house, and I'm so scared," she cried. "I don't know what do."

Detective Wallace replied, "I'm calling the police, Yuri, I'll be there in thirty minutes."

The police arrived at Yuri's in less than seven minutes. Yuri wasted no time running to open the door for them. She was scared out of her wits. She noticed that the same glass window had been shot out, and broken, like the last time. Her Benz was sitting in front of the house, all shot up. She realized with all this happening that she had no one to turn to for support.

Detective Wallace drove up, jumped out of his car, and ran to Yuri. "Yuri, are you ok?" He asked this, not hiding his feelings for her, while hugging her, trying to console her.

Yuri whispered, between sobs, "Yes, but I'm scared. Someone wants me dead!"

Detective Wallace told the cop that was first on the scene to handle the report and he would have someone board up the windows. He told the cop that he would put Yuri in protective custody. Regi knew that she would come home with him so he could hold and comfort her.

Yuri laid next to Regi for the rest of the night. Neither one of them said a word to the other. He rocked her to sleep, letting her know that she was safe in his arms. Yuri stayed with Detective Wallace for the next few days. He told her that he would never let anyone harm the woman he loved.

Three days had gone by, and Yuri was tired of being at Detective Wallace's house. Now that she knew she was pregnant, the morning sickness had gotten worse. She didn't know if it was a mind game, or just what it was, pregnancy. She called an abortion clinic to find out how much it would cost to terminate her pregnancy. Then she thought, what if it was Uno's baby, at least she would have a little Jessy to carry on his name, whether it was a boy or a girl.

Her mind turned to her mother and father. They would not agree with her murdering her child. All kinds of thoughts clouded her brain. Maybe the baby would bring her and her mother back together. She thought about Mason, her godson, and how precious he was. Yuri was confused, not knowing what to do. She hung up the phone and cried some more. She finally called Chanel, "Hello, Chanel."

Chanel replied, "Hey Yuri, how is everything going?"

Yuri was quick to reply, "Not so good, the other day someone shot up my house."

Chanel almost screamed into the phone, "Oh my God, Yuri! Are you ok?"

Yuri was relieved that at least someone cared about her well-being. "Yes, but I think I'm having a nervous breakdown."

Chanel consoled, "I'm sorry, Yuri, that someone keeps torturing you. What did you do for anyone to want to hurt you so bad?"

Yuri was wondering the same thing. She did not know who of all the people she had hurt would be trying to get her back now.

Yuri paused before answering, "Chanel, I have not been very nice to some people. I think it's Candice doing these things, but she's gone too far this time."

Chanel sighed, "Yuri, we all know that she doesn't like you, she told me what you did with her guy, but I don't think she is that bitter."

Yuri did not know what to say, she was embarrassed, knowing Candice had spilled the beans on all of her sexual encounters.

"Yuri is that all that's bothering you? Do you have something else on your mind?"

She paused again before answering, wanting to tell her about the baby. Chanel did not know about her sleeping with Spida or Uno, she was afraid she would tell Shane.

"No Chanel, I'm okay."

"So where are you now, Yuri? Are you at home?"

Yuri lied, "No, I'm at a hotel downtown."

"That's good, I have a class in five minutes, I'll call you later. Oh, by the way, I had a very nice time in California. Except for the funeral, it was very pleasant."

She interrupted, a little annoyed, "That's nice, Chanel."

"Okay Yuri. We'll talk later. Bye."

"Talk to you later Chanel."

Yuri was tired of being crammed-up in Detective Wallace's small, no style, two-bedroom house. She gathered all of her belongings, and left before he came back home. She felt guiltier now, telling him that she loved him when she did not have a care in the world about him. All she wanted from him was his assurance for her safety.

227

Chapter 54

As the months flew by, Yuri was glad that her home was now fully paid for, but without Shane taking care of her, the stash that she had, quickly disappeared. All the shopping sprees came to a halt. The four squirts of Creed perfume narrowed down to two squirts. The shopping at Publix changed to Kroger's.

Shane never once called. Even though she was six months pregnant, she had no one to share the joy with. Detective Wallace was the only one there for her. He had put the murder of Spida on Uno, and no one ever asked her any questions about the robbery. The robbery remained unsolved. Yuri had not had any prank calls, nor any further vandalism to her house. She spoke with Chanel on several different occasions, but never once mentioned her growing baby bump.

The evening was very relaxing. Yuri showered and went to the kitchen, to make her favorite snack. Her cravings were mainly for cookies and cream ice cream with a dill pickle. She wanted to call Detective Wallace to find out what he was doing, but she decided not to because she knew that he had gone fishing for the weekend with the rest of his police buddies. She did not want him to worry about her.

She took her bowl of ice cream and pickles upstairs to her bedroom. She fluffed her pillows and crawled into her king-sized bed, propped her feet, and turned on her 50-inch Sony flat-screen to the Lifetime channel. As the movie played about a man living a double life while he and his mistress plotted to kill his wife, Yuri thought about how she betrayed Shane for Uno, just about the same way. While eating her ice cream, she felt the baby jump for joy inside of her.

She rubbed her belly, talking to her unborn child, "You like cookies and cream ice cream and pickles, don't you Jess? I am going to spoil you and give you all the ice cream you want. Your daddy is gone, but Momma is going to spoil you."

Yuri got up to go to the bathroom, but the lights suddenly went out. The house had a short, and the lights went out on occasion.

Yuri said, "Damn, why tonight?"

She did not feel like wobbling all the way down to the basement. It was already hard enough for her to go downstairs to the kitchen or living-room, but the basement was just too far. She grabbed the Yankee Candle that was lit next to her bed, put on her house shoes, and went downstairs. She realized that the going down was okay, it was the coming up part that was hard, now that she was so big. When she reached the concrete basement, she used the candle to help light her way to the fuse box. She opened the box and reset the main circuit- breaker. All the lights came on. As she closed the door to the breaker box and turned around, she was startled and could not believe her eyes.

"Snake bitch" was the last thing she heard, before she hit the floor.

Yuri was awakened by a bucket of cold water being thrown on her. Yuri was scared, and blind-folded, her mouth shut with duct tape. Her only source of air was through her nose. She felt blood drip down her head, she wiped it with her knee. Her hands were handcuffed to the water heater. The concrete floor was cold.

The voice whispered, "You snake bitch, I am going to kill you."

She cried, as the pain in her stomach was unbearable. She realized that not only she would die, but her baby would too. Yuri did not know how long she had been knocked out, but it seemed like forever. Hours passed by and the torture was just beginning. The unknown intruder smoked on a cigarette while burning Yuri's toes with it. Yuri had silent screams because of the tape across her mouth. After all her toes had been badly burned, vodka was poured all over her fresh wounds.

Yuri just wanted to die; she could not handle the torture. The assailant snatched the duct tape off of Yuri's mouth. Yuri took a deep breath and let out a sigh of relief.

She said the first thing that came to her mind, "Please, just let me go, or kill me. I'm pregnant, and my baby cannot take this. Please don't do this to me. I'm sorry." She was cut off by a punch to the right side of her face.

"Shut up, bitch, and drink," was whispered, while helping Yuri drink the water that was in the cup.

Within twenty minutes of drinking, what Yuri thought was water. She passed out.

Yuri woke up, only knowing that the daylight had come because the sun was shining through the window. She felt dizzy and delusional. She instantly knew that the water she drank had to have had some kind of drug in it. She had even peed on herself. She noticed that one hand had become free, and she started to pull the blindfold all the way off.

As she reached up, the person said, "No bitch, you will never see daylight again."

Yuri felt two punches to the side of her face.

"Please stop. My baby…"

Yuri was weak as she screamed and pleaded with her attacker. She was pulled down, flat to the floor by her hair. She felt her panties rip and come off. Before she had a chance to protest, she felt her legs being pried open. She did not know what they were going to do to her. She felt something hard poking her ass.

"Please don't rape me, I'm pregnant!" she pleaded to no avail.

Next thing she knew, she felt something hard shoved up her ass. Yuri cried. She could not take anymore. It did not take long for her to realize that it was a broom stick being shoved up in her, as it went further and further. Yuri was helpless as she laid there and took the pain. She realized that fighting and screaming would only make it worse. After being violated for thirty minutes straight, all she could do was lay there, drained. She lay there helplessly as the warm blood pooled around her cold body, waiting to perish.

Detective Wallace had been trying to call Yuri all night. It was now morning and he was getting worried because he knew that Yuri always answered his calls on the first ring. Yuri had been craving for some of the fish that she knew he would catch, clean and cook for her. Regi had a gut feeling that something was not right. He told the guys that he would have to end his trip early. He gathered his things, and the fish he caught, jumped in his truck and headed east on 20, leaving Birmingham, heading back to Atlanta.

Chapter 55

Yuri's arms were finally released, but she was too weak to pick herself up off the floor. She laid there, knowing she would die. The blindfold was finally removed, and she struggled to focus on the sight in front of her. She thought she was having hallucinations from the drug she was given because she just could not believe her eyes. She saw two visions of Chanel, looking like a deranged mad woman. Yuri didn't know which of the Chanels she was looking at was the real one.

She asked in a weak voice, "Why are you doing this, Chanel?"

Chanel ran up on her and choked her, "Why did you do what you did to my brother, bitch? As tears ran down Chanel's face, mascara smeared everywhere, "That was you on the tape that was sent to Shannon. You were fucking Chance all that time."

Yuri was sobbing, "Chanel, I'm six months pregnant, please don't hurt me."

Chanel interrupted, "Bitch, I should give you an abortion, like you made my sister-in-law have when you sent that scandalous ass tape. I hope your bastard-ass baby is not my man's child, because he doesn't want to have anything to do with your snake-ass!"

Surprised, Yuri managed to whisper, "Your man? Who is your man?"

Chanel laughed, "Oh, I forgot you didn't know. When I went with Shane to L.A., we ate at his favorite restaurant and had more drinks than we could handle. We went to the hotel suite, and I let him take my virginity. He said this was the best pussy he had ever had. He my man now, bitch!"

Yuri cried, "Chanel, you're going crazy! Please stop what you're doing!"

Chanel jumped on top of Yuri and wrapped her hands around her neck, "I should strangle you to death. Every time I thought about that rope mark around my brother's neck, I wanted to fuck you up!"

Chanel choked Yuri almost unconscious. Chanel stood up and looked down at Yuri, kicking her in the face, "You're a pitiful case. Your mom told me that I should have never run Terrance off. She also told me that you were put out because you fucked Gene, right under her nose. How could you hurt all the people that have ever loved you, even Shane? You set the robbery up after all the shit he did for you? But don't worry, I'll take care of him."

She smiled as she pulled out the .38 special. Yuri cried as she prayed and asked God for forgiveness.

Chanel yelled, "Look at me!"

Yuri would not open her eyes as she kept praying. She knew that only God could help her now.

Before Chanel could finish her off, she heard tires screeching outside the window.

"Shit, who could that be?" Chanel said panicking as she fired three shots.

Detective Wallace heard the gunshots. He ran up the steps and kicked in the door. He ran straight upstairs calling Yuri's name. When he didn't find her in the bedroom, he searched the rest of the house. He ran back downstairs, taking them two at a time. He noticed the patio and basement doors were wide open.

Knowing Yuri never went into the basement, he raced down the stairs, "Yuuuuuuuri," he yelled.

His screams could be heard down the block. Once he reached the bottom of the stairs, he gasped, "Oh my God, Yuri!"

Yuri's battered body was surrounded by a pool of blood. He called for an ambulance, hoping that the woman he loved could be saved. Detective Wallace called for a paramedic and police backup. He lifted Yuri's limp body into his arms. She tried to say something, but only spat blood out. He lifted his head, closing his eyes, begging for God to save her.

Epilogue

"Ms. Jones, it's time for your medication."

Yuri opened her eyes and smiled at the handsome nurse. He handed her the usual dose of Zyprexa and Effexor. Yuri wasted no time putting it under her tongue. Once he left she spit it out and added it to the stash of pills she had been collecting over the past few weeks. She knew that she now had enough to carry out her plan.

Yuri had nothing but time on her hands, and now that she was not medicated, she was starting to remember everything. She remembered Chanel laughing in her face as she worried about her unborn child. She remembered being shot in the shoulder; she was rushed to the hospital. She knew that if it had not been for Detective Wallace showing up when he did, Chanel would not have shot her in the shoulder. The bullet was meant for her head. There was no way that Yuri was going to stay in the psychiatric ward much longer. She had been through a lot, but she wasn't crazy. She was ready for revenge.

The next morning, the male nurse that she had charmed over the past several months, entered the room to give her the daily dose of medication for depression, and to treat her psychotic episodes.

About the Author

Demetria, 'Mimi', Harrison is new and upcoming author who has several books to be released in the near future.

She was born in Omaha, Nebraska but relocated to Kansas City, Missouri as a teenager.

She now lives in Central Florida where she enjoys relaxing time with her family and friends. She especially adores her seven grandchildren and spends as much of her non-writing time as possible with them.

When Mimi is not writing or spending time with loved ones, she enjoys interacting with readers on Facebook and chatting about her books.

Mimi hopes to bring an expanded group of characters to her readers, more dynamic than her first novel "She's Just Like Me". She wants readers to feel that they are a part of the book. Writing is not only her passion, but it has become therapeutic during this difficult time in her life. Readers should expect many more novels from Ms. Dementria 'Mimi' Harrison.

 BossStatusPub

 Mimi@BossStatusPublishing.com

Made in the USA
Middletown, DE
11 September 2021

48069011R00142